STATE OF WAR

Tom Clancy's
NET
FORCE®

STATE OF WAR

Created by
Tom Clancy and Steve Pieczenik
written by Steve Perry
and Larry Segriff

PENGUIN BOOKS

PENGUIN BOOKS

Published by the Penguin Group
Penguin Books Ltd, 80 Strand, London WC2R 0RL, England
Penguin Putnam Inc., 375 Hudson Street, New York, New York 10014, USA
Penguin Books Australia Ltd, 250 Camberwell Road, Camberwell, Victoria 3124, Australia
Penguin Books Canada Ltd, 10 Alcorn Avenue, Toronto, Ontario, Canada M4V 3B2
Penguin Books India (P) Ltd, 11 Community Centre, Panchsheel Park, New Delhi – 110 017, India
Penguin Books (NZ) Ltd, Cnr Rosedale and Airborne Roads, Albany, Auckland, New Zealand
Penguin Books (South Africa) (Pty) Ltd, 24 Sturdee Avenue, Rosebank 2196, South Africa

Penguin Books Ltd, Registered Offices: 80 Strand, London WC2R 0RL, England

www.penguin.com

First published in the United States of America by Berkeley Books 2003
First published in Great Britain in Penguin Books 2003
This special sales edition published 2003
1

Copyright © Netco Partners, 2003

TOM CLANCY'S NET FORCE: STATE OF WAR

For more information on Steve Pieczenik, please visit www.stevepieczenik.com

The moral right of the author has been asserted

Printed in England by Clays Ltd, St Ives plc

Acknowledgments

We would like to acknowledge the assistance of Martin H. Greenberg, Denise Little, John Helfers, Brittiany Koren, Lowell Bowen, Esq., Robert Youdelman, Esq., Danielle Forte, Esq., Dianne Jude, and Tom Colgan, our editor. But most important, it is for you, our readers, to determine how successful our collective endeavor has been.

—Tom Clancy and Steve Pieczenik

PROLOGUE

Solomon "Solly" Bretcher, the Democratic senator from Florida, looked down at the woman beside him.

She had said her name was Joan, and she was young. She'd claimed to be twenty-one when she'd picked him up at that bar back in D.C.—but she had smiled when she'd said it, just a little, just enough so that he had known she was lying. He thought she was probably closer to eighteen.

She was also very slim, almost boyish in her figure, and he believed she must have had some yoga or gymnastics in her background.

Athletic, strong and supple, cute as a bug, and young enough to be, what, his daughter at least. Maybe even his granddaughter.

But none of this was what had drawn Solly to her. No, the reason he was here now, lying naked in some strange hotel room in Virginia, a good fifty miles from his offices, had nothing to do with the way she looked or how old she was or whatever perfume she was—or wasn't—wearing. It was more powerful than that, more compelling, and it had everything to do with the way she had looked at him, the raw, overpowering hunger in her eyes as she approached him.

It had been a long time since anyone had looked at him like that. He couldn't even remember the last time someone had wanted him just for himself and not for whatever access he could grant or the votes he could provide.

She had looked at him like that. She had let him see the naked desire in her eyes. She had told him, not with words but with every gesture, every glance, and every breath, that she wanted him, and he had agreed.

He looked down at her now.

"Joan," he said softly.

She opened her eyes and looked up at him, a slow smile spreading across her face.

"Joan," he said again, liking the way her name slid across his lips. He wanted to say something to this woman in his arms, to thank her, perhaps, to let her know how deeply she had touched him. He wanted to mark this moment before it slipped away.

He never got the chance.

As he reached for his next words, he was interrupted by the sound of somebody kicking in the hotel room door.

Joan reacted faster than Solly, scrambling out from under him and jerking the sheet up around herself while he reached for his glasses.

"What is the meaning of this?" he said, still fumbling with his glasses. "Who the hell are you?" He was trying to sound irate, not the easiest thing to do when you were lying naked in bed with a young woman not your wife. He shut up when he managed to get his glasses on and saw that the man standing there had a gun pointed at him.

"Get your clothes on, you little harlot!"

Solly's gut twisted. Her husband? Lord, Lord, what was he going to do? If Marsha found out—!

"And you, you pervert. I ought to shoot you dead! God would bless me, and so would the po-lice!" The man had a funny accent. Was it French?

"Listen, mister," Solly began. "There's been some kind of mistake! I—I didn't know she was married—"

"*Married?!* You son of a bitch! She's not my wife! She's my *daughter!* She's *fourteen years old!*"

Solly's vision swam with millions of swirling motes. He swallowed dryly and felt light-headed. Fourteen? She couldn't be *fourteen!*

"Daddy, I'm sorry—"

The man strode forward and slapped the girl's face. It was a loud noise in the otherwise quiet room. "Put your clothes on! I'll deal wid you when we get home! First, I got to call the po-lice and get this pervert arrested! They gonna put you *under* the jail, baby raper!"

Cajun, Bretcher realized. *That's what the accent is. Louisiana.*

Joan hurried to obey, holding one hand to her slapped face.

Senator Solly Bretcher felt his life swirling around the drain, going down. Fourteen. He would be totally disgraced. They would crucify him. The press would eat him alive, and if they didn't, his family would. He was a dead man.

As the man reached for the phone, Bretcher raised his hand. "Wait! Wait! Don't do that! Maybe we can come to some . . . arrangement!"

The girl's father looked at him. "What you talkin' about?"

"Anything you want," Bretcher said. "Anything!"

In the car, Joan laughed. "Fourteen?" she said. "That's a stretch, Junior, even for me!"

Driving, Marcus Boudreaux, "Junior," the man who had pretended to be her father, smiled. "Well, fourteen sounds so much worse than sixteen or seventeen, no? And he bought it. You saw his face, yeah?"

"No, I was too busy holding mine. You didn't have to hit me that hard."

He shrugged that off. "I had to make it look good. And like I said, it worked. That senator will do whatever we say."

Joan shook her head. She was twenty-four but had always looked much younger than her age. Being flat-chested, slim-hipped, and skinny had their uses. Convincing a frightened old man you were an adolescent was one that had earned her plenty before now—and had just earned her another ten thousand dollars.

"Now what?"

"Never you mind dat. You just take your money and go lie on the beach down in Biloxi. I'll call you again if I need you."

She shrugged. Ten thousand for a couple hours' work? Beat doing fake pedo-porn on the net. And her tan could use some work. Why not . . . ?

1

It was a Sunday afternoon, hot, muggy, and about to rain—
typical D.C. weather for this time of year. A good day to
stay home. Alex Michaels was doing just that. In his garage, currently without a project car and thus more or less
empty, he was having a short but intense practice session
with Guru. She was the one who introduced Toni to the
Indonesian fighting art of *silat*. Now, all these long years
later, she was still amazing.

She wore a ratty sweatshirt over a long batik skirt and
rubber sandals, and looked about as scary as a stuffed
teddy bear. A really old stuffed teddy bear. But if you
bought that, you would find yourself in big trouble in a
big hurry. One of the first rules of fighting was *Never
assume that what you see is what you get.*

She punched, and Michaels did the block-punch-block-
punch-elbow sequence, that *pap-pap pap!* timing, like two
sixteenth notes followed by an eighth note for the first
three moves.

She nodded. "Not so bad. But watch the low line, be sure the first punch comes from the hip and cuts the angle as it rises. Punch for me."

He did, and despite the fact that she was old enough to be his grandmother, her response was so fast he wanted to shake his head. She could hit him three times before he could blink and, while he was standing there surprised, easily drop him onto the concrete with a sweep or heel-dragging *beset*. A perfect example of technique mastery over physical strength.

"Again," she said.

Ten minutes later, he was picking himself up from the floor after she had put him there with an effortless little sweep when Toni came into the garage. She had Little Alex balanced on one hip and looked like a Polynesian princess in a sarong, her hair wrapped up in a towel. "Are you beating up on Guru again, Alex?"

"Oh, yeah, right. You ever hear what the U.S. cavalry said about what you were supposed to do if captured by the Lakota Sioux? Whatever happens, don't let them give you to the women."

"How droll. You have a call."

She handed him his virgil—the acronym standing for Virtual Global Interface Link—the handy-dandy pocket electronic device that was phone, fax, GPS, homing beacon, credit card, computer line, and other things he hadn't even thought about, including a spy device that told HQ where you were. That the call came in on the virgil meant it was important, since the device's com was also scrambled as well as Net Force's programmers could manage.

Speak of the devil . . .

The tiny screen was lit with Jay Gridley's picture as Michaels took it from his wife.

"Jay."

"Boss. I'm not interrupting anything, am I?"

"Just me getting my ass kicked."

"Toni beating up on you again?"

"Guru."

"Isn't that embarrassing, Boss, getting thumped by a lady old enough to be your granny?"

Michaels grinned. "You're welcome to drop by and stand in for me, if you'd like."

"I'll pass, thanks. I just called to update you on a couple of things. We got another e-mail virus making waves on the web. It's just a filler—clog your system, dupe-and-send thing—nothing real nasty, but it's got good coverage, so you'll be hearing about it. From what I can tell, it's a standard kid-hack kind of thing. No real damage, just counting coup. We should be able to backtrack the guy and nail him."

"Okay."

"The other thing is, we got a funny hit on one of our watchbots I thought you might want to know about."

Michaels grinned again. "A 'funny hit.' Is that a computer geek technical term, Jay?" Net Force had been on a roll lately. Nobody had attacked them, and nothing major had hit the net or the web. Even hackers seemed to be taking the long hot summer off. Michaels knew better than to tempt fate by feeling smug, however. Every time he did that, something came along and Net Force got creamed.

"Are you making a crack about marriage dissolving my brain?" Jay asked.

"Not me. Not with my wife standing six feet away holding a squirming toddler she might throw at me." He smiled at Toni as he said that, and waved and made a funny face at his son. He loved to see Little Alex smile.

Jay caught that on the virgil's screen. "Um, right, Boss. Anyway, yeah, I can send it to your workstation. Nothing major."

"Fire when ready, Gridley."

Jay rolled his eyes. "Oh. Like I never heard *that* one before. Discom, Boss."

Michaels shut the virgil off and went over to give his wife a kiss and a hug, and to hold his son for a moment. Then he would go see what Jay thought was important. At the least, it would keep him from getting thumped around by Granny Death here.

Let it be minor. But he knew in his heart that they were due a major blast.

Jay smiled and shook his head as he disconnected. He'd seen a lot of different sides of Alex Michaels over the years, but this goofy dad thing was a new one. He couldn't help wondering what kind of father *he* would make.

He shook his head again and let those thoughts go. Fatherhood was for the future—if ever. Right now, he had a hacker to track.

He was working from home. After they got back from the honeymoon, he and Saji had moved to a larger place, one that allowed each of them to have a work space. At the moment, Saji was in her office, offering advice to an on-line class of students beginning the study of Buddhism. She'd be working for another hour, so he had plenty of time to do his own job.

The wirelessware he had at home was the same as what he used at Net Force HQ—the latest generations of haptic gear, including optics, otics, reekers, droolers, and weathermesh—so he had full sensory capability when he went on-line. He put on the gloves, the headset with its ear and nose plugs, and the eyecups, adjusting them so they were comfortable. He already wore the tight-fitting mesh suit.

The piece he had sent to Commander Michaels was but a tiny hint of something he knew—he *knew*—was much larger. But knowing it was not the same as finding it. Like the scenario he was about to dive into, there were a lot of submerged logs in the swamp, and while not all of them were alligators, you had to be very careful when you poked at them with a stick. . . .

He grinned at the thought. "Scenario on," he told his computer.

Bayou Baritaria, Louisiana

Jay cruised slowly through the murky waters of Bayou Baritaria, the air boat's throttle nearly closed, watching carefully for submerged logs. Even without an underwater prop, hitting one at speed would be bad—not so much for the air boat as for *him*. Air boats were tough. The $^3/_{16}$"-thick 5086 marine aluminum that made up the boat's flat hull was coated with an additional layer of a Teflon-based polymer, and would slide over pretty much anything, up to and including dry land. A land speed record had been set some time back in the late nineties with an air boat—on asphalt at over forty-seven miles an hour. Bad for the coating, but it worked.

However, hitting anything submerged at speed would put *him* in danger, in case the boat flipped, or spun toward one of the huge cypress trees that stood sentinel, gray Spanish moss draped thickly over their branches.

Only way to tell north on these trees would be to look for the dead Yankee.

Jay recalled a factoid he'd read somewhere, that all statues of southern Civil War generals faced north. They'd lost the war, but never really given up down here.

Beams of sunlight shone through the thick canopy of the swamp, touching here and there upon the murky waters, which, of course, teemed with water moccasins and leeches. The air had that dank, spoiled, rotting-vegetation odor that overlaid everything, a fecund, earthy stink. In the background he could hear the high-pitched whirring of cicadas.

A mosquito hummed by, and he swatted at it.

He grinned. Few took the time for VR details like that. That was the difference between a pro and amateurs: the little things.

His hot-rod air boat, a 560-horsepower V-8 engine with a 2:1 reduction gear, drove the six-bladed carbon-fiber propeller that pushed him along in the deep brownish green waters of the bayou. The flat bottom of the boat would let him float it in as little as an inch of water, and if he had to chase anything, he could be up to forty or fifty miles an hour in just a few seconds—faster, depending on the water conditions.

The air boat was a simple and effective design, invented over a hundred years ago by no less than Alexander Graham Bell. Apparently the inventor had used it as a test bed for early airplane engines, which had been the engine of choice for air boats until the 1990s, when the lower cost of maintenance for automobile engines made them the power plants of choice.

It tickled Jay that the great-granddaddy of modern networking, the first man to get to market with a telephone, had also invented the craft he'd chosen for his VR scenario.

It turned out that air boats were very ecofriendly as well—no submerged screw meant less disruption of the underwater ecosystem. In this case, the metaphor was extended to his investigation: Jay made significantly fewer ripples as he trolled for information.

Sure, he *could* be doing this the old-fashioned way, eyeballing a TFT monitor, a thin window separating him from the data, but who wanted to? The immediacy of all five senses gave him an edge—and Net Force's chief VR jockey liked it that way.

Ahead he saw a brown lump in the water.

He reached down and adjusted the lever to the left of his seat, moved the twin foam-filled airfoil rudders that steered the boat. Like a leaf on a pond, the craft skated to the left slightly, just enough so that he would miss the target by a hair.

He glanced down—a submerged log. It wasn't *really* a log, of course, but a packet of information sliding slowly along this section of the net.

The section of VR he was checking was an older one— one used for datastreams that didn't take as much bandwidth—and data that sometimes wasn't what it seemed to be.

It was a modern variation of Edgar Allen Poe's *The Purloined Letter*: Instead of sending encrypted high-speed data, some of the newer data pirates—and other hackers— hid it in plain sight, risking slower transmission speeds in less observed areas. After all, who would ever suspect anyone of using such a slow section of net to transfer anything critical?

Well, Jay Gridley, for one. Keeping an open mind about everything kept you from getting caught short a lot of times.

He was following a trail he'd started a few days previous, when he'd been rechecking the terrorists of Cyber-Nation. Net Force was being real vigilant with these folks, after what had happened the year before. So far, nothing major had come up.

Another shape drifted by, this time a little faster than the log.

This one was greener, and he could see eyes and nostrils poking above the water—an example of *Alligator mississippiensis*—the American alligator.

The data in *that* packet was obviously a little higher priority than the info in the log, given a measure of protection, and speeded up slightly. Around him, Jay could see more shapes in the water, some gators, some logs.

Another set of gator nostrils and eyes slid past the air boat. Jay looked at the space between the eyes and nostrils—about twelve inches, he figured.

Now there's *a big one.*

It was an old gator hunter's rule of thumb: The distance between the inside of the nostrils and the eyes in inches was the approximate size of the animal in feet. This one should be about twelve feet long.

But when he looked for the gator's wake, it was wrong: Instead of a tail tip sloshing water ten to twelve feet behind the eyes and nostrils, it was way too short—only about *two* feet.

Well, well.

Had he been looking at a computer monitor, he would have just seen that the checksum for the data packet he was looking at didn't match. In his experience, that didn't happen with *legitimate* data. Somebody was trying to make a big thing look small.

Time for a closer look at Mr. Gator.

He reached for his ketch-all pole—an extended piece of stainless steel tubing with a steel noose at one end that could be used to snare dangerous animals—and turned the air boat to follow the gator. The creature must have been imbued with some form of simplified warning system, because as soon as he started tracking it, it sped up.

Fast. Much too fast for a gator, unless it was jet-powered.

Jay grinned. Looked like he was going to get a chance to use his boat after all.

He accelerated rapidly, the roar of horsepower shoving the air boat after the gator. It looked like the critter was making for a branch off the bayou, just ahead. Jay pushed the throttle harder, and cypress trees whipped past. A low-hanging section of Spanish moss smacked him in the face.

Sometimes, he was too good, maybe.

The gator was fast, but no match for his boat. As he got closer, Jay lowered the ketch-all so its noose was just ahead of the gator. At this speed he'd have to be quick, lest the water rip the pole out of his hand.

He dipped the loop into in the water and yanked on the loop that drew the steel rope taut. The pole pulled hard at his arms, and had the gator been as long as advertised, it would have been a very unpleasant experience. But, of course, it was only a shrimp, just as he had figured.

Right yet again. It was a burden, sometimes. People got to expecting it.

He killed the engine and unbuckled his seat belt before lowering the gator onto the deck of his boat.

The two-foot-long beast was most unhappy, it thrashed and smacked its tail against the tough aluminum, making a thunking sound. Jay hand-over-handed his way down the ketch-all. He reached down and squeezed its jaws shut— not difficult, as its more powerful muscles were designed to bite, not *open* its mouth—and slipped another noose over its snout, pulling it tight.

Gotcha.

What he'd *actually* done of course was rascal the address of the gator's destination so that it came to him instead of going to its original destination. But a gator chase was much more exciting than *that*.

Jay flipped the gator and looked at its belly. No seams. *Nice work.*

Well he had ways around that, too.

He took a small skinning knife and slit the belly of the gator open. Instead of warm guts, however, pages of information spilled out, only the top one damaged by his rapid opening of the gator. He glanced at the writing on the first page and grinned.

Well, well. Look at this. How interesting. . . .

2

General John Howard arrived with his son Tyrone. They stopped to talk to Gunny at the check-in station. He was a master sergeant, but he'd always be "Gunny" to the shooters who came here.

"General. And is this Tyrone? You've grown some since I saw you last."

Tyrone, at that voice-breaking fifteen-year-old stage, smiled and nodded. "Yes, sir," he said.

"You shooting rifle today, sir?" Gunny asked the general.

"No, the sidearm. Tyrone hasn't had a chance to shoot the Medusa."

"What load do you want?"

"Some nines, some .38 Special, a few .357s," Howard said.

"Is your ring up to date, sir?"

Howard nodded. The electronic control ring he wore,

that all Net Force and FBI active agents wore, controlled the firing of his personal weaponry. Well, except for the old Thompson submachine gun his grandfather had left him. He hadn't wanted to screw around with that; it was a collectible item, probably worth more than his car—not that he would ever sell it.

"You need me to fit Tyrone with a ring?"

"No, he's got his own. Has Julio shown up yet?"

"Yes, sir, he's already on the line. Lane six."

"I figured," Howard said. "He needs all the practice he can get."

Gunny chuckled.

"Am I missing a joke here, Sarge?"

"With all due respect, sir, you and Lieutenant Fernandez both need all the practice you can get. If all the Net Force ops shot as slow and bad as you do, it'd be more effective for them to throw their weapons than fire them."

Howard grinned. He was, he knew, a better-than-average shooter with a handgun, and superior to most with a long arm. But Gunny here could shoot the eyes off a fly with either hand with a pistol, and with a rifle he could drill neat patterns in targets so far away you could drink a beer waiting for the bullet to get that far. Figuratively speaking. And Howard was never a man to stand on ceremony with his men.

Gunny gave them a box with the revolver ammunition in it along with two pairs of electronic earmuffs and shooting glasses. Howard and his son slipped the sound suppressors on before they went through the heavy doors to the range itself.

There were a couple of shooters firing pistols, and they saw Julio in the sixth lane, blasting away at a holographic target with his old Army-issue Beretta. He had fitted the pistol with Crimson Trace laser sights, built right into the grip, and that had improved his shooting somewhat. With the built-ins, all you had to do was point the weapon, you didn't have to line up the notch-and-post, and you could shoot as well from the hip as from the classical sight-picture pose. When it was properly calibrated, your bullets would hit wherever the little red dot was when you squeezed the trigger. Yeah, you still had to be able to hold the weapon steady, but it was a distinct advantage for older eyes.

Julio, who had talked him into his current sidearm, a Phillips & Rodgers Model 47, also called "Medusa," had been trying to get Howard to put the laser grips on that. So far, however, Howard had resisted. They weren't that expensive, a few hundred dollars, which was cheap when it was your life on the line, but Howard had an old-fashioned streak running through him that made him slow to adopt such things—at least for his personal use.

Julio finished cooking off a magazine, looked up, and saw them. He smiled. "Hey, Tyrone. How's the leg?"

"Doing just fine now, Lieutenant."

Julio looked at Howard. "You told him to call me that, didn't you? Have to keep rubbing it in."

"Well, I figured you might as well get some use out of the title. In no time at all, you'll be a captain."

"Might as well be hung for a sheep as a goat," Julio said.

"Might as well. You okay with Tyrone shooting a few with us today? He's never been much interested in hand-guns, and I thought he might like to see how hard they are to score with compared to a rifle."

"Why would I object to that, sir? I mean, compared to the way the general does it, even a first-timer who didn't know the muzzle from the butt could hardly do any worse."

"A general could have a lieutenant shot for such sass," Howard said.

"Yes, sir, but the only general I know? He'd have to have somebody else do it for him, otherwise he'd waste a whole lot of the taxpayers' money on ammo before he scored a hit."

Tyrone laughed, and Howard grinned again. Twenty-odd years of soldiering together gave him and Julio a camaraderie that was way past commander and enlisted man, at least when there wasn't anybody else around, and Tyrone was family, so he didn't count.

"Well, let's just see, Lieutenant, if your mouth is writing checks your butt can't cash, shall we?"

"Yes, sir. You want me to use my left hand? Stand on one foot?"

"Why? You still owe me ten bucks from last time when you used both your hands and feet. I'm not the least bit worried."

Julio smiled.

Washington, D.C.

Guru was watching the baby—having a live-in baby-sitter was a gift from God, no doubt—and Toni took the opportunity to go for a ride on Alex's recumbent trike. He usually kept the three-wheeler at work, but she'd had him bring it home so she could get back into shape. Since the baby had been born, there never seemed to be enough time to work out, and while she had kept up with her *silat* practice, she had gained an inch on her thighs and hips she just couldn't seem to get rid of, no matter how many times she did her *djurus*. She could get a pretty good burn pumping the pedals, and the trike would allow her to hit the muscles from a different angle than the martial arts moves did. She hoped.

Of course, riding a trike in Washington traffic was an invitation to serious bodily harm, even with strobe flashers and a bright orange pennant flying from a tall whip antenna eight feet up. She had promised Alex she would use the new bike lanes and paths winding in and out of the park not far from their house. She had also chosen to go out in the middle of the morning on a weekday. That was the best time to go out, since there was hardly anybody using them.

She was on a straight stretch that ran for about half a mile along the fenced border of the park. Nobody was in sight, and the paved path was dry. It was cloudy, but still muggy, and the sweat drenched her bike shorts and T-shirt as she upshifted into high gear and began to do some serious cranking on the pedals. The trike was very stable on a straightaway, and the brakes were good, so she wasn't worried.

The warm afternoon air blew past at a speed somewhere about thirty-five miles an hour by the time she peaked, pedaling as hard as she could, and she started to slow down three hundred meters from the end of the run. Trying to take that curve at this speed would have her eating macadam in a hurry.

Her legs burned, but that was what she wanted.

Since Guru had come to live with them, Toni could have gone back to work full-time, but she hadn't. Nor had she wanted to. The baby came first, even though he was not really a baby anymore. He was walking, talking, turning into a little boy more and more every day. He was smart, quick, and beautiful, and even leaving him alone for a few hours was hard. Yes, there were times when she enjoyed the break. And yes, she missed work, because it challenged her in ways staying home did not. Still, if push came to shove and she had to make a choice, she'd be a housewife and mother.

Fortunately, it hadn't come to that. When your husband was your boss, you could be flexible. Besides, since she'd retired from the mainstream FBI job, she was technically a "consultant," which apparently satisfied the legal department. . . .

Her com chimed. She was down to a fairly safe speed now, so she pulled the phone's clip from her shorts' hem. The caller ID sig told her who it was.

"Hey, babe," she said.

"Hey," Alex said. "Where are you?"

"Riding the trike."

"Oh, good."

"What does that mean? You think I need to ride it? That I'm fat?"

There was a long pause.

She laughed. "I'm just kidding, Alex. You are so easy."

"Yeah, right. I've been down this road too many times before, thank you very much. You are not fat. I was merely expressing happiness that you could get out and enjoy yourself. It's supposed to rain later today."

"So I heard. What's up?"

"I've got to fly to New York for a meeting with the director and the Home Defense folks. Should be a quick turnaround, I'm catching the bureau's Lear, so I won't have to wait in the lines for a commercial flight. I should be home for dinner, but just in case I'm running late, I wanted you to know."

"Thanks, sweetie. You be careful."

"I will be. I love you."

"I love you, too."

After he discommed, Toni tucked the phone away and concentrated on her triking. She was glad Alex wasn't taking the shuttle. It had been a while since any bad terrorist stuff had happened on the planes, but after the really nasty events of 2001 and some of the ugly ones since, flying just wasn't the same.

Sure, everyone did it, and mostly they tried to put it out of their minds. Life was full of risk. You could get run over just crossing the street. Still, she always had a twinge of worry every time Alex flew, even on the company jet. Yes, there were sky marshals on most flights; yes, as a federal agent, Alex could carry his taser; and yes, he finally had some skill in fighting. But as everybody knew, against a suicidal fanatic, all bets were iffy.

They would have to get to the root of the cause to stop it, and some of the world's grudges went back thousands of years. How do you change the attitude of somebody whose people had grown up hating since the days when they were building pyramids?

Slowly. Very slowly. Meanwhile, you kept your guard up and if somebody did try something, you flattened them. The price of liberty was vigilance.

Toni rounded the curve. A pair of mothers were pushing strollers, both women wearing broad-brimmed hats, and both strollers with lids up and blankets draped to keep the babies shaded. Toni smiled, feeling a kinship with these women. She had a child. Mothers were all connected in some way, weren't they?

She passed the walkers, smiled, and waved. She could turn around up ahead and head back the way she had come. With any luck, that straight stretch would still be empty, and she could cut loose again. And then go home and see her beautiful, brilliant, wonderful son.

Net Force Shooting Range
Quantico, Virginia

Tyrone had gone to wash his hands and use the toilet, leaving Howard and Julio at Gunny's desk.

Julio was the first to try to describe what had just happened.

"Lord, John, I never saw anything like that," he said. "The kid is a natural pistoleer. Give him a month to practice and he'd shoot the pants off Gunny here."

Howard nodded. It had been quite a surprise to see his teenaged son pick up a pistol and have it become an extension of his hand. No fumbling, no hesitation. He put the first round into the target dead-on and kept putting them there the rest of the session. He did it with Howard's revolver and Julio's semiauto equally well, too. It was as if he had been shooting handguns for years, but Howard knew he hadn't. This had been his very first exposure.

Stunned and amazed, Howard had asked him if he'd practiced in VR, but Tyrone had said no.

Gunny nodded. "You want to send him down here to train, sir, I'll put him on the pistol team. We could use the help."

Howard shook his head. Having his son turn into Wild Bill Hickock had never been part of his vision for the boy. Yes, he wanted him to be able to handle firearms, and yes, he wouldn't be too unhappy if the boy was a little more physical instead of plopped in front of his computer as much as he was. Tyrone had learned how to throw a boomerang, and that got him out into the sunshine more, which was good. And he had a girlfriend, so he was learning those aspects of manhood, too. But a shooter? Howard had never thought about it.

It was obvious the boy had a talent for it. But was he interested in pursuing it? And if he was, did Howard really *want* him to pursue it?

Well, his inner voice said, *it'll keep him off the streets, won't it?*

"I'll ask him," he told Gunny.

"You do that, General, sir. A talent like that, it would be a waste not to encourage it."

Maybe, Howard thought.

Maybe.

3

Mitchell Townsend Ames leaned back in his form-chair and listened as the servomotors quietly hummed and adjusted the unit to fit his new position. The chair was a marvel of bioengineering. Top-grain leather and graded biogel padding covered a pneumatic/hydraulic frame of titanium. Driven by six electric motors, and using pressure sensors and fast relays, it matched his every movement, molding itself to his position within a second. When he sat up and leaned forward, it became a straight-backed office chair. When he leaned back a little, it rearranged itself into a lounger. And if he chose to stretch out fully, it turned into a bed.

Eleven thousand dollars and change, the chair was guaranteed to be the most comfortable thing you ever sat on or your money cheerfully refunded. So far, the company that made the form-chair had sold almost five thousand of the things, and nobody had asked for their money back. It was a great toy.

Ames owned six of the custom-made form-chairs: one in his medical office, the second in his legal office, the third and fourth in his New York apartment and house in Connecticut, respectively, and the fifth at his mistress's apartment in London. The last one he kept here in his "clean" office, which was the only place he met with people like Junior.

Almost seventy thousand dollars for half a dozen chairs. A lot of money for a little comfort. If he wanted, though, he could have bought a hundred more form-chairs without his accountant ever raising an eyebrow. After all, he had won half a dozen class-action tort cases—one chair for each successful suit—against major pharmaceutical companies. Each one had netted upward of a hundred million dollars. His percentage had been considerable. He could retire today with an annual income of well over a million dollars from the interest alone. What were a few toys when you had that kind of resource?

Still, the man seated across from him was in a cheaper and more conventional chair: comfortable, but nothing like a form-chair.

Marcus "Junior" Boudreaux laughed his raucous, crow-like laugh. "You shoulda seen his face, Doc," he said. "He looked like he swallowed a live water moccasin."

Ames shook his head. "Overkill," he said.

Junior looked at him. "Huh?"

"You didn't need to tell him the girl was fourteen. She could have been eighteen or eighty—in his position, *any* kind of sexual impropriety can be fatal. You could have even told him she was a whore who had set him up and it wouldn't have mattered. He's married, he's elected, and it's the family vote that keeps him in office. You don't need to use a cannon to swat a fly."

Junior shook his head. "Better safe than sorry, I figured."

Ames shrugged. It didn't really matter. He dismissed the

senator with a short wave. "What about the new clerk?"

"No problem there, Doc. The man is happy to take our money. He gets fifty up front. If it comes out of Lassiter's office that the court should hear it, he gets another fifty grand. If the court votes our way, he gets two hundred. He's working for us."

Ames sighed and nodded. Yes, having a clerk for a Supreme Court justice on your payroll was a valuable thing indeed. Most people had no idea how much weight these young lawyers carried. The judges depended on their clerks for all kinds of input, and what got read or ignored was in large part due to how the clerks presented it.

As of this moment, Ames had *two* clerks. Better yet, they were from different sides of the political aisle, one a Democrat, the other a Republican. At least, that's what their judges were. Ames didn't care about the clerks' own politics, as long as they did what they were supposed to do.

And what they were supposed to do was further Ames's agenda. Or, more precisely, the agenda that he was being very well paid to further, which was the same thing.

"Very good." Ames unlocked the top right drawer of his desk and pulled it open. Next to a 9mm SIG Neuhausen P-210, the finest production pistol made in that caliber, was a big manila mailer full of crisp thousand-dollar bills. Ames pulled the envelope out and put it on the leather blotter in front of him.

The gun had cost a couple of thousand at most. It had been tuned, so it was maybe worth another grand. Even so, he'd rather lose the fifty grand in the mailer than the pistol. Money was only money, but a good shooter was a treasure.

He had quite a collection of handguns, and the two most valuable were together worth two and a half million dollars. One, a German Luger made for testing as a possible sidearm for U.S. troops back in the early 1900s before they adopted the Colt slabside 1911, was in .45 caliber. Only four of such had been made. Two of those had been destroyed during testing, one was in the hands of another collector, and the last had been produced without records and kept by the man who'd made it, a supervisor at the gun factory in Germany. His great-grandson had sold it to Ames for a flat million.

Someday, Ames hoped to convince the other collector to part with his, so he'd have a pair.

His other prize was a Colt Walker–Dragoon .44 percussion, model 1847. One of the Texas Ranger Company guns, it was in excellent condition. It had been oiled and packed away within a year or two of its manufacture, and stored in a chest in Texas. A massive piece, it weighed more than four and a half pounds and had a nine-inch barrel. Tests had shown that the gun had been fired, but not much, and there was hardly a blemish on it. He had paid one point two million for it at an auction three years ago. He would have paid twice that and considered it a bargain.

Junior reached out and took the envelope. He raised an eyebrow and looked over at Ames.

"Fifty thousand," Ames said. "Call me when that runs out."

Junior nodded. Grinning hugely, he rose and left the office.

Ames glanced at his watch. It was a simple-looking timepiece, really, nothing fancy. Just a concave-backed rectangular black face with hour, minute, and a sweep second hand, art-deco numbers, and a monthly calendar, on a leather band. If you didn't know watches, you would think it was just like dozens of others of the same general design, but it wasn't. It was one of Hans Graven's handmades.

Graven produced only four of these a year, every piece hand-tooled. The case was machined out of platinum, and any spot that had to endure friction within was jeweled with rubies. It was waterproof and self-winding. Ames had a little mechanical box at home that would gently rotate the watch every so often, if he couldn't wear it for some reason, to keep it running.

The watch had a mineral crystal, the band was of select giraffe leather, and the movement was guaranteed to gain or lose no more than thirty seconds a year. It was also guaranteed for a hundred years against *anything*—breakage, theft, or loss. Four hundred and fifty thousand dollars it had cost, not counting the trip to Switzerland to pick it up. Graven did not ship his watches. If he couldn't put them onto a buyer's wrist himself, they didn't leave the shop.

Another toy, but it amused him that it cost so much and looked so simple. The nouveau riche could be ostentatious in displaying their wealth, but Townsend Ames had more class than that, even if he didn't come from old money.

He stood and punched the button on his phone that automatically called the limo. He had to get moving. He had rounds to make at the hospital. None of his patients were about to die, of course. Ames was a family practitioner, after all. When his patients got real sick, he sent them to specialists.

After his rounds, he would head directly to his law offices. Being a doctor/lawyer did tend to keep a man busy. He could have slowed down, of course, but it was all about winning, and Ames was that: a winner.

He intended to prove that yet again in that little matter of the lawsuit regarding the Caribbean gambling ship. His associates should have that ready to file this afternoon. Ames needed to go over everything and make sure it was all in order. After that, he had scheduled a meeting with that Washington lobbyist for a drink around five, what was her name? Skye?

A busy day on the schedule. He glanced down at the gun again and grinned. He wouldn't have it any other way.

Net Force HQ
Quantico, Virginia

"Hey, Boss."

Michaels looked up and saw Jay Gridley leaning against his office doorway. Yesterday's trip to New York was still on his mind. The FBI director had essentially offered Net Force's services to the Home Security folks on some new net-terrorism threat they had uncovered. Michaels wasn't very happy about it. Net Force didn't need another pair of eyes looking over their shoulder. Besides, Home Security wasn't known for its subtlety. Michaels believed that they had a legitimate and vital mission, and he both respected and appreciated the job they had to do. Still, they had stepped over the line a few times in places where even he wouldn't have gone.

Civil liberties tended to get trampled in times of national emergencies. Michaels knew that you had to err on the side of safety when it came to American lives, of course, but he also knew that the nature of any bureaucracy was to perpetuate itself, and the term "national security" could be stretched to cover an awful lot of activities.

"Hey, Jay. What's up?"

"Not much new. I got a little follow-up on that thing I sent you."

"We are talking about CyberNation, here, aren't we?"

"I'm pretty sure we are," Jay said, standing up straighter and taking a step inside Alex's office. "They are dancing their usual twisty dance to distract anybody watching, but yeah, I'd bet on it."

Michaels shook his head. The CyberNation problem had been a nasty one, and in the end had involved a shoot-out on a gambling ship in the Caribbean. Worse, it had put Toni at risk, something he still regretted, even though she hadn't been hurt.

Unfortunately, Net Force had only gotten a few of the

players when all was said and done. Not surprisingly, those arrested had been disavowed by the rest of organization as rogues and traitors. CyberNation itself was still out there, a great, big, ugly can of worms. And it looked as if the organization was about to score a major victory, too.

What they couldn't do with terrorism, the director had told him only yesterday, they might be able to do with the ballot box. The latest round of bills to recognize the virtual nation, as they liked to call it, were being pushed hard, and actually had a chance of getting passed.

The idea just wouldn't go away.

"What have you got?" Alex asked.

"Well, I'm sure they are funneling money to places where it ought not to be going. I haven't been able to nail it down yet, but I will."

"Keep on it. Let me know."

"Sure, Boss."

"What about the other thing? The virus?"

"Still running it down. Nothing yet, but it doesn't look like much of a threat."

The intercom chirped. "Alex, the director is on line one."

Michaels nodded at Jay and picked up the receiver.

"Yes, ma'am?" he said.

Melissa Allison, the first woman director of the FBI, had been a pretty good boss. Mostly, she left Net Force alone, and mostly, she backed them up when they got into deep waters. And since she knew where a lot of political bodies were buried, she had good clout. It could be a lot worse.

"Alex, I just heard from Legal that a five-hundred-million-dollar wrongful death lawsuit has been filed against Net Force as a whole, as well as General John Howard and you in particular, on the behalf of the families of Richard A. Dunlop, Kyle J. Herrington, and S. Jackson Britton."

"Who?" Alex asked. "Those names don't ring any bells. And we haven't killed anybody recently that I know of."

"They were CyberNation employees who died during the assault on the gambling ship *Bon Chance* last year."

Alex shook his head. CyberNation again.

"If I recall correctly, Madam Director, these men were firing weapons at Net Force operatives and only shot in perfectly justifiable self-defense. And the international maritime court that covers such things on the high seas found that to be the case."

"That doesn't matter in a tort action, Commander. This is civil, not criminal. If you sell somebody a cup of hot coffee and they turn around and spill it on their lap, they can sue you and win millions. People who have broken into houses for the purpose of burglary have sued the homeowners because they tripped on the rug while hauling the television set out. What's more, they have actually won damages. We live in a litigious society."

Unbelievable. "Swell," he said.

She ignored his sarcasm. "You'll be getting a call from Net Force legal council Thomas Bender, who'll be coordinating the defense with FBI Legal and DOJ. You are, of course, covered under the governmental umbrella, but you might want to consider retaining private counsel just to be on the safe side. And give General Howard a heads-up, as well."

"Yes, ma'am. Thank you."

She discommed, and he pressed the button for John Howard.

A lawsuit. Wonderful. Just what they all needed right now.

Excalibur Gun Club
White Oak, Maryland

Junior liked to get to the combat range in the middle of
the morning on a weekday when he could. Those were the
slackest times, and he would usually have the place to
himself. The only other people who ever showed up at
those times were some of the cleanup guys working at the
old closed-up Naval Surface Weapons Center just south of
there.

You'd think they could pop off rounds on the base,
though. Clearly there was plenty of room for it. Seven
hundred acres, it had been more or less shut down since
the mid-nineties, but they still hadn't cleaned up all the
contaminants, oil, and PCBs. At least that was what Junior
heard from the reclamation contract guys who came by
here to shoot. Every time they thought they were done,
they'd find some more that needed doing.

Junior laughed at the thought. His tax dollars at work.

Today was a good day, though. There was only one
local deputy cooking off nines down in bay five. Junior's
favorite bay, B1, was open.

He backed his car into the slot. It was just a cut-out in
the side of a hill, probably done with a backhoe and Cat,
with dirt and rock walls rising from the ground at the entrance to about twenty feet high at the back.

He got out, pulled his shooting bag from the trunk, and
put it on the old plywood table.

This bay had a reactive target, a kind of big sawhorse-
shaped thing made out of heavy steel extrusion with falling
plates mounted above, just below eye level. The frame's
crosspiece extrusion was angled so that if bullets hit it, the
rounds would be deflected into the ground. The six targets,
each of which was made of half-inch-thick tool steel and
a little bigger around than a salad plate, were hinged at the
bottom. You simply set up the plates, backed off, and shot

them. A hit would knock the plate over backward. The thing was, they were set for IPSC minor power factor. That meant you needed at least a warm .38 or a 9mm special to knock 'em over, and major power factor stuff was a lot better—a .357, .40, or .45, like that. With what he was using, he could make 'em ring, but not knock 'em over.

But there were ways to get around that.

He pulled the can of flat-white spray paint from his bag and walked toward the target. Along the way, he stooped and picked up half a dozen used shotgun shells. Some shooters always left the brass and plastic hulls, which was good for him.

He set the falling plates up, and used the shotgun shells to lean and prop them in such a way that a light tap would knock 'em over. Then he sprayed each target with a light coat of white paint, enough so that a hit would show up as a dark splotch.

He went back to the shooting table and pulled his earphones out, along with a box of ammo and two speedloaders. The earphones were Wolf Ears—electronic jobs that would shut off loud noises but let you hear regular sounds. He slipped those on, put the speedloaders in his jacket pockets, picked up the spray paint, then stepped away from the table and walked to where he was twenty-one feet from the targets.

He put the paint down. Straightening, he took a deep breath, let part of it out, cleared his jacket on both sides, and fast-drew both his revolvers simultaneously. He didn't use the sights, but indexed the guns like pointing his fingers. He shot the far left target first, using the gun in that hand, squeezing the trigger twice for a double-tap. Then he shot the one on the far right with his right-hand piece, again firing twice. Even as the first two targets clanged and fell, he worked his way back and forth, alternating from left to right.

He cooked both guns dry.

Five seconds, twelve shots, six targets, two each, all hits.

He holstered his left gun, thumbed the latch and shoved the cylinder out on the right one, and popped the empties out with a fast palm hit on the extractor rod. He pulled a speedloader from his pocket and reloaded the revolver, holstered it, then repeated the reload with the left piece. Both guns holstered, he took the spray paint and moved to inspect the targets.

The hits were all close to the center and usually a couple inches apart, except for the second right-hand one, which had two gray splotches in a binocular hit, but slightly high. Not bad, though. They would have hit a man in the mouth.

He set the targets back up, shotgun shells in place, and repainted them.

He was using a pair of tuned Ruger SP101s, two-and-a-quarter-inch barrels, in .22 Long Rifle caliber. "Mouse guns," most serious shooters would call them. The .22 LR round was fast, but tiny. A .38 Special or 9mm bullet would be three or four times as big. According to Evan Marshall's Stopping Power Stats, the smaller .22 would only knock the fight out of a man with a torso hit maybe one time in three. Given that a hot .40 or .357 round would put that same man down and out better than nine and a half times out of ten, most shooters felt that thirty percent was pretty crappy. Sixty-six percent odds the guy would keep coming if you shot him certainly wasn't something they'd want to risk their life on.

Junior grinned as he reached the firing line. A body shot with a mouse gun might get you killed by return fire or an angry guy swinging a tire iron, but a head shot? That was something else. If you put a forty-grain .22 round in a guy's eye, it didn't matter how tough he was.

Junior used to like talking trash to the big-bore guys when they'd laugh at his .22s. *Tell you what,* he'd say, *You let me have the first shot, then you can shoot me as*

*many times as you want with your rhino killer. What you
think about that, hah?*

Nobody had taken him up on it.

Putting the paint down, he turned back to face the targets. Without a pause, he drew, pointed, and emptied both guns.

Six for six.

He reloaded and went to reset and repaint the targets. Yeah, the little Rugers would kill you as dead as a howitzer, if you were good enough to put the bullets where they needed to go, and they had some advantages over the hand cannons. They were small and lighter to haul around. They were quieter. They didn't have any recoil to speak of. And ammo was cheap. You could shoot all day for a few dollars.

Best of all, when he was on the road and couldn't make it to the combat range, he could take a little drive out into the country just about anywhere, walk into some woods, shake up some cans of Coke, put 'em against a backstop, and start blasting away. He could spew fizz all whichaway and not bother anyone more than a few hundred yards away. Fire off a .357 and it sounded like an big bomb going off, *ka-whoom!* You would hear that sucker for *miles.*

Of course, he had given himself some additional advantages. Bill Ruger's little guns were built like bank vaults. You could drop one off a tall building and it would still shoot. The SPs were also head and shoulders above an S&W or Taurus for reliability. That made 'em a little stiff right out of the box, the actions a little hard, but a couple hours with a Dremel and some polish and he had rounded the triggers and hammers. That had slicked up the actions so they each had a nice eight-pound DA pull, and broke like an icicle at just over two pounds single-action, smooth as oil on glass, no creep. New springs and spec lube, too.

Four-inch barrels would have been better, accuracywise,

but they were harder to conceal in summer clothes. The factory stocks were too small for his big hands, so he had switched to Pachmayr's hard rubber Compacs, which were the perfect size, and not going to slip if his palms were sweaty. He could have put Crimson Trace laser grips on 'em, but that was *too* much of an advantage, made it way too easy. He'd had a pair of custom holsters made for 'em, Kramer horsehide, as good as you could get.

And he took care of things from the ammo end, too. He used CCI Minimags exclusively, the solids, not the hollow points. He'd buy a brick, a full five hundred rounds. Then he'd sit in front of the TV with the sports channel on and his little Dillon scale and weigh each cartridge. It turned out that seven or eight out of ten rounds weighed fifty-one grains. All the fifty-ones went into one box, the other stuff into another—he used those for his little lever-action Winchester rifle. It didn't really *matter* how much they weighed; it only mattered that the ones he carried all weighed the *same*.

When that was done, he would use the little headspace gauge he had made. With that, he could check to make sure the bullets were all the same size and shape. Any that were deformed or a hair too long or short went into the rifle box.

Every round he carried in his revolvers or speedloaders was as close to exactly the same size and weight as he could make them. It didn't matter if they all shot a hair high or a hair low, as long as they all went to the same place. Consistency, that was the key. An old silhouette shooter had showed him that, and it worked.

Finally, because rimfire ammo could sometimes go bad, oil or lube seeping into them, he changed the rounds in his guns and speedloaders once a week, and the old ones went into the rifle box.

Of course, a snub-nose revolver wasn't going to be a tack-driver at any kind of range, no matter how good a shooter you were. Still and all, it didn't have to be. All he needed to be able to do was hit somebody in the head at seven yards, which was the longest range of most gunfights. The FBI used to say, "Three shots, three feet, three seconds," was the average shoot-out.

Out to seven yards, he could point-shoot heads all day long pretty damn quick, yeah. But just in case, when he was working on the action, he'd kept the spurs on the Rugers' hammers. That way he could cock 'em for single-action if he had to. Given just a little time to aim, he could hit that same target at twenty-five yards single-action, holding one gun two-handed, nine times out of ten. At fifty yards, the head shot simply wasn't going to happen except by luck, but he could put them all into a torso at that range. The .22s might not be a manstopper to the body, but six hits would give a man something real serious to think about. There weren't too many gunfights at fifty yards anyhow.

Back at the firing line, he reset himself. Taking a deep breath, he drew and cooked 'em off. . . .

Six for six.

He smiled. Damn, he was good.

At least, he was good when the targets weren't shooting back. He was going to have to do something about that soon, yeah, or else stop looking at himself every time he passed a mirror. Pretty soon, yeah.

4

Howard and Tyrone were in the den. Howard was reading the paper. Ty was in the lounger, VR goggles on his head, surfing the web.

In the kitchen, Nadine was fixing supper. She yelled something at him, but he didn't catch it.

"What?" he called out.

She came into the den, a spatula in one hand, an oven mitt on the other. "I asked you if you wanted part of a beer," she said.

They did that sometimes, split a beer while she was cooking.

He smiled at her and shook his head. "No, thanks, babe, you go ahead." He knew she would drink half the bottle, then put the rest back in the fridge. If he didn't drink it, it would go flat. Big party animals, the Howards. Whoo-whoo.

Nadine went back into the kitchen.

"I've been thinking about what you said," Tyrone said.

He took off his goggles and laid them on his chest, but kept the chair almost fully reclined.

Howard put the paper down. At Ty's age, when he wanted to talk, it was clear the decks and stand by or lose the opportunity. "Always a good idea, thinking," Howard said, grinning. "About anything in particular?"

"That TANSTAAFL stuff."

Howard nodded. He wasn't sure of the term's origin. He'd first read it in a science fiction story by Robert A. Heinlein when he'd been a boy: *There ain't no such thing as a free lunch.* It referred, if he recalled correctly, to the old "Free Lunch" signs that were common a long time ago in local pubs and bars. Usually something like boiled eggs in pickle juice, or other snack-y food, given away to patrons. Well, it was free to the extent that you didn't have to pay for it as long as you were buying beers. It was actually a kind of loss-leader for the bars to get the drinkers to stop in.

Not all that long ago, Las Vegas used to offer terrific meals at ridiculously low prices, too. They knew that if they got you into their casinos, and kept you there with free drinks, they would get your money, either at the tables or from the slot machines. At least that way, when you went home broke, you could tell everybody how good and cheap the food was. It was like cheap advertising: *Yeah, I lost my butt at the tables, but I ate great, and it was only like five bucks for a salad, steak, potatoes, and dessert.*

He'd told Tyrone about the concept a while ago, trying to get the boy to see things from a different, more grown-up, perspective. "What about it?" he asked.

"Well," Tyrone said, "according to what I've read, it's one of those capitalist things. Robber barons and industrialists didn't want anybody putting hands into their pockets in any way, shape, or form, no regulations, nothing."

Howard nodded. "That's probably true."

"Pure capitalism doesn't work, Dad, 'cause it screws the

workers," Tyrone said. His voice was becoming louder, more passionate. "If some rich guy owns a big factory, he can hire ten-year-olds to work eighteen hours a day and pay them almost nothing."

Howard nodded again. He thought he could see where his son was headed. "Yes, that was how it used to be, a long time ago, back at the beginning of the Industrial Age or so."

Tyrone sat up, his goggles falling into his lap. "So all regulation isn't bad, then, is it? Without them, we'd have no unions, no Social Security, no welfare."

"I never said *all* regulation was bad. I'm a Republican, not a Libertarian."

Tyrone grinned, as if he had just won a major point. He said, "Right. So sometimes private industry needs to be held accountable, for the greater good of society."

Howard was right. He definitely saw where this was going. He merely nodded, though. He had to give the boy points for getting his groundwork set up.

Tyrone picked up the goggles and held them in one hand, using them to point at his father. "So if some guy, for instance, came up with a cure for cancer and he decided to sell it for a hundred thousand dollars a pop, it might be in the public interest to regulate that."

Howard folded his paper and set it aside. "To a point, I'll agree with that."

"But, see, Dad, that's the whole thing: If you could save ten thousand lives by giving the cure away for free, or only charging a buck or something, wouldn't that be valid?"

Howard shook his head. "Maybe—as long as you didn't put the guy who came up with the cure out of business. We've gone over this before, Ty, but let me say it again. Suppose this guy borrowed and spent, oh, say, ten million dollars researching, developing, and producing this cure. Even if his production cost per dose is fairly low, he still has to repay those loans, and that will drive up the amount of money he needs to keep his doors open. Are you saying it's right to take the cure away from him and have him go belly up? That the people who invested their money in this guy should lose what they put in, for the greater good of society?"

Tyrone shrugged. "If they can afford to invest *beaucoup* bucks somewhere, why not?"

"What if they *can't* afford it? Let's say Social Security goes into the toilet—which is very possible before I get old enough to draw it—and all I've got to live on is my military pension. Let's also say I've invested my money cautiously, and this rock-solid pharmaceutical company that comes up with the cancer cure is where a big chunk of my money went. I'm golden, I can quit work at sixty and live nicely for the rest of my life. But ten years after I retire, you take the cure away from them, they go bankrupt, and there I am all of a sudden, seventy years old, sitting in a cardboard box, eating dog food because my investments got co-opted. Is that fair?"

Tyrone shook his head. "No, of course not, Dad," he said. "But if the choice is you sitting in a box and eating dog food or someone you love dying of a disease because they couldn't afford the cure, which would you go for?"

Howard smiled. He really was getting a lot sharper, his son.

"Ty, in communism, which is a really unworkable philosophy, the saying is, 'From each according to his ability, to each, according to his need.' You know what that means?"

Tyrone nodded. "Of course. It means those who can do stuff help those who can't."

"Technically. What it means in practice is that people with ability carry everybody else. And there are a lot more people *without* special abilities than there are with 'em. Communism says that a guy smart enough to come up with a cure for cancer is exactly the same as somebody who digs ditches. And in the eyes of the law, that's how it should be, when it comes to getting away with murder, say. But the truth is, a guy who can invent a cure for cancer is a *lot* rarer than a guy who digs ditches. I personally have trouble with a baseball or basketball player making thirty or forty million dollars a year while a schoolteacher might make only a little more than minimum wage—that's skewed in a way I truly can't understand. But you have to recognize that talent and skill should be rewarded some-how, otherwise there's no reason to invent that cure except altruism. If you take away the thing a man spends his energy making and give him nothing in return, you take away his desire to do it again. And that of anybody else who looks at all the work needed and says to himself, 'Why bother? It won't help me or mine any.' "

"Yes, but—"

"Look at South America, Ty. Every few years, they have a revolution in one of the banana republics. Everybody in power gets tossed out and a new crew comes in. If you invested a few million in a company down there, and all of a sudden it gets nationalized and taken over for 'the good of the people,' how much do you figure you'll want to invest from that point on?"

"But we're talking about *knowledge*, Dad, not hardware."

"And I'm here to tell you that knowledge is more valu-able than hardware, because without knowledge, hardware doesn't exist. Without the minds that came up with the internal combustion engine, or the steamer, or the electric motor, there wouldn't *be* any automobiles, or freighters, or airplanes. You have to have metal benders, yes, but with-out blueprints all you get is . . . bent metal."

Tyrone frowned, but Howard wasn't finished.

"In our society, Ty, if you do something valuable, you get recognized for it. Could be fame, could be power, could be money, sometimes it's all three, but the bottom line is, if you do the work, you are supposed to get the credit, and all the perks that go along with it. Sometimes it doesn't work that way. Sometimes the inventor gets screwed. But that's how we want it to work. Because it is *right*, and on some level, people know it.

"When you download 'free' music, or somebody's newest novel that's been pirated, scanned, and posted on the web, or the formula for a drug that somebody worked years to develop, you might as well be walking into their house and stealing it at gunpoint. Theft is theft, no matter how you spin it. And it's wrong: 'Thou shalt not steal' is recognized by every civilized society and most major religions, and for a good reason. If there are no rules to protect people, then it becomes anarchy."

"There are exceptions," Tyrone said, his voice stubborn. "What about the aluminum companies in World War II?"

Howard nodded. "Yes, there are exceptions. And, yes, during World War II one company was forced to give its process to the others. But a war for your country's *survival* is not exactly the same as some college student swiping music for his personal collection, now is it?"

Tyrone grinned. "Well, no."

"A great part of common law around the world is dedicated to protecting the property rights of its citizens. When you start skirting those laws, you start down the road to big trouble. If they can take that cancer cure, what's to stop them from taking that software you wrote for a new game? TANSTAAFL means that outside of real estate, pretty much everything of value in our world was, somewhere, somehow, some *when*, thought up, created, developed, produced, and distributed by some*body*. That somebody paid for it, in blood, sweat, or tears, in time or money, for love or whatever, and that anything you think of as 'free,' isn't. You might get it free, but somebody paid for it."

Tyrone shook his head.

"You don't agree?"

"I hear you, Dad. But you make everything sound so . . . mercenary."

"There's not a thing wrong with being a mercenary, son. That's how I make my living. In fact, that's how most people make their living. If you do a job, you get paid for it. What's wrong is making somebody do a job and then *not* paying them for it. That's your CyberNation's basic premise. What you get from them isn't free. They stole it."

Tyrone sat silent for a moment.

"Something?"

"No, what you say makes sense, but I get the feeling there's something else here I'm missing, some argument for my side."

Howard chuckled. Tyrone really was getting better at this. But he wasn't there yet. "You're right, Ty. There is."

"Well, what is it?"

Howard chuckled again. "Oh, no, that's for you to figure out. I'm not going to just give it to you. After all, haven't you heard? There's no such thing as a free argument."

"Dad!" Tyrone groaned.

"Think about it some and you'll get to it. It's a good exercise."

Tyrone went off, muttering to himself and shaking his head.

Howard felt a sense of pride as he watched the boy leave. *Was* there a valid argument against TANSTAAFL? Maybe. He couldn't think of one offhand, but let his son believe there was, and he would keep looking. And sooner or later, he'd find it, bring it back, and hit his old man with it. Which was a good thing. Part of raising your child was teaching him how to take care of himself once he got out on his own. If you could take care of yourself physically, mentally, and spiritually, you had a leg up on most of the world.

November 1935
Port of Newark, New Jersey

Jay Gridley, sworn nemesis of evil, crouched low on the roof of the warehouse overlooking the Kill Van Kull, the waterway connecting New York Harbor with Newark Bay. He looked down upon the south docks, hidden in the shadows.

"Follow the money" was the classic investigative advice, but first, of course, you had to *find* the money.

If Jay was right, he was about to do just that.

It was a foggy night, cold, with the promise of yet colder days ahead. The chill brushed at him with icy fingers as the mist drifted up in slow gray billows, shrouding the farther lights into dim globes. Below, illuminated by fog-edged floods, floated the *Corona*, a rust-streaked tramp steamer just arrived from Spain. Faint trails of coal smoke still drifted from the stacks of the ship, tracing whorls that mixed with the natural mist in the night sky.

In another twenty years they'd call that smog. . . .

He pulled his wide-brimmed slouch hat lower on his head. A carmine-hued scarf covered his mouth and chin. A dark cloak shrouded him. Thin, black leather gloves covered his hands. He blended into the night, nearly invisible, no more than a shadow.

He'd put a high-level watchbot on CyberNation's wire transfers over the last few days. His sniffer had strained thousands of transactions, looking for relatively small chunks of money coming to the United States. Cyber-Nation made all sorts of payments, naturally, so he'd set the bot's sensors to filter out those that went to known companies, leaving only those that seemed to have no immediately legitimate destination, regardless of their size.

The rusted ship *Corona* docked below him was, in the real world, a large squirt of information coming over the net. Within it was a particular electronic payment from CyberNation that Jay wanted to trace. But to do that, he would have to get closer.

Noiselessly, he padded to the edge of the wall facing the river and climbed down the knotted black silk rope he'd placed there earlier. Earlier in the day, he had broken the single mercury-vapor lamp in the immediate area, so his movements now were in near-total darkness. The Port Authority, flush with more money than they'd ever had, despite the Depression, had been refitting the lights to the docks. They would, no doubt, be unhappy with his action.

He shrugged it off. A minor thing, a broken lamp.

However, should anyone look up, they'd see no more than a wraith, and that not for long. It would seem a trick of the light. Nothing more than their imagination . . .

Moving quickly, he hand-over-handed his way down the rope until he was on the docks. The smell of creosote sharp and pungent in the damp air.

A sailor stood guard at the gangway to the ship, waiting, no doubt, for Customs to come and clear their cargo.

Gridley moved slowly toward the man, removing the glove on his right hand as he did so. A gold ring featuring a large girasol, an orange-yellow variety of precious opal, gleamed faintly in the light. Intricate whirls of fire played over the deeply hued stone.

The sailor glanced at Jay and reacted immediately, reaching for the oversized pistol holstered at his belt.

Jay moved his fingers, a subtle movement that caused the opal to glitter in the dim light.

Carefully . . . slowly . . .

The sailor froze, his hand stopping inches away from the black leather holster. His eyes moved from Jay to focus intently on the gem in front of him. Jay moved the ring slightly in a pattern known only to a few in the Far East, concentrating the man's attention, hypnotizing him, placing him in a trance.

There.

In RW, Jay was simultaneously firing hundreds and thousands of passwords and protocol requests to a watchdog program, overloading its capacity to prevent intrusion. Boring. Playing the role of a pulp-fiction hero was *much* more interesting.

Silently, he oozed his way up the gangplank and onto the ship. There he straightened up and pulled off his black cloak and hat, revealing a navy greatcoat and a watch cap underneath. He hid his fedora and cloak behind a lifeboat, and to all appearances became just another sailor on the ship.

Clouding men's minds with girasols was all well and good when you were spotted and challenged. But if he *looked* as if he belonged here, if he could avoid being challenged at all, that was even better.

Jay found a posted copy of the manifest showing the cargo hold he was looking for and made his way there. A single bare, low-wattage electrical bulb cast a thin light upon the scene, just enough to see that which he had come for: The box was unmarked, a plain wooden crate with only an ID number stenciled on it.

Working quickly, Jay pried open one end of the box, careful not to bend the nails. Then he opened his coat and pulled out a cigar box–sized transmitter that he slipped inside the crate.

He grinned. Ah, historical accuracy! He loved it. That was one of the many things that set Jay Gridley apart from other sim writers. It would have been so easy to simply cheat and make the transmitter more modern. It would have been even easier to simply tag the package electronically, avoiding the need for all this skulking about.

But where was the fun in that?

Instead, he had made every single detail as historically accurate as possible. The vacuum tubes that made up the transmitter's circuits couldn't get any smaller. The technology was one hundred percent appropriate to 1935. And the materials were all true to the time period.

He thought about the sailor he had hypnotized with a few mystical gestures and grinned to himself. Well, okay, so maybe the details weren't all true to history, but they were all true to the scenario he was working in.

Reaching into the box, he threw a large toggle switch on the device, activating it. He wiggled the transmitter slightly, nestling it in solid among thousands of greenbacks. The tubes couldn't take much shaking.

Carefully he closed the crate and used the rubber-coated handle end of the pry bar he'd brought with him to quietly tap the nails back in. When he was finished, there was no sign anyone had opened the crate.

Naturally.

He took out a small crystal bottle of liquid with a tiny atomizer on the top and misted the crate several times.

He reversed his path, and within minutes was back on the rooftop. He went to the portable receiver he'd left there and turned it on. A faint glow came from the analog meter on the device showing the signal strength of the transmitter.

Using tracking devices, particularly in this era, wasn't as simple as people thought. Unlike modern GPS devices, older ones relied on signal strength and triangulation to be accurate. With only one receiver, he would be able to tell if the transmitter moved away from him, but he would not be able to trace its direction.

Ideally he'd have placed three receivers around the New York and New Jersey countryside with teams relaying signal strengths from each so that he could triangulate the precise position of the money he was tracking. But as the lone avenger of evil, he only had time to place one on the other side of the river. He had set that one to automatically relay the signal strength of the distant receiver on another frequency, however, so that he could, in effect, have two parts of the triangle. Not the best option, perhaps, but for Jay Gridley, master of the virtual realm, it should be more than enough.

He glanced out at the water, admiring the fog there. The stuff was so thick you could almost cut it with a knife. A tendril wisped past him and he reached out to touch it— and did.

The fog had solid form, it felt like cotton candy, and that was all wrong. It was supposed to be vapor.

And it had an odor, too. It smelled like—like . . .

A sewer.

Hmm, Jay thought. *Must be a problem with those new drivers.*

Now and then there'd be a failure in the hardware/software interface in VR. Usually that happened when something was being upgraded. And, Jay had found, it was generally the drivers for the hardware that had some glitch in them, some incompatibility problem. It certainly wasn't his code.

He waved at the offending fog, shoving it, smell and all, away.

Oh, well. When you lived on the cutting edge of technology, sometimes you got a little bloody.

He grinned. Such things did not deter a pulp hero, no-siree. . . .

On the dock there was activity. Customs had cleared the ship. Longshoremen moved here and there. The process went fairly fast, cargo being offloaded with a speed that surprised him, it being 1935 and all.

He periodically checked the meter. The signal strength didn't move. Were they going to take all night to get to his box?

As if his thoughts had provoked them, the meters on his receiver jumped. The distant one gained strength, and the closer one lost a bit.

He stared at the cargo neatly stacked on the dock in front of him. If the box was among the items there, the signal on the closer meter should have gotten *stronger* instead of weaker.

They're moving it in the other direction—away from the dock!

But there was nothing there—no, wait, there was another ship at anchor a short way off, not yet docked.

This one was Portuguese.

Aha!

Quickly Jay fumbled in the bag near the transmitter for the goggles he'd placed there. He pulled them out, huge fish-eye things that covered his eyes completely, making him look like a mad scientist. He flicked a switch on the goggles and the world suddenly stood out in sharp shades of red. He scanned the other ship—

There! The crate glowed brightly in his field of view. The clear solution he'd sprayed it with contained faintly radioactive particles that would only show up when wearing goggles like his. He could see that a quartet of sailors was moving the crate to the other ship.

CyberNation was slick, he had to give them that. Here in VR they were simply moving the crate to another ship. In reality they were sending the money on another trip around the world. It wouldn't actually hit the U.S. until this Portuguese ship reached the docks. Once there, though, Jay would be able to trace the package easily.

He bet they would transfer it again. Maybe several more times, to further cloud the trail.

Jay left his post at the edge of the rooftop and went to the aircraft he'd stashed deeper in the shadows. In 1935 they didn't have helicopters—they had the autogyro. Like a helicopter, the autogyro used rotors for lift. Unlike it, however, it was driven by a propeller, like a plane. The push from the propeller made the rotors spin, generating lift. A Spanish mathematician, Juan de la Cierva, had made the first successful flight in 1923. The autogyro didn't make a true vertical takeoff and landing—it did have to be pushed forward a little before lifting off, unless there was a stiff wind blowing—but it was good enough for his purposes. Gridley's model was a Pitcairn-Cierva PCA-2, the same kind used for mail delivery by some of the post offices of the era.

God, he loved research!

He fired up the tightly muffled Wright R-975-E2 Whirlwind engine and the craft lurched forward, its thirty-foot rotors beginning to spin. It worked best into the wind, the stiffer the better, but with fog you didn't get much breeze.

Within seconds he was airborne, tracking the crate.

It was easy with the goggles, and he used the transmitter every now and then to confirm its route. These guys were *good*. The crate went to a Libyan freighter next, then a French steamer, followed by one out of Rio, and then to one from Greece.

Then, at last, it was placed on the docks.

Jay used a feature of the goggles to magnify the crate. A clear destination was now imprinted on the box: Washington, D.C. There was an account number, and even the name of the bank branch.

He laughed, a low chuckle building to a sinister rumble: *Moohoohahaaaaaaa!*

He had them now.

5

Washington, D.C.

Three blocks from home, Toni watched Little Alex toddle
down the sidewalk, his lurching run just a hair short of a
fall with each step that he took. He was fearless, her son.
Every time he tripped and went to his hands and knees on
the concrete, scraping himself bloody, he got right back
up and charged off again. Well, usually after a few tears,
just to make sure she was paying attention.

At the moment, the object of his attention was a sparrow. The small bird was cautious enough to keep hopping
away as the boy lumbered toward it, but not frightened
enough to take wing.

Toni smiled. Somewhere in the back of an old photo
album, there was a picture of her as a small child, maybe
two or a little younger, sitting on the steps of her parents'
place in the Bronx. Sitting perched on the stoop in front
of her, not six inches away, was a bird—it had looked like
a blue jay—easily within her reach. How had that bird
come to be there? Why hadn't it been afraid of her?

When she'd first seen the picture and asked her father about it, he had laughed and said it was a stuffed bird. Mama told her different, though. Mama was the one who had taken the picture, and she said the bird had just dropped down and alighted next to her, watching her. Toni hadn't tried to catch it, and it had stayed there for a long time. Mama was convinced that animals knew when there was a threat and when there wasn't, and believed that the bird had known that little Toni meant it no harm.

Alex shambled off the sidewalk onto the lawn, and the sparrow did its little two-foot hop three or four times to one side and turned to look at him again. It wasn't as if the bird seemed to be afraid, except maybe about being accidentally stepped on—which was a real enough danger. It seemed more like it was curious.

A mutual thing, that.

Her virgil beeped at her. She unbelted it and saw it was Alex calling.

"Hey, hon," she said. "What's up?"

"Not much. Just calling to see how your day is going."

"Great. I got home, and now the baby and I are out for a walk. Guru has gone to a movie."

"Really?" Alex laughed. "What did she go to—some action-adventure thing with exploding heads?"

"No, the new Tanya Clements romantic comedy."

"Our Guru? The old lady who can beat up three Marines and a pro boxer at the same time?"

"The very same."

"I'm amazed. Mm." He paused, then changed the subject. "Listen, hon, I'm going to be running a little late. I have to be deposed by the lawyers on that CyberNation lawsuit. What did you have in mind for supper?"

Toni smiled. "Whatever you were planning on bringing home from takeout."

"Ah, I see. How's Indian?"

"Sounds good. Get me the Chicken Masala. And don't forget the dal and nan."

"Your wish is my command, O mistress. Kiss our boy for me. I should be there around seven thirty."

"Good. Love you."

"I love you, too, Toni."

After he discommed, Toni stuck the com back onto her belt and watched as the sparrow took off, having finally decided this monster about to fall on it might best be avoided at a greater distance. The bird flew into a tree, landing on a branch about ten feet up.

Little Alex turned to look at her, his face clouding up. He pointed at the tree. "Mama! Bird! Get bird! Get bird!"

As if she could. And as if he had every right to ask. He wanted it, therefore he should have it.

She laughed. "Sorry, baboo, but Mama can't fly."

He shook his head and looked very determined. "Mama. Get bird."

She laughed again. What a wonderful child he was. Utterly convinced that he was the center of the universe. And why not? she thought. After all, she hadn't done much to disabuse him of the notion. She'd have to start doing that at some point. Otherwise, he was going to have problems when he ran into the other two-year-olds who were just as convinced that *they* were the sun around which all worlds revolved.

More amazing, maybe, was that the boy had become the center of *her* universe. A career woman, marital artist, take-no-prisoners gal who now got mushy whenever her little baboo smiled at her. Who would have thought it?

The sparrow took off again and vanished through the cherry trees.

"Bird go bye-bye," Alex said. He looked crushed.

"Yes. Bird go bye-bye."

But the sparrow wasn't the only amusement on the block. A man walking a happy-looking German shepherd dog came toward them, and Alex's gloom at having lost the bird vanished in a big smile. "Woof-woof!" he said.

"Woof-woof," she said. "It *is* a dog!"

Before her baby was born, she would never have believed that she'd be having these kinds of conversations. When she had heard friends or relatives jabbering at their small kids like this, she had been amused, even condescending. *She* would never talk to her kids that way. Or so she had thought, anyway.

The dog, her tail wagging like a crazed metronome, was straining at the leash slightly, obviously wanting to get to Little Alex. Toni looked at the owner, a fit, largish, fifty-something man in a T-shirt, shorts, and running shoes, with short hair and sunglasses. "Does the dog bite?" she asked. "Is she good with children?"

The owner chuckled. "Cady? She'll lick his face, is all. Maybe knock him down with her tongue. She's the biggest sissy you ever saw. I've seen the cat shove her away from her own food bowl, and all she did was stand there and whine at me: 'Help, Daddy, protect me!' "

Toni grinned. "Alex, you want to pet the woof-woof?"

"Woof-woof!"

"Go ahead, then," Toni said to the dog's owner. "Give her a little slack." She was a little wary, and she edged a tiny bit closer, but she was determined that she wasn't going to walk around her whole life stopping her son from experiencing the world.

The dog, who had to weigh a hundred and fifteen or twenty pounds, surged forward, and Toni tensed up. Nothing happened, though, except that it began to lap at Alex's face.

It surprised him, and he flinched, but then he laughed, reached out, and hugged the big beast around the neck. The dog seemed happy enough, and Alex was ecstatic. "Woof-woof! Woof-woof!"

The owner smiled. "Beautiful little boy," he said.

"We think so," Toni said. "So is your dog."

Alex continued to hug the dog, who seemed to think this was a fine game.

A dog, Toni thought. *Now there's an idea. Somebody to keep Little Alex company.* She'd always wanted a dog when she'd been little, but living in an apartment in the Bronx made that a problem. No reason they couldn't have a dog now, though. Alex liked dogs, she knew. He had even had one for a while. And they had a yard. Kids ought to have a dog, right?

Net Force HQ
Quantico, Virginia

They were in the conference room. There just wasn't enough table space in Michaels's office for all the hard-copy documents they needed to spread out and examine.

Michaels looked at the sea of paper. "God, I hate lawyers," he said.

"Present company excluded, of course?"

"No," Alex said, shaking his head. "*Especially* present company."

Tommy Bender laughed. "Sorry, pal, I don't make the rules. I just try to keep my clients from being skewered by 'em."

"Yeah, well, Shakespeare was right. Come the Revolution, first thing we should do is kill all the lawyers. It would certainly make things a lot simpler."

"That quote is always taken out of context," Tommy said. "King Henry the VI, Part II, Scene II. It's spoken by a comedy relief character named 'Dick the Butcher,' who is a killer, while his buddy Cade muses about what he'd do if he was king. An early lawyer joke is all it was, a cheap laugh."

"Can't have too many cheap laughs," Alex said. "Or lawyer jokes, for that matter."

"Here's one," Tommy said. "A lawyer and his wife are on a cruise in the Caribbean."

"I hate the locale already," Michaels said.

"You should have thought of that before you started shooting people down there. Anyway, the lawyer and his wife are watching the sharks swim back and forth, and the lawyer leans too far forward and falls into the water. The ship's captain, who is passing by, sees the man fall, yells 'Man overboard!' and reaches for a life ring, when all of a sudden the sharks stop swimming. One of them dives under the thrashing lawyer, picks him up on his back, and heads toward the ship, while the other sharks line up in two rows on either side. The shark delivers the lawyer to the ladder, where the lawyer climbs off.

"The captain is stunned. 'I have never seen anything like that!' he says. 'That was amazing!'

"And the lawyer's wife just shrugs and says, 'No big deal. Just professional courtesy. . . .' "

Michaels smiled and shook his head. "Why is it that all the best lawyer jokes I hear are from lawyers?"

"We have to be able to laugh at ourselves," Tommy said. "Everyone else does, and it's easier than crying about it. Nobody loves the undertaker, either, but he's got his niche." He shrugged and pointed at the piles of paper. "All right," he said. "Let's get back to your situation, shall we?"

Alex groaned. "Do we have to?"

"Unless you want to cost the taxpayers a couple hundred million dollars for violating the civil rights of the dead guys, it would be a good idea, yes."

"You know," Michaels said, "I just don't understand this. We were in international waters, and they were shooting at us. Doesn't that help?"

"Yes and no. Mostly, it just muddies things up. A few years ago, it wouldn't have happened, there were actually laws against suing certain agencies in the performance of their duties, kind of like you can't sue a sitting President, and some states won't let cops arrest legislators for piddly stuff when congress is in session. But times change. International Maritime Law is unbelievably complicated, and made even worse by the latest round of rulings from the Hague and by the U.N.'s interpretations of those rulings."

He sighed. "Look, Alex, the way things stand right now, you can get sued in either state or federal court, since the affected persons were all natives of this country, and of Florida, and so are their dependents. American citizens don't lose their American civil rights while at sea, especially if they are being violated by other Americans. Obviously, the violators in this case would be you, although you personally won't have to pay out anything, since you are under the Net Force umbrella, and federally insured and all. Still, nobody in the food chain is going to be happy if we lose this suit."

"What about just settling? Wouldn't it be cheaper?"

"No question, but the people suing you don't want to settle—or, more accurately, the attorney representing them doesn't want to. You know those sharks in the joke? If this guy fell into the water, the sharks would scatter for their lives. Of course, he would just walk back to the ship—on the water, if you get my drift. We are talking about Mitchell Townsend Ames."

He waited a moment, and when it became obvious that Michaels didn't have a clue who this was, he shook his head. "Don't you ever read a paper, Alex? Or watch the news on TV? Ames is the guy who routinely takes on the major drug companies. And wins. He's filed half a dozen class-action suits against the pharmaceutical houses and has never lost one. This guy's a doctor-slash-lawyer, bright as an H-bomb fireball, and meaner than a bag full of hungry wolverines."

Michaels shrugged. "If you've seen one lawyer, you've seen 'em all."

"No, sir, that ain't how it is," Tommy said. "Mitchell Ames eats top guns and spits shrapnel. He's fast, sharp, and he knows both ends of the game when it comes to health suits, plus he is good-looking—and can dumb it down so a jury full of third-grade kids could understand every word of his evidence. He is a very dangerous man in court."

"And he doesn't want to settle the case."

"Correct. Look, I understand how you don't think this should have been filed, that you were justified in your actions, and in a criminal court, I would easily kick Mitchell Townsend Ames's ass and make him write 'I'm so sorry Uncle Michaels' on the chalkboard a hundred times. But this isn't a criminal court. They've filed this as a civil matter, where the burden of proof is different—easier— and where the plaintiff has cause to open all kinds of cans of worms. We can block some of it on the grounds of national security, but he's still going to shine some light on corners you'd rather were kept dark."

"We don't have anything to hide," Michaels said.

"Yes, you do. You just haven't thought about it enough. Did anybody make any jokes about this incident? Maybe some gallows-humor remark that might have gone out in an e-mail?"

Michaels shrugged. "I don't know. It's possible, I suppose, but I don't see every e-mail—or even remember every one I do see."

"Right. So you have this jury looking at some thug's kindly old mama, all teary-eyed, and Ames whips out this e-mail with a remark like, 'Teach 'em to mess with Net Force!' and over that, a picture of her poor dead son taken the day he graduated from high school, or maybe on prom night. Juries are sympathetic to that kind of thing. If he can put a human face on the guy—and he will, even though the bad guy was a cold-blooded headbreaker—he'll be able to cast Net Force as a bunch of bloodthirsty jack-booted storm troopers who laughed as they shot him and spit on his corpse just for fun. Now you and I both know it didn't happen like that, but a good lawyer can convince a jury it did, and Ames is as good as they come."

Michaels shook his head.

"And that's just for starters. Once he gets going, this guy can convince a jury of God-fearing folk that you're the Antichrist, or at least Satan's second lieutenant. I've seen him do it. It will get ugly. Your best defense—your *only* defense—is to show those nice folks on the panel that you *had* to do what you did, no way around it, else the Republic would have fallen, that you hated to do it, and that you are a much, much nicer fellow than the dead guys. Which won't be easy."

"Aren't you *my* lawyer?"

"Sure. But after the trial is over, I'll go have a drink with Ames, if he's interested. We like to pretend that we don't take these things personally."

"Well, excuse me if I do take it that way."

"Yeah, that's allowed."

What a rotten situation this is, Michaels thought.

"All right, let's get the story down to brass tacks," Tommy said. "Our legal status is quite clear, of course. Your military arm technically works under the auspices of the National Guard and not the FBI, and thus can be ac-tivated and sent out of the country when deemed neces-sary. Our charter doesn't say that, exactly, but we can blow smoke and wave mirrors and make that sound good. And we are proceeding on the idea that Net Force had reason to believe that the gambling ship was essentially a pirate vessel. This might be a fine legal hair to split, given the strict definitions of piracy according to the U.N. Conven-tion of the Law of the Sea, Article 101, but when you factor in the Internet and terrorism, I think we can pull that off. You, as a duly authorized representative of a sovereign nation, had the right to board and seize the vessel pursuant to Article 105 of the U.N. Convention."

"I knew it all along," Michaels said.

Tommy grinned. "Sure you did. That's why you need lawyers."

Alex didn't smile back. Somehow, this just didn't seem all that funny anymore.

"All right," Tommy continued, his grin fading. "Start with how you began to suspect that CyberNation was fielding bad guys doing illegal things."

"That'll take a long time."

Tommy nodded. "Then we better get started."

6

New York City, New York

In the kitchen of his apartment, Ames added a bit of Chardonnay—the 1990 Reserve—to the two-quart copper-clad stainless pot holding the lobster and shitake sauce. The pot was from France. You had to give the French that, they did know how to cook. The sauce was for poaching the Yukon salmon he'd had flown in that morning. The fish was a small one, a three-pounder, illegally caught out of season, he believed. When you figured it all up, that salmon probably cost about three hundred dollars a pound, but that wasn't important. Most of these salmon went to the Japanese, but being rich had its perks. Yesterday, the fish had been swimming in the cold waters of Alaska; tonight, it would be dinner at Ames's apartment in New York City.

Civilization was a wonderful thing.

The wine he was using for the stock was eighty-some-odd bucks a bottle, too, but there was no substitute for quality. If you were going to cook fine food with wine, what was the point in murdering the taste with cheap stuff?

Ames was not a wine snob. He didn't bother to learn all the proper terms one used, nose and bouquet and finish and so forth. But he knew a good wine when he tasted it. The first time he had sipped anything from Blackwood Canyon, he knew he'd found a vintner who knew exactly what he was doing. He bought a cellarful of the wines by the case. He had also invested money in the business, as much as Michael Taylor Moore would let him.

He had others now, but Moore's first winery was a hole-in-the-wall place at the end of a gravel road out in the middle of Nowhere, Washington. His first place was hard to find, and it wasn't even listed on the local guides. If you didn't know where the place was, you pretty much had to stumble across it by accident, or else put in a lot of hours doing detective work. It was worth it, though. Back then, the only spot you could buy any of his product was at the winery itself, or by the bottle in a few of the world's finer restaurants.

Moore made his vintages in the old-style European manner, much of it involving a process called "sur lees." Ames didn't quite understand that, but he knew it involved leaving the fruit in the stuff longer than was considered by most to be proper. As a result, the whites had a fullness unmatched by any made in North America. Those whites could run with almost anybody else's *reds*. And his reds? Well, they were just unbelievable.

Moore's cheap stuff alone was better than most other wineries' expensive vintages. And with the exception of maybe two other places in the world, one in Spain, one in France, nobody could touch his expensive ones. He called his vintages his children, and he didn't let them out of the house until they were all grown up and ready to face the world.

He was something of a renaissance man, Moore was. He thought of himself as an alchemist, and considering that he turned water into a wine that eventually turned more or less into gold, it wasn't a bad description. He was as good a cook as many world-class chefs. He also designed catamarans, some of which would fold up for storage and hauling, and assorted hydrogen-powered farm machines.

A lot of his neighbors hated him because they thought he was arrogant. That was to be expected, though. A man who stood up and said and did what he believed always got flak. Especially when he could actually back it up.

Ames knew all about that. He had been driven by his own demons to excel in everything he tried. First in his class in medicine, first in his class in law school, and a top track athlete. But it wasn't enough. It was never enough.

Still, being great was why he had hooked up with CyberNation. They appreciated talent and skill, they encouraged it, and they were willing to pay for it. They always went for the best.

Ames smiled. He had never been accused of hiding his light under a bushel.

He stirred the sauce, lowered the heat on the Thermador gas stove's front burner, and added a few sprinkles of fresh thyme and sage. It would need to reduce for another hour before it was ready to poach the fish. He still had time.

For the dinner with Corinna Skye, he had decided on a Blackwood Canyon Dry Riesling, a 1988. For the appetizers, he had selected a 1989 Cabernet Sauvignon Estate Reserve that should be sufficiently aged by now. A Late Harvest Penumbra Vin Santo would go well with dessert.

When he had bought these, they had been relatively cheap—forty bucks for the dessert wine, a hundred and fifty or two hundred for the others. Now they cost twice that—if you could get them. Moore had sold futures in his wines for a long time, and they didn't have firm delivery dates—it might be a year, it might be ten years before he thought the wine was ready to bottle and ship, and if you didn't like it, you could go somewhere else.

Ames smiled again. A man who could make wines like that was to be admired. And humored. And Ames would be very glad to take Michael Moore's wines on whatever terms they were offered.

He leaned down to check the fire under the pot. That was still the best way, looking at the flame, not the control knob. Satisfied that the sauce wouldn't burn, he went to mix the salad. He would break the lettuce and endive and other greens now to chill, though of course he wouldn't dress the salad until it was time to serve it. He had somehow run low on olive oil. He had only one bottle of the Raggia di San Vito left, the best extra-virgin oil available outside Italy—it cost more than a fair bottle of French champagne—and he made a note to have Bryce order more for him.

So much to do, and it all had to be finished at the same moment.

As he pulled the dandelion greens from the humidity-controlled storage bin, Ames glanced at his watch. Junior was taking care of some minor business with a certain Midwestern junior senator this evening, and should be calling to report on the matter shortly.

CyberNation had tried a frontal assault on the world, attacking the net and web to attract customers. It hadn't worked. They had also tried bribery and legislation, of course, as well as advertising, but in Ames's opinion they hadn't gone far enough in those directions.

Which was where he came in. His job was to work the law. Part of that included buying the lawmakers, or scaring them, and if bribery wouldn't do that, sometimes a fat lawsuit would. Whatever it took. He could get the laws they wanted passed. Get the official recognition they craved.

Personally, he thought the idea was silly. A virtual country? Nonsense. He liked the physical world, with its

poached salmon and its dry Rieslings and its many other
virtues just fine, thank you. But if that's what they wanted,
and if it was even remotely possible, Mitchell Ames would
give it to them. He had taken it on. He would get it done.

He looked at the marble counter with the built-in cutting
board. Where had he put the centrifuge? Ah, there it was,
behind the food processor.

Junior had the number for one of the dozen throwaway
phones Bryce had bought for cash at an electronics store
in Baltimore yesterday. Once a week or so, Bryce would
travel to a city out of state and pick up a case of cheap,
disposable digital cellulars. Whichever ones weren't used
by the end of the week were crushed and trashed, and
never anywhere near Ames's residences.

Every clandestine call Ames made or received was on
a two-hour throwaway. Since there was no way to trace
them to him, there was no real need to worry about en-
cryption. To be safe, though—and Ames was always very,
very careful—they talked in a sort of code, even on these
throwaways. Junior would call and say something like,
"Your order is ready," or "We've had to back order that
item," and that would be enough.

If they needed a longer conversation, or something that
couldn't be said in code, they would do it face-to-face.
Ames had more than one safe location, each with enough
antibugging electronics going so that if Junior had suddenly taken it upon himself to use a hidden wire, Ames
would know it before the first word was spoken.

He'd met Junior at a shooting range and had carefully
checked him out and cultivated him before . . . *activating*
him. He was a rough tool, but he was greedy enough to
be useful. If he stepped out of line, Ames would simply
erase him and find another cat's paw.

And even if Junior ever decided to try to blackmail
Ames—or, more likely, if he got caught and tried to use
Ames to cut a deal—he had nothing solid to give up. Like

the leader of a good pickpocket team, Ames never held a stolen wallet any longer than it took to transfer it to a confederate. All his dealings with the man were in cash, and nobody save Bryce, who would spend ten years in jail before he said a word against Ames, knowing he'd retire rich when he got out, ever saw Junior and Ames together.

So Ames was as safe as he could make himself. Which was good, because Junior was important to his plan. Not irreplaceable, but very important.

Ames had never seen anybody as good with a handgun in a hurry, snub-nosed revolvers at that, and he'd been a shooter himself for most of his forty-six years. A man who could shoot, and who *would* shoot who you wanted him to, was an extremely valuable tool. You just had to be careful that you didn't cut yourself using him.

He washed the greens, put them into the electric centrifuge, and hit the button to spin the water away. The machine's whirr rose in volume, and the scent of the slightly bruised greens wafted to his nostrils. Ah.

Well. Enough about Junior. Corinna Skye was a much more pleasant subject upon which to dwell. After their drink to discuss her further lobbying efforts on behalf of CyberNation, he knew he had to spend some time and energy on her.

He smiled at the double entendre and went to collect the fresh baby carrots. No matter what season of the year it was in New York, it was always harvest somewhere in the world. . . .

Halethorpe, Maryland

Junior was at a drugstore not far from the U of M Baltimore campus, just off I-95, and just a little bit nervous.

He smiled at that, laughing at himself. Big Bad Boud-reaux.

He shook his head. A little nervous? The sweat was practically coming off him in buckets, and he kept wiping his hands on his jeans. It would be really stupid to die just because he was so scared he couldn't get a grip on his piece.

The cop didn't have to worry about that. He wouldn't even know he was in trouble until it was too late to get sweaty.

There came the car now, a single police officer in it just like the last two nights. The drugstore's parking lot was dark, a timer had shut the outside lights off at ten P.M. The inside lights were all dialed way down low, too. Thanks to conservation efforts, cities were a whole lot darker than they used to be. Tonight, though, Junior was glad for that.

The squad car went through the lot of the all-night restaurant across the street. The place looked just like a Denny's, but its sign said Pablo's instead, no doubt catering to the ex-Cubanos who had recently moved into the neighborhood. Junior didn't have anything against those people. Back when he was a teenager, he'd bought his booze at a place called Cuban Liquors, down in Louisiana, and they'd always treated him okay.

The cop looped out of the parking lot and came across the street. There was a pay phone on the front of the drugstore, one of those little half-booths attached to the side of the building, but there was no light to speak of. Junior had busted that out earlier. Still, there was enough glow from the store to see somebody was standing there, even if you couldn't tell much about who it was.

The cruiser came across the street like a prowling cat, and pulled into the drugstore lot. The building sat kind of down in a little hollow, lower than the roads to the south and east of it, and the pay phone was behind the corner of the building. The combination didn't let the headlight shine on the phone when the cop pulled in. The only way to get a light directly on Junior would be if he looped wide from the driveway and turned in toward the front of the place. The cop hadn't done that either of the two previous evenings until he was ready to leave.

Junior wiped his hands again. It wasn't too late to bail out. He could still pick up the receiver and pretend to be talking, just a guy who had to use the phone late at night. Maybe his wasn't working in his apartment, or maybe he was behind on the bill and they'd shut it off. No law against that, just being here to use the phone. The cop would mark him, but probably drive by.

But, no. If he didn't do it now, he never would. He knew that. He had been arrested for simple assault a couple times, and he'd done a nickel for ADW. He had even been busted once for murder, but had gotten off—he should have, since he *hadn't* done it—but he never told anybody that he hadn't, even his lawyer, so people thought he had skated for a killing. They figured a smart lawyer had gotten off another guilty man, and more power to the mouthpiece. That gave Junior the rep, and it had paid a lot of freight. When serious folks wanted a bodyguard, they wanted a man who wouldn't be afraid to drop the hammer when the guns came out, and they thought he had already done it. He'd talked the talk for so long, he had 'em all fooled. They thought he was a killer, but he couldn't fool himself any longer.

Junior had never *killed* anybody. Never even shot at anyone. Not for real. Sure, he had beaten more than a few bloody, and had waved his guns a lot to intimidate people, but he'd never actually killed anybody.

And that ate at him. It made him feel . . . hollow, somehow. He knew he could squeeze the trigger, if it came down to it. He knew it. But he never had.

Time to walk the walk, Junior, or else shut the hell up.

He was scared, no question about that. But he was ready. He knew that, too.

The cop idled the cruiser into the parking lot. It was a big Crown Vic, the car version of Jaws.

He saw the cop spot him. He could see his face in the lights from the computer screen on the car's dash.

Junior could have picked up the phone, now was the time, but he didn't. He just stood and stared.

Cops were used to seeing people look at them, but there were citizen looks and then there were the "up-yours" looks. Junior was giving him one of those. No cop could let that pass, not in the middle of the night, not one on one, not unless he was a wimp.

The cop in the Crown Vic was no wimp.

He pulled over and stopped in the driveway twenty-five feet away. The door opened and the cop, maybe thirty or so, stepped out. He had his big aluminum head-basher flashlight in his left hand, but he didn't shine it at Junior. Not yet.

"Good evening," the cop said. "Something wrong with the phone?"

Junior took a deep breath. The little sleeveless nylon vest he wore had half a box of bullets in each of the side pockets, enough to give them some weight so he could clear them with a little buck and wiggle of his hips. The two Rugers were underneath the vest, secure in their holsters, as ready as they would ever be.

Shit or get off the pot, Junior.

"Nope, no trouble with it," Junior said. His voice sounded pretty calm. He was worried it might break, but it was okay. "I wasn't usin' it anyway, no."

Junior saw the cop shift into a higher state of alertness. He edged his right hand back toward the pistol in his holster. Junior knew it was a Glock, probably a 22C in a .40 S&W, ten rounds in the magazine, one in the pipe, three-and-a-half-pound pull and not the heavier New York trigger. More gun than Junior's, way more. It would knock a man down ninety-five times out of a hundred with any solid hit.

But that didn't matter, not if Junior was better.

"Hey, let me ask you somethin'." Junior took a couple of steps toward the cop. Twenty feet. Eighteen.

"Hold it right there, bud," the cop said, still not too worried, but with his hand now touching the Glock's plastic butt.

So okay. Here it was. The cop was alert, had his hand on his piece, and was looking straight at him. Fair enough.

Junior stopped. He held his own hands low, by his hips, palms forward, to show they were empty. The ready position from which he had practiced drawing his guns a thousand times.

Junior said, "So, how's your sister?"

The cop frowned, and while he was thinking about that, Junior cleared the vest and grabbed his revolvers.

Time slowed to a crawl.

The hard rubber grips felt alive under his hands as he pulled the short-barreled guns and swung them up.

The cop reacted. He jerked his Glock out at Junior's sudden move, but Junior was faster, a half-second ahead. He brought both revolvers up and on target even as the cop cleared leather.

It was like he was in a trance: Everything but the cop vanished, sounds, lights, everything, and the cop was moving so . . . slow. . . .

Junior cooked off two rounds, the right a hair faster than the left, and he would swear that he *saw* the bullets leave the barrels, even through the tongues of orange that washed out his night vision and the jets of greasy smoke; *saw* them fly at better than nine hundred feet a second across the six yards or so, which was impossible; *saw* the tiny lead rounds hit the cop, right one just above his left eye, left one on the bridge of his nose, *whap! whap!*

The cop fell, still in slowmo, his pistol pointing at the concrete parking lot, not a chance of tagging Junior even if he fired, which he didn't.

He hit the ground like a chainsawed redwood tree, dead or most of the way there when he landed. The Glock fell, bounced, and clattered away. Junior heard that, the Glock against the concrete. He couldn't remember hearing the shots, but he heard the Glock land. Weird.

His heart raced like it was on speed, like a shot of Angola meth right into a vein, and after what seemed like years, he finally remembered to breathe. He had a little trouble doing that, and his breaths came and went real fast.

Jesus Holy Christ! I shot the guy dead!

It seemed very quiet all of a sudden.

He looked around. Nobody in sight, but even the little .22s made noise this late at night. Somebody would have heard. They'd be looking around. Cop cars were like magnets, they pulled in the looks.

Time to leave, Junior.

He felt like he had just screwed his brains out. He was flushed all over, and limp, but in a good way. What a rush!

No need to look at the cop. The man was worm food, no question about it.

He reholstered the Rugers, turned, and walked to the north. A brisk walk, but not a run. His car was parked a block over, on a residential street, in front of some apartments. He had swiped a set of license plates from a little pickup truck that was parked outside a repair shop a couple miles away, and put those on his car. If anybody noticed it there—and they wouldn't in that neighborhood—it wouldn't come home to him even if they wrote down the plate number.

If the dead cop had had any smarts, he would have called Junior in before he got out of his car. When he didn't report back, somebody would come looking. By then, though, Junior would be miles away in a car nobody had seen. And an hour after that, he'd be having a beer in his kitchen and replaying it all in his mind.

They probably wouldn't get anything off the bullets. Those itty-bitty nonjacketed lead ones were bad for ballistics. But just in case, Junior would change barrels on both revolvers when he got home. He had three spare sets for each gun. Even if they somehow found him later and tested his guns, which wasn't going to happen, but if they did, the grooves in the new barrels wouldn't match. No way was he going to keep carrying guns that would ID him as a cop killer, no matter how much he loved 'em.

As he drove off, the body rushes just kept coming. He had never felt so *alive* before! He had faced off against an armed cop, a trained shooter, and he had beat the guy, cold. Killed him and walked away. Nothing had ever felt like this before! He was like a god.

Like a god!

7

Toni had planned to go to the supermarket to pick up a few things before Alex got home from work. It was almost dark and she wanted to get back before he did, so she was in a hurry to get going—until she opened the front door and saw the mob of reporters on her front walk.

Well, okay, it wasn't really a mob. There were maybe seven or eight reporters, but it sure looked like more. As soon as she opened the door, they started yelling at her, creating a babble that was loud and only partially understandable:

"Mrs. Michaels, Mrs. Michaels! Is it true you were one of the agents who killed workers on the *Bon Chance*?"

"Mrs. Michaels—how you do feel about your husband being responsible for the deaths of those innocent men?"

"—true that you are a martial arts expert who has killed several people with knives or your bare hands—?"

"—fair to the taxpayers . . . ?"

Guru came to the door behind her. She looked out at

the men and women charging up the walk. She stepped past Toni to face the onrush of reporters. "The baby is sleeping," she said. "You must leave."

The first woman to reach Guru, a television reporter, shoved a microphone into her face. "Who are you, ma'am?" she demanded to know. "What do you know about this?"

Pushing the wireless mike into Guru's face was perhaps not the wisest thing the woman had ever done.

Guru caught the outthrust instrument, twisted, and removed it from the reporter's grip. Adding her other hand, the eighty-five-year-old woman gripped the thing securely and snapped it in half. Then she dropped the pieces.

The clatter of the broken sound gear falling upon the walk was quite loud.

"You must be quiet," she said. "The baby is asleep."

Apparently none of the reporters had ever before seen an old granny break an expensive, hard plastic and steel microphone as if it were a bread stick. They all stopped talking. They looked like a herd of grazing deer suddenly caught in headlights.

Toni grinned.

Guru shooed them with her hands. "Go, go." She took a step forward.

The reporters nearly fell all over themselves backing away.

Guru turned around, gave Toni the smallest of smiles, and went back into the house.

The woman reporter said, "I'm going to send you a bill for that, lady! You can't just destroy equipment like that!"

Toni said, very softly, "Who are you going to send it to?" Then she turned and went inside. She wasn't going to the market now, not and leave Guru and the baby alone with these jackals outside.

∙ ∙ ∙

When Michaels got home, he saw the gaggle of reporters on the walk out front. Son of a bitch. This wasn't right. If they wanted to come to HQ and interview him, that was fine, but no way should they be coming to his *house!*

He pulled the company car into the driveway and hit the remote for the garage. Normally, he left the car parked on the street, to keep the garage empty for *silat* practice, but he didn't want to wade through this crowd.

A couple of them moved into the driveway to block his path.

He rolled down the window, stuck his head out. "Move out of the way, please."

The reporters descended on the car like flies on honey.

"Commander Michaels! Would you comment on the lawsuit against you?"

"—Commander, was it really necessary to shoot those men—?"

"—Commander, why did you send your wife on such a dangerous mission—?"

He tried to inch the car forward, but the pack of reporters stayed with him, like hyenas on a wounded impala. The ones in front wouldn't get out of the way.

He honked the horn.

He stuck his head out again and glared at the two in front of his car. "Listen, I am going to drive into my garage. It would be a good idea for you to move. I wouldn't want anybody to get hurt." He smiled, the expression as fake as a three-dollar-bill.

The pair, both men, both with cameras, stayed where they were.

To hell with you, he thought. He dropped the smile, pulled his head back into the car, took his foot off the brake and let the car idle forward.

They didn't move until the car was almost touching them, but finally, they did.

He pulled into the garage and hit the remote to shut the

door. None of them followed him inside, which was good, because he would have been hard pressed not to toss them out physically.

Once the garage door was closed, he got out of the car. Tommy had told him he'd be seeing reporters, and that whatever he did he was *not* to let them provoke him. Be polite, don't say anything except, "No comment," smile, nod, wave, and get away from them. They were like mosquitoes, Tommy had said. They will bite you and suck your blood, and if you swat one, another will quickly take its place. Better to leave than stand there squashing them.

Toni met him at the door.

"I'm sorry about all this," he said, waving at the garage door.

"It's not your fault," she said. She stood up on her toes and kissed him. "Other than that, how was your day?"

He grinned.

The grin didn't last, though. In the living room Guru sat watching the evening news. He waved at her, and she pointed at the TV.

Michaels looked over and saw himself on the screen. He stopped.

The view was from one of the cameras that had been blocking the driveway, and a tight close-up of his face showed a flash of anger, then a smile that looked more like a leer. "Move," he said, as he pulled his head back into the car and started forward.

They cut out the rest of what he'd said—the "It would be a good idea," and "I wouldn't want anybody to get hurt." A different angle, from another camera, cut in, showed the car heading toward the cameramen in front of the car. They made it look as if he was trying to run them down.

His virgil cheeped. It was Tommy Bender.

"What are you doing, Alex? I'm watching you on the

news trying to run over Channel Nine's and Channel Four's cameramen. Why is that?"

"Tommy, it isn't what it looks like."

"It never is. And remember I told you so."

New York City, New York

Corinna Skye leaned back in her chair and smiled. "That may be the best meal I have ever eaten," she said.

She wore a blue silk blouse with a matching bow at her throat, both of which went with her blue eyes, and a dark maroon pleated silk skirt that stopped just above her knees. He guessed the shoes were Gucci pumps, the leather complimenting the rest of her outfit. Very classy.

Ames smiled at her. "Thank you. I can do better. Ideally, I should have prepared the sauce the day before yesterday to let it age properly. Then it would have been really good."

"I can't believe it could have possibly tasted any better."

"Next time, we'll try something different. You like moose?"

"Chocolate?"

"Not mousse, *moose*, like with antlers, from the forest."

"You'd cook Bullwinkle?"

He laughed. "You know that old TV series? It's one of my favorites."

She said, "Hey, Rocky, watch me pull a rabbit out of my hat!" in a very good imitation of the cartoon character.

He said, "Again? That trick never works!" in as close an imitation to Rocky the Flying Squirrel as he could manage.

They both laughed.

"Shall we adjourn to the living room for after-dinner wine?"

She followed him into the room. He poured her a glass of the wine he'd selected, let her appreciate it to him, then poured his own glass. He directed her to the form-chair, while he sat on the leather couch.

The chair hummed and fitted itself to her exquisite contours. She smiled. "Ah. I've never tried one of these. Very comfortable."

He shrugged. "If it isn't comfortable, what's the point?"

They sipped their wine for a moment. Then he said, "Well, much as I hate to bring up business, I wouldn't want you to think I invited you here on false pretenses."

"Heaven forbid," she said.

"So, how goes the war on the entrenched bureaucracy?"

She put her glass down. "Better than I expected. We've got a couple of unexpected senators who have climbed on board the issue, and believe me, I had nothing to do with it. Also, the unofficial word is that the Supreme Court will be ruling on TransMetro Insurance versus the State of New Mexico next week, and there's a strong rumor that they will rule for TransMetro."

He knew this, of course. The decision concerned some minor litigation about whether or not the New Mexico regulatory agency could force the Swiss company that sold policies exclusively via the Internet to obey certain arcane state laws. By all rights, of course, the agency should be able to, but there was an oddball section of Internet laws that might prevent that. If so, there would be a precedent set that, while it wouldn't seem relevant to most observers, would benefit CyberNation down the line. Ames thought of it as part of a basement wall: unseen, but a part of the foundation that needed to be in place.

"Good," he said. "A little more wine?"

"I'd love some."

He smiled. Things were going along very nicely here. He wouldn't make a move on her tonight. Nor the next time they were together, and maybe not even the third time. Like a fine sauce, some things should not be rushed, not if they were to be enjoyed to the fullest.

And he was certainly going to enjoy Corinna Skye to the fullest. Like everything else he had ever wanted, it was only a matter of "when," not "if."

8

John Howard was not used to feeling ill at ease anywhere on the FBI base. This place, though, he had to admit, had him feeling decidedly nervous.

He was sitting in an exam room in the ENT office at the FBI/Net Force Clinic, having his hearing checked. Nadine had been after him for months to do that. His right ear had been bugging him on and off since that shoot-out in Gakona, Alaska, almost two years ago. Blasting away with a .357 without earplugs was a risky thing. Sometimes, though, if you wanted to stay alive, you did what you had to and worried about the cost later.

Net Force's annual physicals were fairly perfunctory, and didn't routinely include a hearing test unless the patient brought it up. Howard never had. It wasn't as if he was deaf, after all. He could hear the doctor asking his questions, and that had been enough for the physicians to sign off on him each year. Besides, it hadn't really seemed that bad until recently, but it was becoming obvious that his hearing was no longer quite up to par.

Howard said, "No, I don't hear the ringing anymore. But I have noticed if I'm not right next to the phone, I might not notice its cheep. And my wife says I miss half of what she's saying. Sometimes I can hear her voice, but not quite make out the words. We can't talk from room to room, if she's in the kitchen and I'm in the den. She can hear me just fine, but I can't understand her. And my virgil's alarm? I don't pick that up at all."

The doctor nodded, making a note on his flatscreen with his stylus. "What about in a crowded room? Any problems?"

"Sometimes it's hard to pick a single voice out of the background noise. But that's normal, right?"

"Mmm. Let's have a look."

The doctor put the flatscreen down and pulled the ear instrument from where it hung on the wall next to the exam table. He put a little throwaway plastic sleeve on the end, dialed up a light, and stuck it into Howard's ear.

"I always meant to ask, what's this thing called?"

The doctor pulled it away from Howard's ear and showed it to him. "This? It's called an 'ear-looker.' "

Howard grinned. "Funny," he said.

But the doctor, a young guy who looked to be in his early thirties, shook his head. "No, General, I'm serious. The technical name for this is an 'otoscope,' but that translates literally as 'ear-looker.' "

With that, he stuck it back into Howard's ear and resumed the exam.

Howard bore the tugging and poking. After a few moments the doctor pulled the scope out. He slipped the plastic throwaway off and tossed it into the foot-operated trash bin. Switching off the instrument's light, he reracked it and turned back to Howard.

"The tympanic membrane—your eardrum—looks fine,"

he said. "And I don't think there is any damage to the bony structures past that."

"Malleus, incus, stapes," Howard said.

"Yes. Hammer, anvil, stirrup. Good to see you've done your research."

"So what are we talking about here?"

The doctor leaned back against the wall. "Nerve damage," he said. "My guess would be that it's probably in the organ of Corti—those sensory hair cells that make up the auditory epithelium are there. That's pretty common. In fact, unless you live in a quiet forest all alone and don't listen to music or have a TV, you're bound to lose some of your hearing if you live long enough. It's just one of the costs of a mechanical civilization. Mostly, it's gradual, and you don't notice it until it gets bad. Sometimes, though, after a very loud blast very close to one's unprotected ear, the effect is sudden and pronounced."

"Like a gun going off."

"Yep."

"So what do we do about it?"

"I'll have the audiologist give you a hearing exam. When we see what that shows, we'll know what we can do."

Howard nodded, thanked the man, and went straight over to the audiologist's office.

The technician there turned out to be a very good-looking young black woman. She asked Howard to sit in a chair, put a set of headphones on him, and handed him a wireless control with a single button on it. There was a sign on the wall certifying that one Geneva Zuri was licensed to practice audiology in the state of Virginia.

"What kind of a name is 'Zuri'?"

"Swahili." She had a deep, throaty voice. "Some generations removed. My grandfather went back to the old country as a young man and found our distant kin. After that, he started using the family name from before slavery."

Howard nodded. *Interesting.*

"Okay," she said, "I'm going to generate some tones from the computer here. When you hear one, push the button."

"Okay."

She did that for a while, first one ear, then the other. At one point, she introduced a roaring waterfall-like noise in his good left ear while she sent tones to his bad ear. Curious, he asked her about that.

"What we've learned is that people with one weak ear tend to recruit their stronger ear to help out. They are not aware of this, of course. What is actually happening is that the sound is traveling through your head by way of bone conduction. You *think* you're hearing a tone in your *right* ear, but actually you are picking it up in the *left*, compensating without realizing it. So we mask that ear with white noise to prevent that."

After he pushed the button a bunch of times and she made notes on the computer, she gave him another test that checked how loud a noise could get before it became painful.

The next test included a recorded voice that spoke certain words at various speeds and different volumes. His job was to repeat whatever he heard. The voice had a syrupy southern quality, which drew out some of the sounds and made them harder to distinguish.

Finally, the audiologist did a repeat of the tone test, then took the earphones off him.

"All right, sir," she said. "We're all done. Take a look."

She turned the computer's flatscreen around to show him a pair of charts. "This one is your left ear, the other is your right. The red lines on both charts represent the norms. The blue lines show the results of your tests. As you can see, for your left ear you've dipped some in the high frequencies, but you are pretty solid in the middle and bass range. Over here in the right ear, however, it's not so good. You've dropped way down on the high and middle ranges."

He could see that easily enough. "What does it mean?"

"Well, I'm not a doctor. Your physician should be the one to discuss this with you. I'll send these results to his flatscreen right away."

"Come on," Howard said. "You do this for a living. You know what it means."

She paused, then nodded. "Okay. My guess is you are having trouble hearing people talk, or the phone ring, or the high notes on your old Ray Charles CDs. This chart shows that, and it also shows why. It's pretty clear that you've damaged your hearing."

Howard frowned. He'd expected that, of course, but he still didn't like hearing it. "Will it heal?" he asked. "Will it get any better at all?"

She shook her head. "No, sir. Not on its own."

"What about fixing it, either medically or surgically? Is that an option?"

She shook her head again. "No, sir. Not in this case. It's just not that bad a loss, not nearly enough to warrant a cochlear implant. You'd have to be almost stone deaf for that. And we haven't figured out how to regenerate the nerves in the labyrinth via stem cell or gene therapy. So there's no medicine that will heal them. It's a lot like scar tissue, really."

He started to ask another question, but before he could, she added, "We *can* fix it, though, so you will hear pretty much as well as you used to."

That sounded interesting. "How?" he asked.

"Electronic augmentation."

Howard felt his stomach twist. A *hearing aid*, he thought, just like his grandfather used to wear. He shook his head. He was only in his forties, after all. He wasn't ready for some big, ugly lump behind his ear. What would be next? A cane? A walker? He shook his head again, pushing the mental image away.

She could tell what he was thinking, of course. She must have seen that same reaction countless times.

She opened a drawer, reached into it, and pulled out a device exactly like Howard remembered his grandfather wearing. As big as his thumb, it was a big, pale, fleshy-colored thing, with a clear plastic hook on the end. It looked like a little oil can.

He shook his head again. If he wore that he might as well hang a neon sign around his neck: *Yell at me! I'm deaf!*

"This is what we used to use," she said. "And we still use these, for patients with major loss."

She reached back into the drawer. This time, though, when she brought her hand out and opened it to show him, she was holding a tiny, chocolate-colored button, no bigger than the tip of his little finger.

"And here is the state of the art right now, sir. A one hundred percent digital, multichannel, multiprogrammable MC—for mini-canal—signal processing auditory enhancement device. Digital feedback reduction, noise reduction, gain processing, and compression. This little model has a preamplifier, a twenty-three-bit analog-to-digital converter with a one hundred and thirty-eight decibel dynamic range. The processor chip runs a hundred and fifty million operations per second, with all-digital output to the transducer."

Howard just stared. He knew some of the terms, but not all of them.

"The battery is good for about a week, and it can be programmed to your specific hearing loss and cross-coupled to separate channels. What that means is that if you are in a crowded room full of people jabbering, you'll be able to hear the guy next to you when he talks. And if you want to listen to music at home alone, you push this little button here and it will shift to a different frequency so you can hear the high notes. Watch."

She turned away, did something he couldn't see, then looked back at him.

"I have one in my ear. You see it?"

Howard looked. "No."

"Right. And you're looking for it. Nobody will know you're wearing it unless you lean over and point it out to them. And best of all, sir, it will bring your hearing pretty close to what it was before. Not perfect, but not far off."

"Wow," he said.

She grinned. "Yes, sir. We squirt a little rubbery goop in your ear canal, let it set, then take a mold from that so it can be custom fitted. You'll just tuck it in every morning—if you choose to take it out when you sleep. You don't really have to. It's all automatic after that. You'll want to remove it to shower, though. These things are not really waterproof, but if you get caught in the rain, it will be okay."

She pulled the device out of her ear. "See, here's how you turn it off. Open the battery door like this. When you need to change the battery, you just pop it out like so. Put a new one in, close it, and it's ready to rock."

He had to admit, he was pretty impressed. "And do I have to sell my house to buy this technological miracle?"

"They run about twenty-eight, twenty-nine hundred retail, sir, but under the Net Force insurance you only copay ten percent. Two hundred and eighty dollars, give or take. Buy the batteries at Costco or on-line and they'll cost about fifty cents each. It also comes with a maintenance and loss insurance plan free for two years, fifty bucks a year thereafter."

He nodded. "And this will do the trick?"

"Yes, sir," she said. "I believe it will."

"Huh."

"Yes, sir. And nobody will be yelling at you like you thought you had to do to your grampa, because they won't know it's there."

He grinned. "Am I that obvious?"

"It's a youth culture, General. Nobody wants to be thought of as old and decrepit. When that slew of baby boomers started hitting their fifties and sixties a few years back, having trouble hearing after all those years of rock and roll, the demand for things like this skyrocketed. They are working on a model now that will run off a capacitor whose power comes from normal movement. Completely sealed. Put it in and forget about it. Just take it out every three or four months to clean your ears, then pop it back in. Until then, however, this will do the job. Welcome to the future, sir."

He smiled again. Well. It could be worse. And wearing a little electronic gizmo was better than cupping your hand around your ear and saying "Eh?" like some deaf old fart, wasn't it?

A hearing aid. He still couldn't believe it, though. And no matter how high-tech or marvelous they were, he certainly wasn't happy about it.

Washington, D.C.

Jay sat behind his desk and stared at his flatscreen, thinking about how to break into a bank.

They almost hadn't bought this desk. Moving into the new apartment had made more of a dent in their savings than he'd planned. Their furniture plans had been put on hold until one of Saji's uncles at the wedding had suggested a money dance for the couple.

According to tradition, the newlyweds accepted dances from various members of the wedding party, who had to "purchase" each dance with a donation. What made the money dance funny was that the payment wasn't just given to the couple. It was *pinned* to them. By the time the dancing was over, he and Saji had looked like a couple of greenback-stuffed scarecrows. They had made enough from the money dance alone to furnish most of their new condo—including the huge desk in his home office.

It was funny, Jay knew he was the ultimate forward-thinker. His tastes normally ran to ultramodern, usually involving chrome and leather. This desk was different. It was enormous, for one thing, and made out of solid cherry. It was also antique, with absolutely no provisions for hiding computer peripherals and cabling.

But Jay didn't care. He'd fallen in love with this desk the first time he'd laid eyes on it. And Saji had insisted he buy it. No matter that it took up nearly half the floor space in his home office. No matter that it wouldn't fit into the third bedroom, so that if they ever decided to start a family the baby would end up with the smallest room in the house. No matter that the ancient grained surfaces were as un-Gridley-like as you could imagine.

He loved that desk, loved the way sitting behind it got his creative juices flowing.

Except this time it wasn't working. He just couldn't seem to get a handle on this bank he was trying to crack.

He'd worked late at Net Force trying to get his latest VR scenario to work. The bank account number he'd gotten in his trace of the payments from CyberNation had led him to a small branch of the Virginia National Bank out in the suburbs, but no further.

This particular branch had unfortunately kept up with the security bulletins Net Force issued to computer-intensive businesses from time to time. Their firewall was impressive.

He'd spent hours as a Swiss guide attempting to scale the Matterhorn, the VR equivalent of an attack on the

bank's firewall. He had found it was like trying to walk
up a Teflon-coated slide at a ninety-degree angle. He got
nowhere fast.

Jay could hack his way into most international networks
before breakfast. Being shut out by a dinky little domestic
bank was frustrating. More than that, it was embarrassing.

He knew he could go through Legal. There was enough
to get a search warrant, but there were problems with that
approach. For one thing, serving a warrant might alert the
person they were after. That could give them time to pre-
pare, to hide the money or to move it into a legitimate
account.

On the other hand, if Jay could get the name on the
account, Net Force would be able to do a little background
research. Then they could set a trap and spring it when
they were ready. One thing he did not want to do was let
CyberNation get away this time, and that meant not tipping
his hand too early. Once their target was ID'd, *then* he
could request a warrant and build a chain of evidence.
Putting the target under surveillance under those circumstances would probably be much more informative.

The trick was, how to do it?

He'd tried brute force, although he supposed one of the
NSA supercomputers might have a little more juice than
Net Force's own. He could tap them, add them to the mix,
and maybe—

"Hello? Earth to Jay?"

With a start, he realized he hadn't heard—or seen—Saji
come into his office. She had perched on one corner of his
desk, and he smiled as he looked at her. All this time, and
the sight of her could still make him smile.

"Practicing your meditation, darling?" she asked.

He grinned, shook his head. Caught bringing work
home. Again.

"I didn't think so."

She came around behind him and started rubbing his shoulders.

Jay leaned his head back against her and sighed. She had started doing this on their honeymoon. Initially, they had planned to go to Bali, but changed their minds at the last minute and ended up going to Spain instead. They had spent most of the two-week trip on Formentera, an island off the coast of Ibiza. The place they'd stayed had truly been get-away-from-it-all; no electricity, no telephone, or even net connection. He'd felt a little claustrophobic at first—had spent a lot of time with his virgil, bringing up old games he never bothered with when he had VR. Saji had started giving him massages as a way of relaxing him.

After a while the charm of the island—hot sun, the beautiful clear water, and time alone with Saji—had relaxed him more than he'd been in years. She hadn't given him a back rub since they got back. Until now.

He wished they could go back to that island right now and forget about Net Force and CyberNation.

Hmm. Maybe he could try piggybacking a worm with a transfer, capture some keystrokes—

He became aware of Saji's breath in his ear.

"Whoa!"

"Oh, you *are* still here. Good. Remember me? You know, we got married a while back?"

He laughed. "Sorry. I'm here! I'm here!"

"All right, then, Mr. I'm-Here, what did I just say a moment ago?"

"Uh—"

"I thought so." She leaned forward to see his flatscreen. "So what's so important that you managed to go into VR without the gear? Pretty impressive concentration, by the way. You might almost think you had studied with a brilliant Buddhist."

"I did," Jay said, "only he was a *lot* older and uglier than you."

Now *she* grinned, but she also shook her head. "Uh-uh. You're not getting off that easy, Gridley. Now give."

Jay told her about the bank, how he couldn't get in.

Saji listened. It occurred to Jay, and not for the first time, that he was one of the luckiest men on earth to have found her. Someone who listened to him, who cared about his problems. And he'd almost backed out and blown it.

When he finished his explanation, Saji stood there for a few seconds without speaking, her hands motionless on his shoulders. Then she said, "Okay, no problem."

Jay tilted his head back to stare at her. Okay? No *problem?* Was she serious?

"What?"

"Well, I could tell you," she said, "but do you really want me to make it easy for you? Wouldn't you rather earn it? I know how you hate game cheats and all—"

"Saji!" he said, reaching up to grab her shoulders.

She laughed. "You know that old saw about not seeing the forest because of the trees?"

Jay nodded. Where was she going with this?

"That's you and this bank. You're not looking at the forest. You're stuck on one tree."

He shook his head. He just couldn't see what she was talking about.

She laughed again, and then gently bit his earlobe. "You'll get it, Jay," she said, "when you quit trying so hard."

He hoped so. Frustrated, he let go of her and turned his attention back to his computer.

Somewhere there was a way in. He knew it. There always was. He just had to keep looking.

9

Ames was in his clean office at the mall, listening to his hacker's progress report.

"Are you sure this is working?" Ames asked.

The programmer, whose netnom was "Thumper," shrugged. He was a smallish man, young, but nearly bald. He wore a black Metallica tank top and gray cord trousers, with some kind of high-tech rubbery sandals, and no socks. Brilliant in his field, but socially inept. One was probably a result of the other.

"Well, so far, yeah," he said. He had a flat Midwestern accent, nasal and on the edge of a whine. "What I put together was a six-pack, double-threes. That's two sets of three connected programs. The first trio I set for timed release—five, then three, then two days apart. The first one was just a filler. That's a program that infects a system then makes copies of itself until the storage medium—hard drive on your PC, memory stick on your PDA, whatever—

is full. It also attaches itself to your address book and sends copies to everybody on your list. It's not meant to be more than a nuisance, but you have to dig it out and delete it and clean out the drive. That one was on the news already. They think some hacker did it just for the hell of it. They also think they'll get him pretty quick, which they won't."

He grinned and scratched his nose. "The second wave is a blanker, and it should be hitting big this time tomorrow. It doesn't do anything except shut off your monitor. Lots of people won't even know what it means. They'll spend some time jiggering with their hardware before realizing it's a software bug. It, too, will send copies of itself to everybody in your address book. Again, this one's no biggie, but it will be irritating."

Ames nodded. He knew all of this, of course, knew it before Thumper wrote his first line of code. Still, plans changed, so he liked to be kept up to date.

Thumper wasn't finished with his report yet. "The third wave will be a crasher. Once it gets into your system, it will send out copies of itself, and then it will crash your drive. At the very least, you'll have to restart your hardware from external software and do a clean install of the entire operating system. This one will cause a lot of downtime, guaranteed. In addition, a lot of people won't have backed up everything—most people don't, you know—so they'll lose tons of data. Like the others, this one will spread via e-mail. Also, like the other two, it will get around the most common blocks set up to catch it."

Thumper grinned again and leaned forward in his chair. "Now we're getting to the good stuff," he said. "Five days after that last one, the second three will launch. This time they will be set five, six, and seven days apart, just to mess with everybody's head. By then, everyone will pretty much have figured out that more attacks are coming; they just won't have any idea when. Or what, for that matter. This series will do pretty much the same kind of things as the first three. They will be written in different codes, however, so the viral and worm software won't be able to match them to the earlier ones."

"And this assault is going to cause problems nationally?"

Thumper laughed. "Nationally, hell. We're talking global repercussions here. You do have to understand, though, that the better defensive software out there has holographic system capability. That means it automatically looks for a number of things, including certain kinds of activity anywhere in the OS, self-replication, or attachments to e-mail. It flags anything the watcher program doesn't recognize. Those systems will filter out my attacks. They won't be able to break the code, at least not right away, but they will block it from hitting their systems. In addition, they'll sound an alarm as soon as they detect the attacks."

He shrugged, dismissing the idea. "The important thing to remember here is how few people run the good stuff. It's expensive, and very complicated to install and maintain. Most businesses go with the cheap stuff, and that won't stand a chance against my code. Even better, there are still millions of boobs out there on the net and web who don't have firewalls or virusware *at all*. We'll nail almost every one of them."

Ames was not a computer expert by any means, which was why he'd hired this guy. "What are we talking about in terms of lost time and money?"

Thumper shrugged again. "I can't say for sure. A triple-hit like this, followed by a second triple-hit? As far as I know, nobody's ever done that before. Historically it's been a single virus or worm, followed a few days later by some softbrain dragfoot copycat recycling the same virus with a couple of lame code variations. My best guess would be a couple, three billion dollars."

Ames raised his eyebrows. "That much?"

Thumper nodded. "It could be a little less, could be a little more. One thing's for sure, though: It'll keep the troubleshooters jumping and tearing their hair out for a while."

Ames smiled. Since that was the point, keeping Net Force occupied, this was exactly what he wanted. "Good," he said.

Thumper looked at him. "Your turn," he said. He paused, waiting, and Ames knew what he wanted. He reached into his desk and pulled out a big envelope. "Here's the second installment," he said. "Twenty-five thousand dollars. You'll get the next payment when I hear more about it on the morning news." He passed the envelope to the hacker.

Thumper grinned. "Keep your TV on. I'll be back to collect the next payment in a couple days."

After he left, Ames shook his head. If Thumper was right and this worked the way it was presented, it would be amazingly cheap. His price for all six attacks was a mere hundred thousand dollars. Ames routinely paid more than that just to have access to the right law clerk.

Then again, men like Thumper did things like this for free. They were modern-day vandals who got their kicks out of tearing something down for no reason other than that they could.

At least in his case, Ames had good reasons for what he did. More or less . . .

He looked at his watch. It was almost time to take the limo to the airport. The Learjet he'd leased was ready whenever he was for the flight to Texas, and he wanted to miss the traffic.

New York was the heart of civilization. It had just about everything a man could want, and twenty-four hours a day, too. Still, the island and the boroughs were not the best places to be if you had to get somewhere on time. He remembered when there were two rush hours Monday through Friday, one before work and one after. Now, rush hour lasted all day every day.

Oh, well. So things tended to get a little hectic in the city at times. That was the price you had to pay for the other conveniences.

A few days down in Texas would be just what he needed. There was nothing like getting away from it all to recharge your capacitors. He smiled. Well, not exactly away from it *all*, but close enough, close enough. . . .

Net Force HQ
Quantico, Virginia

Alex Michaels was headed toward the exit when he heard a strange whirring sound behind him.

He turned and saw Julio Fernandez just stepping off one of the two-wheeled Segway HT scooters. Once he was clear of it, the scooter wobbled back and forth like one of those round-bottomed dolls.

Alex remembered when those things had first come out. The creator had claimed it was going to be to the automobile like the automobile was to the horse and buggy. Well, they hadn't done *that* well, but you did tend to see them in city cores fairly often these days.

The problem was not that they didn't work. They did. He had ridden one himself, and it was fun. The initial cost was high, though, and the range was pretty limited. The first commercial ones had run . . . what? Seven or eight thousand? The smaller ones started out around half that amount, which meant they were a lot more expensive than old-fashioned bicycles. And while bikes were muscle powered, they had a more or less unlimited travel range. The scooters were only good for a dozen miles or so and then needed to recharge for six hours.

Great in theory, and fun to ride, but they certainly hadn't lived up to their promise or their hype. At least not yet.

"Lieutenant," Alex said. "What's up?"

Fernandez pointed at the scooter. "We're testing some new Segways," he said. "We've got two HT beta models. One runs on compressed hydrogen, the other on a fuel cell. They are both supposed to have more oomph than the old battery-powered electrics. This one, the fuel-cell unit, will supposedly haul a fully equipped soldier—we're talking a two-hundred-pound trooper with a hundred pounds of gear—for thirty-five miles at twenty miles per hour before refueling. That's twice the electrics' maximum range."

"Sounds pretty good," Michaels said.

"Yes, sir. Unfortunately, this one just died after what I figure is about five miles. On top of that, I just learned that when the power goes out, the nice little stabilizing gyroscope stops whirling around. It's got safeties so it doesn't slam to a stop and throw you nose-first onto the concrete, of course, but once it comes to a stop, you need to get off quick. Otherwise, you will fall."

"So you're not impressed, I take it?"

Julio shook his head. "The thing is, Commander, it's a great idea, but it's got to work. If one of these shuts down in the middle of a hike, say, I just don't see a lot of guys in the field hoisting this sucker over their shoulders to add to their packs, or towing it behind them like a tired old dog." He shrugged. "In other words, sir, what we have here right at this moment is your basic eighty-five-pound *lawn ornament*." He touched the thing's upright post and handlebar.

Michaels laughed. "I guess this means you're not going to buy one for yourself anytime soon."

"Well, actually, Commander, these things are a lot of fun, and the electric ones work pretty well, even if they don't have much range. And there are definitely field applications where extended capacity would be very useful, mostly flat terrain stuff, of course. Now, granted, all our troopers can hike ten or fifteen miles in full gear anyway, no problem, but going twice as far at a time, and getting there rested, sure wouldn't hurt their operational capabilities any."

He sighed and kicked the scooter lightly, just to watch it wobble some more. "I guess you have to expect glitches with beta models. I'll drag this one back to the mechanics and see if they can figure out what's what. At least the manufacturer built in a motor/wheel disconnect so you can at least push a dead one."

"Careful," Michaels said seriously. "I hear they are rigged to blow up if anybody tries to open them."

Fernandez chuckled. "Yes, sir, I've heard that, too. But I'm going to let the shop boys worry about that. That's their job."

Michaels watched him go, then turned back toward the door. As he reached it, however, he heard Jay Gridley call out, "Hey, Boss!"

Michaels turned back around. "Jay," he said. "What's happening?"

"There's another virus making the rounds. This one is a little odd thing that shuts off your system's monitor. From its language and construction, I'm guessing it's from the same guy who built that first one I told you about, the filler."

Michaels frowned. "How bad?"

"It's nothing major, Boss, but it'll be aggravating to a lot of folks. I have a couple of the boys working it."

"Okay," he nodded. "Good work. Anything else?"

"It's pretty quiet on the electron front. Just some low-rent scams, porno, the usual. The big news is that I think I've figured out a way to get that fund transfer from CyberNation I've been tracking nailed down. I'm going to take a shot at it and see."

"Excellent. Keep me posted." He paused, then switched

gears. "So, how's everything at home, Jay? You've still got that newlywed glow about you, you know."

The younger man grinned. "Well, I can't complain. Saji is pretty much the perfect woman, as near as I can tell."

Alex grinned back. "Hold to that thought, Jay. *Nisi defectum, haud refiecendum.*"

Jay frowned. "Which means?"

"If it ain't broke, don't fix it."

Jay laughed. "I hear that, Boss."

Michaels grinned and turned away. This time, no one stopped him as he made it through the door and headed for his car.

10

The hearing aid was just a tiny little thing, Howard thought. It certainly wasn't very impressive looking.

Geneva Zuri held it in the palm of her hand, showing it to him. "I'll give you an instruction booklet to take home," she said, "but the basics are pretty simple. If you pull this little door open, you can see where the battery goes."

Howard took it from her and did as she had suggested. At first he thought he was going to drop it, it was so small, but after a few moments he started to get the hang of it.

He frowned slightly when he saw the button-style battery. At maybe half the size of an aspirin tablet, it was going to take a pair tweezers to load and unload it.

"That's how you turn it off at night," Geneva said. "Just open the door and take out the battery. We recommend that you keep it in its case with the silica granule packet to dry it out. In the morning, pop it back in, close the door,

and you're good to go. Try it. It helps if you pull your ear
out with one hand and use your thumb to shove it in."

"What's the little button on top here do?"

"Changes the channel. Put it in, I'll show you."

Howard was used to using earplugs for shooting. He had
no trouble inserting the hearing aid.

He didn't know exactly what to expect, but he was just
a tiny bit disappointed. He didn't notice any change at first.

He frowned. Was that somebody talking? He shook his
head. No, they were *singing.* . . .

He turned to look, and saw somebody walking past outside the window. He grinned.

Zuri leaned forward and looked into his ear. "Nice fit.
Shake your head."

He did. It didn't move in his ear at all.

"It won't fall out by accident," she said. "In fact, it'll
take a little effort to remove it. Some people have problems
with that." She leaned back, rustled a paper at him, and
that sounded very loud. She knew it, too. He could tell by
the way she smiled. "You expected to hear some kind of
roaring sound when you put it in, didn't you, like the wind
or static or something? Maybe some feedback squeal, like
a cheap PA system?"

"Yeah, I did."

She smiled again. "What it's supposed to do is make
the bad ear work like the good one. It won't be perfect,
but it should seem as if both ears are working better.
You'll be able to pinpoint sound location better, too."

He nodded.

"That button you mentioned?" she went on. "Reach up
and push it."

He did and heard two soft beeps.

"Again."

He heard only a single beep this time.

"One beep is the normal mode," Zuri said. "That's the
default when you turn it on in the morning. The second

channel, the two-beeper, is for very loud environments, those with a lot of background noise. In the two-beep mode, it will pump mid-ranges, like most speech, but not the hum of your computer drive or car's engine. All you have to do is toggle back and forth until you get it where you want it."

She reached over and snapped her fingers by his good ear. "Cover this ear."

He did so.

She snapped her fingers by the one with the aid in it. "Sound about the same?"

"Yes."

"Good. Now pop it out. It'll help if you come underneath, use your thumb, and pry a little."

He removed the device. She was right. It took a bit of effort. That was good. He didn't want his expensive electronic ear falling out on the sidewalk where somebody could step on it. . . .

"Now let see it."

He handed it to her.

"Here's a little wire loop tool, to clean the wax out of the speaker channel, like so. Hold it angled down, so the wax falls out, see. And you can use the little plastic poker, right here, to clean out the air channel, that's this hole here. Don't clean anything else, except with a little brush, or maybe wiping it with a soft cloth. No cleaners, no soap, no water. Don't shower or go swimming with it in, you don't want to get it wet. A hat should protect you in the rain, a drop or two probably won't hurt anything, but if it looks like you are going to get deluged, stick it into this little waterproof packet and put it in your pocket until you get somewhere dry."

He nodded again.

"I want you to wear it for a couple days, go on about your business as usual, then come back. We can adjust it if something is too loud or harsh or not loud enough. It

only takes a minute to do that. I just hook it to my computer and program the changes."

She handed it back to him and he put it back in his ear.

"You'll have to change the battery about once a week,"
she said. "I'll give you a package of spares, and a little
holder you can carry a couple around in. Don't drop it on
the floor if you can help it, or in the bathtub. Like I said
before, if you lose it or break it, it's covered for two years.
By then, we'll probably have a new model anyway."

"Sounds pretty simple."

"It's not particle physics. If you can stick your finger in
your ear, you can use these things." She paused. "Are you
a betting man, General?"

He raised an eyebrow at her.

"I'll wager ten dollars that nobody but your wife notices
you're wearing it unless you tell them—and another five
that even she doesn't notice."

"You must be pretty sure of yourself."

She nodded. "Like I told you, it's not visible from the
front, and you can't see it from the back. The only place
someone *can* spot it from is directly to the side, and even
then, most people don't look at your ears."

He grinned at her. "Do you make that bet with all your
patients?"

She nodded. "All of the ones who get this model. In
fact, I usually bet them twenty bucks, not ten, but you're
a tougher case. Cops, federal agents, those folks who automatically mark you for purposes of ID, they're the most
likely to notice it, and they are exactly the kind of people
you work with."

"Great."

"Even so, it's better than going 'Eh, sonny, what's that?'
all the time, isn't it?"

He felt a little stab of vanity. "Yeah, well, that's easy
for you to say."

She suddenly went very serious. She looked at him silently, not smiling at all. After a moment she gave a small nod and turned her head to the side so he could see her right ear. Then she turned to show him the left.

She had hearing aids in *both* ears.

"One of the reasons I went into this field was because of a nasty virus I had when I was a child. It caused a high fever and burned out part of the wiring in both ears. I've worn hearing aids since I was eleven."

"I'm sorry, Ms. Zuri," he said.

"Don't be. I'm not. Not anymore, anyway. These things really do work great, General."

Howard sighed. She was right. A little piece of plastic and circuitry and a computer chip sure beat the other option, no doubt about it.

He stood up and shook her hand. "Thank you."

"You're welcome. See you in a couple of days."

Howard nodded and headed out the door, whistling as he left.

Ames's Hideaway
Southeast of Odessa, Texas

Ames stood in the middle of a dry and dusty plain, alone. All around him was emptiness and desolation.

From where he stood, there were no signs of civilization whatsoever. No roads. No cars. Just the tire tracks his own driver had left, and they were already crumbling in the sand.

A hot wind was trying to take his hat off. The summer sun played upon the mostly barren ground. Tumbleweed, the only sort of life he could see, bounced slowly along the sun-baked sand.

If you didn't know any better, you might think a man out here alone would be in trouble.

Ames smiled, feeling a certain sense of, well, superiority. He had a secret.

Everybody knew about Cheyenne Mountain, near Colorado Springs. The bombproof military operations center had been obsolete for *that* purpose before it was ever finished. By the time the excavation was done, and before they had even built the massive doors, the Soviets had targeted the complex. Rumors were they had enough megatonnage of ICBMs aimed at Cheyenne Mountain that, if the shooting ever *had* begun, the complex would have become a radioactive crater.

The best part was that the government had known all this, and they went ahead and built it anyway.

The cold war had produced more than a few such "secure" sites. Some of them probably would have survived a nuclear engagement, if for no other reason than that they really *were* secret. The ones the Soviets knew about, like Cheyenne Mountain, would have been destroyed, of course.

There had been a handful, however, that had been carefully and secretly constructed. Usually—but not always—this was under the guise of mining or heavy industry. The locations were never bandied about, and, through great diligence and great luck, their very existence was kept secret. Some of those would have probably made it.

Ames knew about three of these. One was outside Washington, D.C., for congressmen and senators. There was another one in Mississippi, and Ames knew that one would always be safe. Nobody in their right mind would waste missiles on the Holly Springs National Forest in northern Mississippi. Not unless they knew for sure there was something worth shooting at there, anyway, and probably they didn't. Fifty-odd years after it was built, most of the locals didn't even know the bomb shelter was there.

The third site was in central Texas.

Some miles southeast of Odessa, this third one had been

designed to house close to two hundred people. Ames guessed that the intended guests were probably big oil barons who had contributed significantly to certain politicians' election campaigns. It had been stocked with water, food, medical supplies, diesel engines and fuel, and power generators to run the lights, and air-conditioning, refrigeration, air filtration, and sewage systems. It would keep that many people alive and well for six months. The fewer people inside, of course, the longer they could survive.

Built in the mid-1950s, it had a fair-sized library. It also had dozens of radios and little black-and-white televisions, all with vacuum tubes, most of which still worked. And it had a gold mine of vinyl records—LP albums and 45 rpms that had never been played and were probably worth thousands to collectors.

The contractors had dug an underground garbage pit a quarter mile away from the compound. Electric golf-style carts could haul trailers of trash to it via a concrete tunnel buried thirty feet under the ground.

It had cost millions to build and stock, and it had never been used. The cold war ended. The threat of nuclear winter didn't go away completely, of course, but it had been greatly reduced. And the underground hideout had become a great white elephant.

So Ames had bought it. A real steal at six million and change, with both sides of the arrangement convinced they had suckered the other. Ames smiled at that. He had spent almost that much simply restocking and updating the supplies.

It had come with a huge pantry of canned goods, much of which were still useable, even after more than five decades. He had added smart-freezers and refrigerators stuffed with high-quality produce and meats. If he ever had to come here for an extended period, the only thing he would miss would be fresh fruits and vegetables. With freeze-drying, however, he could keep all kinds of foods not quite as good as fresh, but better than canned, almost forever.

Ames also installed a commercial-quality gas stove with a thousand-gallon propane tank to fuel it. He hid a satellite dish or two and put in state-of-the-art electronics, including televisions, computers, and sensor and communications gear. When he was all done, his little hideaway was perfect. Safe. Isolated. Secret.

Even if you knew it was there, it was almost impossible to get there without being spotted, by land or air. On top of that, its security system included both radar and heavy equipment sound detectors, and Ames had surrounded it with a minefield full of nonlethal noise poppers.

He was confident no one would be sneaking up on him, but he wasn't worried if anyone did manage to defeat his security. The place itself was impregnable. Built of hardened concrete and rebar with walls six feet thick, it was a veritable fortress. Best of all, it lay under twenty to thirty feet of very solid ground.

Safe and secure, but comfortable, too. Like everything else in his life.

He looked around again, feeling very satisfied, then headed for the secret entrance to the stairwell. It was far too hot to spend much time out here, especially since it was much nicer inside.

11

The Middle Ages
Sherwood Forest, England

Perched in a large old oak tree, Jay Gridley studied the castle in front of him. It had all the usual features: a wide moat, a high stone wall, an iron portcullis raised just beyond the drawbridge. He could see large iron pots between the crenellations at the top of the walls, pots that he knew could be filled with boiling oil. There were also dozens of firing slits in the thick walls. Those narrow, protected openings would allow long- and crossbow men to loose a rain of shafts and bolts on any who attempted to storm the castle.

But Jay had no plans to storm the castle. He had something far different in mind.

He smiled. What was it that Saji had said about not being able to see the forest for the trees? And here he was, looking *from* a tree in the forest.

He sobered, then, thinking about Saji, and how much he appreciated her help. It had taken her comment to get him thinking. She had been right, too. He *hadn't* been looking at the entire bank when he'd tried to follow the money here. He had been focusing on the area where wire transfers were sent, and that was a mistake.

The vault was, of course, heavily armored. Banks protected their customers' money, after all. If they lost it, they would be out of business. Which meant that trying to get to where the money was would be practically impossible, even for him.

He smiled again at the thought. He knew himself well enough to realize that the phrase "practically impossible" was like a challenge to him. There was a part of him that was still tempted to go that route, just to prove that he could.

He shook his head, laughing at himself. No, he needed the information, and he needed it fast. He needed to do this the easy way.

Besides, he could always come back later and crack the vault.

He climbed down from the tree and went over to a leather-covered chest near the base of the old oak. Opening the chest, he took out a brown robe. His forest green doublet, which worked well to hide him in the trees, wouldn't be suitable for what he was about to attempt.

Before changing, he unstrung the longbow he carried and laid it on an oiled skin. A pity he couldn't bring it with him, but it just wouldn't fit with his disguise. He admired the carefully worked and sanded wood before wrapping the oilskin around it.

Amazing things, longbows. With their superior range and penetrating power, they'd given the English the Battle of Hastings, which had pretty much kept the entire nation from having thereafter to speak French.

He pulled on the brown robe, picked up a heavy wooden quarterstaff that leaned against the oak, and moved toward the small settlement outside the castle.

As he neared the village he smiled and nodded at people who nodded back.

Just another friendly friar going to pay respects, that's me.

As Saji had said, once he revised his view to look at the entire aspect of the problem, he'd seen openings. Once he'd spun this VR scenario with the bank as a castle, he had noticed something interesting. Toward the back, and outside of the main fortified walls, was a smaller building, a humble village chapel. Many people came here, including townspeople, clergy, knights, and merchants. Which meant Jay could get in there, too.

It hadn't taken him long to identify the real-world equivalent of the building, and he realized that it was indeed a part of the computer he was trying to penetrate.

Banks strived very hard to provide convenience to their customers. These days, convenience meant access. They couldn't make the access to the money itself too easy or the money wouldn't be safe. That was the very problem that Jay had been fighting. They could, however, make it easy for customers to access things like bank balances and account histories.

This chapel housed that information, behind a *much* less daunting firewall.

If he was right, this chapel would give him access to the information he was after. It wouldn't be in the same form, necessarily, and it wouldn't have as much information as he would have liked, but it should have enough for his purposes.

He hoped.

Jay walked toward the small gate in the side of the castle wall. A pair of monks sat at a table outside, welcoming people. As he neared the table, he heard people giving their passwords to the friars. The silver-haired one on the left would nod if the password was right, and the person would be allowed to go inside the chapel to pray—although in the real world they were accessing their banking records. Not withdrawing their money, just checking on its status.

This whole process of finding the security hole had been a perfect example of why VR worked better than just peering through a flatscreen or at a holoproj. His instincts, his eyes and ears, all worked better in an environment like this than in one of pure text.

He stepped up to the table.

The older monk spoke. "And your account number, my son?"

Jay gave him the number of the account he was tracking.

"Your password?"

Jay spoke the Sanskrit word "om," drawing it out as Saji had taught him. She had told him once that some Zen masters believed that the word contained all the sounds in the universe happening at once.

In the real world, tens of thousands of passwords slammed into the on-line banking program simultaneously.

In the VR world, time stopped. The monks froze, and everyone in the village stood motionless. A woodcutter near the smithy paused in mid-stroke, splinters of firewood to the left and right of his axe, hanging in the air. The flames in the blacksmith's forge stood out as sharply as a three-dimensional marble statue.

Only Jay could look around. Only Jay was free to move.

And then time clicked back in, reality's hiccup over.

The silver-haired monk nodded, as though nothing had happened.

"You may pass, my son. God be with you."

Jay bowed his head, a smile on his face. "And with you as well, brother." He entered the small gate to the chapel within the castle.

He made his way to a vast array of pigeonholes alongside one wall of the chapel. Huge Roman numerals marked the account numbers of each of the bank's members.

Way to go, Jay, he thought. *Outsmarted yourself again,*

didn't you? You know you hate *Roman numerals.*

He paused the scenario for a second and made an adjustment.

There, he thought. *That's better.*

The account numbers were now in Arabic numerals. Much easier to follow. He located the pigeonhole with his account number. Within lay a single sheet of parchment that contained a summary of all the account activity for the last few months.

He picked it up and scanned it. There was the name of the account holder: Otis E. Levator.

He smiled at the name and turned his attention back to the details. It sure looked like Mr. Levator had been getting some serious cash from CyberNation over the last few months.

Jay grabbed the parchment and headed for the exit of the chapel. Time to change scenarios and track down old Otis. He left and headed out beyond the castle wall. Once he was back in the forest, he modified the virtual world around him.

One of the joys of being a net demigod was the ability to wave one's hand and change reality. Too bad it only worked in VR.

Tuscaloosa, Alabama

This new environment was also a forest, but one far different from the majestic old oaks of Sherwood. Jay had also traded in his Robin Hood outfit for a frayed flannel shirt, a pair of raggedy denim overalls, and worn combat boots. A pack of six bloodhounds bayed beside him, straining at the leashes he held in his hand.

Jay took a handkerchief from his pocket. It looked a lot like the parchment from the previous scenario. He waved it under the dogs' noses, giving them the scent.

The hounds sniffed the handkerchief, whuffled, and got more excited.

"Let's git 'im, dawgs," Jay hollered, and set them free of their leashes.

The pack took off, following the scent, with Jay chasing after the baying hounds.

This scenario was an old favorite of his, running through the Alabama backwoods like some old moonshiner chasing white lightning thieves from his still. He smiled at the image.

After a few minutes, the dogs' barking changed in pitch.

He moved faster, pushing through saw-grass plants and low bushes. Ahead he could see the dogs surrounding a small shack.

He called up the ID program for the shack and frowned.

Someone had been clever. This little shack wasn't Otis E. Levator's home after all. It was a mail delivery box at a Postal Plus—one of the tiny commercial post offices at mini-malls everywhere. They were all sterile, with a built-in irradiator that was guaranteed to keep your letters germ-free.

Another cutout.

"Thanks a lot, Otis." To the bloodhounds, he said, "Okay, pups, you can shut up now."

The dogs obeyed.

So what he had was some clown's idea of a clever pseudonym. Elevator. Probably something to do with moving up in the world. But that was all that he had.

Now what?

Jay left the dogs behind and went into the shack. He did a VR shift—

Postal Plus Shipping Service

Jay didn't bother loading one of his custom scenarios. Not
much point in it. He was pretty sure there was nothing to
be found here. Instead, he just ran a standard VR website
visual of the place, and tapped into the security on the
shipping store's computer.

The address left by the mysterious Elevator was *also* a
post office box, only this one was U.S. Mail.

Well, that was just great. All that work seeing the forest
for the trees, all that time hacking a bank to get *this*—

He looked up and noticed something. Hello?

A security cam hung down from the ceiling. The oper-
ator of the mail place must have had some problems with
people vandalizing mailboxes late at night. That was pretty
typical of a place like this. Whatever the reason, he had
installed a video surveillance device.

Jay recognized it as a pretty standard device. The cam
took a mid-ranged resolution video of the lobby, capturing
images of everyone who came in. Usually the files were
stored for a week or so before being either destroyed or
archived.

Now if only the data was kept on *this* hard drive. . . .

Jay went past the boxes and into the shop proper. The
clerk was busy with some customers. Jay saw the door
behind the vidcam and eased over toward it. When the man
behind the counter went into the back with a package, Jay
tried the door's handle. It opened, and he quickly slipped
into the little room where the monitor and hard drive for
the cam were. He closed the door behind him and crossed
over to the computer.

It only took a couple of commands to start the playback.
In the background of the video Jay could see a few parking
spaces to the right of the wall of boxes. He narrowed the
picture and located the box he wanted. There it was. He
then sped through the data, hoping the owner of box 1147

had been in sometime within the past week.

Movement caught his eye and he slowed the recording.

A tall, dark-haired young man in a very nice business suit—Armani, it looked like—opened the mailbox, pulled out a parcel, and left.

Jay widened the frame. The man headed to a vintage Porsche Boxter parked just in front of the place.

Jay froze the image, narrowed the focus again, and got the license plate of the vehicle. He could just barely make it out: LAWMAN9.

Jay frowned. A cop? That didn't make sense.

He made a quick copy of the video, sent it to his own e-mail address, and then bailed from the scenario—

Washington, D.C.

In his home office, Jay checked the time. Almost midnight. Saji would be asleep; she was an early riser.

He did a quick check with the DMV databank and found a name for the owner of LAWMAN9: Theodore A. Clements.

Gotcha!

Jay pulled down a few more files, a basic search, and scanned them quickly.

Not a cop. A lawyer. Clements worked for the Supreme Court. He was a clerk.

Well, well, well. Why would CyberNation be sending money to a Supreme Court justice's clerk? Not for anything legal, he'd bet.

Just wait till Alex heard about *this* one.

U.S. Capitol Building
Washington, D.C.

Commander Alex Michaels was not happy. It wasn't even eight in the morning yet, and he needed another cup of coffee. Instead, he was due at a briefing session for a congressional committee.

The worst part was that there was nothing he could tell the Subcommittee on Internet Security that they couldn't have gotten from a com or e-mail, nothing that an assistant couldn't have delivered just as well. But of course, that wasn't how things worked in this town. When a committee chairman wanted to be briefed, he didn't want to hear it from some flunky, and he certainly didn't want to actually sit down and *read* something. No, he wanted it from the lips of the man in charge.

It was just another part of the political gamesmanship that went on every day of life here. Who had to go where, and say what, was part of how clout was defined in the corridors of power. Alex knew all this. He also knew that the head of a small agency like Net Force couldn't say no to six congressmen, no matter how stupid those congressmen were being.

He was supposed to meet Tommy Bender here first. Nobody from Net Force, or even the mainline FBI, went before committees without a lawyer at his elbow.

He checked his watch and looked around again before finally spotting Tommy. The lawyer was talking to a tall blonde in a gray power suit, low heels, and red silk scarf. The skirt was cut just above her knees. She was gorgeous, no question about it, and Michaels thought she looked vaguely familiar, but he couldn't place her.

Tommy caught his eye and motioned Alex to join him. "Hey, Commander," he said when Alex came over.

"Counselor." Alex nodded.

"This is Corinna Skye. She's a lobbyist. Cory, this is Alex Michaels, of—"

"Net Force," the woman said. "Yes, I know. Commander, nice to meet you, though I think we're on opposite sides of an issue right now." She gave him a small smile.

He took her hand. She had a firm grip. He caught the scent of some subtle musklike perfume from her, just a hint. Very nice.

"What issue would that be, Ms. Skye?" he said, releasing her hand.

"One of my clients is CyberNation. I hope you won't hold that against me?"

Alex didn't reply.

Tommy glanced at his watch. "Sorry, Cory, we have to run. We're in front of Malloy's committee in five. I'll catch you later."

She smiled again. "Go. The congressman hates it when you're late. Nice to have met you, Commander. Maybe we might get together later this week? I would like to try to correct some misconceptions about my client, if you wouldn't mind?"

What misconceptions? Alex thought. *That they are evil scum who happily use terrorism to further their ends? That they are suing me and my department for a couple hundred million bucks?*

But he didn't say any of that. He only smiled in return and said, "Sure. Give my office a call."

As they walked toward the committee meeting room, he asked Tommy, "What do you think that was all about? And why were you talking with a lobbyist for Cyber-Nation, anyway?"

Tommy shrugged. "Hell, Commander, I'll talk to anyone, even the enemy—no, make that *especially* the enemy. I'm not going to pass up any chance to gather some information."

Alex frowned. "Don't you worry that they might pick up some information from you?"

Tommy laughed. "About what? Our strategy is no secret. The guys on that boat were criminals. They fired first, your guys reacted in self-defense. We don't have any secrets to give away."

"So you think I should meet with her if she calls?"

"Oh, she'll call, Commander. And, yes, I think you should meet with her. A word of warning, though: Corinna Skye has a reputation for doing anything to get what she wants. And I do mean anything. So be on your toes."

Michaels just shook his head. He had the feeling it was going to be a long day. . . .

His virgil beeped. Great. Now what?

"Excuse me a second, Tommy." He stepped to one side and glanced at the ID. "Jay?"

"Hey, Boss. I have something real interesting here."

"Can it wait? I'm sitting in front of a committee in two minutes."

"I guess it can. The quick version is, I traced a nice chunk of change from CyberNation to a clerk for a Supreme Court justice."

"What? That's incredible!" Michaels said.

"Yeah, I thought you'd think that. I'll fill you in when you get back to HQ. Have fun at your committee thing. Discom."

Michaels thumbed the virgil off. CyberNation was sending money to a Supreme Court clerk? If Net Force could prove it and backtrack the money, it would be a huge victory for them. Assuming, of course, the money was for something illegal, but it just about had to be. Jay had been working this one. If the money was legit, Jay would not have had so much trouble tracking it.

"Alex? We've got thirty seconds."

Michaels nodded. "We can make it. The door is right there."

They hurried to do just that.

12

Bailiff Hollow
Williamsport, Indiana

Junior didn't like small towns. He'd grown up in one, and he knew how they worked. If somebody spit on the ground at ten o'clock in the morning, they'd be talking about it at the barber shop by noon. Everybody knew everyone's business, and they paid extra attention to any strangers who came to visit.

This particular little town was exactly the kind of place where a man would get noticed if he wasn't a local. In the middle of corn country, its people were mostly farmers, with the odd airline pilot or ex-military retired to the country thrown in, and maybe some weirdo artists who worked in stained glass. People like that.

This particular little town was also home to a United States senator whose family had owned property here since they stole it from the Indians. That senator was about to learn which way the wind blew.

Junior grinned. Senator David Lawson Hawkins, the up-

standing Republican, was a buttoned-down widower with
three grown kids and eight grandchildren, and none of that
mattered. Senator Hawkins was either going to toe the line
or he was going to get stomped.

Junior glanced at the GPS reader mounted on the rental
truck's dash. He had selected a pickup truck, one a couple
years old, so he wouldn't stick out as much. The truck was
a big old Dodge Ram that looked like a dozen others he'd
passed on the road here from Indianapolis, via the long
way through Lafayette. It should buy him a few extra
minutes before the locals took note of him, and that would
be all he needed.

He didn't have an appointment, and the senator's bodyguard wouldn't be thrilled to see him, but there was no
question in Junior's mind that Hawkins would talk to him.
Junior had a conversation starter that guaranteed the man's
attention.

Junior smiled. And if the bodyguard gave him any crap?
Well, maybe he would cook the sucker. Just like that cop.

He got another rush thinking about the shooting. It had
been all over the papers and the news services for days.
They thought it was gang-related, and that was fine with
him. He'd changed out the barrels on his Rugers and used
a grinder to turn the old ones into steel filings that he had
flushed down a storm drain. He'd bought a new brick of
ammo, too, and thrown out all the old rounds, just in case
there was some way they might match the lead or something.

He was golden. They didn't have a clue. He had bagged
himself a cop and gotten away with it. One on one, *mano
a mano*. And that feeling he'd had when he did it? He
wanted it again. Soon.

Of course, you couldn't keep going around zapping
cops. Once was a skate, but twice was a pattern. If another
cop turned up with a pair of .22 rounds in his head, they'd
crank up the hunt for sure. As long as they thought it was

gang-related, they'd bring in the usual suspects and he should be safe. But if he deleted another policeman somewhere else with the same MO, they'd start up enough steam shovels to move heaven and earth.

Shooting somebody out here would be even worse. There was only one main road in or out, and even in the blend-in truck, some fool with nothing better to do might remember it, maybe even the license plate number: *Nossir, it warn't Bill's truck, warn't Tom's, warn't Richard's, it was a stranger's Dodge, and yessir, I just happened to write down the numbers, kinda made me curious and all. . . .*

He had that part covered, of course. He had switched plates with a used truck on a lot in Indianapolis not far from where he'd rented the Dodge, and he'd switch 'em back when he was done. Still, it wouldn't be smart to underestimate the cops even out here in the sticks.

Junior knew a con once who had swiped a bunch of computer gear, then put an ad in the local paper to sell the stuff. Junior thought that was crazy, but the guy hadn't been worried. The cops wouldn't think anybody would be that stupid, he'd said. They'd never look in the classified ads.

He'd been wrong. They looked. And they nailed him.

There were a lot of guys in cages who thought they were smarter than the police, especially the ones out in the middle of nowhere.

Junior knew better. He knew how they worked. If they were looking for a certain kind of truck, if they had that much, they might check every rental place for three states hoping to get lucky. And while he'd used a fake license and a credit card that couldn't be traced to him, that old cowboy hat he'd worn pulled low might not be enough of a disguise.

He shook his head, letting go of his fantasy of shooting the bodyguard. He knew it was better not to get their blood up looking for him. Besides, bodyguards were like dogs, they did what they were told, and the man's boss would tell him to stand aside. Junior was pretty sure of that.

He glanced at the GPS unit again. He had the coordinates for the farmhouse programmed into it. All he had to do was follow the map. It shouldn't be much farther.

Ten minutes later, Junior came to the property's gate, a large steel-frame swinger, complete with cattle guard. It wasn't even locked. He slipped the cable off the gate post, opened it, got back into the truck, drove in, and then got out and shut the gate. No point in drawing any attention to himself. People who left gates open on property where there might be livestock stuck in your memory.

The house was an old two-story place, recently painted and kept up real well. A half a mile from the gate, it sat at the end of a curvy road that wound through a section of cornfield. The corn stood about six feet high and looked as if it would be ready for harvest soon. Junior knew a little about crops. Though they'd grown mostly sugarcane and soybeans on his uncle's farm in Louisiana, everybody had a truck garden—corn, tomatoes, carrots, pole beans, like that.

By the time he'd parked the truck under the welcome shade of a cottonwood tree, next to a GMC pickup newer than his, the bodyguard/chauffeur was already on his way across the yard.

He was a big man, six-three, maybe six-four. In shorts, T-shirt, and running shoes, Junior could see that he was also very muscular. A weight lifter, for sure, and probably a boxer or martial artist to go with the muscles.

He was wearing his gun hidden in a belly pouch under the T-shirt. Some of those were rigged with Velcro so all you had to do to access the piece was to grab it with one hand and peel it apart, going for the gun with the other hand. They weren't as fast as a belt holster, but in the middle of the hot summer, it was hard to justify wearing a jacket or even a sleeveless vest.

Junior smiled. He liked his method better. He wore an unbuttoned denim shirt with the sleeves rolled up to his biceps and tails out, over a white T-shirt. It was a little warm, but you could get away with it. The little revolvers rode close to his body, and the shirt was enough to hide them as long as he didn't move too fast and flare the tails.

Before Junior could open the door, the bodyguard was there. Up close, Junior saw a small tattoo on the man's forearm. Junior nodded. It was a prison tattoo, blue ink, probably ballpoint, a little spider web, not bad.

"Hey," Junior said.

"You don't have an appointment," the bodyguard said. It was not a question.

"No. But the man will want to talk to me."

"How do you figure that?"

"Give him this."

Slowly and carefully, Junior reached down to the seat and picked up a sealed 9 × 12 manila envelope.

The bodyguard took the envelope without looking at it. His eyes were still locked on Junior's.

Junior glanced at the tattoo. "Where'd you do your time?"

The bodyguard frowned. "I printed validation stickers at Wabash Valley. Six years, man-two." He looked at the envelope, just a glance, then back at Junior, his eyes hard. "You're not going to cause my boss any trouble, are you? The man has been very good to me."

Junior grinned and shook his head. "Not a bit. I'm just here to talk business."

"Wait here. Don't get out of the truck."

The bodyguard backed away, keeping Junior in sight, then turned and went back into the house.

I can take you, Junior thought. *You're not fast enough coming out of that belly pouch.*

Of course, he'd have to make the head shot. A .22 to the body wouldn't even slow that bodyguard down. He played it out in his mind, smiling. Yeah. He could take him.

It didn't take long. Five minutes and the bodyguard was back. "Leave any hardware you're carrying in the truck," he said.

Junior nodded. There was no point trying to pretend he didn't have any, though he had already pulled the two Rugers out and stuck them under the seat.

He got out, stood there while the bodyguard patted him down, then followed the man into the house.

They went in through the back door and straight to a big paneled office—Junior thought it looked like pecan wood—with lots of bookshelves. There was music coming from hidden speakers, an old show tune. He grinned.

The senator sat behind a big desk made of the same kind of wood as the paneling. It had a burl to it. Pecan, he was sure of it, or maybe some kind of maple.

"Have a seat, Mr. . . . ?"

"Just call me 'Junior,' Senator."

Hawkins was sixty-something, leathery, tanned, and fit. He had salt-and-pepper hair cut in a flattop. He wore a plaid cotton shirt, jeans, and work boots.

Senator good ole boy, Junior thought, but this time he hid his grin.

"Wait outside, Hal," the senator said to the bodyguard. "And close the door, would you?"

Hal nodded, stepped out, and shut the door softly behind him.

As soon as the door closed, Senator Hawkins turned back to Junior, his expression growing ugly. "Now you want to give me a good reason why I shouldn't have Hal take you outside and stomp you into a pile of greasy hamburger?"

"Your call, Senator," Junior said. "But you know I'm

not so stupid as to come here with the only copy of that picture. You can also be sure that I have people who know where I am, and who have more pictures like it—and some a lot worse. Something happens to me, you know what comes next."

"You son of a bitch."

Junior frowned. "You're a smart man, Senator, and you've been in politics half your life. How long did you figure to keep something like this a secret?"

"It's been forty years so far," he said.

Junior nodded. "The wife, the kids, the grandkids, they're all good cover, but that doesn't matter now, does it? What's done is done."

The senator sighed, and Junior could see him give up. "What do you want?" he asked. "Money?"

"No, sir."

Hawkins stared at him.

"I need one thing, one time only. I need a vote. In return you get all the copies of all the pictures, and we never say another word to each other as long as we live."

Senator Hawkins glared at him. "And I'm supposed to trust a blackmailer."

"It's not like you have a whole lot of choice here, Senator."

Hawkins thought about it. "What if I say no?"

"Then the pictures—all of them—show up on the web and tomorrow's front page. You want your grandchildren knowing you've been sharing long weekends up in Pennsylvania with another man? The brother of an appeals court judge? That you've been swinging the other way since before you met Grandma?"

Hawkins shook his head. "No, I don't want that."

"Fine," Junior said. "Then we can do business."

There was a long pause, and Junior felt just a twinge of nervousness. You could never be sure in a situation like this. The guy might just lose it and go off, and with his guns in the truck, he didn't feel real comfortable. Hal would stomp him like a roach. Sure, the senator would pay for it, but that wouldn't help Junior any.

Finally, Hawkins said, "I don't know who you work for, *Junior*, but let me tell you this. If this gets out, I'm ruined. If that happens, I won't have anything left to lose. Hal out there has friends. They'll find you, and you will tell them who sent you, before they put you out of your misery, and whoever your people are will suffer the same fate as you. You understand me here?"

Junior felt a chill. This man was dead serious, Junior had heard enough people calling it straight to know it when he heard it. The senator was telling him it was easier to do what Junior wanted than it was to kill him, but that if it went wrong, he could do that. Would do that.

He nodded. "Yeah, I hear you."

"All right. What is it you want?"

Junior told him.

"That's *it*?" He looked stunned. "My God, you didn't need to do this. You already *had* my vote."

"The man I work for doesn't take chances," Junior said.

Junior left. After he was back in the truck, with his guns in their holsters, he felt a whole lot better. Hawkins would be a nasty enemy, and Junior was just glad to be done with him.

Washington, D.C.

There were some good things about living in Washington, Toni thought. One of them was that news got old fast. The phone would still ring now and then with calls from the media, but at least the reporters were gone from the sidewalk. They were off making somebody else miserable, which meant that Toni's life could begin to get back to normal.

She was even thinking about going into the office today. Alex needed her help, no question about that. Between the lawsuit and normal Net Force operations, things were getting a little thick.

Toni had lost a few steps, she knew. She wasn't quite as sharp as she'd been before she quit to have the baby. Like *silat*, work was a skill, and if you didn't hone it, it got a little dull.

That didn't worry her, though. She knew she could get it back if she really wanted. The question was, did she really want it? And that question did worry her, at least a little.

A year ago, two years ago, it would never have occurred to her that she might not want to go back to work. Before Alex—and especially before Little Alex—her work was her life. She had never imagined that anything—*silat*, her parents or siblings, or any future family of her own—could ever replace her job as the single biggest focus in her life.

She had been wrong. She had found something that mattered more to her. And it was making her think about things in a way she never had before, to ask herself questions that would have been unthinkable just a short time ago.

It didn't have to be that way, of course. She had known plenty of women who had done both, raised a family and maintained a career, but it had seemed to Toni that something always suffered, even among the best and brightest. It was a matter of time, not effort or ability. There were only so many hours in a day, only so much you could do, no matter how much you wanted to do more.

And that was the point she kept coming back to. There were other people who could do her job at Net Force. Other people could help with investigations and administration. But who could step up and be a mom to her son?

No one, of course. She knew that. Even Guru couldn't replace Toni. Not when it came to her family.

The worst of it was, there was just no way to know. Not in time, anyway.

At Net Force, at the FBI, at most jobs, the results of your decisions showed up quickly. Oh, some investigations stretched out over months or years, but for the most part you made a decision and you knew pretty quickly if you were right or wrong.

Being a parent didn't work that way. You made your decisions on how to raise your child. You figured how and when and why to discipline him and how to encourage him. You determined when to lead by example and when to give a lecture. And after each decision, after each opportunity to teach or scold or praise, you had no idea if you had made the right call. You wouldn't know—couldn't know—until someday in the far future when your son was grown and you saw the fruits of your labor.

But even then, really, how would you know? If your child turned out happy and productive and successful and loving and all the other things you hope and pray for him, how would you know how much was due to your parenting and how much was just luck, or genetics, or other influences?

You wouldn't. You couldn't. And knowing that made making parental decisions—and especially major parental decisions—that much harder.

She sighed. Why hadn't anybody told her about such things before? How did she go from having all the answers to her life, to having things all planned out and comfortable, to feeling as if she were standing on a trail leading into an unknown wasteland, next to a sign that said, "Beware! Here Be Dragons!"

Being Mommy was a lot harder than being a federal agent. Or kicking somebody's tail in a fight. Much harder.

13

John Howard shook his head. Julio hadn't been able to make it today. He had said something about having to take his son to somewhere to apply for pre-preschool classes. That meant that John was the only one here with his own son. It was probably just as well, though. After all, there was no point in both of them being embarrassed.

Tyrone brought the K-frame revolver up and squeezed off two shots, double-action. He paused a second, then squeezed off two more double-taps, with only a half-second between the second and third pair.

Howard looked at the computer screen in the shooting bay. The computer displayed an image of the "bad guy" target. Hits showed as bright points of light against a darker shade.

Howard let out a low, soft whistle. Six shots, all neatly paired, all hits. Two in the head, two in the heart, two in the groin. No question about it, the boy had fired quickly,

smoothly, and accurately, using a handgun he had only
shot one time before.

"That's good, son."

Tyrone smiled. "Thanks, Dad. It just feels so, you know,
natural."

Howard shook his head. Unbelievable. "Try the .22."

Opening the Medusa, Tyrone ejected the empty shells
into his palm and put them into the plastic bin. He put the
revolver down and picked up the little .22 target pistol, a
bull-barreled Browning semiauto. The gun had iron sights
and was front-heavy, but it was an accurate enough
weapon. The sights were frame-mounted and not on the
slide.

Tyrone slid the half-loaded magazine in, chambered a
round, and thumbed the safety on. He kept his trigger finger outside the guard, the gun pointed low and down range.

John nodded, giving the boy high marks for safety, too.

"I'm going to change the target to a bull's-eye," Howard
said. "Take your time, remember what I told you about
breathing, and shoot five rounds slow-fire."

Tyrone nodded.

Howard tapped a control on the computer. The image
blinked and shifted into a standard black-and-white
concentric-circled twenty-five-meter pistol target.

Tyrone took a couple of deep breaths, raised the pistol
one-handed, and extended his arm, duelist-fashion. Formal
target shooting discipline allowed only a one-hand hold.
The gun would not be as steady as when held in a two-
handed combat grip, so he shouldn't do as well, even with
the smaller recoil of the .22 round.

The little *pap!* of the .22 target load was very quiet
under the sound suppressors, even though Howard hadn't
taken his hearing aid out.

Tyrone lowered the weapon, took a couple more breaths,
and raised the pistol again.

Pap!

Howard watched his son, not as interested in the score as he was in how Tyrone shot. He paid particular attention to how he stood, his grip, trigger control, his breathing, and his eyes. Behind the shooting glasses, Howard could see that Tyrone kept both eyes open.

Tyrone lowered the gun again, relaxed and breathed, then brought it back up.

After five rounds, the slide locked open. Tyrone ejected the magazine, checked the chamber, then put the pistol and empty magazine onto the bench and turned to look at the computer. At this range the bullet holes were too small to see with the naked eye.

Howard looked at the computer screen at the same time.

All five rounds clustered into a ragged hole an inch below dead center, tight enough so you could cover them all with a quarter. There were no fliers at all.

A one-inch group, one-handed grip, twenty-five meters out, and the first time he had ever fired the pistol. Now *that* was good shooting!

But Tyrone frowned. "I missed the bull's-eye," he said. "I was aiming right at it."

Howard laughed and shook his head. "No, son," he said. "Those sights are set for my eyes. What's important is not that you shot low, but that you put them all essentially into the same hole. You can always adjust the sights. Try it. Just give them one or two clicks, that'll raise the point of impact."

Tyrone adjusted the sights, reloaded, and fired off another slow five. This second group was almost the same as the first, with four centered in the ten ring and one round slightly off.

John shook his head again, amazed. If you threw out that one flier, you could cover the other four with your thumb—and even with the flier included, all five were still within an inch or so of each other. Amazing.

"I pulled the third shot," Tyrone said. "It felt off."

Howard said, "Son, there are men who have practiced regularly for years, burning tens of thousands of rounds, who can't do what you just did. This Browning is a very good gun, but it's not close to being a world-class free pistol. With a precision weapon and match-grade ammo, you'd do even better." He paused, then finished, "Ty, if you can do this consistently, you could win Olympic medals. You're a natural born shooter. I've been around guns all my life and I've never seen anybody with as little experience do as well."

Tyrone looked at him. "Really?"

Howard smiled. "Really. You have a talent. I don't know that this is one I'd have picked for you, but God has His plans, and we're not always privy to them. If you are interested in pursuing this, I'll see that you get whatever equipment and training you need."

"Sir," came Gunny's amplified voice over the PA system, "are you screwing around with my target computer out there?"

"Negative, Gunny," Howard called out. "It's Tyrone."

"Tell me he wants to join the junior pistol team, sir. Please."

Howard looked at Tyrone. "Well?"

"Yes. I'd like that."

Louder, Howard said, "Only if you promise not to teach him any bad habits."

"Sir, when a man can shoot like that, there's nothing I can teach him at all."

Net Force HQ
Quantico, Virginia

Corinna Skye was a little softer than when Alex had seen her last. As before, her suit was well-cut and expensive,

but today it was a pale, less-formal gray, her jacket unbuttoned, and she wore a red blouse beneath it. She sat on
the couch facing his desk, her legs crossed, showing a few
inches of stocking above her knees.

"Thank you for seeing me, Commander."

He nodded. "Before you get started, there's something
you should know."

She looked at him expectantly.

"Your client, CyberNation, is suing Net Force—and me
personally—for two hundred million dollars. On top of
that, we've caught them doing all manner of illegal things
in the past, and there is an investigation that has been ongoing since then."

She started to say something but he held up his hand.
"Now I know that the organization managed to throw a
few sacrificial bodies off the sled, as it were, but I don't
believe that all the guilty parties have been brought to justice. In fact, I fully expect that we will catch CyberNation
doing all manner of illegal things in the future, too. I think
CyberNation's higher-ups all ought to be wearing eye-
patches and peg legs and going 'Har, matey!' when they
talk, that they are as twisted as a boxcar full of corkscrews,
and if I can, I'll see them all in prison for a long, long
time."

She smiled, what looked like a genuinely happy expression. "Oh, go on, Commander, don't sugarcoat like that—
tell me how you *really* feel."

He had to laugh at that. "I'm sorry," he said. "I guess I
came off pretty righteous and pompous, didn't I?"

She laughed, too. "That's all right, Commander. I appreciate honesty. I seldom get to hear it as much as I would
like in my work."

He nodded. "In that case, Ms. Skye, I have to warn you
that you're wasting your time lobbying me."

She smiled and shook her head. "I don't think so. Besides, there's no challenge in convincing somebody who already agrees with you."

Well, he thought. *This ought to be interesting, at least.*

"Let me lay out some facts, Commander."

"That's the third time you've called me that," he said. "We don't stand on titles around here. Please, call me 'Alex.' "

She smiled again. "All right, Alex. My friends call me 'Cory.' "

He nodded.

"Let's assume for a moment, hypothetically speaking, that all the bad apples in CyberNation were removed from the barrel. Or maybe even that there are a couple you missed, but that the rest of the organization is not intrinsically evil."

"That's a big assumption, and like I said, I don't agree with it."

"For the sake of argument."

He shrugged. "Okay."

"If that were the case, if all those who did anything illegal were gone, how would you feel about the organization then?"

"You mean about those fine, upstanding people who are suing me for all that money?"

She smiled. "Well, as long as we are speaking hypothetically, suppose that lawsuit did not exist. That it just went away?"

"No crooks, no legal action," he said. "In that case, I suppose I might not think much of CyberNation one way or another."

She frowned. "Are you saying that you have no opinion whatsoever regarding their basic premise?"

He leaned forward a little, clasping his hands and resting his elbows on his desk. "Not at all. I think it's a silly idea. A virtual country whose citizens live and work in the real world but do not have to pay taxes to the countries they actually live in? A phantom government that can still issue IDs, credit cards, even driver's licenses?"

"It's not a phantom government and you know it," she said. "Its leaders are elected through the same democratic process as the President of the United States."

He shrugged. "There's no White House, no Capitol Hill, no physical analog to any of the traditional seats of power. Without that, it's all just pixels on a screen."

She smiled. "Actually, with VR there are no pixels and no screen, but you know that, too, of course. Besides, I see your point. I just don't agree with it."

"What about the rest of my comments?" he asked.

She waved her hand dismissively. "You already get most of your IDs and credit cards on-line," she said. "When was the last time you mailed in a credit-card application instead of just visiting a website? This is no different. And I've heard that several states are considering doing their driver's license testing and renewals on-line as well. Sure beats standing in line, doesn't it? If we can do it, why can't CyberNation?"

"It's just not the same."

"Why not, Commander? Alex? Why isn't it the same?"

He shook his head. "Look, I'll grant you that some of this, maybe even much of it, is happening already or is going to happen. But not just on-line. The virtual world we live in is just a convenience, a time-saver. The Department of Motor Vehicles still exists. It still has all its same branch offices. And you can still go down and talk to someone face-to-face if you have a problem. The same is true for all the branches of government, and all the banks, and all the other companies who have a presence on the net. Their virtual offices haven't replaced the physical ones, and that makes all the difference."

"Why?" she asked. "What difference does it make if I have the option to go downtown and stand in line in some old office building? If I can get the same level of service—

no, if I can get better and faster service on-line, with the same level of accountability—then why should that make any difference at all?"

He frowned again. He knew he was right, but he couldn't find the words to explain it to her.

"It just does," he said.

She just smiled.

"All right," she said. "Let's table that part of the discussion for now. Why don't you tell me what really bothers you about CyberNation, Alex?"

He sighed. "It just doesn't make sense," he said. "Let's say CyberNation exists right now, and that you're a citizen there. But you work here, in the real world, in the United States. You spend all your time here, regardless of whether you're working on-line or off. You're here, receiving all the benefits of being a citizen, all the protection of our laws, all the freedoms of our land, and yet you're not a part of it."

"And I'm not paying for it."

"Exactly."

She smiled. "That's it, isn't it, the fact that I'm not paying taxes and you are?"

He nodded. "That's part of it, certainly."

"But don't you see, Alex, that happens all the time. If I were a citizen of Saudi Arabia, for example, or France, I could live here and work here—part of the year, at least—and not pay taxes to the U.S. government."

"That's different," he said. "Those are real countries. Our government has reciprocal agreements with them, so our citizens can live and work there under the same arrangements."

"And that will be true with CyberNation, too," she said. "We'll have arrangements with every government on the face of this planet. We'll have to. It's the only way our citizens will be able to live and work where they want to."

"But . . ." He stopped.

"Yes?"

He shook his head. CyberNation was wrong. The whole idea was ludicrous, and he knew it. He just couldn't seem to make her understand that.

"And what happens to the real-world countries?" he asked.

"Ah, now *that* is the best question I've heard so far," she said. "And I believe it's the real heart of your concern, isn't it? The fact that people becoming citizens of CyberNation, of not paying taxes to the U.S. anymore, would be bad for this country that you love so much."

He nodded. He hadn't really thought of it in those terms before, but she was right. It would be bad for the United States, just as it would be bad for Saudi Arabia, and France, and every other country. It would have to be.

"But maybe, just maybe, that would be a good thing. After all, the United States is supposed to have a government 'of the people, by the people, and for the people.' Can you honestly say that the current tax structure works that way? Never mind for the moment that fewer than ten percent of the population pays more than eighty percent of the taxes. Never mind for the moment that for tax purposes the poverty level is set at an unbelievably low level, so that families making far less money than they need to feed and clothe and house their children are nonetheless paying taxes. No, for now, just look at where those taxes go. Tell me that you're happy with all the pork barreling that goes on, and that you believe the monumental waste you see all around you is 'of the people, by the people, and for the people.' "

She paused and looked at him. "Maybe, Alex, just maybe it isn't CyberNation that's bad for America. Maybe America has become bad for itself."

"No, Ms. Skye," he said in a flat voice. "We've got problems, I'll admit that. We always have and we always will. But that's exactly because we *are* of the people. Any human endeavor will always be flawed. It's part of our makeup. CyberNation would be no different."

There was a moment of silence as they both looked at each other. Then she nodded. "Well," she said, "I won't take up any more of your time. I appreciate the opportunity to talk with you. If ever I can help you with information regarding CyberNation, or anything else, please give me a call."

He nodded, rose, and shook her hand.

She paused, still gripping his hand lightly. "Promise me one thing, Alex. Promise me you'll at least think about what I've said."

"Oh, I think you can count on that, Ms. Skye."

She left and Alex turned back to work. A virtual country? No taxes? Preposterous.

Wasn't it?

14

Jay Gridley walked across the huge laboratory's hard li-
noleum floor toward the test chamber. A low, dry rustling
sound, as if thousands of leaves were being tossed about
in a huge lotto machine, echoed through the room. The air
was heavy with the smell of ozone. Across the room, two
Jacob's ladders, the epitome of mad-scientist decor,
buzzed, sending hump-shaped blue sparks up their V-
shaped electrodes. Close at hand, a bank of Tesla coils
radiated even more intense sparkings, and Van de Graff
electrostatic generators added their cracklings. A large
Lava lamp stood off to the side, and on one of the lab
benches, a Rube Goldberg forest of beakers, retorts, and
Bunsen burners drove multicolored liquids through tubes
and distilled them into yet more containers. At the end of
another bench, an old oscilloscope displayed a revolving
sine wave. The topper was the huge computer lining the
entire wall at the end of the room. Huge rolling reels of

magnetic tape rolled back and forth, interspersed with banks of flashing lights. The sound of clicking relays was a touch he had added himself.

Jay grinned. This particular scenario wasn't actually all his, but since he had the final word in most Net Force VR work, his suggestions had carried some weight.

Frankenstein would be proud of this setup. Or at least the moviemakers who did all those science-gone-mad flicks of the thirties, forties, and fifties would be. Jay was proud, too. His people had done their usual great work.

Around him on the other three walls were hundreds of museum-quality display cases, each one lined with cotton and filled with odd-looking insects. On top of the lab benches, in huge wooden boxes, were thousands upon thousands more bugs: Their assorted wings, legs, and pincers were what made the leaf-rustling sound.

This wasn't Jay's usual VR scenario. It wasn't intended to help him break into other net sites. It wasn't even connected to the net at all. Instead, it was quarantined in a stand-alone Net Force computer, with no links to the outside net at all.

This scenario was a holding cell. It was also a visualizer and a synthesizer. It translated computer viruses, worms, and Trojan horses into distinctive insectoid shapes, complete with whatever features made each particular program unique. When it came time to see how a new attack program worked, Net Force personnel came here, to the test lab, to see what they were up against.

If the virus ate data, for example, it might have oversized mandibles along with a big abdomen and colors to match the data it went after. If it propagated by hiding in other data, or by catching hold of it, it might have a chameleon-like ability to change color, or spinnerets to ensnare its prey. Each mode of operation, combined with the bug's delivery and goal, would give Net Force's software enough info to make a distinctive-looking bug.

Naturally they still had to look at the actual code that made up the cores of the viruses, but the visualizations gave them a better way of tracking how the virus actually worked.

Like now, for instance.

Behind a thick Plexiglas wall was the virus test chamber, itself an analog representation of data transfer between computers. An old-fashioned punch-card printer sat at one end of a long conveyor belt. At the other end was a scanning array and punch-card reader along with a large diagram of a computer that looked like an ant farm.

Everything was a brilliant white, like some scientific version of heaven. Cameras and magnifying lenses surrounded the apparatus to make it easier to watch the process from start to finish. A long section of the Plexiglas wall had been built to make a huge lens that brought sections of the conveyor belt up several levels of magnification.

Jay walked over to the punch-card printer and sat at a terminal. He tapped a few buttons and the printer began to spit cards. What he'd actually done was to upload an e-mail that had been infected with the new blanker virus going around. High-end security software had caught it, but the virus had slid past standard virus-checker stuff, and he wanted to find out why.

He moved to a magnifying glass in front of the printer, one half of which was cut away like a "how it works" kind of drawing, and took a look. There, near the punch card being printed, was a small insect shape. He flipped a larger lens down over the area he was watching and took a better look.

The bug was fairly large. Pale, almost clear, without color, it was segmented into three main sections. It had six legs and six pincer arms, with one pair of each per section. The head was surprisingly small, with tiny feathered antennae, and it had large eyes.

As he watched, the middle thorax—if it could be called that, there being three of them—went completely transparent, and he could see through it.

Clever. The author of this little bug had come up with a new invisibility routine, a don't-look-at-me-I'm-not-here bit of misdirection that made viral data less noticeable.

As Jay watched, the bug worked its way toward a small pile of punch cards.

The first batch of cards dropped down from the printer onto the belt, which inched itself forward just enough so that the next batch of cards wouldn't hit the first, and then stopped. The bug didn't go yet, though.

It waited for the second set of cards—which actually represented a packet of data—to begin stacking up. Then it reached between the second and third sections and did something to detach the last set of arms and pinchers. That segment moved toward the cards, went transparent, and began cutting at them with its claws. When it had made enough room, it burrowed in and pulled a section of torn card back to cover itself. The bundle of cards dropped onto the conveyer belt a few seconds later, and packet number three began printing.

Fascinated, Jay watched as the bug split itself apart again several packets later and the second segment burrowed into another stack of cards. The very next stack got the last third of the bug.

Impressive. A trinary virus—and, if he was right, one coded to ride different packets.

The last stack of cards dropped onto the conveyer belt, and then the belt sped up, taking the cards toward the scanner at the other end of the test chamber.

The cards were VR representations of packets of information: the e-mail he'd forwarded broken down and sent in little bunches. The way it worked was the first packet had a list saying how many packets were coming, kind of like a cover sheet for a fax. The last packet had a little tag saying, "The end." The packets in between contained the actual e-mail itself.

The computer or server getting the data would watch for all the packets and confirm delivery of each one before forwarding on to the next link in the chain. If there were any errors, the problem packet would be re-sent.

Early virus writers had taken advantage of the fact that each packet was a set size. That meant that if your message was, say, ten point two packets long, eleven packets would still be sent. The point oh eight unused space would usually be filled with zeroes, and that was where the virus would hitch a ride.

The virus checkers had gotten wise to this, though, and started carefully checking the size of messages against the number of characters sent.

So the innovative virus writers had gone one better, and had their creations cut out sections of legitimate data in the middle of the stream and hide there.

This would change the size of the packet, of course, which would throw an error, but that wouldn't set off any alarms. Errors in transmission were pretty common. Line noise, bad connections, time-outs, there were many, many legitimate reasons why errors occurred. The receiving computer would simply flag the error, the entire stream would get sent again, and the recipient would get their data unaware of the hitchhiker that had come along.

This had led to binary viruses, where the virus would split into two innocuous-looking sections that didn't do anything until they were reassembled at the other end of the chain.

This was the first time he'd ever seen a trinary, however. In addition, the way the bug had not spaced the packets it was riding evenly led him to think it was randomly selecting them, which would make it tough to get a handle on.

At the other end of the test chamber, Jay watched the

packets slide past the scanning array, which was actually a standard, off-the-shelf virus detector. He wanted to see how this bug got past them, after all. Putting one of his own cutting-edge programs there and squashing the bug with it wouldn't tell him anything.

He was disappointed, though. The bug didn't do anything special to defeat the security program. The off-the-shelf killware wasn't designed to detect trinary bugs, and so it didn't.

Jay saw the virus-bug reassemble itself, and then proceed to a large clear sheet of glass that represented the video subsystem of the computer setup. Once there, it sprayed the glass with some kind of ink, blacking it out. If he had been in the real world, he would have just seen his computer screen blank out.

Jay ran the test several times to confirm that the virus was indeed randomly selecting packets to leap onto, his thoughts turning over the same question.

Why?

Why would someone go through so much trouble to develop a virus that couldn't be defeated by modern checkers, just to make someone's screen go blank? It seemed like a lot of work for not much gain. Somebody that smart could be making good money programming.

Maybe they were, of course. Though that still begged the question of, Why bother?

As he watched the bug on the third test, something else occurred to him. There was something familiar about the way it moved, the shape of the antennae.

He walked toward the most current bug case on the wall of the lab and started looking. He glanced at hundreds of recent viruses, red, green, big, small, all kinds of them.

There.

It was the filler, the really recent one that had made the rounds a few days before, the virus that had been eating up hard-drive space.

He took a closer look, pulling it carefully from its cage.

The antennae were identical to those of the blanker he was running in the test chamber. He turned the bug over, and saw it shimmer: another invisibility routine.

Hmm.

Jay got a live sample of the filler and took it to the test chamber. After a few runs, he was satisfied that whoever had made the filler had also made the blanker. An analysis of the written code showed portions that were exactly the same. This, plus the fact that the bugs had been released only three days apart, told him that they'd probably been developed at around the same time.

Which led to a particularly nasty thought, one that offered a possible answer to the "Why?" question.

There's more to come. This guy is seriously messing with the net, and not just for fun, either.

In addition to everything else going on, it looked like they had a serial hacker piping cutting-edge viruses out onto the net. Jay cleared the VR scenario and reached for his virgil to com Alex.

Kim's Business and Industrial Center
Dover, Delaware

Junior had made the drive from D.C. across the bay, taken Highway 301 north to SR 300, and driven east over the state line into Delaware. From there, it was only another dozen or so miles to Dover.

It had been dusk when he got there. Dover wasn't much of a town, but it was big enough to have a branch of Hopkins Security. Like Brinks or Pinkertons or the other big security firms, Hopkins offered service patrols and electronic alarms for homes and businesses. They also offered armed guards.

If you were their customer and your alarm went off, they didn't just call the cops like most agencies did. They sent an armed response of their own.

This was a huge selling point for them. In most places, the local police forces were stretched pretty thin. Answering a security call to an empty house, no matter how much money the owners had, just didn't rank right up there with burning homes or 911 calls where individuals could be in danger. Oftentimes that gave smash-and-grab thieves enough time to kick in a door and steal half someone's furniture before the police showed up.

Hopkins claimed that its armed response teams were the best private security around. They promised security personnel who were sharp, smart, and could all shoot. Every one of them had to qualify on the pistol range quarterly, and Hopkins's standards were higher than those of seventy-five percent of the major metro police departments in the country.

All of which was exactly what Junior was looking for.

The way he figured it, shooting another cop would be too risky. Cop killings were rare enough that somebody might try to link them together, and he definitely didn't want that. Even an armed security guard killed with a .22 might raise some eyebrows, though he had done all he could to protect himself there. He was planning to use only one gun this time, and the ballistics report would show that the bullets came from a different weapon. Doing it in another state should help, too.

It still wasn't smart. He knew that, but just the thought of it thrilled him more than anything else he could think of. Yeah, sex was great, but it was nothing like clearing leather and pulling steel against a man who was trying to kill you. No drug he had ever tried—and Junior had tried more than a few while in the can—no drug came close.

This was the ultimate rush. Lose, and you were dead.

Win, and you were like a god. You got to say who lived and who died. What could match that?

He ought to have made this trip before. He should have scouted it out, gotten the lay of the land and all, but Ames had been keeping him too busy running around lately. So what he ought to do now is to make this the scout—find a good place, set it up, check the response time and all.

That's what he ought to do. He knew it, too. But it wasn't what he was going to do. He was hooked, a junkie looking for his next fix, and he just couldn't wait any longer.

He drove toward the outskirts of town, looking for a place that would work. It didn't have to be perfect, but he wanted to find a spot far enough outside the city limits that they'd have to call the sheriff's office, or even the state troopers. It had to have a Hopkins sign posted, of course, and it also needed to be some kind of business or warehouse or something that, after five o'clock, would be mostly empty. A residential neighborhood was riskier. Too many people, too many eyes. Sure, he had swiped a set of license plates from an old car parked on a D.C. side street, and those were now on his car, but he still didn't want a crowd around. People in a neighborhood sometimes did weird, unpredictable things.

He remembered a time down in Mobile ten or eleven years ago. He'd been driving a car for a couple of guys who had said they knew where there was a gun safe full of cash. The house didn't even have a burglar alarm, they told him, and it was in this middle-class neighborhood full of soccer moms and working dads. The two guys—Lonnie and Leon—had waited for a night when the homeowner had gone bowling. The three of them drove up, Lonnie and Leon went to the house, kicked in the door big as you please, and waltzed on in. Junior sat in the car with the engine running. What they figured was, Lonnie and Leon would crowbar and sledge the safe open inside five minutes, grab the cash, and run.

It was Leon and Lonnie's plan. Junior was just the wheel man.

The safe turned out to be a better model than they had figured. After five minutes all they'd done was make a lot of noise, clanging and banging away at it. Junior could hear them out in the car even with the house's doors closed, the car window rolled up, and the air conditioner going.

The neighbors must have had good hearing, too, because lights went on all over the place and people started coming out of their houses to see what was what.

The neighbors clearly knew that the guy who owned that house was bowling, it being eight o'clock on a weeknight, because they spotted Junior right off and started his way. That alone would have made him real nervous, but he also saw that some of them had guns.

Junior was a pretty good handgunner even back then, but he wasn't about to try and take on five or six guys with shotguns and squirrel rifles coming at him in the dark on a hot summer night in Mobile. People up north might hate guns and all, but men in this neck of the woods knew how to use them, and there was no way that he was going to hop out of the car and shoot with them. He'd signed on as a driver and lookout, not security.

Junior laid on the horn to warn Lonnie and Leon as best he could, then put the car into gear and left rubber halfway to the corner.

The neighbors didn't shoot at him, fortunately. A man who had grown up knocking squirrels out of oak trees wouldn't have had any trouble hitting a car pulling away at all.

Later, he heard from a guy he knew who shared a lawyer with Lonnie and Leon that they hadn't heard the horn, and were still banging away at the gun safe when the neighbors snuck up behind them and started clicking off safeties. He'd lost track of Lonnie and Leon after that. Which was just as well; neither one of them was too swift.

So, no, Junior didn't want any neighbors coming to help out the security guy. The fewer people around, the better. He didn't need an audience, either. He wanted it to be man against man, with no witnesses except the guy who walked away. Which would be Junior.

This one would be more dangerous than the last time. A guy coming out on an alarm would be expecting trouble. And if what the company said in its advertising was true, he'd be a better shooter than most cops. Plus the whole thing would have to go down quick, because the cops would show up eventually.

Which was just fine with Junior. He didn't want it to be too easy after all. If there wasn't a chance that the security guy would drop him, then there wasn't any point. He might just as well sneak up behind somebody and shoot him in the back. There wasn't any challenge in that, no victory, no glory.

He passed a couple of possible prospects before he found the one he wanted. *Kim's Business and Industrial Center*, the sign said. There was an "Armed Response" sign warning that the property, which looked to be some little prefab shop and offices, all single-level and joined, was protected by Hopkins Security. He had passed a city limit sign, so he was in the county. Exactly what he wanted.

There was always the slight chance the local sheriff or state trooper might make it here first. If that happened, Junior would have to decide how to handle it, but he was betting the security guy would show up before the others.

He parked the car under the shadows of a big tree in the first corner of the dimly lit parking lot, got out, and walked around the building. There was an old flatbed truck in front of a little machine shop down on the east end, but

the truck was locked and the engine cover was cool. There
were no other cars. A few windows had lights on, but it
didn't look like anybody was home.

Perfect.

He found a nook between two buildings where a car
pulling through the lot wouldn't see him. After running
over it a couple of times in his mind, he nodded to himself
and went to kick in a door. The window had a Hopkins
sticker, and a blinking sensor showed the place was
alarmed.

He hit the door and it popped open on the first kick. An
audible alarm blared, hooting over and over like one of
those European ambulance sirens, *eee-aww, eee-aww!*

That ought to do it.

Junior strolled back to his hiding place. He loosened his
Rugers in their holsters, pulled them from under the vest,
then reholstered them. He felt the sweat break out, his
heart cranking up faster. *It's killin' time, Junior.*

15

The deposition had barely begun and Alex Michaels was already uncomfortable. Mitchell Townsend Ames was smooth, no doubt about it, and Alex was more than ready to have this all over and done with. He just wanted to get back to work.

Ames was striking in appearance: tall, well-built, and undeniably handsome, with wavy, almost blond hair and cleanly chiseled features. He was dressed in a dark blue pinstripe suit that had to run at least five thousand dollars, and his shoes were clearly handmade.

"Please state your name, address, and occupation for the record," Ames said, his voice low and even.

Michaels did so.

"Thank you, Commander Michaels. I realize you are a busy man, and I'll try to get this done as quickly and painlessly as possible." Ames smiled.

Michaels returned the smile automatically, despite what

Tommy had told him: *Alex, Ames is a shark getting ready to chomp you in half. This man is not your friend, no matter what he says or does, no matter how polite he seems to be. Don't ever forget that, not for one second.*

They were in the Net Force conference room nearest Alex's office. There were five of them present: Mitchell Ames and his assistant, a young woman attorney named Bridgette who was flawlessly beautiful; Tommy Bender; a certified court stenographer named Becky; and Michaels. This wasn't the first time Michaels had been deposed— you didn't get to his rank in the federal LEO hierarchy without dealing with herds of lawyers—but it was the first time he had personally been a defendant in a lawsuit.

A DVD recorder took it all in, and the court reporter keyed in a transcript as backup. Whatever got said here would be preserved for posterity.

"Commander Michaels, is it true that you were in charge of Net Force operations in January of 2013?"

"Yes."

"And that the assault by Net Force military operatives, led by General John Howard, upon the CyberNation-owned and Libyan-registered ship the *Bon Chance* was by your order?"

"Yes." Tommy had cautioned him to answer direct questions with no more than "Yes" or "No" whenever possible, and not to expand on his answers unless absolutely necessary. The less you said, the less you gave away.

"Because you believed it was a pirate vessel? And as such, you had the right to go after it, even in international waters?"

"Yes."

Ames paused, looked at a yellow pad in front of him, and made a note on it with a pen.

So far, so good. Tommy had told him the kinds of questions he was likely to get. Alex wasn't going to lose his cool and give away anything that the man could use against him.

"I understand that prior to the assault, you sent Net Force agent Toni Fiorella Michaels to the vessel as an undercover operative for the purpose of gathering information."

He hadn't expected this kind of question so soon. "Yes, I did."

Ames looked up from his pad, raised an eyebrow. "You sent your *wife* onto what you believed was a ship full of *pirates*?"

The scorn practically dripped from the man's voice. *What kind of man would do that? Send the mother of his child into harm's way?*

Or is it that you didn't really think there was any real danger on the boat, hmm? Not a pirate among them?

Given a choice, Alex would have explained that one. He would have preferred to tell the man that he hadn't expected there would be anything for Toni to worry about that early in the game. He would also have liked to mention that Toni had only been stuck on the ship due to a passing hurricane. But Tommy's instructions had been clear.

"She was, and is, a qualified field operative," he said, keeping his voice bland.

"I see. Well, sir, you are a better man than I. I cannot imagine sending my spouse into a situation like that." He glanced down at his pad. "Oh, but wait. I also see that your wife is an expert in an Indonesian fighting art, called *Pukulan Pentjak Silat Serak*, is that correct?"

"Yes."

Ames nodded. "Well, I suppose your wife's abilities might mitigate the worry some—that she can slaughter a man with her bare hands, not to mention what she can do with a weapon? And that she has, in fact, maimed and killed people using this art? I see here incidents on 8 October 2010, right here at Net Force Headquarters, wherein she beat an alleged assassin until you shot and killed that person; again on 15 June 2011, in Port Townsend, Washington, when she broke a man's neck; and, let's see, again in October 2011 at your home in Washington, D.C.—no, wait, it was you who killed that one, too, wasn't it? With a pair of little daggers, wasn't it? Tell me, Commander, do you believe that the family that *slays* together *stays* together?"

A year ago that might have gotten to him. Two years ago he certainly would have risen to the challenge. And as little as five years ago he may have risen to his feet and punched this insinuating little lawyer right in the mouth.

But *silat*, like any true martial art, was about more than fighting. It was about discipline and control, and while Alex still had a long way to go before he considered himself proficient, he had come far enough to be able to deflect Ames's little gibes.

Tommy answered for him. "Is there a question in there, counselor, or are you just trying to bait Commander Michaels?"

Ames smiled. "No, I'm just trying to establish what kind of people work for Net Force, counselor."

"People whose actions have all been justifiable under the law," Tommy said. "Let's move on, shall we? Like you said, my client is a busy man—wasting his time with character assassination is hardly productive."

Ames's smile grew wider. "I wouldn't think of impugning your client's character, Mr. Bender. I'm only trying to uncover the truth, in the name of justice. That your client has a propensity for violence goes to the heart of our action, doesn't it? Runs in the family, too."

Alex could see all too clearly where this was heading. This was going to get ugly, just as Tommy had said. He wouldn't mind so much getting dragged through the mud by this guy—he wouldn't like it, of course, but Alex was a big boy whose actions could stand a little scrutiny. The part that would be most likely to get to him was hearing his wife impugned. *That* was going to be hard to take.

"Now, then, Commander, let's return to the reasons you came to believe that my clients' duly registered recreational ship, minding its own business in international waters, was infested with cutthroat pirates that were somehow a threat to the United States. . . ."

Michaels stifled a sigh and settled back into his chair. This was going to be a very long morning.

Ames smiled to himself as he left the Net Force building at the FBI compound. Alex Michaels was made of a little sterner stuff than most bureaucrats he'd gone up against. He wasn't going to lose his cool in front of a jury unless Ames could rattle him more than he had at the deposition. Attacking the wife was a possibility—Ames had thought Alex had shown some vulnerability in that area—but you had to be careful with those. Sometimes even if they worked, a crack about somebody's spouse could alienate a jury enough to hurt you. Ames didn't want to risk that. He always presented himself as the soul of good-heartedness, and even when he used personal attacks he made them seem reluctant and only tendered for the cause of truth, justice, and the American way. As if he was genuinely sorry that the defendant was a wife-beating creep, but that the jury had to decide if that mattered.

Next to him, Bridgette said, "What do you think?"

She was bright—top of her class at Lewis and Clark two years ago, as smart as any of the other dozen assistants and associates at his firm. Lovely, too. But she still believed that law and justice were synonymous, which of course they were not.

He couldn't begin to tell her the real reasons he had instigated this deposition. He had wanted to see his opposition face-to-face. He wanted to get Michaels's home address from his own lips, because it might come down to nasty and personal, and he wanted that information without leaving a more obvious trail. Mostly, though, he wanted them to see him and be afraid.

Little things, taken separately, but they were all part of a great lawyer's affect. In this business, presentation was every bit as important as the law itself. It didn't matter how many statutes you could cite if the jury didn't like you.

Bridgette wasn't ready for any of that, however. "It went as well as could be expected," he said. "You'll be second chair on this one, so I want you to know everything there is to know about maritime law and U.N. treaties and pirates by the time we are ready to go to trial. Not to mention Commander Alex Michaels and his wife, Toni."

"Understood."

"Good." In truth, though, the results of this action did not really matter. Of course, if it ever actually got to trial, he wanted to win it. Mitchell Townsend Ames didn't lose, period, but the real point here was to bury Net Force in problems so that he could end-run them legally. If congress and the senate passed an acceptable bill and the President signed it into law, then all this was moot. Net Force would be bound by the results. As much as they might hate it, once it became law they could jump up and down and rant until they turned blue and it wouldn't make any difference at all.

Ames did not care about the men killed on the *Bon Chance*. He didn't care about their surviving relatives. The dead men had been thugs, shooters who had gotten shot instead. They were criminals, and deserved none of his worry. This entire suit was a smoke screen, and if it served its purpose, that was all that counted.

Once he had a goal, Ames always figured out whatever means was necessary to achieve it. If he could do it with a threat of a legal action, great. If it took a trial, fine. If it took sending a knuckle-dragger like Junior to bribe, blackmail, or assault anybody who stood in the way? That was acceptable, too. Whatever was necessary. Second place was for losers. Winning was all.

The chauffeured limo pulled up, and the driver hopped out and opened the door for them. Bridgette climbed in first, Ames followed. As soon as he was seated, he reached into the door's map compartment and pulled his pistol rig out, the SIG P-210, and slipped the crossdraw holster back onto his custom-made horsehide belt, locking the one-way snaps into place on his left side. Crossdraw was best for in a car. It wasn't uncomfortable, and was easier to get to in a hurry. This one had been designed for drivers to thwart carjackers. Hard as they were to get, he had a permit to carry a handgun in D.C., Virginia, Maryland, and New York, and in most of the easier shall-issue states as well. That was just one more advantage of big money and a legitimately recognized need. He'd been threatened with death in public by angry men more than a few times. But such permissions did not extend to federal courts or law-enforcement buildings, passenger aircraft, or post offices, among other places.

All in all, this had been a productive visit. He had a better sense of Commander Alex Michaels. He knew where to find the man and his family. If push came to shove, he could always have Junior pay them a late-night visit. A man like Michaels wouldn't roll over for bribery, blackmail, or even physical intimidation, Ames knew that, but he had a family. And even if his wife was some kind of martial arts death on two legs, they had a little boy who wouldn't be so adept.

And a man would do just about anything to protect his children.

Chalus, Iraq

Howard's group was badly outnumbered. On top of that, his four-man scout team was only lightly armed. They had come to gather intel, not to fight. The Iraqi foot patrol, on the other hand, was more heavily armed, and they outnumbered Howard's unit by at least four to one. There had to be sixteen, maybe eighteen of the enemy soldiers.

Howard and his team were already off the road. He waved his team down. In the dark, they'd be hard to spot.

The liquid Arabic flow of the Iraqis talking among themselves drifted through the rocks and scrub growth. The men were joking, laughing, not expecting any trouble, on a routine patrol that had probably never stumbled across anything more dangerous than a lizard.

They were in the El Burz Mountains. The peak elevation along the road from Chalus to Karaj was a thousand meters above sea level, maybe a little higher to the west. They weren't that far inland yet, only about thirty kilometers from the Caspian on the north coast of Iraq, but that was far enough so that it would take an extraction copter a few minutes to get here. One more good reason to lay low and let the patrol pass.

Contrary to what a lot of people thought, especially after the Gulf War, not all of Iraq's soldiers were half-witted camel jockeys who ran around yelling "Allah ackbar!" and couldn't shoot straight. Some of the elite units were battle-hardened vets who could hike all night and then fight all day, men with training as good as that given by any army in the world. In a stand-up fight against B1 bombers dropping daisy-cutters and Navy ships firing rockets from a hundred miles away, the Iraqis would get creamed. You couldn't use World War I tactics in the twenty-first century and expect to win. But on a narrow road in the mountains at night—in *their* mountains—against a recon force not wearing SIPEsuits or heavy armor, a quarter their strength? Those AK-47s still worked just fine.

Howard and his men had come to find out if there was a biological weapons plant buried here in the hills, possibly buried deep in a cave where it couldn't be spotted from spysats looking for it. Cutting loose on a larger and better-armed force was *not* the way to do that.

The fact that the patrol was here at all probably meant the intel about the bio-weapons plant had some basis. So far, the Big Birds had not been able to pinpoint the location, but the amount of traffic they had tracked in and out of one of the canyons not far from here indicated that there was something going on.

Whatever it was they were doing in that canyon, Howard needed to find out. Once the patrol was past, they'd get to it.

One of the Iraqi soldiers wandered off the road in their direction.

None of the Net Force squad moved. They were statues, hardly even breathing.

The man drew nearer. He came to an outcrop of rock no more than three meters in front of Howard, and rounded it, out of sight of the road, and unzipped his pants.

His back was to Howard, but the noise of his urination was loud in the dark.

Great. Guy had to take a leak, and he picked here to do it.

Howard drew his knife. It was a Loveless-style hunter with a short, stubby, drop-point blade no longer than his middle finger. It was the kind of knife used to skin and gut game, but it would cut a throat just fine. The steel had been blackened with a baked-on powder coating, a flat, matte black that reflected no light.

Howard gathered himself to move. All the man emptying his bladder had to do was to turn slightly and he would see an American trooper prone in the night behind him. If that happened, Howard and his group were in big trouble.

But if Howard moved first, he could get to the man before he realized what was happening. A stab to the brainstem at the base of the skull would do it. He didn't like that, having to kill some poor soldier whose only crime was answering the call of nature, but it was too risky. *Better one of them than four of us.*

Three regular steps, two long ones, less than a second to get to the man, grab his mouth with one hand, drive the blade in with the other.

Howard came up from his prone position carefully, onto his hands and knees, then to a squat. He leaned forward to push off—

The Iraqi, warned by something, looked over his shoulder as Howard leaped. The man screamed, already reaching for his rifle.

Uh-oh. They were in for it now—

"General Howard?" the computer said, interrupting the VR scenario. "You have a Priority One call."

Net Force HQ
Quantico, Virginia

Howard dropped out of VR and pulled the headset off. "Who is calling?" he asked.

"Commander Michaels," the computer said.

"I'll take it. Put it through."

Though it probably wasn't anything drastic, Howard had put Michaels on his Priority One list a long time ago. He wasn't going to snub his boss while he played war games in VR.

"Commander."

"Hello, General. We have a small problem here. Tommy Bender is in my office, and he wants to talk to you about the good ship *Bon Chance*."

"The lawsuit," Howard said.

"Exactly."

"I've already been deposed, sir," Howard said. "A young woman came by on Friday."

"I know. I met her, along with the big gun lawyer a little while ago, for my own deposition. Apparently there is some additional information about one of the dead security men our lawyer thinks we need to know about."

"I see."

"That is, of course, if you aren't too busy," Alex said. "I can put him off if need be."

"No, sir, Commander. I've got the time. It's been pretty slow around here. I'll be over in about ten minutes."

"Thanks, John."

"No problem."

Howard showed up three minutes early and exchanged greetings with Alex and Tommy.

"All right," Michaels said, "what's this all about, Tommy?"

The lawyer smiled. "You're going to love this," he said. "Richard A. Dunlop, as near as we can tell, was the man John shot and killed during the raid."

"The man who shot me first," Howard said. He touched his side, low. "Right in a gap where my borrowed vest didn't cover."

"Yes, well, we'll certainly point that out. Did you know Mr. Dunlop before you shot him, General?"

"No, sir. The moment he shot me was the first time we'd ever met."

"Ah."

"Why?" Michaels said. "What's this all about, Tommy?"

"Well, it seems that Mr. Dunlop was a member of the WAB."

"Which is . . . ?"

"The White Aryan Brotherhood," Howard answered, beating Tommy to it.

"So?" Alex asked. "I've heard of them. They're a prison racist group. How does this affect anything?"

"Well," Tommy said, "if General Howard—who, I must point out, is a black man—knew that Mr. Dunlop was a racist, that might have given him motivation to shoot Mr. Dunlop beyond simple self-defense."

Michaels shook his head. "You know, Tommy, that might be the stupidest thing I have ever heard."

Tommy shrugged. "Have you ever been to Las Vegas, General?"

"Yes, I have."

"And were you in Las Vegas on April 3, 2011?"

Howard thought about it for a moment. "Yes, I believe I was. As I recall, that was just before we mounted an operation in the desert nearby. Our unit was on hold, waiting for a computer glitch in the surveillance sats to be resolved. We were holed up in Vegas while we waited for the go order."

Tommy nodded. "And did you have an altercation with Mr. Dunlop while you were in Las Vegas, General?"

"Of course not. Like I told you, I never met the man."

"But the plaintiff's lawyer can produce records showing that Mr. Dunlop was, in fact, in Las Vegas on that same day."

Howard frowned. "So what? So were a million other people."

Tommy leaned back in his chair and smiled. "But you didn't shoot a million other people, John. You shot Dunlop. Here's what Ames will do: He'll show that the two of you were in Vegas at the same time. He'll postulate a hypothetical meeting, in which you and Dunlop met, and got into an altercation over the man's racist behavior. He bumped into you on the sidewalk, called you a name, and you nearly came to blows over it. Then he'll link it to the shooting on the ship, implying that you killed Dunlop because of your earlier meeting."

Howard shook his head. "That's unbelievable," he said. "None of that happened."

"That doesn't matter, John. He doesn't have to prove it. He just has to make a jury believe that it might have happened that way."

"What do you mean?"

"Look, you and I both know that he will be able to find a lowlife Las Vegas wino who, for the price of a bottle of cheap bourbon, will swear he saw you with Dunlop. The jury might very well recognize this man as a liar. They might very well not believe a word that he says. But they won't be able to forget what he says, either. The judge can direct them to disregard it, of course, but that's like not thinking about the elephant in the living room."

"I still don't get it," Howard said.

Tommy rubbed his eyes. "If you blow enough smoke and wave enough mirrors, you can dazzle an audience," he said. "Ames is a master at this kind of illusion. He is a magician. He can make people think they saw something they couldn't possibly have seen. Trust me, Ames will manufacture all the mud that he can, and then drag everybody involved right through the middle of it. Even if none of it is legit, some of it can stick. Remember, this is a civil case, not a criminal one. Reasonable doubt doesn't apply in the same way. All he really needs to do is to get the jury to doubt, even just a little bit."

Howard frowned again.

Tommy sighed. "You've shot a few other people in the line of duty, haven't you, John?"

"Yes. But every one of them was justified."

Tommy shook his head. "Not necessarily. And certainly not in the eyes, ears, and minds of a civil jury. Any Net Force operation in which any person was severely hurt or killed will be fair game for Ames. He will haul every one

of them out and do a body count. He will show morgue
pictures, offer testimonials of the families, whatever he can
get past the judge.

"Ames is going to paint the picture that every Net Force
op who ever stepped into the field was a bloodthirsty killer
who couldn't wait to go out and shoot, stab, or stomp
somebody. More than that, he is going to show that these
ops were not only directed by, but *led* by a commander
and general who love to go out and get their own hands
bloody. He'll have us looking like the Mongol hordes,
murdering and plundering for sport."

"My God," Howard said. "Can he really do that?"

"If he can convince a judge that such things go to es-
tablishing a pattern of behavior, or that a particular incident can be linked directly to his case, yes, indeed. As I've
said, civil law is not the same as criminal, and the standards are not as high. And for Ames, no stoop is too low.
When he's on a roll, he has to jump up with his arm out-
stretched to reach a snake's belly."

"My God," Howard said again.

"If you have an in with Him, I'd pray for intervention,"
Tommy said. "Ames stepping into an open manhole or
suffering a fatal heart attack would be good. Anything less
won't slow him down. He'll spin fantasy so thick it'll seem
like you've been dropped between Sleeping Beauty's castle and Mr. Toad's Wild Ride. . . ."

Michaels shook his head, too. How could somebody do
stuff like this and get away with it?

"There's another thing you need to know," Tommy
added after a moment.

"What is it?" Michaels asked.

"You have to be very careful in your ongoing investigation of CyberNation. Every 'i' needs to be dotted, every
't' crossed."

"We do that in all our investigations," Michaels said.

Tommy nodded. "I know, but understand this: If you

bend the smallest rule, it will cost you. Ames obviously knows about the investigation, and you can be sure that he will wave it back and forth like a flag in a Fourth of July parade. He'll claim Net Force is harassing his clients because of the suit, that there is no other reason to have such a procedure going since they are all law-abiding and upstanding corporate folk just trying to make an honest living."

"But our investigation predates this suit."

"Doesn't matter," Tommy said. "Remember, Ames deals in perception, not reality. And as far as your normal investigations, can you honestly say that there have never been any instances where you or one of your people didn't step outside the lines, even a little bit, in order to crack a case or put away a bad guy? Well, Ames will have copies of all your files—everything that isn't classified, anyway—at his fingertips, and he'll be going through them looking for any sign, any hint, of anything he can wave in front of the jury."

He turned to Howard. "For example, General, every time you got tired of being a desk jockey and went into the field yourself, Ames will use that to show that you like to be personally involved. That you like waving guns around and shooting people."

"But that's my job," Howard said.

Tommy shook his head. "Generals don't lead the charge into battle anymore. They sit back and direct from afar." He turned to Alex. "And it's even worse for you," he said. "You're not even military. By being hands-on, you demonstrate a certain zeal, which can easily be fanned up to look like full-blown fanaticism."

Michaels leaned forward. "Are you suggesting we drop this whole CyberNation investigation? And has it occurred to you that this whole lawsuit might be nothing more than an attempt to get us to do that? Stop our inquiry? Or force us to back off enough so CyberNation can do whatever illegal activity it wants without having to look over its shoulder?"

"Of course it occurred to me, and that's not what I'm suggesting. I wouldn't object if you put it on hold until this was over, but you don't even have to do that. What you need to do is exactly what I said: Proceed very carefully and pay extra attention to all the little details here."

Michaels looked at Howard. Neither of them had anything to say.

"I told you this was going to be a big can of worms," Tommy said. "And we don't even have it halfway open yet."

Michaels sighed and nodded. "I'll pass the word along to be careful."

"Good. Well, I'm off. Have a nice day."

After Tommy left, Michaels looked at Howard. "I think we need to have a staff meeting."

"Yes, sir," Howard said. "I believe that would be a very good idea."

16

There were four of them in the conference room: General Howard, Jay, Toni, and Michaels himself.

Alex said, "So that's the situation regarding the legal stuff. Obviously we are not going to drop our investigation of CyberNation, or even put it on hold, especially in light of what Jay has turned up. We are, however, going to take Tommy Bender's advice and make sure we are squeaky clean on this one." He looked at Jay as he said that.

There was a moment of silence. Toni broke it by asking, "How sure are we about the clerk, Jay?"

"I'm positive about the money transfer. I haven't been able to find any reason why a Supreme Court justice's clerk should be getting any money from CyberNation. I've also gone through this guy's files looking for anything to indicate that he might be a special case—like if he'd done some legitimate work for CyberNation and was still receiving payments from them—and I've found absolutely nothing. I am convinced this is a bribe."

Howard said, "We had better be absolutely certain before we go public on this one. The judge will chop us all into tiny pieces if we are wrong. They don't like even the smallest hint of improper behavior over there."

"Amen," Toni said.

Michaels looked at Jay. "Get us something bulletproof, Jay."

"I will."

"Anything else that we should know about coming down the pike?"

Jay shrugged. "Just about these worms and viruses that have been hitting the web recently. I am convinced that the same guy is doing them, and they are getting progressively worse—which means I think there is more to come. There is not much you guys can do to help with that, it's pure net stuff, but I thought you should know."

Michaels nodded. "Look, I know this lawsuit is a real pain, and that we all have better things to do. I also know that there is a very good chance this might all be a big smoke screen on CyberNation's part to keep us from focusing on our investigation. Still, we have to pay attention to it. We're under the microscope on this one, even more so than normal. Let's not do anything that could come back to haunt us."

He got a group murmur of assent.

Alex looked around the room at his team, the people he trusted most in the world. This was where he was supposed to say something inspiring, but he realized that he just didn't have the words.

Besides, he realized something else as well: There was a reason why these were the people he trusted most in the world. Every one of them was a consummate professional, the best at what they did. They didn't need inspiration from him. They just needed his confidence and support.

"All right, guys," he said. "Let's go get 'em."

Jay was mad. Saji had called him as the meeting was breaking up, and now he felt like going out and killing someone.

He went into his office and sat behind his computer, still fuming.

It all started with the pictures. Saji had loaded their honeymoon pictures on her computer in the living room. Which was fine, of course; she wanted to share them with the family. He could understand that. But she had disabled their virus protection during the install.

That wasn't what was bothering Jay, though. He understood how it had happened, and even understood why it had happened. Saji had spent some time editing the photos as she loaded them, and you usually wanted to turn off any virus checker while working on graphic-intensive programs. Even with power machines like he had at home, there was just too great a chance of conflicts if you didn't.

But Saji hadn't turned it back on.

Jay's systems were protected behind a double firewall— including one that he had coded himself—but that only protected his machines from hackers trying to break into them from the net. Firewalls didn't work against viruses or other programs loaded—accidentally or otherwise— through e-mail, which was why he also ran the top-of-the-line virus checker, which constantly automatically updated both its code and its data files.

None of which meant a thing *if somebody turned it off!*

The software was even programmed to turn itself back on when the system was rebooted, but Saji hadn't done that. She finished her uploading and editing just fine, with no signs of system instability, so she didn't think to restart the machine.

The worst of it was that Jay had programmed his virus checker to restart itself anytime it had been turned off for more than half an hour. He had done that because he knew how easy it was to forget such things. Saji had spent quite a bit of time editing, however—far more than half an hour—so she had disabled its restart as well, which meant that her computer—and, consequently, his entire home network—was vulnerable to a virus.

And they got hit.

Jay hadn't traced it yet so he didn't know if it came from someone in Saji's family or one of her friends or one of the listservs she belonged to. For that matter, it might have been a random e-mail generated by an infected system. It didn't really matter where it came from. It only mattered where it started from.

The virus that hit them was the newest one, the crasher, the one that reformatted hard drives. It got their pictures, and her e-mail address book—after popping copies of itself to everyone in it, including Toni, Alex, and several of their other Net Force friends. And it got his machine, too, jumping the LAN connection and wiping out his hard drive as well.

Yeah they had back-ups of everything, even of the pictures, but that wasn't the point. The point was that they got hit. The point was that Jay's own machine, as well as his wife's, had sent out copies of a virus to everyone in their address books. Jay Gridley himself, head techie and virus guru for Net Force, laid low by a simple virus.

He was not happy.

If Saji hadn't shut off the virus checker, nothing would have happened, but she had, and it had, and she was very sorry.

Dumb. He didn't say that, having learned at least a couple of things since he'd gotten to know her, but he'd thought it. Even a schoolkid knew better than to touch the net without virus protection. Even kindergarten kids knew that. . . .

But it wasn't Saji he was mad at. She didn't live in a world where every electronic move was automatically covered. She didn't think about such things like he did.

It was the *hacker* Jay wanted to stomp, the author of the

virus, the jerk who had taken advantage of Saji's good nature. *He* was the one to blame.

Jay was going to nail this hacker. This guy was going to learn that you did *not* mess around with Jay Gridley, and you sure didn't make him look bad by using his wife.

He stared at his computer a moment longer, still fuming, then reached for the keyboard and set his system to accept no intrusions less than a Priority One. It was time to get to work. Under normal circumstances he loved his job and couldn't wait to begin the hunt. This time, though, it would be even sweeter. This time it was personal.

Jay had written and released his own share of viruses back in his college days—just the usual "Gotcha" type programs to show that he could. He'd never coded anything really *damaging*, of course. He'd also hunted a good many of them as Net Force's chief safari leader, so by now the opening steps were pretty routine for him. The key was to track the time trail, see when computers got infected to centralize a point of origin. Once you had that, you'd start tracing from there, working your way back toward the source.

Naturally, these days people could pipe things all over the globe, but they had to start *somewhere*.

Unfortunately, by the time he'd realized the first two bugs were related, a lot of information had gone by the wayside. The first two viruses were pretty mild; they hadn't done any real damage, so they hadn't been followed very closely. This would make it harder for him to gather data on them.

It would take a lot of testing, which would take a lot of time.

If he did it the normal way.

Jay put on his VR gear and called up a scenario he hadn't played with since his college days.

The Wizard's Workshop

Jay stood in a large, circular room, dimly illuminated by a scattering of candlelight. All around him were various arcane devices, jars of rare herbs, odd-looking mechanical contraptions, and musty old books, bound in various animal skins, from lizard to ostrich to what looked like human. . . .

A crystal ball and a small but stout wooden cage sat on a clear area of the bench. Next to that was a long, thin wand, intricately carved with golden runes that glimmered slightly from within.

A faint musty smell hung over the room, and the air tasted stale. It felt as though it hadn't been aired out for hundreds of years. Jay was impressed. He hadn't been in the workshop for years, and the details were excellent.

I am *good.*

Nothing he didn't already know, of course, but it was nice to be reminded, particularly by his own work.

He picked up the wand. It felt slightly warm, exactly as he remembered. It vibrated in his hand, a tool of creation waiting to be unleashed.

There was a reason Jay hadn't played with the workshop for a number of years. This was where he had made his own viruses. Those days were gone, of course. He'd chosen the high road, gone with the good guys, and ever since making that decision he'd refrained from playing with such things—except when he needed them to figure out better ways of defeating the bad guys.

Sometimes it did take a thief to catch one.

This wasn't precisely one of those times, but he was going to take the latitude he had as Net Force's chief hacker and use it. The hacker who had destroyed his wife's hard drive, and through her had gotten Jay's own system at home, was going to be very sorry.

This was not an easy decision for him. He remembered all too well Alex's warning about playing this one by the book, but he wasn't too worried. For one thing, this had nothing to do with CyberNation. For another, what he was about to do wasn't really wrong. Oh, it violated the spirit of the "non-self-perpetuating-code" laws that were on the books—he had served as a consultant on some of those laws—but the code he was about to write would be completely harmless . . . except to a certain hacker out there.

Mostly, though, it came down to the fact that this was the only way Jay could see to stop this guy quickly, and at the moment that was all that mattered.

He took a deep breath and began.

He waved the wand in the air, forming a star-shaped pattern with it, and a fiery glowing pentagram appeared on the solid floor of the small wooden cage. He tap-tap-tapped the wand in the air, and alternate points of dark and light appeared around the vertices of the star.

He paused for a moment, trying to remember the incantation. He'd been seriously into fantasy gaming for a few years in college, had gotten into a wizard's role, and done all kinds of research into ritual magic.

Oh, yeah—he remembered.

Jay spoke, and as he did so, the sounds of his words burst into the room as colored balls of fire, illuminating the chamber in flickers of rich red and gold. Details in the room stood out, more supplies and old tomes became visible, all casting hard shadows as the globes moved toward the cage.

Within the cage the glowing balls of light that represented his words of power combined over the pentagram. He heard a popping sound as a formless *something* appeared within the wards he'd set up. It slowly took on shape and color, coalescing into a minor demon.

"WHO DARES CALL ME TO SERVICE?" The little thing's voice was *deep*.

Jay smiled a bit at his younger self. Pretty melodramatic stuff.

"It is I, Jay Gridley." When he said his name, the little demon cringed as he'd programmed anything he summoned to do. Even though he knew it was infantile, he couldn't help but think it was kind of cool.

Well, some things hadn't changed.

He spoke to the demon, laying out what it was to do. As he gave it instructions, it gradually assumed a somewhat different shape to match its goals.

It ceased glowing and became smaller, more transparent, like the viruses he'd analyzed. It resembled a tiny devil, with horns and a tail, but more squat, dwarflike. Its eyes grew huge, so it could see better, its nose longer to sniff out traces of the target viruses, and it grew wings, tiny batlike things that spun quickly, like a hummingbird's.

Jay reached into the pocket of the wizard's robe and removed the bug-forms of the three target viruses. He tossed them through a gap in the top of the cage. The creature grabbed them, sniffing and probing each one before ripping it open to devour the buglike guts of each.

"I AM READY, MASTER," it said.

"About time," Jay said. *"Go."* He waved the wand. The cage dissolved in a shimmer of gold sparkles, the wards fell dark, and the creature flew up and out through a tall window by the bookcase.

He let out a breath he'd been holding. Well. He'd done it now. All the old adages came to him—*it takes a thief to catch a thief, absolute power corrupts absolutely, it's a slippery slope.*

Although he had certain powers and rights as Net Force's chief VR man, releasing a virus on the public wasn't one of them. On the other hand, if he called it a tracker program, he might be able to get away with it.

Not that he was going to call it anything unless someone came asking. Since he was the chief cop on the block when it came to viruses, it was unlikely anyone would.

Besides, he'd made it good. Although he hadn't used it in years, he'd kept the workshop program updated on the latest techniques for virus construction. That was part of the overhead of keeping on top of things: updating software you might never use.

It was hard work, being king of the mountain.

The virus wasn't going to damage anything, or even make itself noticeable. It would piggyback on incoming and outgoing traffic only, and only report to him information about when the three viruses had hit—and where. It would erase all tracks it had ever been there, and no one would be the wiser.

He hoped.

He waved the wand again and the crystal ball on the table grew to the size of a beach ball. He uttered a word, and a tiny simulacrum of the United States appeared within it. As he watched, tiny dots of red, blue, and yellow began to appear on the map, each one corresponding to a computer which had been infested with one of the three viruses.

The dots expanded at a geometric rate, getting faster and faster as his imp-virus multiplied and expanded in its own wave of infestation.

Pretty soon now he'd have an idea of what to check next. The hacker who'd messed with him had better enjoy his last few free computing hours.

Mess with the best, go to jail like the rest.

17

The security guard turned out to be much better than the cop had been.

The guy came in dark. He had turned his car lights off far enough away that Junior never even caught them. He didn't hear the motor, either, which meant that the guard must have coasted the last couple hundred yards in neutral, maybe even with the engine turned off. The first Junior saw of him, the guard was on foot and working his way toward the office with the kicked-in door.

He wore a dark gray and black uniform and some kind of dark-colored baseball cap. He was using cover and shadows and had his piece already drawn. He held the weapon in a crosshands grip, gun in the right, with a flashlight in the left hand above, pointing along the sight line but not turned on.

From the position of his hands, Junior could tell that the flashlight must have a button in the butt. It was probably

one of those fat, stubby, tactical cop lights, most likely a
Sure-Fire M6. If so, it was going to flare like a movie
spotlight when the guard turned it on. Those things put out
five hundred lumens, and cost two-fifty, three hundred
bucks.

Junior had gotten one like it in a trade with a drug dealer
once. He lost it somewhere later, but it was a fine piece
of machinery. Anyone carrying one of those flashlights
that he probably paid for himself was serious about his
work, that was for sure.

Whether he was the real thing or a wannabe, that was
something else. That was what they were going to find
out.

This guy wanted to catch somebody, no question. If all
he'd been looking to do was scare a burglar off, he'd have
come in code three, those silly rent-a-cop orange rack
lights flashing, siren howling, giving plenty of warning he
was on the way.

But no, not this guy. He sneaked in quiet, gun in hand,
GuardMan to the rescue! He was *hoping* somebody would
still be there, hoping the door-breaker would be armed,
hoping he'd resist. Then he'd blind him with that light
cannon, and if the guy didn't get his hands up fast enough,
he was going to drop him.

Junior could tell that by watching the guy. He'd bet the
farm on it.

It put a different spin on things. GuardMan there already
had his gun out, so it wasn't going to be a fast-draw con-
test. Junior didn't get a great look at the hardware, but he
saw enough of it silhouetted to see it was a semiauto, and
his impression was that it was a SIG, could have been a
9mm, a .40, even a .45, they all looked pretty much the
same at a distance, and all of which were fine combat
weapons not likely to jam when the guy started cooking.
Probably a .45, if he had to guess. The serious shooters
still liked those best.

How good was he? No way to tell for sure, but he moved well, he kept his hands low and ready, to shine-and-shoot, and you had to figure the guy had some ability, given the company's ads and all.

So Junior's idea of stepping out of the shadows and yelling at the guy straight out went away real quick. If he did that, and if the guy was any good, the guard would spin and, flame on, light Junior up like a Christmas tree, and as soon as he saw him go for his heat, GuardMan would cook faster than a hot dog in a microwave, *ka-blam!*

No, Junior decided, he couldn't do it that way.

But he also couldn't mess around out here. He was pretty sure that the company dispatcher had called the cops at the same time that he sent the guard. If so, the official heat would be along, and probably sooner than later.

Junior would bet that Dover, Delaware, was not exactly a hotbed of serious felonies on a weeknight. A bored cop, county mountie, or smokey would be looking for something interesting to *passe le temp*. So letting the guard root around in the office for a few minutes and waiting for him to come out all relaxed thinking nobody was around was also not such a good idea. He wasn't ready to rock with a hotshot guard *and* a state policeman, with maybe even a local shurf or two coming along just for grins at the same time.

As GuardMan worked his way toward the door, getting ready to make his move, Junior decided how he was going to play it. He squatted and picked up a handful of gravel from around the base of the building next to him, using his left hand. With his other hand he pulled his right-side Ruger.

Edging out of the dark, he stayed low and duckwalked toward the guard. He angled to his left a little, so the guard would stay backlit by the office lights. He was still thirty feet or so away when the guard reached the door and, after checking it out, got ready to shove it open.

Junior softly tossed the gravel at the wall to the man's left, underhanded, and came up from his squat and into his isosceles stance.

The little rocks, all pea-sized or smaller, pattered against the metal siding like a sudden gust of hard rain, making a lot of noise in the quiet night.

GuardMan was wired tight. He twisted fast, lit the wall up with the flash—and it *was* bright, even not pointing at Junior, who had slitted his eyes tight to protect his night vision. Had to be bad on the guard's eyes. The guy held the light and his weapon right at chest-level, textbook perfect.

The guy started to sweep the light his way—

Junior had already brought his left hand over to cup his right; now he shoved the revolver out like he was punching somebody in the throat, and yelled, "How's your sister?!"

The guard was good. He never paused to think about that, but came on around, that big ole floodlight beam of his leading, but Junior started pulling the trigger as soon as he yelled, indexing his hold just above the flashlight and walking his aim up. Three double-taps, *pow-pow!* to the high chest, *pow-pow!* to the neck, *pow-pow!* to where he figured the guy's head had to be—

—the guard's pistol roared, adding its yellow-orange blast to the bright light. A .45, like Junior figured.

Between the flashlight and the muzzle blast, Junior's night vision was pretty well shot, but he wasn't hit—he wasn't hit! A moment later the light fell, and then the guy did, too. Junior heard him thump hard on the concrete, and the guard's shot, wherever it went, hadn't hit him!

Junior came up from his crouch, holstered the empty gun with his right hand as he drew the full one with his left, fast and smooth like he had practiced a thousand times. He hurried forward, ready to cook again if the guy moved, but when he got there, he could see in the reflected gleam of the still-lit tactical light on the ground that the guy was done. Had a vest on, GuardMan did, and if it was as good as the rest of his gear, it stopped the first two rounds, but the higher ones got him. Junior saw three entry holes, one in the neck just under the chin, one in the right cheekbone, the last one into the hairline on the same side. An inch or two higher and that last one would have missed. One of his six *had* missed, but so what? In the dark like that, five were enough, especially with three of them hitting paydirt. He'd take it.

Junior's breath came and went like an express train flying down a steep grade. He forced himself to slow it some, but his heart kept pounding hard. It was true what he had heard. There was nothing in the world that felt as good as being shot at and not hit, nothing like it!

Especially when you took out the guy shooting at you.

He saluted the dead man. "*Bon soir, ma frien. See you in Hell.*"

Junior turned and hurried to his car.

Washington, D.C.

Mitchell Ames decided that, as long as he was in town, he might as well make a different set of rounds. He always had business he could do here in the nation's capital. You didn't get big things done without making connections here. He had a few lawyers, a couple of doctors, and several senators and congressmen he wanted to touch base with, and he spent the rest of the day and evening doing just that.

He had sent his assistant back to New York, so he was at loose ends for dinner. On a whim, he called Cory Skye's number. She answered on the second ring.

"Mitchell. How are you?"

"Fine," he said. "Actually, I'm in D.C. on business."

"Really? Are you free for dinner?"

"As it happens, yes."

"Let me take you to Mel's. It's a new Northwest Cuisine place, fresh crab, planked salmon, that kind of thing. I think you'd really like it."

"Great. What time?"

"Ten okay? It doesn't start to clear out before then. You have a car?"

"Yes."

"Good. I've got some business over drinks. Why don't I just meet you there?"

"Sounds fine. Ten it is."

After she discommed, he grinned at the phone and slipped it back into his jacket pocket. She was bringing her own transportation, so she was still keeping her options open. He liked that. No reason to hurry this. He had gotten a preliminary report from his investigators on her, and so far he liked what he'd heard.

Corinna Louise Skye, parents Holland George Skye and Gwendolyn Marie Sherman Skye, who lived full-time in Aspen, Colorado. Her father was a retired corporation president, her mother a college professor, also retired. No siblings for Cory. She'd gone to school at Columbia and graduated first in her class with a major in political science. She had gotten into lobbying after working on Marty Spencer's winning senatorial campaign two terms back and had been immediately successful at it. She was beautiful, personable, bright, educated, and had, as far as he could tell, gotten to the top on her own—she'd never slept with a current client, nor with anybody she'd been lobbying. A member of Mensa, decent chess player, scratch golfer, and a qualified aerobics instructor. She had done a little sky-diving, some hang-gliding, and she liked to ski.

Her love life was somewhat sparse, and it appeared she tended to go for active men. She'd had brief affairs with a fireman while she was in college; an Olympic-class cross-country skier in Aspen; and, most recently, just a year or so back, a police detective-lieutenant in D.C. Nothing since that he'd been able to find. Jocks and authority figures.

Ames had noticed that kind of thing before. Sometimes, among intellectual women, there was a fondness for men with physical attributes, with a different kind of power, as if that somehow balanced things. Well, he wasn't in bad shape, he certainly could run with her when it came to brainpower, and she seemed to enjoy his company.

He wanted her, and he was used to getting what he wanted. Determination counted for a lot. In fact, most of the time, determination to achieve a goal was more important than anything else. Given two people chasing the same rabbit, the man who wanted it the most had the edge.

The next report he was to get on dear Cory should include specifics on what kind of entertainment she liked— what DVDs she rented, movies she downloaded, plays, operas, concerts she went to, and the like. It would also tell him where she shopped, what brands she liked, what her favorite toothpaste was. All the little things would become his. The devil was in the details, and nobody knew that better than Ames.

Cory Skye was going to find herself on the receiving end of a lobbying effort unlike any she had ever known. When somebody knew everything that could be found out about you, that man could be a formidable opponent, especially when that man was an expert in waging winning campaigns for the hearts and minds of supposedly unbiased jurors.

Ames knew how people worked, mentally, socially, psychologically, and physically. He went after what he wanted, and he didn't fail to get it.

He wasn't planning to start now.

18

Alex Michaels was in the garage, beginning another light workout. It was almost eight o'clock. Toni was bathing the baby, and Guru was cooking supper. Alex had to admit that the old lady's Indonesian recipes had been pretty good, so far, at least.

Michaels was still stretching when Guru stuck her head out and said, "Telephone for you." She tossed the portable unit to him. He caught it and thumbed it on.

"Alex Michaels."

"Alex. Cory Skye."

Calling him at home? "What can I do for you?"

"I came across some information you might want. Nothing illegal or immoral or anything, but possibly of some use to you."

"Well, I appreciate that," he said. "You can upload it to my computer—"

"Um, no, nothing in writing, I'm afraid, it'll have to be from my lips to your ear, and even then, you didn't hear it from me. Why don't we meet for a drink? It won't take long."

Michaels felt a chill frost his spine. Was it just his imagination, or did this seem a little too coincidental? A beautiful lobbyist calling him at home to set up a circumspect—some might even say clandestine—meeting?

And she *was* beautiful, no question about that.

"I have a dinner at ten, I'm afraid," she continued, "so we'll have to make it a quickie."

His chill turned into goose bumps, and he felt like Toni—or maybe Guru—had just kicked him in the belly.

Of course, he could be wrong. It could be absolutely innocent. The term "quickie" could mean nothing more than a short meeting, people used it for that all the time. But something about the tone of her voice told him that if he went to meet Cory Skye for a drink and a quickie, he was pretty sure that there wouldn't be much *drinking* going on. . . .

He wasn't tempted. He'd been down that road, and even though he had never actually cheated on Toni—or on Megan before her—he had come close enough to know that he just wasn't interested in that.

Besides, he wasn't gullible enough to imagine even for a moment that the beautiful Ms. Corinna Skye was interested in him for himself. If the signals he was picking up were accurate—and Alex was very aware that he could simply be misreading her words—then he was certain it had nothing to do with his own personal magnetism and everything to do with the fact that he was the head of Net Force and the lead defendant in CyberNation's lawsuit. Given what Tommy Bender had said about Mitchell Townsend Ames, Alex had no trouble imagining what that cutthroat lawyer would do with photos of himself and Corinna Skye.

And so he said, "Ah, I'm sorry, but I'm really tied up

this evening. Maybe you could come by the office tomorrow?"

There was a short pause.

"Ah, well, of course you're busy, it was just a last-
minute thing, no problem. I was hoping I could work you
in, but I understand. I'll drop by your office."

"That would be fine. Any time."

"I'll take you up on that. Good night, Alex. I'll see you
soon."

Her voice must have dropped an octave on that last part.

He hit the disconnect button and dropped the phone onto
his workbench. Then he pulled out his virgil—he had it
clipped to his waistband even while he was working out—
and sent a quick memo regarding the phone call to his files
at the office. Corinna Skye's phone records would show a
call from her phone to his house; he wanted an answering
memo on file in case Mitchell Ames tried to make something ugly out of it.

Corinna Skye. For a moment an image of her filled his
mind. Then the image changed, morphing into Toni at
work, and Alex felt himself smile.

No, Corinna Skye had nothing to tempt him with. He
was happily married, and he had everything he wanted and
needed right here. Everything.

While Alex read the boy a story—something about not
teasing weasels—Toni watched him from the bedroom
doorway, smiling. Her son laughed at his father as Alex
read part of the book, doing voices for the characters.

"Again, Daddy, again!"

"Well, okay. But this is the *last* time."

Guru appeared behind her, ghostlike.

"Baby is happy with his father."

"Yeah, me, too," Toni said, turning to look at her old
teacher.

Guru had a funny look on her face. "Something wrong?" Toni asked.

Guru nodded. "My second grandson called from Arizona. My great-grandson David, he's twelve this year, is sick. Summer cold."

"Sorry to hear that."

Guru nodded. "He has never been a healthy child, David. Has bad lungs, even in the desert. He catches every bug that passes by. Not like our baby here, who is healthier than a water buffalo."

"Thank God for small favors," Toni said.

"Yes."

They both watched Alex read to their child. For Guru was as much his great-grandmother as Toni's real grandma was. No question.

Mel's Restaurant
Washington, D.C.

Ames walked into the restaurant at ten P.M., crossing the threshold just as the sweep second hand on his watch touched the twelve. Perfect.

He saw Cory standing at the bar to his left. She saw him come in and waved at him.

He went over to stand next to her. "Been here long?"

"Nope, just got in. They haven't even had time to bring my drink yet."

Even as she spoke, the bartender came toward them, bearing a bottle of champagne and two glasses. "Veuve Cliequot Private Reserve okay?" she said. "Twenty aught seven?"

Ames smiled. Twenty aught seven was a good year for champagne grapes. The Veuve reserve went for what? A hundred, one-fifty a bottle if you bought it by the case.

Probably twice that in a restaurant. If not the absolute best, it certainly wasn't something you'd use to make mimosas with.

The bartender set the glasses down, poured a taste for Cory, and, when she nodded that it was okay, filled both glasses. He left, taking the bottle with him.

The hostess came to get them before the second sip of the wine, which was crisp, dry, with a hint of apple— Ames knew that much of the jargon. The rest of the bottle was waiting for them in an ice bucket at their table.

He looked around. Nothing fantastic insofar as decor, but the service so far was good, and the place was still filled with patrons this late in the evening. A beautiful woman, nice restaurant, good champagne. Definitely a promising start to the evening.

"So, tell me about your day," she said.

He shrugged. "The usual. Gadding about, taking depositions, talking to clients, stroking a few political powers."

"How is the suit against Net Force going?"

He sipped his champagne. "Right on schedule. Bureaucrats are easy. These have a decent lawyer, Harvard man, smart, but they always leave such paper and electron trails you can follow them blindfolded in the dark. It's a slam dunk."

She smiled over the rim of her glass. "Does being a doctor help more with being a lawyer, or does being a lawyer help more with being a doctor?"

"About the same. Saves me having to hire one or the other without some idea of what they know. But enough about me. How was your day?"

She dipped her fingertip into the champagne, then rubbed it gently around the lip of the glass. The stemware emitted a clear, bell-like tone. She stopped. "Sorry. Bad habit. That's how you tell if it's good crystal, the tone. This is pretty good."

"We all have our little habits," he said. "Do you know about toilet lids?"

She raised her eyebrows.

"It's customary to stamp the date of manufacture into the underside of ceramic tank covers. So if you are in a house, and you want a quick check to see how old it is, you just look under the toilet tank's lid."

"What if it's a replacement?" she said.

"It's not a perfect system," he said, "but if the date under the lid is, say, 'November 1, 1969,' then you know the house is at least that old. Could be older, but unless it was built before indoor plumbing, it probably isn't any newer than that date."

"Ah. Good to know."

"A real estate agent showed it to me. If somebody is trying to sell you a house they claim is twenty-five years old, and the toilet was built thirty years ago, chances are likely they are lying."

She laughed, took another healthy swig of her champagne.

"Am I missing a joke?"

"Not at all. We've been sitting here for two minutes, and already we're having a deep philosophical discussion about bathroom plumbing."

He laughed. A sense of humor, too. Ah, he was going to enjoy this conquest. "But let's get back to your day," he said. "We'll always have Kohler. . . ."

19

Net Force HQ
Quantico, Virginia

Alex Michaels looked up and saw Tommy Bender standing in his doorway. "You're like the bad penny, aren't you? You just keep turning up."

Tommy didn't smile, though. "I thought I'd better warn you, Alex. You'll be getting a copy of the records request later today, pursuant to the lawsuit."

Michaels frowned and shook his head. "Oh, good," he said. "That's just what we need, putting an operative on duty, spending part of our budget pulling files so they can be used against us."

Tommy nodded. "That's how the game is played, Commander. And a word of caution, even though I know it's totally unnecessary: There will be judicial review, with input from assorted federal agencies as to whether or not any material requested is vital to national security. If something should be kept secret for such reasons, it will be tended with appropriate deletions. Don't decide that the list needs to be trimmed here. If they ask for it, give it up."

"Of course," Michaels said. "We wouldn't want to do anything illegal, would we?"

"Exactly what you are supposed to say. I'll drop by later and see how it is going."

"It might take days," Michaels said. "Weeks, even."

Now Tommy did smile. "Of course. The initial order won't set a deadline, it will merely specify that said documents be delivered in a 'timely manner.' They don't expect you to shut down operations for this. But if it looks as if you are deliberately dragging your feet, the judge will not be amused."

Alex nodded. "I understand, Tommy. We'll be sure to smile, nod, and tell everybody we are going just as fast as we can. And thanks for the heads up."

Tommy left, and Michaels leaned back in his chair. Just another day in paradise. He glanced at his small top drawer, the one he reserved for personal items. Inside it was an envelope that came the other day, and inside that was a job offer to head up a computer security service for a big corporation headquartered in Colorado.

He got two or three similar offers pretty much every week. He read them all, but most of them he just threw away. This one he'd kept, though he wasn't sure he could really say why. And now, in the wake of Tommy Bender's latest announcement, it was starting to look awfully appealing.

Colorado was certainly beautiful, and the job would be a lot less work. It pretty much had it all, a lot more money, a lot less stress, and more time for his family. On top of that, Colorado was a great place to raise a child, and it was closer to his ex-wife and his daughter, which would make it easier for her to visit. They could learn to ski. Hike in the summer. Enjoy the fresh air, if they could get far enough away from Denver.

Maybe he should talk to Toni about it. This job was

never easy, and it seemed like it had gotten worse lately. There was something to be said for working in the private sector. . . .

"Sir?" came his secretary's voice over the com.

"Yes?"

"Ms. Skye is here to see you."

Michaels sighed. He had forgotten all about Cory. She'd said she was coming by.

"Send her in."

And leave the door open, too. . . .

John Howard was walking toward his office with Julio, talking about the latest revision to the official requisition forms, when he heard something. It sounded odd, like an electric motor's hum. "What's that?" he said.

Julio looked at him. "What's what?"

"That noise, kind of a low drone."

"I don't hear any—wait. Oh, that. It's one of the scooters I told you about."

As if to punctuate his words, Sergeant Franklin Kenny rounded the corner of the hall heading in their direction, riding on what looked like an old manual push lawnmower.

Oh, yes, the Segway, Howard thought. He had seen those out in the real world, and Julio had mentioned they were testing some new models.

Sergeant Kenny rolled past at a pretty good pace.

Julio frowned and said, "You know, General, I couldn't hear the scooter until after you did. Maybe I ought to look into getting one of those little earplugs like yours."

Howard smiled. He hadn't told anyone about his new toy. He certainly hadn't mentioned it to Julio. On the other hand, he hadn't made any real effort to hide it, either. He'd just been waiting to see who would say something—or even notice—and who wouldn't. That Julio had spotted it

The flight was a hassle with all the security and lines, but that was just how it was. He always took his hardware to FedEx in a big box marked "Survey Equipment," insured the box for ten grand, and put down that it contained expensive electronic gear for survey work. When a box was insured for ten thousand dollars, FedEx didn't lose it. He sent it same-day delivery, to be picked up at the FedEx place nearest the airport, and his guns were waiting for him when he got wherever he was going, since they didn't have to put it on a truck to go elsewhere.

Some shooters simply packed their weapons in their checked baggage. Some had even found ways around the security and actually carried them right onto the planes. Junior didn't do that. As a convicted felon, he couldn't risk being caught, and since the airlines did random hand-searches of checked baggage now and then, even a small chance was more than he wanted to take.

He didn't much like being without his revolvers on a jet—you never knew when some whacko was going to go nine-eleven—but he wasn't completely unarmed. He had a pair of short knives he carried tucked into his socks. Made of hard plastic—they were called CIA letter openers—the metal detectors didn't see them. He could walk right though the security checkpoint, no problem.

He'd also been meaning to get himself one of those Israeli two-barreled derringers. Made out of what was essentially layers of carbon fiber and superglue, with scandium barrel liners and titanium springs and firing pins, they shot some kind of boron-epoxy round. The barrel itself was essentially the shell, like an old-time black powder weapon.

Like the knives, metal detectors didn't spot them, but you had to take them apart to reload. They weren't rifled, either, but smoothbores, so they were only accurate up close. Expensive little devils, too. They ran three grand each, if you could find 'em, which was also a problem.

Still, any gun was better than no gun when the shooting started. That's all he'd need, to have his jet taken over by someone who thought he was on a mission from God. If that ever happened, and if the guy didn't have a gun of his own, Junior was going to slice the fool like he was a watermelon.

One good thing you could learn in prison was how to do nasty stuff with a shiv, even a plastic one. While he was in the Louisiana pen in Angola, he'd met some South African guys who could make a knife do everything but stand up and whistle "Dixie," and unless the terrorist was one of those, he was going to be dead real fast if he struck at a flight Junior was on.

Junior knew he could gut the guy and be a hero for doing it. If they questioned him about the plastic knife, he would say he found it in the bathroom—the terrorist must have dropped it while doing whatever it was terrorists did to psyche themselves up for their suicide missions. He could plant the second one on the body to make sure. The way he figured it, if a guy saved a plane full of people, nobody was going to give him too hard a time about how he did it.

They landed, and Junior collected his carry-on bag. In and out, quick and dirty, that was the drill. He'd get a car, go collect his guns, and then make a call on a certain congressman who was getting too big for his britches. He'd give him some advice the congressman would be hard-pressed to refuse, what with the pictures Junior had of him with a woman other than his wife at a motel in Maryland and all.

Another day, another dollar.

He smiled. *Wonder what the poor folks are doin' today.*

20

Alone, Jay Gridley meditated in the Place of the Dead.

Or, rather, he *tried* to meditate. He shivered as he exhaled. His eyes were closed, but he knew if he opened them he would see his breath cloud the air before him. It was always cold here at the top of the world, where the snows lay deep and eternal. In the summer the top layers were stale and crisp, crusted into snow-cone ice, and the daylight hours were longer—but the cold never went away. Even inside, out of the wind, with fires and lamps burning, warmth was far more illusion than reality.

Jay smiled ruefully. It was all an illusion, of course, but it made Saji happy, and he was glad he had created this scenario for her. He just wished he could get the place to work for him as well as it did for her.

Seated upon a reed mat worn thin by generations of student monks, Jay felt the smooth rock floor claim what meager heat his flesh generated: It was *cold*.

The patchouli incense smoldered in a big clump on the altar in front of him. Along with the rendered-yak-fat oil lamps, they sent entwined tendrils of greasy smoke up to paint yet another layer of soot on the already tar-colored ceiling forty feet up. The carbon must be a centimeter thick up there, Jay thought.

Most of the lamps in the monastery used kerosene or white petrol. The fuel for them had to be carried dozens of miles up the mountain trails in ten-liter plastic bottles. Here in the traditional meditation chambers, however, the ancient, smelly, smoky oil lamps were still used. The combined aroma of bundled incense and burning fat was an oily, metallic odor, powerful but not unpleasant.

Nice touches, if he did say so himself.

Jay took another deep breath and exhaled slowly. He was supposed to be calm. He was also supposed to be finding out about the Supreme Court justice's clerk, and not focused on some small-time programmer's inconsequential net viruses. But it was personal now, after his own computer was infected—

He would never achieve a still mind this way. He opened his eyes.

The legions of the dead surrounded him.

The four walls were lined with shelves made of long planks stained a dark green, from a time when wood was not so scarce in the region. And on those shelves were—*artifacts*, Jay thought, repressing another shiver. Artifacts—a safely ambiguous term.

Artifacts—which had once been human beings.

Tibetan Buddhism taught that there was no worth in a dead body, except whatever use it might be to those left behind to dispose of it. A corpse was like a house destroyed in a storm—once the spirit was gone, a body was not to be revered any more than an empty, wrecked building would be. And if somebody had need of the timbers or shingles or window glass of that building? Why, then, let them make what use they could of it.

Which is what the monks of the Avalokiteshvara Monastery had done. There on the top shelf, visible in the flickering yellow light of the largest of the brass lamps, was a prayer wheel. It was an ingeniously constructed device, a cylinder inscribed with prayers and litanies designed to spin during devotions.

The shaft of the wheel had been made from the thigh bone of the first head of the Avalokiteshvara Order. The wheel itself was cleverly carved from sections of that same holy man's skull. Both had been overlaid with fine layers of hammered gold leaf, but there was no mistaking what they had once been. Next to the prayer wheel was a drinking cup, also made from the trepanned top of a monk's skull. And next to that was a scroll composed of human skin, counting beads made from finger bones, a necklace fashioned of yellowed teeth. . . .

The shelves surrounding him were full of such *mementos mori*, dozens of them, all neatly dusted and arranged.

Brrr. Jay shivered again, but this time the involuntary reflex was not caused entirely by the cold. He was alone physically, but not spiritually. The dead swirled around him unseen, traces of their essences clinging to that which had once been part of them.

Of course, before he met Saji, his western, rational, scientific mind would have been amused at such things, would have laughed at the idea of ghosts and revenants. But here in the depths of the monastery, science ran into its limits. Here, in this charnel dug deep into the raw stone heart of Mount Changjunga, here, in the bottom levels of these labyrinthine tunnels and chambers, here, in the Place of the Dead, Jay had more than once thought he heard the spirits call to him when, on rare occasions, he had managed to still his thoughts long enough to slip into meditation.

Spooky.

To sit alone in the Place of the Dead was definitely that.

Some of those who had left parts of themselves here had not been quite so holy as their contemporaries had thought them to be. Some of them had not advanced so far along the path as they had pretended. Their essences were strong and sinister, it was whispered, still full of unfinished business, of lusts and hatreds and fears, and woe to the initiate who sat among them unprepared. Legend had it that they would beat upon the walls of a student's mind, clamoring to be let in, to experience once more the red pulse of life, to leach warmth from his spirit as the floor did from his body.

Saji had spoken to him of the fear Jay had felt on such occasions, especially when he had been recovering from his stroke.

"But of course you will be afraid," she had said. "Fear is natural. Confront it often enough and it will lose its power over you. There will come a day when you will embrace fear as you would a woman, and it will serve you as well as the warmest love."

Uh-huh. Right.

Jay realized that his breathing had become more rapid and shallow. He could feel fear rising in him like the mercury in a thermometer. He concentrated on breathing deeply and slowly, focusing his awareness on his breath.

It seemed to him that the light had grown even more wan and pallid, that the darkness was pressing in hungrily around him. He noticed the skull of some ancient monk sitting on a nearby shelf at eye level. An unnamed artisan—perhaps existing at the same time as the monk, perhaps centuries later, there was no way of knowing—had outlined the skull's eye sockets with filigreed silver and placed within them a pair of faceted rubies, each worth a king's ransom. The gems glittered in the weak light, seeming somehow to focus on Jay with malign intensity. . . .

Jeez, how good were you at creating a scenario when you could scare yourself with something you had made?

Jay turned his gaze from the skull, trying to still his mind, to concentrate on following the breath as it entered and left his body.

He sighed. There was no denying it—the monkey mind was in full control now. His thoughts scampered from one subject to another like primates leaping from tree to tree. Before his mental eye arose the image of his own infected computer, and of the anger he had felt at that. He wanted to hurt somebody. Oh, boy, did he.

He also wanted very much to be able to be calm, and to not let his emotions run away with him, and so he kept trying to get there. And if that had to include sitting on a frigid stone floor among human body parts, meditating and fighting off the attacks of restless spirits, then so be it. Saji could do it. He could learn how to do it, too.

Jay closed his eyes again. He blew his breath out through his left nostril, inhaled slowly through his right nostril. Once more he blanked his mind as best he could and sought the "om," the sound of all sounds, the drone of the entire universe as it spoke with a single voice.

In the embrace of the "om," it was said, all things were possible.

Even tracking down the lowly little hacker who'd created that virus—

He shook his head. There he went again. He was never going to get this. Never. Maybe he should—

His priority alarm chimed, kicking him abruptly out of the meditation scenario—

Net Force HQ
Quantico, Virginia

"What?"

"WE HAVE FOUND THE EVIL ONE," his tracker imp said.

Jay grinned. He could get his head together later. Right now, he had a criminal to catch and a very personal score to settle.

21

"Smokey Jay" Gridley leaned against the cool blue tuck-and-roll Naugahyde cushion in a back booth in the disco, doing his best to appear relaxed as he watched the drug dealer and his buddies in a booth a dozen feet away. Thick smoke drifted through the air, with much of the bluish haze coming from low-grade marijuana, to judge from the smell.

The dealer was a pig. Jay guessed he weighed three, three hundred fifty pounds at least. His bald, bullet-shaped head gleamed in the flashing lights from the dance floor. Three sets of heavy gold chains glittered on his chest in the large gap of the lime-green polyester shirt he wore unbuttoned down to his navel. He moved his hands in the air, tracing a Coke-bottle shape, and laughed.

His two friends, who looked as if they could have been cast in a *Superfly* movie, laughed uproariously at his apparently obscene comments. One man wore a black hat with big peacock feathers in the band, a poster boy for "pimp of the week," and the other sported black leather pants and a jacket, both studded with chrome buttons. A few safety pins through his cheek and a mohawk and he'd be a punk rocker. Thankfully, they weren't quite to that era yet.

A few people moved on the dance floor, fairly graceful considering the platform shoes they all wore. The *chukkita-chukkita-chukkita* of the disco beat was underscored by a lot of percussion, particularly cymbals, and a nasally male singer.

What awful music.

Jay glanced around the room and caught a view of himself in one of the mirrored pillars that framed the dance floor. He wore amber-tinted horn-rimmed glasses and a brown leather jacket. A thick gold medallion with an upraised fist lay on his chest, framed in a gap that was nearly the equal of the fat man's, and his dark blue bell-bottomed jeans almost completely hid the snakeskin boots he was wearing.

He'd combed his hair into a huge pompadour, the front of the ridge extending a good inch out from his forehead, and held in place by the strongest hair spray you could find in 1973—which was almost shellac. You could bounce quarters off his hair, he was sure.

Jay Gridley, human chameleon.

A burst of static echoed in his right ear. He wore an earpiece there that was 1973's version of a high-tech receiver.

Jay pushed the fist in the middle of the medallion—the microphone—and spoke: "Yeah?"

"Hey, hey, Smokey Jay, looks like the connection has done arrived."

It was the undercover cop outside. Jay knew that he needed help on a major bust like this—not because he couldn't handle a simple pickup like this one. No, it was more political than that. Whenever possible, Net Force tried to bring in the locals, share some of the credit as it were, especially on the big busts.

A crew of undercover officers also ringed the inside of the club. The guy in the big afro on the edge of the dance floor and the foxy chick in the bright orange micro were another pair from metro.

"I read you. Keep an eye on his ride, and leave the rest to me."

"You got it, Smokey—and hey, uh, leave a little for us, will you?"

Gridley grinned and pressed the fist again.

"We'll see what goes down."

Naturally, what was going on here wasn't really a bust in the traditional sense, but the analogy was apt enough.

What they were waiting on was the hacker who had been creating viruses.

After running the imp for about a day, Jay had gathered information on the start points for all three viruses, but the data had been inconclusive. This guy was smart. He had launched from several different places geographically, all with quick-start AOL accounts that he'd registered with cash cards, paying a full year in advance. The trail had gone cold pretty quick.

Not ready to give up, Jay had started analyzing the virus trail. And in the curious and backward non-barking-in-the-night-dog manner—and thank you kindly, Mr. Sherlock Holmes—he'd found something lacking.

Deep within some of the heaviest concentrations of the virus, he'd found a scattering of computers that hadn't been infected. These machines weren't just free of one or two of the viruses. They were free of all three, which seemed to Jay to stretch coincidence a bit.

There were possible explanations for such anomalies, of course. Those machines could all have great firewalls or antivirals. They could have been off-line when the viruses hit. They could be new systems that hadn't been up until yesterday. There were a lot of reasons, and some of them were even logical.

Well, he'd thought. *Let's just see which it was.*

Jay had refined another tracker, this one even more subtle, and hit the unaffected systems with it.

He found that while most of the immune systems had pretty good firewalls and bug squashers, several of them had off-the-shelf stuff that should have let at least one of the bugs past, which pretty well shot the first theory.

All of them had been on-line at the time of the general infection, which took care of the second theory.

But most interesting of all, he found that there was a fair amount of traffic between most of the unaffected machines.

Aha. That gave him an even better reason why they hadn't been hit:

It was a hackers' ring.

Oh, it was nothing obvious. It wasn't like the website said anything like, "Geek Friends of Computer Viruses," but visiting the on-line VR chat rooms where some of these SysOps hung out, it was easy to read between the lines. These were virus fan boys.

Which could only mean one thing. Someone in the network of unaffected websites, or someone close to them, had made the viruses Jay was tracking. And, like many hacker rings, these guys would send out immunizations of anything they made to everyone else in the group.

Jay had hacked one of the computer's virus software packages and had found patches and virus definitions added just hours before the release of each of the three viruses.

Honor among thieves, and it was going to cost them. . . .

A stream of sunlight blasted into the darkened club's interior as the door opened.

In came the connection.

He wore a white leisure suit, big collar and all, a low hat over dark sunglasses, and a big Mongol moustache flanked by bushy sideburns. Disco forever.

The hacker walked with a swagger, carrying a white plastic briefcase which matched his outfit. He made his way over to the fat man and they exchanged high fives.

Leisure Suit sat next to the Dealer and opened his briefcase so that only they could see what was inside. The fat man reached down and came back with something on his finger, a whitish powder which he touched to his tongue. He smiled and nodded.

Jay tapped the medallion.

"All units close in. We have delivery."

There was the sound of rushing feet out of synch with the disco music, as the undercover dancers charged, whipping out hidden revolvers as they moved.

But Leisure Suit wasn't going down easy.

"No way, pigs!!"

He leaped from the booth and pulled his own weapon, a chrome-plated .45.

The Dealer yelled, too: "It's the fuzz! Sonny—Randy—take 'em!"

The henchmen pulled out their pieces, and lead filled the air.

Jay pulled out his own gun, a custom-tuned .44 Smith & Wesson Model 29, one of the most powerful handguns in the world, and let go a shot.

BOOM—!

He grinned again. That was *loud*—!

Black leather flew backward as the huge bullet took him in the chest.

Pimp Hat fired at the dancers as the hacker turned over one of the tables. Jay saw him crawling toward the back entrance of the club.

"Stop, police!" he yelled, and started crawling himself.

More cops joined the fight, pouring into the club with

vests on. Within a few seconds the Dealer was down, and
Pimp Hat would not be henching anymore—if that was a
good term.

Jay reached the back entrance and heard a shot before
he saw the hacker dive into a big Cadillac. The undercover
cop was down.

"You'll never get me!" the hacker shouted, and his car
lurched forward, tires squealing.

"Man down!" Jay shouted as he ran for his own car, a
huge Dodge Charger custom fitted with a 360-cubic-inch
overbored engine. He hopped in and fired it up. The machine roared, the Holley carb pumping like crazy, and he
took off after the fleeing hacker—

—who was cresting a hill just ahead. Jay flattened the
gas pedal, enjoying the rush of acceleration and the feel
of the wind blowing in through his open window.

He sailed over the steep hill in a classic car-chase maneuver and braced himself as the car hit, undercarriage
tapping the pavement for a second as the shocks tried to
take the dynamic load of the falling Dodge.

This was way cool.

The Caddy rolled around a corner, and Jay tore into the
intersection, turning hard right as he passed the midpoint,
as he'd been trained to do. His car skidded right, under
the minimum control necessary for it to stick to the road,
and he punched the gas again.

"Hi-ho, Silver!" he yelled.

As he did, he toggled a switch on the medallion: "Julio,
you ready?"

"You got it. My team's ready to rock. You just give us
the location. We've even got a warrant waiting."

Jay gave him the address.

On the straightaway, the Dodge started to catch up to
the Caddy, and Jay pushed the accelerator down as far as
it would go.

Closer . . . closer . . .

The suspect threw a small package from the car, and Jay swerved right to avoid it. Good thing he did, because it exploded as he drove past it.

He grinned. "You've got to do better than *that*, pal!"

Oh, this was fun.

And the best part was yet to come.

Because Jay already knew where the guy was going. Jay had figured the guy would probably be releasing more gunk onto the net, and probably more immunizations to his hacker buddies, so he'd set a watchdog on the hacker site's chat room, primed to alert him about any new patches.

The dog had barked just before lunch. Jay had checked it out and saw that something new was coming in. So he'd alerted Julio and headed in for his stakeout scenario.

Since he'd already backtracked the trail of the previous antivirus shots, all he'd had to do was trace the last few steps, which he'd done after the guy had been spotted outside the club.

He'd had the address before the shooting started.

The chase was a stall. They could have picked the hacker up back at the disco club—Jay had worked hard figuring out how to stage the scene so the hacker would believe he'd really gotten away on his own—but Jay needed to track him back to his safe house, and they needed to get there before the guy either launched the new virus or destroyed it.

There were other ways he could have handled this, but he had felt this was the best way to both preserve the chain of evidence and involve the locals in a meaningful way.

Besides, he thought, grinning again, it was more fun this way.

Imagine how surprised this hacker will be when he pulls off his VR gear and finds Julio and his team standing there, machine guns pointed at him.

So when the hacker threw another bomb and Jay

swerved into a light post, which stopped the chase cold, he didn't mind.

He just hoped that Julio remembered to take a picture.

He *really* wanted to see the look on the guy's face when they got him.

22

Mojave Desert
Between Joshua Tree and Twenty-nine Palms, California

It started out okay.

The congressman, a California representative named Wentworth, had wanted to meet somewhere private rather than in his home or office. Junior had agreed—it didn't matter to him where they met, as long as they got their business done. Wentworth gave him directions to a little dirt road that ran into the Joshua Tree National Park. Junior wasn't sure, but he thought the congressman's district included the national monument and maybe the Marine Corps base to the north. That didn't matter to him, either. A park in the desert was fine with him.

Wentworth had been an easy blackmail. Like Senator Bretcher, Junior had used Joan to set him up. They had played this one a bit softer, though, no confrontation, no threats to call the cops, no lies about Joan's age. Instead, Junior had simply hidden in the closet with a digital camera. He'd gotten some highly detailed photos, and had e-mailed a few of them to the good congressman, along with a request to meet. The congressman had agreed, as Junior had known he would, and Junior had flown out to California to conclude their business.

He drove the rental car from LAX out I-10, past San Bernardino and Banning, and then cut north on State Road 62 at Palm Springs. He passed several small towns—Morongo Valley, Yucca Valley, Joshua Tree—then he started looking for the dirt road, which Wentworth said would be off to the right, between Park Boulevard and the Boy Scout Trail. If he got to Indian Cove Road, the congressman had told him, he'd gone too far.

He passed the park entrance sign, and almost missed the dirt road, but he didn't. He pulled off, and wound through the dusty and dry country, looking for the congressman. Hot out here, it had to be pushing a hundred, hundred and five. If the car broke down, it was going to be a long uncomfortable walk back to civilization. Junior knew enough about riding through the desert, even the high desert, to carry a jug of water, just in case, but he still didn't like the idea of having to walk ten or fifteen miles in the summer sun.

Why would anybody want to make this a national park anyway? There was nothing to see but more of what was on the other side of the road, which was nothing to get excited about. Still, Junior was always careful and thorough, when he had the time, and he'd done his research on the area. Most of his information had come from the Park Service, which had told him the park covered eight hundred thousand acres. So far it was all rocks and sagebrush. Full of African killer bees, too, according to the Park Service, and you didn't want to mess with them.

National monument? A waste of the taxpayers' money, that's what it was.

A couple miles along the very twisty road, he spotted a clump of stubby trees and more creosote bushes. Must be some kind of water there, a spring or pond or something. A black Lincoln was parked in the shade, the motor running, and the license plate matched the congressman's car.

Junior pulled over into the shade and killed his engine. The hot engine ticked, and even in the shade and through the tinted glass, the reflected sun was fierce; he could feel the car getting warmer even though he'd just shut the AC off.

Well, might as well get to it, he thought.

Junior opened the door. A blast of arid desert wind hit him like a blanket right out of the clothes dryer. He broke a sweat immediately. But he was used to heat *and* high humidity, and this wasn't as bad as New Orleans in September.

He walked over to the congressman's car. The window rolled down, and the congressman looked up at him. Junior peered inside and checked the vehicle out, taking no chances. Unless somebody was hiding in the trunk, in which case they'd be cooked by now, the representative of the great state of California was by himself.

He was a thin man, pale, about forty-five or so, his hair too long and foofy. He wore a short-sleeved button-up shirt and khaki pants. His hands were in plain sight, one on the steering wheel, one resting lightly by the side mirror.

"Hey, how y'all doin'?" Junior asked.

"Screw you," the congressman said.

"Congressman Wentworth, I'm surprised at your language, you being a gentleman and a Democrat and all."

The congressman glared at him. "I'm not some jailhouse trash like you're used to dealing with. Just say what you have to say."

"All right, you want to play it hard, here it is. We got us a nice collection of X-rated pictures of you and that sweet young *cher* in that little motel in Maryland. I'm thinkin' you probably don't want to see those pictures posted all over the Internet, now do you?"

Wentworth didn't say anything.

"So the deal is, you give us a little help, we'll give you a little help."

"Let me get this straight. You want me to do you a favor. Something illegal, right? Or what? You'll blackmail me with those pictures?"

Junior frowned. He didn't like the tone of that at all. That had the sound of something a man would say if somebody was listening and he was trying to get an admission of criminal intent. So far, Junior hadn't done that, he'd just mentioned some pictures, and he wasn't about to go any further until he checked some things out.

Junior leaned down and looked into the car. The congressman leaned back away from him.

"You wouldn't be wearing a wire, now would you, congressman?"

"A wire? No!"

Too fast and too hard, Junior realized.

Junior stood up straight and looked around. Could be a hundred feds hiding in the rocks out there, waiting to jump him, and he wouldn't know it until it was too late. All of a sudden, the sweat started bothering him.

The power window started to go up, and he saw the congressman reaching for the gear shift at the same time. What the hell?

Junior reacted without thinking. He shoved, hard, caught the window with the heel of his hand, and shattered it. The safety glass broke into hundreds of little squarish bits, showering the congressman with sharp glitter.

Junior reached in, grabbed the latch, and opened the door—Wentworth scrabbled across the seat toward the passenger's side door. Trying to get away—?

Nope, he wasn't. He was going for the glove box. It fell open and Wentworth reached in—

It could have been a cell phone. Maybe an envelope full

of money. But where Junior came from, a scared man who went for the glove compartment?

He was looking for a weapon.

Junior went for his revolver on the right side. Good thing, too, because the congressman came out of the glove box holding a little silver pistol, trying to get it up and pointed at Junior—

Junior fired first, twice, *pap-pap!* and at four feet, he would have had to try real hard to miss.

He didn't miss.

Junior found that he was breathing fast and sweating even harder.

Why did he do that? He must be crazy!

Of course, Junior now had problems of his own. If the man was wired, Junior was in deep trouble. There was only one way out of this hole in a car, and he sure wasn't going to try to run on foot.

They'd be on him like ducks on a june bug any second now, if the congressman was wearing a wire, and what Junior didn't want was to have a gun in his hand when they came charging over the hill. A good lawyer might get him off, but waving a gun in the faces of a bunch of ticked-off feds was sure to save the government the cost of a trial.

He holstered his piece, stood straight up, and looked around.

Nobody screaming and hollering, "Get him, boys!" No PA from a helicopter telling him to "Freeze!" Nothing but the hot wind and a buzzard way up, circling something that was probably dead a long time before the congressman bought it.

Junior waited another minute. Two. If they were coming, they should have been here by now.

Another minute passed. Maybe they weren't coming. Maybe he ought to see why the congressman there had been trying to get Junior to say something. Or if he actually *had* been trying to do that.

He went around to the passenger side and opened the door. There was a fair amount of blood, but he was used to working around that, and it took only a minute or so to turn out the dead man's pockets and find what he was looking for.

There was a little electronic pen-sized device clipped inside Wentworth's shirt, and it was recording. Junior hit the replay button, and sure enough, everything the two of them had said was on it, plus the two gunshots.

Junior wiped the recording and stuck the pen in his pocket. He'd destroy it first chance he got, but he didn't want to leave it lying around anywhere near this place.

He shook his head. What an idiot his guy had been! He was just going to record the conversation on his own, no backup? What, did he think he was James Bond or somebody? He must have not expected any trouble, otherwise he would have had that little pistol—looked like a chrome-plated Beretta .25, a poor choice in a gun—closer to hand.

The congressman obviously didn't know how these things worked. He couldn't simply blackmail Junior and balance the threat. Wentworth had a whole lot more to lose. Unless maybe he was getting a divorce or something anyway, and he didn't care if somebody knew he was getting a little on the side?

Junior sighed. Well, it didn't much matter now, did it? The congressman was dead, and so was this deal.

Better clean it up a little, if he could, then split.

Junior used a handkerchief to pick up Wentworth's hand, which still had the Beretta in it. He pointed the gun at the opening on the driver's side and capped off a couple of rounds. He dipped the handkerchief in the dead man's blood until he had sopped up a fair amount, then, holding his other hand under it so it wouldn't drip, he walked around to the driver's side, stepped back a couple of feet, then squeezed the sodden handkerchief.

Blood oozed out and pooled on the dirt.

Junior walked about fifty feet away, heading toward the desert, and squeezed some more blood out.

A third time, another fifty feet, and the last of the blood made another little puddle on the dirt.

He scuffed the ground a little, but it was mostly rocky, so not much in the way of footprints showed.

So the congressman got killed, but he had returned fire, maybe even shot first, and he'd hit somebody. Somebody with the same blood type, so Junior hoped it wasn't one of the rare ones. But at least when they first found Wentworth's body, they'd think they were looking for somebody who had gotten shot, and hospitals had to report bullet wounds.

There wasn't anything he could do about the rental car's tire tracks. It wasn't going to rain out here anytime soon, so the tracks would be here, and you could count on the fact that the FBI would be in on this. They'd know what kind of tires they were pretty quick, and probably what kind of car, too. At least he had rented the car under a phony name, and in L.A., so it would take them a while to trace it, if they could.

He had his travel bag in the rental car, and he'd lose the shoes and the clothes he was wearing when he could. He didn't need to stop for gas anytime soon, and he'd drive up to San Francisco to turn the car in. That way they wouldn't have a rental at LAX that had the same number of miles on it from there to here and back.

What bothered him the most, outside of the fact that he was going to have to tell Ames he had been forced to kill a United States congressman, was that he was going to have to lose the Ruger. He didn't have a spare barrel with him—he hadn't planned on shooting anybody—and how stupid would he be by putting a gun that could be traced to a homicide of a VIP into FedEx or UPS or even the U.S. mail? If somebody opened the package and found a gun, they'd probably go straight to the cops. The ballistics boys at the FBI would sacrifice a goat to their gods or something when they got *that* news. They'd have half the G-men in the country waiting for Junior to come by and pick up the package.

He'd have to make do with just the one until he could get a replacement. He hated that.

But, done was done. Best he get going before some hiker or nature type happened along and spotted this scene. By the time the sun went down, Junior wanted to be a *long* way from here.

And he surely wasn't looking forward to telling Ames about this. The man would have a kitten when he heard it. For sure. What a screwup, and not even his fault.

23

Dutch Mall
Long Island, New York

Mitchell Ames was angry. Junior had blown it, and he couldn't figure out how. It was a simple job, something Junior had done dozens of times. How could this one have gone so wrong?

"Look," Junior continued, "the man was nuts. He came out of the glove box with a gun. What was I supposed to do, let him shoot me? It was him or me."

"You killed a United States congressman, Junior. Do you have any idea what kind of heat that is going to cause?"

"Yeah, I know. Like I said, I had no choice except to let him kill me."

Ames sighed. "All right. It's done. Obviously, I'm not happy about it, but there's nothing that can be done about it now. The next question is, how clean are you on this?"

"Nobody saw me. The car is four hundred miles away from where I rented it. The clothes I wore, shoes, socks, everything, got burned. I wiped the gun clean, I stripped it down, and it's in pieces scattered on the bottom of San Francisco Bay. I flew with fake ID, in and out of Atlanta, and switched both planes and IDs there."

"What about the pictures?"

"I burned them up, too, disks and everything, and scrubbed the stored files off the computer. I didn't just erase them, either, but made sure to overwrite the sectors with other data so no utility in the world could re-create them. Not even Net Force. It's all gone. I'm telling you, anything that might tie me to the man is gone."

"What about the woman?"

Junior frowned. "What about her?"

"Where is she?"

"Down in Biloxi lying on the beach I reckon. No problem there. She was a part of it, but she can't say anything to anyone. She'd go to jail if she did."

Ames frowned. "Junior, don't be stupid. You've been in prison. You know how this works."

Junior ducked his chin and shook his head stubbornly. "Joan would never give me up to anyone. Never."

Ames sighed. "Sooner or later your friend is going to be arrested for something. She's a bad girl. If it's a soliciting bust, it won't be a problem, she's in and out, but what if they catch her with serious dope on her? Or playing blackmail games with somebody who carries some weight? She knows how to do that now. You taught her the game. You don't know that she might not get ambitious and branch out on her own. When they catch her—and they will—and if she's looking at hard time, not in county lockup but in prison, and she's got something to give them that gets her out of it, you think she won't do it?"

"Not to me. Besides, she knows what I'd do to her if she did."

"And you think some sweet-talking cop or fed can't convince her you won't be able to do anything because you will be locked away? She slept with this congressman and she knows that you were hiding in the closet taking pictures, Junior. When this guy turns up dead, she is going to notice, because it will be on the front page of every paper in the country and all over the radio, television, and Internet news. CNN will beat it to a pulp every half hour for days. She's going to know one of the guys she set up for blackmail is dead, and unless she's got cotton candy between her ears, she is going to know you probably had something to do with it."

Junior just sat there, looking stubborn.

"Junior. She might be a great lay. She might be somebody who rings your chimes, but there are other women in the world, women who can't send us to the death chamber. It's a get-out-of-jail-free card, and you gave it to her. The murderer of a congressman? That's a career-maker for any cop in the land if he solves it."

"It wasn't murder. It was self-defense."

"You killed him in the commission of a felony. Blackmail. They'll make it work. I sure could."

"Joan doesn't know about you."

"But *you* know about me. And if you face the choice between giving me up or getting the gas chamber? I don't trust you that much."

"So what are you sayin'?"

"You know exactly what I am saying. And do it fast, before she has a chance to think about things too long. I don't want this hanging over us."

Junior didn't say anything. He stood there for another moment silently. Ames could see his mind working, see him trying to figure out an alternative, but there wasn't one. They both knew that.

After a minute or two, Junior gave a single sharp nod and left. When he was gone, Ames sat for another twenty minutes, thinking about the situation. This was never in any of the scenarios he'd postulated.

Junior, like the woman he'd hired to honey-trap his victims, was now a liability. Junior was going to have to go away, and Ames was going to have to do the deed himself—he couldn't afford to get anybody else involved at this stage.

Maybe he'd have Junior meet him at the underground hideaway in Texas, do it there. He could grind him up, flush him away . . . no, better yet, once Junior was no longer among the living, he could leave him somewhere with enough evidence that he'd killed the woman and the congressman, something subtle, but something the investigators wouldn't miss. Once they ran that down, that would dead-end the hunt. Sure, they would suspect Junior had been working for somebody, but once you had the actual shooter, the pressure would be off; that's how it worked in cop shops around the world. "He did it" was much more final than "Maybe he was working for somebody who told him to do it."

Ames nodded to himself. Yes. Once Junior was gone, there wouldn't be any provable links to himself. Of course, the CyberNation legislation wasn't final yet, there were still some things that had to be done, and Junior needed to be around to do those, but as soon as the last pieces were put in play, which wouldn't be too much longer, then Junior would be leaving for his final destination.

Outdoor Shooting Range
Quantico, Virginia

John Howard looked at Julio and frowned. "What is so important that you are willing to irritate the Marines, Lieutenant?"

Julio grinned. "Well, sir, I believe anything we can do to irritate them is important."

Howard didn't grin back. He merely shook his head. They were at the Marines' outdoor pistol/rifle range, not Net Force's smaller, private facility. They were there because Julio had asked General Howard to meet him there.

Julio, seeing Howard's expression, grew more serious himself. "Gunny won't let us play with ballistic gel on his range," he said. "Says it's too messy, so I had to find somewhere else. This place was closest and most convenient. And speaking of Gunny, he says he's got a line on a Hammerli SP20 target pistol in .22 LR, convertible to .32 S&W. It's got an adjustable buffer and anatomical trigger and grips, and is supposed to be in Very Good condition. A real nice gun for Tyrone to learn with."

Howard raised one eyebrow at him. "How much?"

"Gunny says he can make it happen for three hundred."

Howard's other eyebrow went up. "You're kidding," he said. "One of those in rotten shape ought to go for more than twice that. VG would run fifteen, eighteen hundred minimum."

Julio grinned again. "You've been checking prices."

"I want the boy to have a decent tool to work with."

"Well, you know how Gunny works. He's a horse trader from way back. He'll swap something for something, kick in something else, and wind up with a deal that everybody is happy with. Should I tell him you're interested?"

"Three hundred bucks for a world-class pistol that sells for five times that much used? Yes, I'm interested."

"I figured. But you know, if you hold out, I expect Gunny will shave some off that—he sees Tyrone as the son he never had. Watching the boy shoot brings tears to his cynical old eyes."

Howard nodded, then changed the subject. "Okay, so other than Tyrone getting some new hardware, why are we here?"

"You remember those trophy-winning XM-109A Wind Runner BMG rifles we got?"

"I seem to recall them," Howard said, his voice as dry as the Sahara. He'd remember them as long as his memory worked—one of the BMG—for Browning machine gun—rifles had saved his life when that gone-bad federal agent started plinking at him during the California-druggie situation last year. In addition, the fifty-caliber takedown rifle had allowed Net Force shooters to win the most recent Thousand Meter Special Teams Match for United States Military Services at Camp Perry. First win ever. Outstanding piece of hardware, that weapon.

"Well, the fifty-caliber ammo our shooters used to win the match was made by RBCD, down in Texas. Stuff uses BMT—that's Blended Metal Technology, a high-tech bullet design—and blended powder. We're talking a real tackdriver here, John."

"And we're talking about this, here, now, because . . . ?"

"Because RBCD makes handgun ammo, too. I don't know how I missed it, but they do."

"And . . . ?

"And it will not only outperform just about everything else out there in accuracy, it also has some tactical advantages as well. Check out the targets."

Howard followed Julio to the bay. Twenty-five meters downrange was a big deflective-steel target table, upon which were six large, rectangular blocks.

"The two on the left are ten percent ordnance gelatin wrapped in four layers of ballistic nylon. The next two are the same, but with a sheet of tempered glass set up a foot or so in front of them. The two on the right are clay blocks."

"I can see that, Lieutenant."

"Well, General, if you would, please put one round into the gel on the left side with that Medusa of yours."

Howard drew his sidearm. The Medusa was a revolver with a patented chamber design that allowed it to fire doz-

ens of different calibers of ammunition, from .380 auto to
.357 Magnum. It had a three-inch barrel, which was a bit
shorter than most issue sidearms, but it was match-grade,
and it shot better from a rest than Howard could do offhand. He carried it loaded with .357 Magnum copper-
jacketed hollowpoints, and as such, it was better than a
ninety-five percent one-shop stopper with a solid body hit.

Howard took an isosceles stance and a couple of deep
breaths, then brought the revolver up two-handed. He lined
up the sights and squeezed off a round. The backlash from
the .357 was fairly stout, but his hearing protectors damped
out the noise. He lowered his weapon.

"And now the third target, sir, behind the glass."

Howard lined up and shot the second round.

"And finally, General, the first clay block."

Howard snapped the revolver up and fired again,
quickly. He didn't need to hurry, but it never hurt to re-
mind his old friend that he could shoot fast and accurately
when the situation required it.

"Thank you," Julio said. "Now dump and reload these,
sir, if you please."

Julio handed him a half-dozen cartridges. They looked
like standard .357 ammo, far as Howard could tell. Brass
cases, lead-nosed, copper jacket.

As he reloaded, Julio said, "While these look pretty
much the same as any solid-jacketed round, they are actually made up of several powdered metals and a polymer
similar to the plastic used in Glock frames."

Howard nodded and continued loading them into his
Medusa.

"The jacket is an alloy with a slick moly-coat. Not pre-
fragged, but a solid unit. Not plus-P, either, standard pressure stuff. If you'll shoot the second, fourth, and sixth
targets."

Having made his point earlier, Howard took his time,
ten seconds or so to hit the three targets.

Julio nodded. "Now we wait for the Marines to stop firing so we can go downrange."

When the range officer called a cease-fire, Howard and Julio walked the short distance to the six targets. Julio pulled the nylon off the tops of the ballistic gel blocks, a substance designed to replicate muscle tissue, revealing the stretch cavities.

The one on the right, the new rounds, was much larger than the one immediately to its left.

"The stuff you carry is one-twenty-five-grain jacketed hollow point. It comes out of your barrel at about fourteen hundred feet per second. The energy in foot/pounds is around four hundred. RBCD's .357 Mag bullet is only sixty grains, but it leaves a three-inch barrel at better than eighteen hundred feet per second, with an E/fp of around five hundred. Expands like a balloon when it hits, you see. That's a *permanent* stretch cavity, twenty by twenty-seven centimeters. It dumps the energy into the target without overpenetration."

"Impressive," Howard said, and he meant it.

"The best is yet to come, sir. Look at the glass-protected blocks."

They did. The impact of his usual round with the glass had partially deformed the bullet. It shattered the glass, then went through and hit the gelatin, and it still penetrated and left a big hole, but it was shallower and smaller around than the block without the glass. Which was to be expected. Glass was a serious pain.

However, the cavity in the second glass shot, the one with the new ammo, was virtually the same as the one without the glass in front of it.

"See, the RBCD stuff is designed to punch right through a solid, almost like military ball ammo, but when it hits a hydraulic substance, the expansion cranks up. The powder is progressive-burn, so you get standard pressure for the full length of the barrel. That way you don't have to worry about blowing your gun up."

Howard nodded. It definitely seemed like superior ammunition.

"Now for the fun stuff." Julio pulled the covers off the clay blocks. The left one had the usual small entry hole, and was ballooned up with a big cavity.

The one on the right? The whole block was splashed open wide.

"More accurate, more powerful, better penetration through cover, better expansion on soft targets. Though you can't tell with that old hog leg you carry, it feeds very nicely through a semiauto, and they have a nine that will feed like oil through a full auto. What's not to like?"

"I know you well enough to know there's another shoe. Drop it, Lieutenant."

Julio grinned. "Well, sir, it's a tad more expensive than standard ammunition."

"Why am I not surprised?"

"But when it is your life on the line, you aren't going to begrudge a few cents, now are you?"

He had a point.

"I'm not saying we should buy carloads of it to practice or plink with, but as a duty round, this is the top of the line. I'm going to carry it in my Beretta even if I have to pay for it myself, and you ought to use it in your wheelgun. At the very least, you could order a few cases for evaluation. Think of it this way—if you have to shoot somebody, you'll save money 'cause you'll only have to shoot them *once*. . . ."

"Given our experiences with the legal system of late, Lieutenant, you might have to explain to a jury why you are carrying these rhino-stoppers in your sidearm if you do have to shoot somebody."

"Better twelve men trying me than six men carrying me," Julio observed.

Howard nodded. Yes. You didn't want to shoot anybody unless it was a matter of life or death, but if you did have to shoot, you wanted them to cease their attempts to kill you immediately.

"All right," Howard said. "Get a few cases. Nines, forties, forty-five, thirty-eight Special, and a couple boxes of .357 Magnum."

"Yes, sir!"

"A *few* cases, Lieutenant. Not a warehouse full."

"You wound me, sir."

"I don't think so, Julio. I think even these things would bounce right off—you're bulletproof when it comes to this kind of thing."

"I try, sir. I do try."

24

"They can't be serious," Michaels said, looking at the list of requested documents. It had come via e-mail and certified letter, both. He had the e-mail open on his computer.

"They are, Commander," Tommy said. "They are quite serious."

Michaels shook his head. "They want copies of every e-mail sent by every operative of this agency between these two dates? We're talking about eight or ten thousand letters, maybe more."

"That's correct."

Alex pointed at a line on his screen. "And all these work files, personal notes, and official reports? If we printed them out, we'd have to rent a moving van to haul them!"

"Electronic copies are acceptable, Commander, as long as they are certified by a DOJ or GAO inspector."

"Do you know how much time we'll waste pulling all this up? Time that could be better spent solving crimes—or stopping new ones from happening?"

"The only option is to allow Ames or his representatives access to your computer systems, which, of course, we can't do, in the interests of national security—unless they hire somebody with adequate clearance, and that's not going to happen since just about anybody with that kind of clearance already works for us. You have to cough it up, Commander. It's the rule."

"But it's stupid," Alex said. "Stupid, inefficient, and wasteful."

"I understand. And I'm sure they'll be happy to take it in small pieces."

Alex glared at him. "Yeah, well, you know what? That's not how they are going to get it. I'll wait until I have a chunk big enough for them to choke on. And you know what else? I am going to print it all out, too."

"What about that moving van?"

"I'll eat the cost. If we send it to them as hard copy, then they'll have to *read it all*. They won't just be able to do a nice and easy word search to find stuff they want. I don't have to make their job easy for them, do I?"

Tommy smiled. "I believe you are finally beginning to get into the spirit of things, Commander. No, you don't have to make it easier for them. You may, within the bounds of the law, make it as difficult as you can." He smiled again. "Of course, we are all looking for truth and justice, but it's up to a judge and jury to decide that part. Ames will have readers go through it, and I don't expect they will miss much, but if it takes them longer to find it than they'd like, that is their problem. By the time this comes to trial, and that will be months from now, key witnesses might decide to come clean and tell things straight. Or they might skip town and not leave a forwarding address. Or have a heart attack and pass away. Lots of things can happen, and you can never figure on a sure win in advance. It doesn't hurt to take all the time you can get when you're on the receiving end of one of these suits.

"On the record, as your attorney and as an officer of the court, I must instruct you to move with all deliberate speed to comply with judicial orders. But you must be the judge of what is appropriate celerity and manner. If you can justify it to a judge—which means if *I* can, and I can—then you can bury them in a snowstorm of paper. They won't like it, the judge won't like it, but he knows how the game is played, too. Time is the plaintiff's friend when it comes to gathering evidence, but not necessarily when it comes to being able to utilize it."

"Thanks, Tommy."

"Just doing my job."

Tommy took off, and as he did, Michaels's private line chirped. He picked it up.

"Alex? It's Cory. How are we?"

He blinked, caught unawares by her call. How did she get this number?

"Cory. What can I do for you?" His voice was guarded, giving nothing away.

There was a part of him that couldn't help being flattered by her apparent interest in him, even though the larger, more logical, more experienced part knew that she wasn't really interested in him. She was just doing her job, and if her job meant appearing to be interested in him— or if, as he suspected, her job meant going farther than that, well, he suspected she was pretty good at that, too.

But he just wasn't interested, and his job didn't require him to give any such false impressions. Besides, the "information" she'd given him earlier turned out to be nothing he didn't already know about CyberNation.

After a brief pause, she said, "I think I have something more useful to you this time."

"Uh-huh," he said.

"I had dinner with Mitchell Ames recently."

Despite himself, he perked up at that. "Really?"

"Yes. He had a few things to say I'm sure you'd find interesting."

"I'm sure I would. Why don't you drop by—?"

"Can't," she said, cutting him off. "I have to fly to the west coast tonight, won't be back for a couple of days, and I've got appointments all day. But I can make time for that drink. Meet me at the Roosevelt Hotel in the lobby at seven P.M. Bye."

Cautious, he had drawn a breath to tell her he couldn't make it, but she hung up before he could speak.

He frowned, then thought about it for a second. What could it hurt, to meet her in a public bar? No danger in that. And maybe she could give him something he could use against Ames, some kind of shark repellent.

Okay, he'd do it. He'd have a drink with her. But he'd do it his way.

He touched the intercom control.

"Sir?" his assistant asked.

"See if you can find Toni for me, would you please, Becky? I think she's in the building. Ask her if she would stop by."

His new executive assistant, a young woman from Oregon who was apparently part Indian, said, "Yes, sir."

Jay showed up before Toni did.

Leaning against the wall near the door, his arms crossed in front of him, Jay was grinning like a cat. "His netnom is 'Thumper,' " he said, "but his real name is Robert Harvey Newman. Julio Fernandez's report ought to be along soon with all the details of the takedown, but I can give you the gist of what we know so far."

"Go ahead."

"We got him by backwalking the thing and finding out there was a hacker's group that didn't get hit. We found one of them and squeezed him, and he gave Thumper up.

Rolled over quicker than a lubed steel ball bearing."

"Go on."

"So once we kicked in his door—I used the royal 'we' here, since it was Julio and his team who did the actual kicking and collecting—Thumper was brought in. He is being, um, 'interviewed' as we speak."

"Who's got it?"

"Toni."

"Good," Michaels said. "And thanks, Jay. Good work."

"How about a lawyer? Don't I get a lawyer?"

Toni shook her head. She was alone with the hacker, but a digital camcorder recorded every word and gesture that either one of them spoke or did.

"No, Mr. Newman, you don't get a lawyer," she said. "You're a terrorist, and we have different rules for dealing with people like you."

She sat across the long table from the hacker, in the back conference room. They didn't really have interrogation facilities here to speak of. Net Force hunted and found a lot of criminals, but didn't normally do much in the way of actually arresting them. The way it usually worked was they'd track down a guy scamming the net and call in the regular FBI or, when it worked out that local laws were better, the local cops, to bust the perps.

Still, they were good at improvising. The back conference room was a designated safe area. If somebody dangerous somehow slipped into the building, some guy waving a gun up and blasting his way down the halls, you could come in here and deadbolt the door against him. The door was steel, and the walls had sheets of Lexan in them that would stop most small arms' fire. It would do just fine for interrogating a white-collar crook like Newman.

"But— I'm not a *terrorist!* I'm a *computer programmer!*"

"Not according to the law," Toni said. "You unleashed a

series of debilitating viruses upon the Internet and the web, causing millions of dollars in downtime damage. It was an attack upon America, upon the world, clearly a terrorist act, and as such, qualifies you just fine under the statutes."

"That's absurd!"

Toni gave him a toothy smile. "A man who calls himself 'Thumper' needs to watch very carefully for predators. You are a rabbit in among the wolves, Mr. Newman. What you are is *lunch*."

"I'll sue you!"

Toni let an edge creep into her voice. "What, you mean if we let you ever see daylight again? Listen, pal, I can ship you to a cell so deep it'll take until noon Friday for Monday morning's sunshine to *get* to you. By the time you come up for trial, and I think I can guarantee a military tribunal, open-and-shut and you get to go right back to your hole, you'll look like Rip van Winkle's clone. All alone. No contact with anybody, and no computer to play with, just you and four walls. Ten, fifteen years. That's if they don't decide to *execute* you."

Not true, of course, almost none of it, but this guy didn't know it. And right now, Toni's job was to gather as much information from him as she could, not be his best friend or act as his attorney or his civil-rights activist.

"You—you can't do that!" Thumper said. "It—it's not *fair!*"

Toni gave him the big-cat-about-to-feed grin again. "Welcome to the real world, Mr. Virtual Reality. The clock is running. If I don't hear what I want to hear starting in the next sixty seconds, I'll have that big, mean, nasty guy with all the guns who arrested you take you for a walk to our basement elevator."

She let him think about that for a moment, not saying anything.

Thumper sighed and sagged back in his chair. "What do you want?"

Toni looked at him. "I want to know why you did this."

"I was *paid!* I got hired by a guy to do it. It wasn't my idea!"

"And his name?"

"I—I don't know his name."

Toni stood up and made a point of looking at her watch.

"No, it's true, I *swear!* He called me, I met him at an office, we did everything face-to-face. He paid me in cash. I never got his name."

"Where is this office?"

"At a mall on Long Island."

Toni shoved a small flatscreen across the table. "Key in the particulars. Name of the mall, where it is."

He took the flatscreen.

"I want a description of the man who hired you. Height, weight, hair, eyes, everything you can remember. And when we're finished I'll send a technician down to work with you on an Identi-kit to come up with a picture of this guy."

Thumper nodded, already typing.

"Are you supposed to see him again?"

"Yes, yes, for another payment, as soon as he sees evidence of the virus's effects."

"How do you make contact?"

"I have a secure phone, no visual, signal scrambled coming and going. He calls me."

"Where is this phone?"

"Your people took it from me."

"You use a vox-changer when you talk?"

"Yes."

She nodded. "Good. Maybe you won't have to turn into a cave fish after all, Mr. Newman."

Toni went to the door, already planning the next step. She would have Jay put out a press release that the hacker's next virus was out there doing damage. When the guy paying this clown called, they'd set up a meeting, nail him, and that would be that. This was no sweat, no problem.

25

Dallas was like a whole bunch of other places in the southern U.S.—hot and humid in the summer, and very uncomfortable if you didn't have air-conditioning. It was ninety-five degrees out there today, with ninety-one percent relative humidity. As bad as back home.

Well, Junior figured, it didn't matter. He'd be in and out of here in a day or so.

He'd rented a house for a month via the net, a college area near the U of T, out in Arlington, about halfway between Dallas and Fort Worth, using a legit credit card he had under a phony name and post office box. He'd had to cough up a thousand bucks extra, a guaranteed "cleaning" fee, and he sure wasn't going to get that back. Between the rent, the extra fee, the airplane tickets, and the rental car, this would end up costing him five thousand and change, but that was part of the cost of doing business. You had to spend money to make money, and you had to spend whatever it took to cover yourself.

As he drove from DFW airport to Arlington—he had to take the International Parkway to I-30, jig west, and then south on State Road 360—he replayed the shoot-out with the security guard in his mind. It had been much better than the cop. The way he figured it, he could have waited for the county mounties to show and killed them all.

He was invincible.

Joan wouldn't be that kind of rush. There wasn't going to be any challenge, no real risk. She was a skinny little thing.

He already knew that he wasn't going to shoot her. There wasn't any need to do that. He'd give her a couple of drinks, maybe find some enjoyable way to tire her out, then, once she was asleep, he would put a pillow over her face and she would just wake up dead. Clean, no blood, and he'd be careful not leave any of his DNA around.

Once he had everything cleaned up, scrubbing every place he touched, vacuuming, taking the bag with him, he was out of there, and Joan was no longer a problem. It would be a month before the rental agent came around looking for more money. He'd leave the air conditioner going full-blast, maybe even put Joan's body in the tub and dump a few bags of ice over her. She wouldn't start to stink for a while, and God knew college flops didn't smell like rose gardens anyhow. It would be at least a week or two before she got ripe enough so any of the neighbors would likely complain about the smell. All he needed was one day.

In college towns, Junior knew, people came and went all hours, hopped on a bicycle or scooter or in their cars, and nobody paid any attention to them. Turnover was high in such neighborhoods, kids flunking out or transferring or graduating, so it was hard to keep track of who was living where. He had a cowboy hat and a pair of pointy-toed boots and Levi's cut for them, a big ole silver belt buckle, and aviator shades. He even had a fake moustache. He

looked like any other Texan. What they'd see would be
the clothes, and if he was a little older than most students,
big deal. He wasn't planning on interacting with the neighbors.

Come tomorrow, he'd be long gone. And when the cops
eventually came round and discovered the body of a
woman who had a record for prostitution busts in at least
four states Junior knew about—Texas, Louisiana, Mississippi, and Florida—they would hardly call out the Texas
Rangers in full battle gear to hunt down her killer. A
hooker dead halfway between Dallas, with hundreds of
whores to go around, and Fort Worth with almost as
many? The cops would figure she'd come in from one of
the big cities and had pissed somebody off.

They'd probably figure it for a professional hit once they
got to poking around the real estate rental office and hit
walls trying to trace the renter, but even so, figuring out
motive and who could have done it was a long way past
that.

The odds were good that they'd just drop it at that point,
leaving the case open but not putting any serious effort
into closing it. And if they didn't? Well, he'd been careful.
There was absolutely nothing linking him to that house,
nothing to give them even a hint of a trail to follow.

He may be invincible, but he was also very, very careful.

He found the house, made a pass by, and checked out
the situation. He wouldn't be back here until well after
dark—he was picking Joan up at the airport at seven,
they'd stop and get something to eat on the way, grab a
bottle of bourbon, she liked to drink Southern Comfort, he
knew—so it'd be nine, maybe ten P.M. before they got
back.

It was too bad, 'cause he really liked her. She was useful
for his game, and she was great in bed, too, but this was
business. Ames was right. There were plenty of other fish
in the sea who didn't know squat about Junior. Better to

swim with them and make sure this one went belly up and quiet. Dead women tell no tales.

Net Force HQ
Quantico, Virginia

"You wanted to see me?" Toni asked, standing in his doorway.

Alex grinned. "Always," he said.

Toni smiled back. He loved that, making her smile.

He could see she was carrying a manila folder under her arm. He nodded toward it. "What's that?" he asked.

Toni shrugged. "My report on that hacker, Thumper, who released the latest viruses. I've sent a copy to Jay, of course, but I thought you might like to see it, too."

Alex nodded. "Thanks, hon," he said. "I'll look it over first chance I get. First, though, there's something we need to talk about."

Toni came over and sat down in a chair on the other side of his desk. "What is it?"

Alex spun his flatscreen to face her. On the screen was a photo and brief dossier of Corinna Skye.

"Her," Alex said, nodding toward the screen. "She's a lobbyist for CyberNation, and she's been working me pretty hard."

He gave her a moment to read through the short file. When she was done, she shifted her eyes to look at him, and he saw there was steel in those eyes.

"Working you how?" she asked. Her voice was soft, but carried an edge.

Michaels shrugged. "Nothing specific," he said. "She's come by the office a couple of times to make some points and deliver some information. She even called the house the other day."

"When you were working out in the garage?"

He nodded.

"Guru told me someone called. She didn't say who, though."

"She called again earlier today," Alex said. "She said she had a meeting with Mitchell Ames and has some interesting information to pass on to me. She wants to meet me at her hotel at seven tonight for a drink."

Toni's eyes flicked to the flatscreen and then back to him. "And?"

"And I have a bad feeling about this."

"What has she done?" Toni asked, her voice still soft and low, but still with that edge of steel.

"Nothing. Nothing specific, anyway. It's just that she's been a bit too . . . suggestive, I guess. But between her innuendos and the timing with this CyberNation suit, I just have this feeling that I'm being set up. And I don't want to take any chances."

"So you're not going to meet her?" Toni asked.

Alex shook his head. "I have to meet her. But I want you to come with me. If Guru won't mind watching Little Alex for a while longer, that is."

Toni smiled at that. "I'll call her right now," she said. "And I'll be ready to go by six."

She rose to leave, but paused in the doorway and turned back to face him. "And by the way," she said. "I love you. And thanks."

And then she was gone.

Alex just sat there for a moment, enjoying the warm feeling she had left behind, and then he picked up the manila folder holding her report on the hacker.

In spite of himself, he couldn't help feeling that one more virus-strewing hacker was not Net Force's biggest problem. CyberNation and their lawsuit, their bribing a Supreme Court judge's clerk, their devious ways to get their agenda across, that was a problem. This was nothing.

They had caught the guy. End of worry about him.

He looked at the folder. Best he read it, though, and be ready to tell Toni what a good job she had done.

It didn't take long. It *was* good work, both on Jay's and Toni's parts, even though they didn't have quite all of it. According to what she had written, there was still this man behind the scenes, supposedly, but that would be a simple enough sting: Wait until he called, set up a meeting, go and collect him.

As Michaels read the description of the suspected king-pin, he thought the man sounded familiar somehow. Like somebody he knew.

He couldn't pin it down. Ah, well. It would probably come to him in the middle of the night. Besides, a lot of people looked alike. Sometimes when the anchor described a criminal suspect on the evening news, it was all he could do to keep from laughing out loud. *"Police describe the suspect as a white male, age twenty-five to thirty-five, five-foot-nine to six-feet-two inches tall, one hundred and sixty to two hundred pounds, with brown hair worn moderately long. He was last seen wearing a T-shirt, shorts, and running shoes."*

That could be any of a million people in any big city on any given day. Maybe one of two million. Who did they hope to collect with such a description?

Well, he didn't need to worry about it now. He had to talk to the secretarial staff and the ops who were going to be amassing paperwork for that shark Mitchell Ames on behalf of CyberNation.

Just what he needed.

Arlington, Texas

As they came out of the Indian restaurant, Junior said, "I spotted a liquor store down the road a piece. You want to get a fifth of Southern Comfort to take to the house?"

"Sure, why not?" Joan said.

She wore a disguise to match Junior's, just like he'd told her to—cowboy boots under a long blue denim skirt, and a shirt with mother-of-pearl buttons under a white cowgirl hat.

Even so, the clerk in the restaurant had looked at him like he was some kind of pervert, since Joan did look young enough to be Junior's daughter.

"So tell me more about this gig," she said, after they had collected the bottle and gotten back into the rental car.

He shrugged. "It's just like the last couple," he said. "This one is a fat, rich Texas oilman who got into politics. You'll be working as a temp secretary in his office, romance will blossom, we'll set up a photo shoot at a motel, the usual."

"My fee?"

"Same as last time."

She was silent for a moment, only the deep drone of the car's AC to break the quiet.

"What?"

"I was thinking, maybe I need a raise."

A cold wind seemed to blow across the back of his neck. That wasn't like Joan. "Why?" he asked. "You're making good money for not much work."

"Well, I heard on the news about that guy out in California. The Democrat? Turned up dead in a park a couple days ago?"

He managed not to react to that. Ames had been right after all. "What's that got to do with you getting more money, *cher*?" he asked.

"Come on, Junior, do I have 'Stupid' tattooed on my forehead? We caught him with his pants down. You went and had a talk with him, he flipped out, and you capped him. At least that's how I figured it, unless it is just one huge monster coincidence, which I don't believe it was."

He made a show of thinking about it. After a moment he said, "I don't know what you're talking about, but okay, maybe I could come up with a little bonus."

She smiled at him, a big, happy grin. "How much?"

"What you think is fair?"

"Ten thousand. Since people are getting dead and all."

"No way. I maybe could go three thousand."

"Eight."

"Five."

"Seventy-five hundred."

Junior pretended to consider it. It didn't matter how much he agreed to, she wasn't going to get any of it anyhow, but he had to make it look good. If he'd just rolled over and agreed to the ten, she'd have been suspicious.

He sighed and shook his head. "All right. Seventy-five hundred."

She reached over and laid her hand on his thigh. "Always a pleasure doing business with you, hon."

26

Jay breathed in, and the scuba tank strapped on his back fed him air with a cold, metallic taste. The regulator clicked and he exhaled, bubbles of carbon dioxide hemisphering and heading for the ocean's surface, thirty feet straight up.

Ahead of him, a gray green moray eel peered from within a small opening in a reef of dying coral. The eel was as big around and as long as Jay's arm. One beady eye watched him above needle-sharp teeth. It didn't seem disposed to venture out, though, and Jay flippered past him a good fifteen feet away, staying wary. He had a speargun, one of those air-powered jobs with a trident point, but he'd just as soon not waste one of his two shots on the moray. There were more dangerous predators lurking in the warm Hawaiian seas.

There was a little water in the bottom of his face mask, not enough to worry about clearing, and the glass itself was unfogged. Jay had learned the trick of spitting into the face mask and rubbing it around with his fingertips to keep it from misting up. Worked pretty well, too.

He cruised along slowly, waving his legs, driving himself along with the stiff rubber flippers, only using his hands to hold the speargun. The water was warm enough that he didn't need a wet suit. He wore regular bathing trunks, a diver's knife strapped to his right calf. It had a long, thick, stainless steel serrated blade with a black rubbery handle. He wore a watch with a depth gauge, an extra spear for his gun Velcroed underneath the barrel, and, around his waist, a webbed nylon belt strung with lead weights. As he used up the compressed air in the tank, he would start to get more buoyant, and the weights would help compensate for that.

The water was a clear, gorgeous blue, visibility easily a hundred feet, and all manner of tropical fish schooled back and forth in his panoramic view. The sunlight dappled the bottom, shifting with the currents, and the clean sand was only forty-five, fifty feet from the surface here, but sloping away deeper as he moved seaward. The fish were bright with all the colors of the rainbow, from minnows shorter than his little finger, to angelfish, platys, and groupers as big as his leg.

Jay wasn't looking for fish, though. He was after a different kind of prey.

Ahead, just barely visible in the distance and under an overhang of coral, was the wreck of the pirate cabin cruiser *Elise Matilda*, a mid-twentieth-century vessel that had made herself infamous by attacking tourist boats in the islands during the late 1950s and early 1960s. Manned by a gang of cutthroat Australians and a couple of New Zealand Maoris, the *Elise Matilda* was a seventy-foot diesel craft that had, for two years, managed to avoid the authorities while its crew boarded and robbed more than a dozen vessels in the warm waters, collecting, it was estimated, more than four million dollars in cash and jewels. Late in the summer of 1961, during a storm that blew in unexpectedly, the U.S. Coast Guard had spotted the *Elise Matilda*, fresh from an attack on a tourist steamer that had been running for shelter to escape the storm. The winds were already above gale force, the rain slashing down and turning the world gray, when the cutter gave chase. As the cutter drew near, she was fired upon by a .30-caliber machine gun mounted on the cabin cruiser's aft deck.

This was a tactical error on the part of the pirates, because the Coast Guard gunner was a crack shot. From a thousand yards, he hit the pirate vessel with his first round from their five-inch gun, holing the hull. His second round blew away the *Elise Matilda*'s steering wheel and most of the man holding it. Without any control, the cruiser turned broadside to the wind and was rolled hull-up by a big wave.

The *Elise Matilda* began to sink quickly. Some of her crew might have made it off, but it was dark, and nobody on the cutter spotted them in the choppy waters if they did.

The pirate ship remained afloat in the heaving seas no more than five minutes after the shelling, then she went down. The cutter stayed for as long as they could before heading for port.

As it turned out, the Coast Guard cutter stayed too long hunting for survivors. They didn't make it all the way back. Under the storm's pounding, the vessel lost power, foundered, and began to sink. By some miraculous luck, the sinking happened close enough to land that most of the crew made it back ashore, despite the huge surf. The location of the pirate vessel's sinking had, however, been lost. None of the survivors seemed to be able to remember, in the dark and foul weather, exactly where they had been, and the ship's navigator and the commander were two of the six men who had gone down with the cutter.

However, Jay "Sherlock" Gridley had managed to find

a survivor of the cutter, and with peerless investigative techniques had gotten enough of the old man's memory working to determine where the pirate ship had gone down.

Jay grinned at himself. Hunting for sunken treasure might be a bit florid as a metaphor, but it worked for him, and when it came to virtual sleuthing, he was the only person he had to please.

On board the sunken ship, aside from the bones the fish and crabs didn't get, was a treasure chest of money and jewels. The chest represented the hidden bank account belonging to the Supreme Court justice's clerk. Once Jay located it for certain and determined its worth, the clerk was going to be cooked.

If it contained as much money as Jay suspected, there was no way the man could have earned that much honestly. His family didn't have any money to speak of, he'd gone to school on scholarships, and he was going to have some tall explaining to do. And the way they'd do it would be via the IRS. Unpaid taxes had brought more than one criminal low.

Jay grinned into his mouthpiece and moved toward the wreck.

He caught movement from the left.

A shark, bearing right at him. Great white, a good thirty feet long.

Now there was a firewall metaphor. All he needed now was the theme music from *Jaws*.

He swung the speargun around and pointed it at the shark. . . .

Arlington, Texas

Junior lay naked on the bed next to Joan. She was wearing a long T-shirt with a picture of Albert Einstein on the front.

She was asleep, on her back, the shirt reaching only a little way down her thighs.

It had gone pretty much as he had expected it to go. They had gotten back to the house and had a few drinks, talking about old times, and also discussing the fake "plan" a little more. After a little while they had gotten undressed and gone to bed. When they were finished, Joan took a quick shower, came back in the T-shirt, and dozed off.

Once she was asleep, Junior's next move was clear: Grab the pillow, lean on her face with it, bye-bye, Joanie, *au revoir*, sorry it had to be this way, kiddo.

But: He couldn't do it. Not yet, anyway. He had curled up next to her, intending only to let her breathing deepen and even out, letting him know she was sound asleep. He didn't want her waking up too soon. He knew from experience how strong she could be.

The thing was, he fell asleep himself, lying there all relaxed and cozy and thinking warm thoughts about the woman he was about to kill.

He woke up around six A.M. cursing himself for a fool.

He couldn't delay any longer. Joan would be waking up soon, and he would have lost his chance to do this the easy way—and for her sake he wanted it to be easy.

Picking up his pillow, he moved to straddle her. He planned to sit on her hips so she couldn't move, lean into the pillow, and just do it. Couple, three minutes, she'd be choked out, and once she stopped struggling, he'd hold the pillow there another five minutes to be sure.

But as he swung his knee up and over Joan's hips, she woke up. Her eyes went wide as she saw the pillow, and she must have somehow realized what he was doing. Before he could get set, she screamed like a fire truck siren and kneed him in his exposed crotch.

The pain made him want to puke it was so hot and sudden. He couldn't even *breathe* it hurt so bad.

Joan scrambled and slid out from under him before he

could catch her. She fell off the bed, hit the floor hard, but was up in a second.

He started after her, slowed by the blinding pain. Before he could do more than scoot toward the edge of the bed, however, she grabbed the bedside table lamp and smashed him over the head with it.

Pieces of the ceramic lamp base shattered all over him.

Junior's vision flashed red, then filled with sparkling stars.

Stunned, he fell back. He wasn't out, he didn't dare lose it that way, she'd probably kill him if he did.

His guns were under the mattress. He lunged for them, but Joan picked up the television set, a little portable on the chest at the foot of the bed, and threw it at him.

The TV came at him in slow motion, and Junior swung one arm to try and block it. He didn't have any choice, he had to bat it aside or it would bash his head in. He connected with it all right, but his arm was bent, and his elbow hit the glass. The screen *popped!* and spewed glass everywhere.

He felt a shard slice open his arm above the elbow, and worse, his elbow was caught in the busted TV.

While he was prying his bleeding elbow out of the TV and cutting himself more, Joan vanished. He finally jumped up, blood slinging all over the place, and lurched after her. Before he cleared the bedroom, though, he heard the front door open, and the screen door slam shut behind her. He ran, started outside, then realized he was naked.

It pulled him up short. A naked, bleeding man running after a half-naked woman? That would draw attention in any neighborhood, even this one. He could not have somebody calling the cops before he shut Joan's mouth for good.

He ran back for his pants. He could take a few more seconds. She wouldn't get far on foot.

He sprinted into the bedroom.

His jeans were gone.

Joan must have grabbed them on the way out.

He cursed, then grabbed a hand towel and wrapped it around his bleeding arm. He took another one from the floor and pulled it around his waist. Then he ran for the front door.

The rental car was gone, too.

He stood there. The keys had been in his jeans' pocket. So had his wallet, with most of his ID and cash, plus a couple of bogus credit cards. She was dressed, at least partially, in a T-shirt, and she had his pants. He was bleeding like a stuck pig wrapped in nothing but a towel. He couldn't go out like this.

Oh, man. He was well and truly up the creek now. What was he going to do? He had to find her!

But, how?

The Roosevelt Hotel
Washington, D.C.

There had been a few hotels in the area named after the two U.S. Presidents who'd worn the name "Roosevelt." This one was new—actually, it was an old hotel that had been called something else and refurbished a couple years back, and as a result it had the old elegance, but with clean new furnishings.

Toni and Alex arrived and went to the bar. He didn't see Cory Skye, but they weren't there twenty seconds before a tall and skinny bellhop appeared and approached them. "Are you Commander Michaels?"

"Yes?"

"Ms. Skye begs your pardon, but she has to pack and leave earlier than she expected. She asks if you would meet her in her room."

Alex glanced at Toni. The bellhop hadn't seemed to notice her, or at least hadn't been bothered that she was there.

"She's in three-sixteen," the bellhop said.

Alex turned to Toni. "What do you think?"

"I think your suspicions were right," she said.

Alex nodded. "Let's go home," he said.

Toni frowned. "What? Why? I mean, seriously, Alex, how does this change anything?"

Alex glanced at the bellhop, who was still standing there, apparently waiting for a tip. "Would you please convey my regrets to Ms. Skye," he asked. "Tell her I was called away on an emergency, and ask her to call me when she gets back into town."

The bellhop, who was maybe twenty or so, said, "Are you sure about that, sir? I, uh, got the impression the lady was really looking forward to seeing you."

"I'm sure." Alex pulled a twenty from his wallet and handed it to the bellhop.

"Yes, sir. Have a nice night."

Alex turned back to Toni. "I've been thinking about what Tommy Bender says about this guy, Mitchell Ames. The thing is, hon, he deals in suggestion and innuendo every bit as much as he deals in facts. With you along, I had no problem meeting her in a bar. No one, not even this shark, could twist that into anything that could be used against us."

"I know, Alex," Toni said. "That's why I came along. What I don't understand is how it's different now."

"Because it's not a bar anymore. It's her room. Can you imagine him putting her on the stand and asking her, 'I understand, Ms. Skye, that Alex Michaels, the commander of Net Force, came to your hotel room.' Can you see what that would plant in the jury's mind?"

"But we'd have the chance to set it straight," Toni said.

"Yes, but by then it would be too late. Tommy wouldn't

have the right to protest the question, so he wouldn't have a chance to clear things up until he got to cross-examination, and by then the idea would have sat in the jury's heads for too long. It's kind of like the judge instructing them to ignore something they've heard. They can't do it. You can't unhear something, and you can't forget something just because the judge tells you to."

"Suggestion and innuendo," Toni said.

"Exactly. If I had come alone, nothing would have happened. You know that. But for him to say that we met for a drink would have been enough. It would have damaged me in the eyes of the jury, made it easier for them to believe the other things he'll say about us. Going to her room, even with both of us there, does the same thing."

She nodded. "You're right," she said.

Alex sighed, suddenly feeling very tired of all the political maneuverings. "Let's go home," he said.

27

Long Meadow Pond, Connecticut

Ames was tooling along in his new chocolate-colored Mercedes, pushing it a little. He was doing seventy-five and was still a dozen miles or so south of Waterbury on I-84, on his way north.

He was driving up from the city for an estate sale in Wolcott, just north of Waterbury. A rich old lady he had met a couple of times, Marsha Weston, had recently passed away, leaving a medium-sized fortune and some outstanding antiques. She had owned a grandfather clock brought over from Europe a couple hundred years ago that he thought would go perfectly in his entry hallway, and he didn't expect there would be anybody showing up for the sale who could outbid him for it. The Westons were old money, though the younger ones had gone into computers and had a fair amount of stock in several of the larger hardware companies. It was his hope that they didn't have any interest in Granny's moldy old furniture. But he figured if they had, the clock would never have been put up for sale.

Thinking of computers, he remembered he was going to call his pet hacker today to make arrangements for another payment.

Ames reached into the center console and removed one of the four throwaway cell phones he had there. He used a memory trick he'd learned in med school to bring the hacker's number to mind, thumbed it in as he passed a refrigerated tractor trailer hauling frozen fish sticks, and waited for the connection.

"Thumper," came the deep voice.

He shook his head. The hacker used a voice-altering device on his calls, a precaution that Ames thought was a waste of time. They never said anything that would identify either of them, and the cell phone Ames was using was never going to be used again. Surely the hacker wasn't stupid enough to use his own phone for this kind of thing?

"I see our project has continued successfully," Ames said.

"That's the idea," Thumper said.

"Indeed. If it is convenient, meet me at the usual place tomorrow, one P.M. for remuneration."

"I think I can make it," Thumper said.

Ames smiled. Of course he could make it. The man spent ninety percent of his time parked in front of a computer, he had no other life. Walking to the kitchen for another Twinkie was probably the most exercise he ever got.

Ames thumbed the disconnect button on the cheap phone and tossed it onto the passenger seat. He would take it out at his next stop and stamp it under his heel, distribute the smashed parts into a couple of trash bins at different locations, and that would be that.

He frowned and gripped the wheel tighter. He was a little irritated that he hadn't heard from Junior yet. The man was supposed to have dealt with that loose end and called him. So far, however, Junior hadn't made contact.

He sighed, then, and made an effort to relax. Junior would call eventually. In the meantime, Ames would get himself a nice antique clock, and enjoy a leisurely drive to his place in the country for lunch before heading back to the city.

Everything was going along as it was supposed to be going.

Net Force HQ
Quantico, Virginia

Toni smiled at the phone that belonged to the hacker who called himself "Thumper."

"Gotcha," she said.

Jay Gridley, passing by her office door, paused. "Huh? What did I do?"

She shook her head. "Not you. Thumper's boss just called."

"Ah."

"Thumper is going to meet him tomorrow at one—at least that's what he thinks. We'll bag him then."

"Are you going to have the local cops grab him?"

"Yes," Toni said. "No point in stepping on anybody's toes if we don't have to. Besides, some businessman on Long Island is hardly a case for the Net Force troops."

Jay nodded. "It'll be interesting to find out why he was doing it. I'm thinking maybe he's making money on se-curityware or something. The Net gets attacked and people buy more of his product. Find a need and fill it. If there isn't a need, make one."

Toni nodded, too. She would have Liaison call the regular FBI, who should call in the local cops—she wasn't sure who the police agencies in charge on Long Island were—and that would be that. Once they picked the guy up, she'd zip up, maybe take the train, interview the man, and her part would be done. Another strike for Truth and Justice.

Atlanta, Georgia

Junior had broken down and gone to an ER at a hospital fifty miles away from the rental house in college town. Three of the worst cuts on his arm needed sewing, and when the doctor was done there were forty-seven stitches on the outside, plus a bunch of the dissolving ones that would itch like crazy later on the inside. He told the doc, who looked like he was about sixteen, more or less the truth—he'd put his elbow through a TV screen, though he told the guy it was an accident, of course. Young as he looked, the doc had heard stranger stuff.

With the bandages and all, his arm was hardly inconspicuous, so he bought a cheap sport coat and hid the dressings. Nobody remembered a guy in a bad jacket, but a guy whose arm looked like it belonged on the Mummy might stick in a few heads.

But his arm was the least of his worries. Somewhere out there, Joan was on the run. If she used his credit cards or her own to buy tickets, he'd be able to trace her. The problem was, she was smart enough to know that. In fact, she knew most of the ways he had to trace her, and she'd be avoiding all of them. So the question was, where was she going to go?

Junior had a good memory. Somewhere along the line, a year or two back, Joan had let it slip that she had a sister, her only living relative, who lived in Atlanta. The sister, she'd said, worked as a bartender in some biker bar on the outskirts of town. Joan had been pretty plastered when she told him, so chances were probably good she didn't remember she had told him.

When a woman like Joan wanted to hide, she'd go where she had friends or family. As far as Junior knew, she didn't have any friends. She sure wasn't going back to Biloxi, because she'd know that's the first place he'd check. And he didn't think she would go to the cops—at least not yet. He knew Joan, and he knew that her first thought would be to see if she could get something out of the deal.

She knew Junior had tried to take her out, no way around that, and that was bad. She'd be on her guard constantly, knowing that if he tried to kill her once, he'd do it again. But she also knew that he had to have had a pretty good reason to try and kill her, and that made her valuable.

Joan was smart, but she was also greedy. She'd see this as a chance to squeeze some serious cash out of him, and that was his only hope right now.

Someone other than Joan would likely flee across the country, maybe to Canada, change her name, and lay low. But not Joan. Not when she saw an opportunity like this. And that bought him a little time, but not much. He had to get to her before she started setting things up so she would be covered. Once she told some people, maybe put a file somewhere with a lawyer in case she accidentally got run over crossing the street, that would be the game.

So, he had to find her fast. And the sister was the place to start.

He didn't know her name or where she worked. He figured, though, that there weren't that many biker bars with women bartenders, and even fewer where the bartenders looked like Joan. He was also pretty sure he would recognize her if he saw her. Once he had her, if she had any idea where Joan was, he would get that out of her.

It wasn't much, but it was what he had.

By now, Ames would be sweating bullets wondering

what was going on, but it wasn't a good idea to bring him up to speed just yet. Not until Junior had something good to tell him. He would wait. Ames being angry at him for not calling was a lot better than how he'd react if he found out Joan was loose and knowing Junior had tried to kill her.

He did have one other advantage. White guys hung together in prison, and he'd gotten to know a few bikers when he was in Angola. A couple of them ran around Atlanta, so they'd know the bars. He'd give them a call. You didn't want to walk into a biker bar without some friendly faces around.

He'd find the sister, somehow. And then he'd find Joan and finish the job.

Washington, D.C.

Michaels was in the kitchen looking for something fatty to eat after his workout when the phone rang. He picked it up, and a man asked for Mrs. DeBeers. He started to tell the caller that he had the wrong number, but then remembered that Mrs. DeBeers was Guru's real name. They never called her anything but "Guru," which meant "Teacher."

"Hold on a second," he said.

Guru was in the living room, telling a story to Little Alex.

"—and then the Garuda *snatched* up the little monkey and flew him away from the tigers!"

Little Alex laughed, certainly one of the most delightful sounds on Earth, and said, "Again, Guru, again!"

He hated to break in. "Guru, telephone for you."

The old lady nodded and went into the kitchen to take the call.

Michaels squatted down and picked up his son, twirled

him around, and got him to laugh again. After his daughter had been born, he had thought he would never feel that kind of love again. When he and Megan had fallen apart and gotten divorced, the time he could spend with Susie became much too short. She was almost a teenager now. But Little Alex was another joy, and Michaels was, he thought, a better father now than he had been when he'd been on the upward career track. At least he hoped so.

Guru came back into the living room.

"Everything okay?"

"My great-grandson in Arizona is sick," she said. "Gone to hospital with pneumonia. My grandson and his wife are worried. The doctors tell them the boy will be okay, but they are worried. I think maybe I need to go and be with them."

"Yes, of course," Michaels said.

"I can take *laki-laki* with me," she said, nodding at Alex. *Laki-laki* meant "little man." Michaels nodded. "You could," Alex said, appreciating her offer, "but you need to be able to concentrate on your grandson."

That he would even consider allowing an eighty-five-year-old woman to take his young son on a plane across the country might seem strange to anybody who didn't know them, but Toni trusted Guru with any of their lives. She was as much the baby's great-granny as any of their blood kin, and she was here with him every day. She knew the boy as well as he or Toni did, and Little Alex loved her. And even at her age, she was a formidable nanny. She could still knock most men down before they had a clue she was dangerous.

She nodded. "That might be best, if you are sure."

Guru took her responsibilities very seriously, so Michaels nodded. "You have more than one family," he said.

"Yes. I will make preparations."

"Toni will be home in a little while," he said. "And she can call our travel agent and set things up."

Guru nodded gravely.

After she had gone to her room, taking Little Alex with her, Michaels wondered what it must feel like to be as old as she was and still bear the responsibility for all the generations of her family. And that a grandson had called his grandmother about his child when he was ill, probably knowing she would hop on a plane and come out there. Did they think she could somehow fix the boy, with some old-country magic?

He shook his head. Probably not. But it was amazing that they would call her, and that she would pick up and go, just like that.

Toni was going to have to take some time off from work to watch the baboo. He paused, then. No, he thought. Maybe *he* could take a couple days off and stay home with Little Alex.

He thought about the pending lawsuit and Corinna Skye. He thought about the meetings on the Hill, and the thousands of other time wasters and frustrations that were all a part of running Net Force—or any government agency.

He thought about all that, and then he thought again about that latest job offer he'd looked at the other day.

Yeah, maybe he should take a couple of days off. He'd think about it some more and talk with Toni about it when she got home.

All at once it seemed like he had a lot of thinking to do.

28

Ames had made his rounds at the hospital and then headed over to his law office. His staff there had things under control. The clock he had bought at the estate sale was being delivered today. The sun was shining, and it was a hot one, but the air conditioner kept the car's interior most comfortable. He'd had an early and great lunch.

All in all, he was feeling pretty good as he tooled the Mercedes through the thick traffic toward his safe office for the meeting with the hacker.

Then he saw the two men sitting in the unmarked car parked on the street in front of the little strip mall. They wore suits and sunglasses, sat inside a car in the hot summer sun. Cops. They had to be.

Ames didn't slow. He just drove on past. Half a block up the street he saw a second unmarked car, and his belly twisted.

Maybe they hadn't set up surveillance on the mall offices to catch him. It was possible they were looking for

somebody else, but when you were engaged in illegal activities, it paid to be paranoid.

That he was supposed to be meeting Thumper here in a
few minutes and that there were at least four men watching
the place? That was worth worrying about.

He frowned, assessing the situation with the same speed
and efficiency with which he would size up a new case.

He'd have to abandon that office. That was clear to him,
but it wasn't that big a deal. One of the reasons he had
selected it, however, was that there were no security cameras installed in the building, at least not in any of the
common areas. They were going to do that eventually, they
had told him, but he would have left to find another safe
office before that happened.

Inconvenient, but at least there was nothing to connect
him to that office. He had rented it under a phony name,
and each time before he departed the office he wiped all
surfaces that might have collected his fingerprints. Even
the furniture had been bought via a dummy corporation
that ended in a cul-de-sac. He was clear.

But what had tipped the cops? Thumper must have
screwed up and gotten himself caught. And naturally, he
would have given his employer up.

He turned off the AC, feeling a sudden chill. Even
though the hacker couldn't do anything to him, Ames realized that he himself had been less than careful. He had
gotten complacent. Once upon a time, he would have sent
his man ahead to check the place out. He had done that
the first few times he'd met people there. After a while,
though, it had seemed a waste of effort so he had stopped.

If he had gone into the building, into the office, they
would have had him. Not that they could have convicted
him of anything, there wouldn't be anything but
Thumper's word against his, but even to be taken in and
questioned? Scary, that thought. At the least, he would
have been marked as a person of interest, which would

have made things much more difficult for him.

He sighed. He had gotten lucky this time, but he refused to rely on luck. He would simply have to move with extreme caution regarding such things from now on.

He turned at the next intersection. He would go home for a few hours, run over things in his mind until he was sure he had considered everything.

Commander's Bar and Grill
Atlanta, Georgia

Junior waved at the waitress, a woman of forty with most of her bare arms and bikini-topped upper body covered with tattoos. He caught her attention, made a horizontal circle with his finger, and pointed it at his table.

The waitress, who carried a tray with eight bottles of beer on it, nodded back at him.

Junior was buying. So far, he'd bought four rounds, and he was willing to keep 'em coming all night, if that's what it took.

He only knew one of the three men at the table with him. Buck was a former Gypsy Joker who'd gotten into some trouble over a saddlebag full of crystal meth and wound up doing four-to-six at Angola when Junior had been there. Buck was big, mean, stupid, and he liked to fight.

One day in the showers, Buck had let himself get a little overmatched, going up against four black guys without any help nearby. The biker had been giving a fair account of himself, but the other guys were big and mean, too, and it was just a matter of time before they nailed Buck. That was when Junior stepped in and helped out. Buck was the kind of guy who remembered a thing like that, so when

Junior called him, he was happy to do this little thing for him.

The smoke was so thick in here you could bounce quarters off of it, and the copy of "Born to Be Wild" playing on the jukebox must be about worn out, since somebody played it every third song.

The other two guys at the table with him were friends of Buck's, Dawg and Spawn.

Dawg said, "So what was it you want her for again?"

Junior, who had put some thought into a story so as not to get in trouble with somebody who might be involved with Joan's sister or something, said, "Not her; I'm looking for her sister. She stole my car, my watch, my credit cards, and split."

It was always better to put some truth in whatever you passed around. If it got to it, that much would pan out, plus you didn't have to remember which lie you had told.

Spawn, a bodybuilder obviously on steroids, shrugged shoulders that looked like split cannonballs under his sleeveless denim jacket. "Big deal. That's worth chasin' her from Texas?"

Junior caught Spawn's gaze and put a little macho into it. "No," he said. "But she ran over my Soft Tail when she left. Knocked it into the street and it got totaled by a UPS van. Twenty-six thousand dollars worth of upgrades on it, including a handmade, eighteen-coat, hand-rubbed candy-apple red Space Cadet gas tank with psychedelic green flames."

"Oh, man," Dawg said. "That sucks."

Even Spawn had to shake his head at that.

Junior nodded. The way to a biker's heart was to talk about somebody damaging your scoot. Hurt worse than a kick in the balls to think about a restored bike getting wrecked any way except the rider dying with it.

"Let me see the picture," Dawg said.

Junior produced the picture, one he'd cropped from a vid on one of the blackmail shoots.

He looked, but shook his head. "Ain't seen her."

He passed the photo to Spawn, who squinted at it through his cigarette smoke. "You know, she looks a little like Darla, at the Peach Pit."

Dawg took the picture back. "Yeah, now that you mention it, she does, kinda."

"Well, I could go check it out," Junior said.

"Better take some company," Spawn said. "That's Gray Ghostrider's turf. We have a truce with them, but they don't much cotton to strangers."

Junior looked at the three men. "Think you might be interested in keepin' me company a while longer?"

"Long as you're buyin', that'll be no problem at all," Buck said. He grinned.

Washington, D.C.

Gunny had come up with the pistol, just as he'd said, and Howard had collected it to bring home to Tyrone. He thought his son would be pleased—he really seemed to be enjoying practice.

When Howard knocked on his son's door, Tyrone yelled, "Come in!"

The boy sat in front of his computer, staring at the holographic projection. The image was of a tall rectangular building, angled slightly, with what looked like a huge, orange-neon tiger on it, frozen in mid-leap. It took a second for Howard to realize what it was.

"Hey, Dad."

"Hi, Son. What are you working on?"

"Homework. English. Maybe taking a summer class was not such a good idea. This chomps." He looked at his father and smiled. "Hey, maybe you can help. You know about dinosaurs, right? Didn't you grow up riding one?"

"Sure. Fifty miles to school and back every day. In the snow. Uphill, both ways."

"That's what I figured. Check this out."

He touched a button and the tiger dimmed and faded and was overlaid by a block of text.

Howard moved to where he could see it. It was a poem called "Dinosaurs," but it clearly wasn't about fossils or lizards. There was the writer's name under it, but it wasn't one he recognized.

Howard nodded. "Yeah. So?"

"So, what does it *mean?* I'm supposed to analyze it, but I don't have a clue what it's about."

Howard reread the poem. He nodded. "You can't figure it out?"

"C'mon, Dad, you don't know."

"Sure I do."

Tyrone gave him a baleful stare. "You want to enlighten me?"

"Easy clue," Howard said. "Go back and look at the picture."

Tyrone waved his hand and wiggled a finger, and the words and the building swapped brightness.

"What you are looking at is the back of a drive-in theater screen," Howard said.

Tyrone frowned. "A what?"

Howard said, "There are probably still a few of them around. They were mostly gone before my time, products of the late forties and early fifties. Your grandfather and grandmother used to go as teenagers. They were outdoor theaters. You'd drive your car to them at night. You had to pay to get past a gate, then park facing the screen. The ground had little ridges that let you angle your view. Movies would be projected onto the giant screen, and you'd sit in your car with a speaker on a wire to hear the sound. It

STATE OF WAR 265

was a cheap date, and couples could, um . . . cuddle inside their cars without bothering anybody."

"Cuddle?"

"An old person's term," Howard said.

Tyrone grinned real big.

Howard said, "People used to live inside some of the buildings, like this one. See that window on the side, right there? Usually the people that owned or managed them."

"No kidding?"

"Nope. Your gramma took me to one when I was a little boy, when they were living down in Florida. I still remember it. If you didn't want to sit in your car, there were benches next to the snack bar where you could sit outside and watch the show. They were only open in the late spring, summer, and early fall. After it got cold, they shut them down for the season, even in Florida. They were huge places, took up a lot of real estate. I think television mostly killed them off."

"Huh."

Tyrone looked at the poem again. "So, okay, it's a theater. But what's all this about toothpick vampires and Kools and Pik and stuff?"

Howard cast his memory way back, trying to recall the experience. He had stayed with his grandparents one summer when they'd still lived in Florida. He had been young, six, seven, and they had gone to the drive-in five or six times. And maybe a time or two when he'd been in California, as a teenager.

"Well, the vampires would be mosquitoes. Kools were a brand of cigarette—that's what the older kids used to do, sneak off from their parents and smoke—and Pik? I think that was a coil of bug repellent you burned, kind of an incense, that kept the mosquitoes away."

Tyrone nodded. He tapped something into his keyboard. A sub-image lit, a crawl of words. "Oh, okay, here we go—'The Merry Go Round Broke Down.' That's the name of the music they play on the Merrie Melody cartoons!"

"Really?"

Tyrone was getting into it now. "I guess this part had to do with sucking face in the cars," he said.

Howard smiled. The boy was fifteen. They'd had the birds and bees talk a long time ago. Though he couldn't imagine having this kind of poem to deconstruct when he'd been in school, things changed.

"And this part is easy. I got it, Dad."

"Yeah?"

"Well, I understand what the writer was talking about. He's wishing they still had outdoor movies, right?"

Howard said, "Well, English was never my best class, but I think he's talking about more than that. What I think is that he's looking back on his innocence. That's what he's wishing he had—the good old days when his life was mostly in front of him and not behind him. The drive-ins were just a part of it, they represent something larger than just themselves."

"You really think so?"

"Yeah. And that youth is wasted on the young. You don't miss it until you are too old to do anything about it."

"Huh. You think that's true?"

"How would I know? I'm still a young man myself. Ask Gramma next time you see her."

They both laughed.

Tyrone said, "This idiot teacher does this all the time. Gives us stuff to analyze that doesn't have anything to do with our lives. Why couldn't he give us a poem we could understand based on our own experience?"

"Because then you wouldn't have to stretch," Howard said. "If you only work from inside your own comfort level, if you don't have to sweat a little, you don't learn anything new. Maybe he's not such an idiot."

"I'll reserve judgment on that."

"Oh, I almost forgot. Gunny found something for you."

He handed Tyrone the box. And was rewarded with a very large grin as the boy opened it.

Maybe all youth is not wasted on the young, he thought. Maybe the old folks benefit from it a little now and then. . . .

29

Michaels scanned some files on his flatscreen as he walked down the hall on his way to grab a quick lunch. There was a time when he would have changed into spandex and a T-shirt and taken his recumbent trike to a local Chinese or Thai restaurant and burned off a few calories in the process. But not today. The weather forecasters were predicting temperatures near body heat, and humidity almost as high. On a day like that, the air-conditioned cafeteria didn't sound so bad. Besides, the trike was at home for Toni to use, if she wanted.

And the food was usually pretty good.

He saw John Howard just ahead, also heading toward the cafeteria.

"John," Michaels called.

"Commander." Howard slowed for him to catch up.

"You see the new EHPA/HEL from DARPA?"

Howard shook his head. "No, can't say as I have."

Michaels passed his flatscreen over. "Check it out."

EHPA stood for Exoskeletons for Human Performance Augmentation; HEL the Human Engineering Laboratory, at UC Berkeley; and DARPA was for the Defense Advanced Reasearch Projects Agency, which was funding the beast. The project had been around for ten or twelve years, and was finally to the stage where they had a full-strength product they thought worth field-testing.

Howard looked at the screen. It showed a soldier in chocolate-chip camo outfitted in the experimental exoskeleton. He was holding a barbell loaded with plates over his head in a military press.

Michaels hadn't had time to do more than scan the article, but already knew quite a bit about the project. The basic unit was a blend of tightly wound carbon fiber, spider silk, and lightweight metals, securely strapped to the soldier's limbs. The suit had articulated aircraft-aluminum and titanium joints at the shoulders, elbows, wrists, hands, waist, hips, knees, and ankles. It came with special boots and metal half "gloves," too.

A series of hydraulic pistons attached to the geared joints were dual-powered. The bulk of the work was done by Nanomuscle's revolutionary memory-metal actuators, like those found in cars and boats. These memory-metal "muscles" were backed by several standard electric motors clamped to the frame. Everything was run by a small backpack tank of hydrogen and a fuel cell, and operation was coordinated by an onboard computer chip with a built-in failsafe.

With sensors that picked up normal muscle movements, developed originally by medical technicians for artificial limbs for amputees, the exoskeleton would greatly augment a man's abilities. A trooper who could bench press two hundred pounds without the suit could push five hundred with it. Any movement that the frame could handle was likewise augmented. One moment, a man could be standing at ease; the next, he could squat and lift a car's rear end clear off the road, with the suit doing most of the work. They weren't good for running faster, but using one you could climb longer, work harder, and even lock it so you could stand unmoving for hours. It would even let you sleep standing up.

The exoskeleton could make a small woman stronger than any man. A man would be almost as strong as a gorilla.

"We can get one for testing, if you want to try it out," Michaels said. "The National Guard has six available, and I have the clout to snag us one."

The general grinned, teeth flashing white against his dark skin. "That would be interesting. Not to mention it would be nice to have something to surprise Lieutenant Fernandez with for a change." He passed the flatscreen back to Michaels.

"I'll put in a requisition," Alex said.

"Thank you, Commander."

Michaels nodded. "Toni wanted me to tell you she's still working on your gun grips," he said, changing the subject.

Toni, who did scrimshaw, had decided to do a set of faux-ivory stocks for Howard's sidearm, the Net Force logo on one side, and, unbeknownst to him, a portrait of his wife on the other panel.

"She doesn't need to do that," Howard said.

"She wants to. She'll have a little time to play with them, since she's going to be home for a few days."

"Trouble?"

They reached the cafeteria, collected trays and flatware, and stood in the food line.

"Not for us," Michaels said. "Guru's great-grandson is sick, Phoenix or somewhere, and she's gone to visit him."

"Nothing serious, I hope?"

"Pneumonia, and she says the doctors aren't too worried. Anyway, we're without a sitter until she gets back."

"You looking for one? A baby-sitter?"

Michaels arrived in front of the fried chicken. He took two pieces, then added a third. "You have somebody in mind?"

"Well, my son Tyrone could use some work. He missed out on a regular job because he had a class he wanted to do this summer. He's on the fast track to graduate early. I'm pretty sure he wouldn't mind baby-sitting Alex. He's been doing that kind of thing for the last year or so, mostly neighbors, and little Hoo—Lieutenant Fernandez's son."

"Really?"

"Sure. Only the Good Lord knows why, but he likes kids. If Toni wanted to work half-days or something, I imagine he'd be up for it. He has some new computer gear he wants to buy, and I told him I'd go half but that he had to earn the rest."

Howard passed on the fried chicken, selecting a hamburger steak for himself.

"Well, that would be helpful. Let me ask Toni."

30

Junior sat at the table with the three bikers, Buck, Dawg, and Spawn. Seemed like half the businesses in Georgia had the word "peach" in their names.

Even armed as he was with two guns, Junior wouldn't have wanted to be in here alone. At the very best, he'd only get twelve shots off before the remaining gang members stomped him. The basic biker code that the Hell's Angels had come up with a long time ago was simple: One on all, all on one. Most other clubs took that one for their own. If you looked funny at one rider, you were looking funny at the whole club.

He might shoot six, eight, ten of them, but then they'd get him. And that was assuming none of them pulled their own pieces when the first round cooked off, which would be a stupid assumption. He'd bet dollars to pennies that every one of the people in that bar—men and women both—was carrying something lethal.

As long as he had an honor guard, though, he was probably okay.

The Peach Pit was like a dozen other biker bars Junior had been in: loud music, a lot of smoke—a mix of tobacco and marijuana—and worn-out dancers and waitresses. There was the usual mix among the riders, too: Little weasely looking ones, and others the size of small countries; young, old, fat, buffed, long hair, skinheads, bald; all wearing their colors. They sat at tables or the bar, played pool or the old-style pinball machines, and drank beer by the bottle or pitcher. The big image on their jackets, their colors, was a skeleton wearing a Confederate uniform with a cap, one hand up, giving the world a bony finger. "Gray Ghostriders" was written over that, and "MC" underneath the rebel skeleton.

The women here were hard-looking, sporting a lot of blond and red dyed hair, with purple and blue eye shadow. Most of them wore tank tops and jeans, no bras, and there were enough tattoos on the bikers and old ladies visible to make a mural that would practically cover the whole outside wall. There was a row of bikes parked out front that together probably cost as much as a fleet of Cadillacs. You might not have the rent, your old lady could be in jail and you couldn't make bail, but you didn't cheap out when it came to your scoot. A man had his priorities, and in the biker's world, it was his ride.

Darla, who might or might not be Joan's sister, wasn't in yet, but her shift was supposed to begin in half an hour.

Junior figured God owed him one on this whole deal, and if Darla showed up, Junior was willing to call it even.

He was starting on his third beer when Darla came in, through the back door, because he didn't see her until she was at the bar.

And glory be, right behind her was *Joan!*

God had paid off, in spades. About *time* something went his way.

Now the next part might be a little tricky, since Darla was known to the local bikers and Junior wasn't. He wanted to ease into this, get close enough to Joan to grab her and run before any ruckus.

But before he could even think about the best way to go about it, Joan looked right at him. He saw her see him.

A cold feeling washed over him.

Joan leaned over and said something to her sister—and there was no doubt about Darla being related, they looked like two peas in a pod—who nodded. Then in a voice that could shatter glass and must have carried five hundred yards, Darla *screamed*:

"Yankee MC!"

Everybody stopped what they were doing and looked. Darla was pointing her finger right at him.

Junior didn't know the name, but he wasn't slow. Being a member of the Yankee Motorcycle Club was definitely *not* the thing to be in this bar. It could be fatal.

Any idea he had of talking his way out of it went away when Buck, his buddy, looked at him and said, "Junior? You ride with the Yankees?"

"No way," Junior said. "She's lying!"

But the time for talk was done. Junior jumped up and ran. He angled for the bar, and as he gathered speed, he reached for his guns. He had maybe a second before the bikers came to life, and he'd have to stretch that to get clear.

He pulled his revolvers and started blasting as soon as the barrels were clear of the holsters. It didn't matter what he shot, he just wanted to make a lot of noise in a hurry, get people scrambling for cover. When guns start going of in a bar, any bar, people hit the floor. They might reach for their own guns, but only after they made sure the first shots didn't hit them and they could get a fix on the shooter.

He swung his right hand up and pointed it at where

Darla and Joan had been, hoping maybe to tap Joan on the way out, but they had already moved, and he didn't see them.

Then the back door was there in his face. Junior twisted and hit it sideways, shoulder leading. It popped open. He went through, realized he was clicking on empty with both revolvers, and churned his feet for all he was worth. The rental car was to the side, fifty yards away, and if he could get to it and crank it before the riders raised their heads and then boiled out of the bar, he'd be okay. They'd be looking for a man on a hog; serious bikers didn't ride in rental cars. Maybe they wouldn't even notice him, but if they did, he'd be reloading first thing he got rolling.

It was a lot easier to shoot out of a moving car than it was from a two-wheeler, especially those with long rakes on the front forks: You needed both hands on the handle-bars until the scooter got going enough to steady it. He couldn't outrun them in the rental, but he could drop a couple, maybe three bikers in the road. The rest would have to slow to get around them.

And with any luck, enough of them would be paranoid enough so that they'd worry that this whole deal was a trap. After all, they had to know that no Yankee MC biker would be stupid enough to go into enemy territory alone. They'd have to think—once they had time to think at all— that he'd have a posse waiting out there to waylay anybody chasing him. Bikers didn't mind fighting, they'd do it at the drop of a hat, knock each other's teeth out just for fun, but they didn't like to be suckered. They liked things on their own terms.

Junior got to the rental car, which he'd left unlocked, jumped in, and shoved the key into the ignition. As soon as the engine was running, he rammed it into gear and peeled out. He thumbed open the cylinder on his right-hand gun, tapped the ejector hard with the butt of his other gun, and spewed empties all over the seat. He dropped the second gun, pulled a speed-loader from his pocket, shoved it into the cylinder, twisted the release, dropped the loader, and snapped the cylinder closed. He rolled the window down and fired two rounds at the bar's front door as he passed it, reached the street, and floored the accelerator.

He was half a block away before he saw anybody in the parking lot. By then, he had reloaded his left-hand gun. Out on the road, he had a chance, even if they came after him. They'd have to come from right behind him and he was good enough that he could pick them off if they got too close.

He shook his head. Well, this was royally messed up. Now Joan knew he was after her, and after he had gotten this close, she'd really go to ground. This was bad. This was a disaster.

The mirror stayed clear after a mile, and Junior decided that maybe the Gray Ghostriders weren't that interested in running him down. Of course, Buck, Dawg, and Spawn were going to have some explaining to do, and even if the bar crowd bought it, and probably they would, that wouldn't do Junior any good. Junior was in deep trouble now, no matter what.

Washington, D.C.

Toni said, "Here is his diaper bag, in case you want to go for a walk or something. The stroller is on the front porch, and he can walk for a couple of blocks okay, but then he'll get tired and want to ride or be carried."

"Yes, ma'am," Tyrone said. He was a polite young man. His mother had dropped him off and would be coming back to pick him up later. Toni liked Nadine Howard; she seemed a down-to-earth person, and a great mom, too, if Tyrone was any indication.

"He likes peanut butter and jelly sandwiches, but he'll eat tater tots, ham and cheese, or fish sticks. In the fridge and freezer." She waved in the direction of the kitchen.

"Yes, ma'am."

"He can have two peppermint candies if he eats his lunch. He'll try to get you to give him more." *And he usually manages to finagle his mama out of three, sometimes four.*

"Yes, ma'am."

"He might want a bottle of milk if he gets sleepy. Sometimes he takes a nap after an outing. That's okay, to give him a bottle."

Tyrone smiled.

"Here is my office number, and here is the number for my virgil. If you have any problems, anything at all, call me."

"Yes, ma'am," Tyrone said. "I'm sure we'll be fine."

Toni was a little amused at herself for being worried, but worried she was. *C'mon, girl, John Howard's son can certainly keep a two-year-old in check for a few hours.*

When it came time to leave, Toni was afraid that Little Alex might get teary-eyed and clingy, but he was busy stacking Lego blocks with Tyrone. "Bye, sweet boy. Mama has to go to work for a little while."

"Bye, bye, Mama," he said. He glanced up, then back down at his toy construction. "Ook, I-rone, ook!" He waved at the toys excitedly. He still had trouble with his "l"s, "g"s, and "t"s sometimes. He called her mother "Ammaw," which everybody thought was incredibly cute.

It bugged her, just a little, that he seemed so blasé about her leaving. Not that she really wanted him to cry and be upset . . . Well, okay, maybe she did a little.

So much for being indispensable.

She fretted in the car, but she knew in the long run it was for the best. The boy needed to get used to being with other people. He was shy around strangers, although it had taken all of forty seconds for him to warm up to Tyrone, a factor much in Tyrone's favor. She didn't want him to turn into a little recluse who never went out into the daylight.

Halfway to the office, she shifted into work mode. She'd been disappointed that the man who had hired the virus-spewing hacker hadn't shown up for the arranged meeting. Could be it was just a coincidence, but he hadn't called back, and Toni's thought was that the man had somehow spotted the trap. Which, when she thought about it, probably wasn't that hard to do. When they wanted to, the regular FBI could become invisible—they knew sub rosa surveillance techniques as well as anybody. But they probably wouldn't have been in full-stealth mode for this kind of arrest. A businessman, in a mall office, in Long Island? How worried about him seeing them would they be? Not to mention what the local cops might have done.

The background check on the office renter had come up negative. The references had been fake, the rent paid via no-trace electronic transfers. The guy had been hiding something, all right, and smart enough not to leave an obvious trail.

Well. She would get Jay to poke around it some more. Maybe he could find a lead. Not that it was a major attack on the Republic or anything, but it was her case now, and she wanted to clear it successfully.

She had gotten a call from Guru earlier in the morning. Her great-grandson, who had apparently taken a turn for the worse just before she had arrived, was apparently doing better. Another few days and he would be out of the hospital. Guru would come home, then, which was good because Toni missed the old woman. Both Alex and the baby did, too, though Big Alex would never admit it.

The sun was broiling the city, and it was going to be another hot day, but all in all, Toni couldn't complain. She had a wonderful husband, a gorgeous and bright little boy, and a job that allowed her to stretch now and then. Her *silat* teacher, who had been a part of Toni's life since she was thirteen, would be coming back to occupy the spare bedroom in a few days, to be nanny and live-in great-granny to her child. Everybody was healthy. Life could be a lot worse.

She had a lot to be thankful for. A whole lot.

31

Ames sat in his inner office at the clinic, brooding.

Something was wrong. Junior had not called, and Ames's attempts to contact him had failed. Junior had never kept Ames out of the loop before.

And then there was that little incident at the clean office, with the cops staking it out. Could there be a connection?

Probably not, he decided. Most likely it was just what he'd thought: The hacker had gotten busted and tried to bargain his way out of trouble. It might not have even been him on the phone the day before the meeting. With that vox-changer Thumper used, it could have been anybody. It could have been some cop. The only thing Thumper had to give to them was the location of that office, nothing else, so that's what he would have given them.

He couldn't see how Junior could be connected to that. He certainly didn't think Junior had been arrested. Junior was smarter than the hacker, at least when it came to street work. If he had been picked up, he'd sit tight, get word to Ames he'd been arrested, and wait for Ames to send a lawyer and money to bail him out.

There were all kinds of ways Ames could do that without leaving a trail, and Junior would know that he would do whatever he could to get Junior freed. Having Junior in police custody was not advantageous to Ames. Dead, yes. In jail, no. Once he was out, he could always jump bail, take off, and not look back, if he thought it was going to go badly for him later. And no doubt he'd expect a nice piece of change from Ames to run with, if he needed it.

So, Junior wasn't in jail. Where was he, then, and why hadn't he checked in?

He sighed. It could be a lot of other things, some innocent, some not so innocent. Junior could have gotten into an auto accident, been hit by a drunk driver out in Small Town, Mississippi, or somewhere, and be on life support in the local hospital, full of IVs and catheters, EEG flatlined, in an irreversible coma. Simple as that.

Or the accident, if there was one, could have been worse, and maybe he was wearing a toe tag in the county morgue and they were trying to run down relatives using his phony ID. Or waiting for the fingerprints to come back from the police, which would put a whole different spin on who the victim had been.

It was also possible that Junior could have changed his mind and decided that his little woman was worth the risk that she might turn him in. He might have decided to run off to Mexico with her rather than kill her. Right now, the two of them could be on the beach in some snazzy resort, drinking tequila, licking salt off each other's hands, and cooking up ways to make Ames pay for it from now on.

He didn't really think Junior was that sentimental, but people had made stranger choices.

Or maybe Junior had decided to go ahead with his plan,

but had screwed up and been killed by the woman instead. Unlikely, maybe, but possible.

Or he could have run a red light, gotten pulled over by the cops, found to be a felon in possession of a firearm, and now be lying on a dank mattress in a small town lock-up somewhere where they decided he didn't rate a phone call—or the phone wasn't working.

Ames could easily conjure up a dozen more scenarios, most of them bad for him. Without any hard information, he could speculate for the rest of the day and it would all be meaningless.

The facts were, Junior had told Ames he was going to get rid of the woman, and he hadn't called to say it was accomplished. He had supposedly gone off to do it, and enough time had passed that the job should have been finished.

Whatever the deal was, Junior had not called. That was what Ames knew.

He leaned back in his chair, steepled his fingers, and ran through it again. He could see other possibilities, but the essence was unchanged.

So, what did it mean? More importantly, what could he do about it?

For that matter, did he really have to do anything about it at all? Yes, having Junior out of touch was inconvenient. There were still a few jobs he needed done. But having Junior in custody, or on the run, didn't hold any real danger for himself.

After all, Junior was the shooter. *He* was the guy who had killed a United States congressman, and certainly *not* on Ames's orders. If Junior was ever tied to that killing, there was no way he would be able to bargain his way out of it. He might be able to deal himself a life sentence instead of the death penalty if he gave up Ames. Without proof, however, it would be his word against that of a well-respected attorney. And there was no proof, nothing concrete to tie Junior to Ames.

Absolutely nothing.

And if Junior could be believed, there was nothing to connect him to that murder, either. Unless he was involved in some other bad business Ames didn't know about, the biggest risk to Junior was that woman, and Junior was supposedly in the process of getting rid of her.

The only other risk that Ames could see was if any of the politicians Junior and that woman had up came forward, which wasn't that likely. The one who had been ready to talk was dead, and Ames had to figure he was a rare beast to risk it. Politicians who are screwing around are not the bravest of men.

So he didn't believe Junior was in trouble with the law. And even if he was, Ames wasn't too worried about it. But he was worried about the silence.

Junior should have reported in by now, even if he'd failed his assignment. If he wasn't in jail, it must be one of the other myriad possibilities. But, which one?

And how could he find out?

Atlanta, Georgia

The motorcycle that finally caught up to Junior didn't belong to one of the Gray Ghostriders. No, this one had flashing lights and a siren on it, and a city cop in the saddle, waving for Junior to pull the rental car over.

Wasn't *that* just great?

Junior found a residential side street off the main road and turned, pulled the car to a stop three houses in, and put his emergency flashers on. He had a vague idea of where he was, but Atlanta was not his town. Somewhere fairly upscale.

The cop stopped his bike thirty feet behind him. He waited a minute or two, probably running the car's plates, then got off and strolled up to the car.

Junior already had the window down, and the cool air inside was quickly sucked out into the hot, damp night.

"Evenin'," the cop said in that honey-voiced Georgia drawl. "Can I see your license and registration, please?"

Junior had his latest fake license, this one from Alabama, already in hand, along with the rental car's contract, and he offered them to the cop. "What's the problem, officer? What'd I do?" He could be polite, too.

"You changed lanes back there without signaling."

Junior blinked. Was this guy serious?

"I'm sorry about that, officer," he said. "I thought I hit the blinker. I must have not pushed it down hard enough." That's what a citizen would do, try to talk his way out of it. Not that Junior cared about the ticket. He wasn't going to be around when the ticket came due. But he didn't want to make the cop suspicious by acting out of character.

The cop nodded absently, looking at the Alabama license.

"Wait right there," the cop said. He walked back to his bike to do a radio and computer check.

The license wouldn't come back on him, because he hadn't done anything with it in Georgia, and the rental agreement at the car company matched the license, if they had any way of checking it. There was no way they would be hooked into a net that would let them access the Alabama Department of Transportation or whatever that fast, and even if they *could*, the fake was supposed to be good enough to come up no-want, no-warrant, and a legit name and number.

He'd take the ticket, smile, and be on about his business.

The cop came back in a minute, and sure enough, he had a ticket book his hand, Junior's fake license clipped to it.

But when the cop got there, he said, "You're not carrying anything illegal in that car, are you, sir? No guns or explosives?"

"Me? No. Why would you say that?"

The cop said, "Can't be too careful these days. You, uh, of Middle Eastern descent, Mr., uh, Green?"

Junior was insulted. "Do I look Arabic to you?"

"Well, sir, yes, you do a little."

Junior almost blurted out that he was a Cajun, but that wouldn't have been smart, since he was supposed to be a redneck named "Green" from Tuscaloosa, Alabama.

"Well, I'm not. I'm as American as you, pal."

"I wasn't trying to insult you, sir."

"Yeah, well, you did. Just write the goddamned ticket and let me get on about my business, would you?"

That was a mistake. He knew it the second it left his mouth. It rubbed the cop the wrong way. Never tell a cop what to do, especially if you have the slightest whiff of ex-con on you.

"Step out of the car, sir."

"What?"

"I said, 'Step out of the car.' "

That was bad. Junior was wearing the fishing vest over his T-shirt. If the guy patted him down, and he was definitely going to do that, he'd find Junior's guns. Even though they'd be clean—a new barrel in the left one and a whole new one on the right since he'd shot anybody— well, except if he hit anybody at the bar. But even so, it would be an automatic trip to jail, and once they got his prints and started poking around, they'd realize pretty quick that Junior was not named "Green," and who he really was. Felon, firearms, fake ID. That would be bad all the way around.

"Okay, okay, don't get riled, I'm sorry. I'm getting out right now."

The cop had his hand on his pistol, but it was still holstered, so Junior kept his hands raised and away from his body as he carefully and slowly stepped out onto the warm macadam.

The cop got a better look at him and nodded. "Assume the position," he said. "You look like a man who knows it."

"You got me wrong, officer. By the way, how's your sister?"

The cop had time to frown, and when he saw Junior move, he pulled his piece, but Junior had the beat and he was faster. The guy was five feet away, he couldn't miss.

Twice in the face—*pap! pap!*—and the cop went down.

Lights went on inside the houses closest to them, and people started opening window shades and doors. It was a pretty good neighborhood, they probably didn't hear a lot of shooting around here. Some of them had probably noticed the bike's flashing lights when it had first pulled in.

Go, Junior, now!

He jumped back into the car and floored it.

As he drove away, he kept shaking his head. How much worse could things get?

32

Jay was bugged. He'd spent several hours ripping apart his code for that superhero scenario he'd written, the one that he'd used to locate the inflow of CyberNation money into the country, and he just couldn't find anything wrong with it. Which was what he'd expected, of course, except that he still couldn't explain that weird patch of fog he'd run into, and Jay didn't like things he couldn't explain—especially not in code he'd written himself.

The problem was, he was almost out of options. The only other thing he could think of to try, now that his software had checked out, was replacing some of his hardware. He kept duplicates of most items on hand—he couldn't very well tell Alex Michaels that some bad guy had gotten away because his DVD drive had broken down. He also tried to keep up with upgrades in the industry, both because it was his job and because it was his passion, and usually ordered new models as soon as he heard about them. With some companies, ones he'd worked with for years and had a lot of confidence in, he had standing orders to ship at least one unit of everything they made.

And there were a few companies he helped out by serving as a beta tester, getting a chance to try out some items before they were even ready to hit the general market.

It always helped to stay ahead of the game, especially in this business.

He'd gotten a new reeker in the other day, an Intelli-sense 5400 olfactory presence generator, guaranteed accurate to within 500 PPM, and he wanted to try it out. This seemed as good a time—and as good a reason—as any.

He opened the box. The new reeker was a little slimmer than the one he had, a brushed-aluminum finish with tiny air intakes and little nozzles where the chem was mixed to make smells.

He smiled as he looked at it, all shiny and modern and new. His best guess was that almost all this hardware would be gone within five years, replaced by direct stimulation of the brain through induction. In the meantime, however, you used what was available.

Jay moved back to his computer, removed the old one from his VR rig, and plugged the new one in. Pulling on his gear, he toggled his hardware-room scenario.

Instantly, he was in a huge space, dimly illuminated by hundreds of readouts—old analog dials, LED projections, backlit LCDs, and various screens. Over in the corner, under a large blue-neon nose-shaped icon, a red light was flashing. A computerized voice sounded an alert.

"Warning. New hardware detected. Initializing virus hardware check. Warning. New hardware detected—"

Jay snapped his finger and the voice went silent. A few seconds later, the drivers for the new reeker loaded, and he was ready to calibrate.

A green light shone near the nose.

"Let's try some . . . *candy*," Jay called out.

A moment later he was in a old-fashioned candy store, filled with hundreds of huge glass jars of every kind of sweet, tooth-rotting treat imaginable. He went to a container of fat red-and-white-striped peppermints and lifted the lid. The distinct smell of mint blossomed as he inhaled. Ah. Nice.

He took a deeper breath and was pleased to note an increase in the odor's intensity.

Must have an airflow rate sensor.

He tried several other pleasant-smelling jars, noting each time that the scent was as close to the real thing as he could recall.

After five minutes or so he decided it was time to try some other olfactories.

"Outdoors, swamp," he said.

He stood in a swamp, looking out at cypress trees thick with Spanish moss. The trees weren't as well rendered as they could have been—he would have done better if he'd written the calibration proj—but he was here for the smells, not the visuals.

The air had just the right combination of suffocating murkiness he remembered from his one trip to a real swamp. Jay was pretty much a VR guy, not much RW, but a VR programmers' convention he'd attended in New Orleans back in the early days of VR had included a tour of the surrounding bayous as part of the "get it right, make it real," theme of VR work. He'd been bitten probably ten or twenty times by mosquitoes while he'd sniffed, touched, and looked around the swamp, and had contemplated briefly going into another less nature-based life of coding.

But no. VR was the way—using human senses to interpret digital data. It worked with what nature had given man and extended it. Jay had always wanted to be at the cutting edge of things, and VR was it. So he'd put on anti-itch cream and gone back to the convention, and every time since he'd taken whatever tour was available for wherever that year's meeting was.

He inhaled slightly and got a hint of woodsmoke. A thin breeze wafted against his face, and the smell intensified.

Nice. Good resolution on this hardware.

"Clear scenario, reload Pulp Hero."

The scene flickered for a second, and suddenly he was at the New Jersey docks again, dressed as he had been when he'd traced CyberNation's payment to the clerk when it had entered the U.S.

Let's see—he'd been over *there*. . . .

Jay moved across the rooftop, the cold wind blowing against him as he headed for the vantage point where he'd had the stinky fog glitch.

Got some soap for you, you dirty little glitch.

SOAP was an acronym one of his college professors had been fond of using. The man had repeated it so often it was just about the only thing Jay could recall about him. Old Doc Soap. The word's letters stood for the steps taken while troubleshooting: Subjective, Objective, Assessment, Plan. Jay had found out later that his teacher had borrowed the method from the health profession, where it was used to assess a patient's state of mind, but it served equally well in the tricky business of finding soft- and hardware bugs.

Subjective. What had happened? He'd been standing *here*, and a few tendrils of fog had drifted past. He'd reached out to touch them, and he'd been able to *feel* them, which wasn't supposed to happen. Then he'd smelled something that made him think of a sewer. Bad feel, bad smell, not supposed to be there.

Okay, so much for the subjective. Objective: He'd done a full check of drivers after the VR run and everything had been up to par. He'd also just finished checking out his own code and knew for sure that the problem wasn't his fault. The properties of the fog object had *not* been set to stink, at least not in that particular way.

Assessment time. It wasn't the drivers, it wasn't the software, but there had definitely been a problem. So try a new reeker, which rolled him right into Plan.

Here we go.

A thin tendril of fog rolled past, and as he had before, Jay reached out to touch it. This time there was no sensation other than a slight coolness on his fingers. The fog smelled a little like the ocean. Perfect.

So it had been the reeker after all. Another problem solved.

He snapped out of VR and disconnected his gear, and then decided that as long as he was working on his system, he might as well load another little item he'd gotten in the mail recently. This one was a small package sent to him by Cyrus Blackwell, a sensory artist and one of the best.

Cyrus took real-world scenery and collected it into VR: odors, tastes, visuals, feelies—everything. While it was true that Jay worked hard to get every detail right for his VR scenes, it helped sometimes to have the legwork done for him. He'd had Blackwell do a custom set of scans on a series of bank vaults for a robbery scenario he'd been planning.

Jay took the data cubes out of their media protectors and jacked them into the computer terminal he was using. He put his VR rig on again and went to a blank workspace.

This was supposed to be an analog for his next firewall breach, a huge bank that he was going to "rob."

He called up the directory, and large red letters appeared in front of him. He scrolled them up until he saw what he wanted.

Interiors.

An info blurb explained that the vaults and bank interiors were taken from several large metropolitan areas in both the U.S. and Europe. He reached forward and pulled out the VR thumbnails, tiny models that were slightly translucent so he could see inside of them.

There was one with gorgeous neoclassic columns on the exterior, and high-vaulted ceilings within. Jay threw it on the blank space in front of him and activated it. The tiny model grew rapidly in size, translucent walls giving way to RW textures, and Jay enjoyed the perceptual shift that made it seem as though *he* was getting smaller.

Suddenly he was inside of the bank. He could hear an air conditioner running, and there was a clean but not over-powering scent to the place. The ceilings were high, like something from a movie set, and a long row of teller cages stretched from one side of the large room to the other.

Perfect.

Jay scrolled through the building, working his way to the vault. There was a set of stairs leading down to an underground chamber with a barred door in front of it.

No—I want something bigger.

Jay brought up a list of individual items and scanned for vault doors. He popped out several that looked prom-ising before he found one that he liked. It was a huge circle, maybe a foot or two thick at the center, with huge gears that had to be thrown by a large wheel before it would operate. The door was shiny chrome steel, an ultra-modern crimestopper that had just the look he wanted.

He grafted it onto the opening in the bank cellar and saved the file. He had the basic form now; he would work on some of the functional elements later.

Michaels decided to skip lunch and hit the gym instead. He'd been indulging in snacks a little more than he should have lately. He had found that he tended to eat when he got tense, and had decided that being unhappy wasn't as bad in his mind as being *fat* and unhappy.

As he changed into a pair of baggy cotton shorts and a T-shirt, he thought about his morning. It wasn't as if the lawsuit was the only thing on his plate, but every time Michaels saw another cart stacked high with papers go by, it reminded him that it was a pretty big chunk of it.

He hadn't gotten into federal law enforcement to spend his time playing games with lawyers. It was a waste of time and energy, and he was finding it increasingly frustrating.

Back in the early G-men days, the bad guys had taken their lumps when they'd been caught, gone off to prison, and done their time. It would never have occurred to them to sue the cops who'd caught them doing wrong. Definitely a better class of criminal in the old days; guys who knew what they were.

He shut the locker door, spun the combination lock, and grabbed his towel. Toni was coming in at noon. John Howard's boy had been watching Alex half-days, and that seemed to be working out okay. Guru was supposed to be back soon—her great-grandson had gotten worse, then better, then worse again, and as of this morning was still in the hospital. Apparently the doctors were worried about some kind of secondary infection, maybe a virus. The worry was that it was one of those things that mice carried.

As he padded out onto the workout mats, Michaels wondered for the hundredth time if maybe it wasn't time to get out of this business. He had gone about as far as he could, he figured—farther than he'd ever expected, to be honest. He had, on a couple of occasions, even briefed the President himself—pretty high circles, admittedly, but his chances of moving any higher in the federal system were very slim. The director of the FBI was a political appointee, as was the CIA's head. NSA usually had a working agent or military officer running the show, but you had to come up through that system to get a shot at it. Alex Michaels didn't have any clout to offer anybody for putting him in charge of a bigger agency. And in truth, he really didn't want the headaches that came with that kind of job; this one was bad enough.

Besides, Alex had never worried much about promotions. He hadn't taken this job in the first place because of what he himself could get out of it. He had taken it because Steve Day asked him, and because he felt he could make a difference.

These days, watching the carts of paper go by, feeling the pressure from Mitchell Ames, he felt that all he was doing was marking time.

He began stretching, working his legs, watching himself in the mirror. There was a handful of people around the place exercising instead of eating, though most of them looked to be pretty fit.

Did he even want to stay in Washington? Yes, this was an important job, even if it didn't always seem like it, and somebody had to do it. And, he had to admit, he was pretty good at the job, but there was so much about the work that he didn't like. The politics. The groveling for appropriations. Things like this lawsuit, which called into question almost everything he had done during his entire term as commander.

Who needed it? All it did was stress him. When he'd been alone, he could deal with it all right. He was remarried now, though, with a young son, and there were things in life that seemed a lot more important than lying awake at night worrying about a lawsuit without merit.

He shook his head. He still couldn't understand how this lawsuit could have ever gotten this far. How in the world could anybody feel sorry for a murderous thug who'd been shooting at his men? How could that thug getting shot in return be worth a lawsuit, be worth all the cost and all the waste?

Probably some jury would give his widow ten million dollars. Where was the justice in that?

Alex could get other work. He knew that. He'd been offered good jobs, making more money and doing a lot less to earn it, in places where you could hear yourself think, too. Wouldn't it be nice to have a house in the country somewhere, trees, fresh air, a home for his son to grow up among normal people? Wouldn't it be great not to be at the mercy of congressional whim, to not have to sit in front of a committee while some bozo from Wide Patch, Ohio, who didn't have two IQ points to rub together, asked questions that a third grader should know the answers to?

Yeah, that sounded pretty good. Kind of like a dream.

Of course, he had to think about Toni, what she wanted. Was she ready to bail from the biz, go off to some rural spot, sit home and make cookies or spend her time at PTA meetings? She could work, too, of course, the net gave a lot of freedom in that way. She could probably even work at whatever company hired him, if she wanted. But he'd have to discuss it with her before he started gathering himself to jump, find out what she really felt like.

Toni had told him, during those times when things got really bad and he found himself complaining about work, that she would go wherever he wanted. All he had to do was point at a place and she'd go looking for a house. But that had been him just venting steam, and her saying what he needed to hear at that moment. Would she still feel that way if it was real?

He sat on the mat, stretched his legs out in front of him, and bent to grab his feet, working his hamstrings and calves. Maybe it *was* time to move on. He really needed to think about it.

33

Sitting in a decent motel just off I-95 on the north side of town, Junior stared at the audio-only throwaway cell phone and blew out a big sigh. Might as well get it over with.

He punched in the number, a one-time use that should connect to one of Ames's throwaway cells. Maybe he'd be lucky and Ames wouldn't answer—

"Where have you been?" Ames said, a hard edge in his voice.

"Busy," Junior shot back, instantly defensive. Yeah, okay, he should have called the man by now, and yeah, he had screwed it all up, but he did not like being talked to like he was some wet-behind-the-ears kid. Ames didn't know what had gone down. Junior had killed men with guns, straight up, face-to-face. He was a man to be reckoned with. He didn't have to take anything from any *lawyer*, even one he worked for.

"What happened?"

Junior took a deep breath, and went with his plan:

He lied.

"It's all done. It was a little trickier than I expected, which is why I couldn't call before, but I got rid of the old unit."

"Permanently?"

"Of course."

How would Ames know he wasn't telling the truth? And this gave him some time to think things through. Come up with a plan.

"Well, that's good."

"You need me to, uh, get a replacement model?"

"No, I don't think we'll be doing any more business in that particular arena. How far away are you?"

"Day or so."

"Head on back. Call when you get to town. We, uh, are relocating headquarters."

Junior frowned. Something must have spooked Ames if he'd dumped his safe office. Could it have anything to do with Joan?

Nah, he decided. It couldn't. She didn't know anything about who they worked for. Her only contact had been Junior. It must be something else.

Junior broke the connection, dropped onto the king-sized bed, and stared at the phone. Joan was out there, but she sure wasn't in Atlanta anymore, he'd bet his life on that. And even if she had stuck around, he couldn't. He needed to get back to his place, change out the barrel on his right-hand Ruger, and ditch the old one. It wasn't likely anybody was going to tie a dead Baltimore cop to one in Atlanta, but he wasn't going to take any chances. There were all kinds of guys in gray-bar hotels who had hung on to a favorite piece after they'd capped somebody with it.

No, he would go by his place and pull a new barrel out of the safe. He was running out of them. He'd have to get some new ones—but not for a while, not until enough time had passed that the feds wouldn't be checking *that*, too. It would be safer to buy a whole new gun and switch out the barrel with that. More expensive, and since he'd already had to replace one gun altogether, he was getting low on his preferred hardware. He only had a couple left, but when the alternative was maybe going to the gas chamber or a lie-down on the needle gurney, you didn't decide to go cheap all of a sudden.

He still didn't think Joan would be talking to the heat anytime soon. Oh, that would get her off on the prostitution and blackmail stuff, maybe even let her sell her story to the *National Enquirer* or something, but she had to know that as long as Junior was alive, she'd be in danger. And if she ratted him out, he had ways of getting to her, even from prison. She'd have to stay in hiding her whole life, and Joan wasn't that kind of girl. She liked to get out and party down. So he should be okay, even after what had happened in the bar. She'd still be trying to figure out a way to turn it into gold. Until she did—and figured out a way to contact him and cover herself while she did it— he ought to be okay on that score.

So, he was safe, for now. For a little while.

There wasn't anything he could do about it now, anyhow.

Net Force HQ
Quantico, Virginia

Toni stared at the documents that had been scanned into the computer, copies of the police and FBI field-agent reports on the unsuccessful surveillance of the office building on Long Island. They couldn't afford to keep men on the place, but they had gotten the building manager to watch. The man who'd rented the place had never come back.

Must have gotten spooked, Toni figured.

While she was looking at the projected images above her desk, one of the little LEO NewsAlerts flashed and ran across the bottom of the holoproj. An Atlanta policeman had been murdered during a traffic stop. Shot twice in the face by a man who had escaped in what turned out to be a rental car. The suspect was still at large.

Toni shook her head. Life in the big city. She wondered if the dead policeman had any family. A wife, children who would never know their father? So awful. As well-trained as she was as a fighter, she knew it didn't make you bulletproof. Some loon with a gun could take it all away in an instant.

She remembered Steve Day. And the times when both she and Alex had come close to being killed. They had a child now. They shouldn't be putting themselves in that situation anymore.

Something tugged at her memory. Something about the dead cop . . .

She read over the story again, but the details were sparse. Witnesses had heard the shots, seen a man jump in a car and drive off, but there was no good description of him. It had been dark, it had all happened so fast. . . .

Toni was about to move on to other things on her agenda when she noticed a reference to the caliber of the gun used on the dead cop. It had been a .22 Long Rifle, and the investigators suspected it had come from a short-barreled handgun.

Hmm. Hadn't there been another cop shot recently with a .22 somewhere not that far from here?

Her voxax circuit was open. Toni said, "Search: Shootings-slash-twenty-two-caliber-slash-time-frame-slash-two-weeks."

As the searchbot's screen popped up, she realized she

should have narrowed the parameters to include "police officers." Well, she'd see what came back, and narrow it if she needed to.

Apparently there had been more than two dozen such shootings in the country in the last fourteen days, including Arlo Wentworth, a United States Democratic congressman from California, and wasn't that another awful note? There had been three incidents on the east coast, and one of them was indeed what she'd remembered, a policeman in Baltimore. And here was an armed guard, in Dover. . . .

And somebody was also shot in a bar in Atlanta, same night as the cop down there had been.

Hmm.

Toni frowned. Surely if there had been any connection between the cops, the ballistics boys would have caught that.

Curious, Toni put in a call to the Net Force shooting range.

"Shooting range," came Gunny's voice.

"Sergeant, this is Toni Michaels."

"Yes, ma'am. What can I do for you?"

"Answer a couple of questions."

"Shoot. So to speak."

"I was looking at CopNet's LEO bulletins and saw that there have been some police shootings on the east coast recently."

"Yes, ma'am. Baltimore and Atlanta."

"You know about them."

"Yes, ma'am. I keep track of LEOs who are getting shot, and with what. Professional interest."

"My question is, how unusual is this?"

"Cops getting shot, or getting shot with mouse guns?"

"Both, I guess."

"Not many get killed in the line of duty each year, but some do. And .22 is the most common caliber for civilian firearms. Probably followed by 12-gauge or .410 bore shotguns, deer rifles, .38 Specials, .25 autos, like that. A .22 isn't a very good man-stopper, though, even out of a rifle, and these were all handgun shootings."

"How do you know that?"

"MEs can usually tell by penetration. A twenty-two solid point out of a rifle is moving two, three hundred feet a second faster than one coming out of a short-barreled handgun. From a long barrel they sometimes punch right on through."

"So you are saying these shootings are not that rare?"

"No, ma'am, I'm not exactly saying that. These particular shootings? They aren't normal. The Baltimore cop, a security guard in Delaware, a congressman out in California, and the Atlanta motorcycle patrolman? They were all shot in the head."

"Ah. And that is unusual?"

"Yes, ma'am. If you were going to shoot somebody with a .22, a head shot would be the way to go, and more than one round. If I'm not mistaken, all of these guys were hit at least twice. My guess? Same guy did them all."

Toni blinked, taking that in. "Really?"

"Yes, ma'am. I have a friend in ballistics over at the regular feeb-shop. The cop in Baltimore? He was hit twice by two different guns. According to the forensics wound-angle stuff, they are pretty sure the bullets hit him at about the same time, and from the same height and distance. That tells me you either got shooters standing side by side and aiming for the same spot, or one guy with two guns."

Toni nodded. "Go on. Please."

"Yes, ma'am. Ballistics on the congressman say both rounds in him came from the same gun, two head shots, from inside five feet—there were powder speckles on the car and dead guy. The security guy in Delaware caught a bunch of rounds, in the body and neck, only one in the head, but that's probably because the shooter started cooking and walked them up to be sure. Probably too far away to be certain of a head shot right off. All of those wounds were from the same gun."

"And the Atlanta cop?"

"Nothing in on him yet, but if the shooter was the same guy who opened up in a bar forty-five minutes earlier, and it looks like he was, he was using a snub-nosed revolver."

"There were witnesses?"

Gunny laughed. "A whole bar full of bikers, but none of them saw a thing. There was a security cam installed there. Atlanta PD is going over that recording with a microscope right now."

"So what do you think?"

"Well, the revolver fits with the other shootings. The guy didn't leave any used brass, for one thing, which implies it was a revolver. Of course, he could have hunted it up and collected it, if he'd been using a semiauto, but the two cops and the guard were done at night. Brass from a .22 flies a long way, and it would be very hard finding it all in the dark. At the Atlanta shooting, people looked out and saw a car pulling away right after the shots were fired. Not much chance of him stopping to hunt for expended shells. A revolver makes more sense."

"Hmm."

"Another thing. I think we're dealing with a sportsman here."

"Excuse me?"

"All the dead guys? They all had guns. And they had all cleared the decks when they got hit, all had hands on their weapons. I think we're talking about a hunter. He only shoots people who can shoot back. Most-dangerous-game kind of guy."

"Lord. Does the FBI think this?"

"I'd bet big money they've considered it, ma'am. They got some pretty swift folks over there."

"Thank you, Gunny."

After she hung up, Toni sat staring at the computer

screen. It wasn't her job to find the shooter or shooters who'd done this. But it did pique her interest. She knew some people over at the regular shop. Maybe she could get a copy of the tape showing the shooter?

It wouldn't hurt to look at it.

34

Jay was working at his desk when Toni stuck her head into his office.

"Hey, Jay. You got a minute?"

"Always," he said. "What's up?"

Toni stepped into the office. She held up a mini-disk in her right hand and showed it to him. "This. It's a surveillance vid of a guy who shot somebody in a biker bar in Atlanta."

He took the silver-dollar-sized disk from her and slipped it into his station's reader. "What's the deal?"

"Well, it's not really our business. At least nobody has asked us to do anything with it. I stumbled over this while I was looking for something else."

The holoproj lit, and Jay saw it was from a cheap video recorder, a low-res cam set high on a wall. Sure enough, it was one of those dewdrop inn kinda of places, full of men in biker colors, women in garish eye shadow, and a lot of tattoos on both sexes. The angle was wide, showing much of the floor. Off to the right were four men, three in colors, one not wearing biker gear. The civilian suddenly jumped up. He started running, and as he did, he pulled two small handguns from under what looked like a fishing vest, and began shooting. There was no sound. The shooter raced out of the viewing field and was gone in a couple of seconds. The recording jumped, and a new scene appeared, a parking lot full of motorcycles, with a few cars.

As Jay watched, the guy who had done the blasting in the bar came into view from the right, ran to a car, hopped into it, and drove away.

The recording stopped.

He looked up at Toni. "Okay."

"This was taken by the interior and exterior security cams at the Peach Pit," Toni said, "a bar on the outskirts of Atlanta. Less than an hour after this was recorded, an Atlanta policeman was shot and killed at a traffic stop. Witnesses got a look at the car leaving, and it seems to be the same make. I just talked to a contact across the compound who says preliminary ballistics make the cop-killer's guns the same as the one used by the shooter in the bar."

"So unless he sold his hardware real quick, the biker bar guy shot the cop," Jay said.

"Yep."

"And what, exactly, is our interest in this?"

"I talked to Gunny at the shooting range. He thinks this guy has been shooting other folks recently. Including Congressman Wentworth out in California."

"Really? The regular feebs know this?"

"Probably. But they don't have Smokin' Jay Gridley working it. It would be very nice to hand it to them on a platter. They'd owe us one."

He smiled. "Hooyah," he said. "It sure would. What do you want me to do?"

"I've sent you a file with other possible shootings by this guy. Enhance the image as much as you can, then start looking at car rental agency security cams around the times

and places of those other killings. See if you can find anybody who looks like this guy renting a vehicle around
then."

Jay nodded. "I can do that. I could also check local
motel and hotel cams while I'm at it. Would you sign off
on an hour of mainframe time for the Super-Cray if I can
get eight face-match points on him?"

She nodded. "Yeah. If we catch him, nobody will complain about that. If not, we'll worry about it at the budget
meeting next month."

"I'm on it," Jay said.

Toni nodded and left, and Jay started right in on it. Fid-
dling with his enhancement program, he used the holographic fill to zoom in and augment the features of the
shooter. The man was dark, almost swarthy, had black hair,
and, oddly enough, blue eyes.

Jay ran the stats, the ratio of forehead to nose, to eye
spacing, ear proportions, all like that, trying for an ethnic
tap, but it came up inconclusive. Still, he had nine pretty
certain points on the Segura Facial Structures Grid, and he
needed only eight to come up with a greater-than-seventy-
five-percent match—if he could find other pictures as good
as this one. The SFSG had been developed for use in airport and bank surveillance cams to catch robbers and potential terrorists. It wasn't altogether accurate, but seven
out of ten was more than enough for a field agent to start
checking out somebody's alibi.

The SFSG program on the Super-Cray routinely accepted and catalogued input from thousands of commercial
surveillance cams in the U.S. every day. That translated
into hundreds of thousands, even millions of pictures. The
computer could compare the facial grids of a suspect
against a day's worth of those and spit out possible
matches in ten minutes. With an hour's worth of time, Jay
could check six days of tapes. Of course, the bill to Net
Force for the computer's time would be more than he made

in a month, but if he caught a guy who shot an elected federal official? It was congressmen who approved their budget, they wouldn't kick over a few bucks to nail the guy who got one of their own.

If Jay limited himself to the days immediately before and after one of the shootings, he could check three of them. If he held it to just the day before, say, he could check six. He only needed to run four, according to the file Toni had e-mailed him. No sweat.

His system was on voxax mode. "Call the Super-Cray," he told the computer. Boy, he loved saying that—that was real power.

Michaels was, figuratively, knee-deep in legal wranglings, and not pleased about it. When Toni came by, he was happy enough for any distraction.

"Hey," he said, waving hard copy at her. "Have I mentioned that we really need a vacation?"

"I hear you," Toni said, grinning. "Meanwhile, I have something interesting. You want to come to the conference room? Jay's there."

"Sure."

At the conference room, Jay sat at the table, smiling like a cat who had swallowed a whole aviary full of canaries.

"What?" Alex said as soon as he walked in.

"Toni?" Jay asked, looking at her.

"Go ahead," she said. "Shine."

Jay grinned even wider. "Toni came across some information about that congressman who got shot recently," he said. "Not really our case, in that the local cops and the regular feebs didn't ask us in on it yet, but it seemed like a good idea to run with it."

Michaels nodded. "And . . . ?"

"And we got the shooter," Jay said, trying for an offhand ease he didn't quite pull off.

Michaels raised an eyebrow. "Got him?"

"Well, not exactly, but we know who he is."

Both Jay and Toni looked inordinately pleased with themselves.

Jay said, "Toni gave me a security tape of a guy who shot some people in a bar in Atlanta, then a cop. I entered his face into the Super-Cray and ran it through SFSG. Got a match on a guy renting a car in California the same day the congressman got hammered. Also got a match on a rental in D.C. the same day a cop in Baltimore was killed."

Jay passed over a trio of hard-copy photographs. In one, a man wearing a cowboy hat and sunglasses stood in front of a counter. In the other, a man wearing a baseball cap and a large moustache occupied the picture from a similar angle. The last one, from the scene in the Atlanta bar, showed a man with guns in both hands, with people in the background ducking for cover.

"Same guy in all three pix," Jay said. "Nine point match on two, eight on the last one—the fake moustache hides the upper lip. Of course, he used a different name and ID for all the rentals, and they were pretty good—ID thefts that checked out on first hits."

"So you have a man who rents cars and wears a false moustache. Doesn't prove anything."

"Well, if that's all we had, him being in the area, that'd be pretty circumstantial. But that's not all we've got."

He slid a fourth picture across the table. Michaels could see it was the same man, and the image appeared to be an ID photo. It had that ugly driver's-license look to it.

"Marcus 'Junior' Boudreaux," Jay said. "We got a visual match from Louisiana penal records—he did a stretch at the state prison, Angola. He's a legbreaker, general all-around thug, and professional bad guy. Arrested once for killing a man, but he got off. He fits the profile."

"Well, I'm impressed. I'm sure our brothers and sisters across the compound will appreciate it."

"Oh, but that's not all," Jay said. "You have to figure

that a guy like Junior wouldn't just go off and start shooting congressmen on his own, for no reason. He's got to
be working for somebody."

"And . . . ?"

"And so we ran Junior's picture and various fake IDs
through some other places. Since he's a shooter, we hit all
the public gun clubs we could find in and around his last
known place of residence, which was, by the way, in the
District of Columbia. Up and down the east coast."

Jay paused dramatically.

"Okay," Alex said when he didn't go on immediately.
"Are you going to drop that shoe or stand there holding it
all day?"

Jay grinned. "We found that Junior is a member at four
shooting ranges, including one in New York City. Under
different names."

"Uh-huh. Get on with it."

"And so we ran membership lists of those clubs, with
the idea that maybe we might come across a name of
somebody else we recognized there. Just on the off
chance."

"Come on, Jay—"

Jay slid another sheet of hard copy across the table. On
it was a list of names, one of which was highlighted in
yellow.

Michaels looked at the highlighted name. "No," he said.
He shook his head. "No way."

Both Toni and Jay grinned like baboons.

Jay was gone, and Michaels sat at the conference table
with Toni. Something was nagging at him, but he was still
distracted enough with all the legal paperwork he was dealing with that he was having a hard time coming up with
what it was.

He stared at the hard copy. "It's just a coincidence," he
finally said. "It doesn't mean anything. Why would a guy

like Ames stoop to something like this? He doesn't have to."

"Somebody hired our boy Boudreaux," Toni said. "I don't know why he'd be shooting up biker bars and cops, but Congressman Wentworth was leading the fight against CyberNation on the House side, wasn't he?"

"Hon, that's a stretch on the order of the Golden Gate Bridge."

"Maybe. But what if it's true? You have to check it out."

"Come on, Toni. You know what that will look like? Us going after the lawyer who is suing us over wrongful deaths for a Net Force operation?"

"Well, we'd have to be careful."

He laughed. "Careful? This is a guy who can subpoena our records, e-mail, phone logs, everything! If we start snooping into his background, we have to *tell* him."

"No, we don't. Technically, all he can ask for is material regarding operations against CyberNation. Investigating him for potential conspiracy charges doesn't necessarily fall into that category. Maybe he hired Junior for something else. We wouldn't know until we got there, would we?"

Michaels shook his head again. "One misstep and we'd be drawn, quartered, and our heads mounted on pikes on the city walls."

"So we watch where we put our feet."

He thought about it. It probably was nothing more than coincidence. The shooter belonged to four clubs. Between them, the memberships at those four clubs totaled more than two thousand people. He didn't have to have any connections to any of them. But—what if he did? And what if Ames was the connection?

It couldn't happen to a nicer guy, as far as Michaels was concerned. Maybe Toni was right. At the very least, they should check it out, right?

"If we can find this guy Boudreaux," Toni said, "and

persuade him to talk to us, that would be good."

"And how are we going to do that?"

"Jay is working on it even as we speak," she said. She smiled.

In that moment, he was very glad she was on his side. There was something of a hungry she-wolf in that expression.

Alex nodded. Something was still nagging at him.

He glanced at the list of names again, looking at the one that was highlighted. "Oh," he said. "Of course."

"What?"

He shook his head, thinking. "Hon, can you bring up that hacker's statement?"

Toni went to the flatscreen computer on the conference room's table. She hit a few keys, inputting her login code, and then called it up.

"Got it," she said.

"Read his description of the guy who hired him."

There was a pause while Toni scanned for that section and then read it. A moment later her eyebrows shot up.

"Alex," she said. "It's Mitchell Ames."

Alex nodded. "Or his twin," he said. "Get some photos down to that hacker, and include one of Ames in the mix. See if he picks him out of the batch."

"I'm on it," she said, already heading for the door.

"Oh, and Toni?"

She paused and turned back to face him.

"Good work, hon. And tell Jay I said so."

She flashed him a big grin, nodded, and went out the door.

35

Ames subscribed anonymously to a very expensive netweb
service called HITS—a specialized search engine, updated
twice a day, that kept track of inquiries on major databases
and servers. He didn't know how they managed it.

It was probably illegal, but he didn't care. All that mattered to him was that it provided him with valuable information. He simply plugged in a name and, after a couple
of minutes, the seekbot came back with records of inquiries about that subject on the web search engines it covered.
These included those open to the general public, as well
as some supposedly restricted to military, police, and federal agencies. It also searched a few that were subscription-
only, for hospitals, medical record companies, and the like.
While not totally comprehensive, the coverage was very
wide.

With all those sites being covered, he had to be careful
in his construction or he would download an enormous
number of results. A lot of people shared names. Ask it

about "John Smith," and he'd be a long time reading the list. It was best to narrow things as much as possible. Ask about a specific person for example, using first, middle, and last names if he had them. Even then it was a good idea to limit the time to one day or less, otherwise, he might be elbow-deep in hits.

Ames felt that if somebody was asking questions about him or his people, he needed to know about it. He also needed to know who was doing the asking so he could try to determine what they wanted. HITS was his insurance policy.

It was with a cold, stomach-twisting dread that he looked at the computer image floating over his desk. The HITS program had come back with more than a dozen queries after the name of "Marcus Boudreaux," and the databases being searched—police, prison, rental car, and hotel agencies—made it chillingly clear that the searcher was some kind of law-enforcement officer, and that the Boudreaux in question was none other than Junior.

One of the hits was about a cop-killing in Atlanta, Georgia. Another for a dead policeman in Baltimore. And there were inquiries about the congressman in California, too.

How could this have happened? he wondered. What had Junior done?

That the searcher had a NO ID AVAILABLE status could mean several things, but most likely, it meant "cop," and probably a fed.

Which meant to Ames it was Net Force.

Junior had screwed up somehow. He'd tripped an alarm somewhere, the dogs had scented him, and now they were baying on his trail.

This changed everything. His earlier calculations of the risk Junior represented assumed that Junior hadn't gone too far across the line. The kind of blackmail Ames had used him for wasn't all that bad. The penalties for it, if Junior were ever caught, weren't that steep. He knew that

Junior would simply ride that out, trusting that Ames would help him out—and knowing that Ames would kill him if he turned on him.

But murder? Especially the murders of cops? That was a whole other ball game. There was no way Ames would be able to bail Junior out of this mess. Which meant that Junior would have no reason to protect his boss. Quite the opposite, in fact. Facing life imprisonment, or worse, he would be eager to work a deal. And the only card he had to play was Ames himself.

Ames shook his head. What was he going to do about this? They wouldn't be able to substantiate any of Junior's claims. They would certainly never be able to prove that he had even known Junior, much less hired him. But an accusation by a man arrested for murder would throw mud on his good reputation. Even the hint of scandal would be bad for business.

No, they'd never prove anything, but it would be an embarrassment, and that was something he'd rather not endure.

He had to lose Junior, no question about it, and he had to do it quickly.

As these things sometimes did when he was under sudden and intense pressure, a plan came to him, all of a piece, *bam!* just like that. The way to be rid of Junior, without any real risk to himself. Once that link was gone, he was in the clear.

He smiled, impressed with his own cleverness. He really was brilliant. Back him into a corner, and he did not turn into a rat, he turned into Einstein. . . .

Brooklyn, New York

It was just after sunrise. Ames sat at his desk in the new safe office. This was the third one in as many weeks.

Across from him was the man who was shortly going to be leaving this world, though he didn't know it.

Junior shook his head. "Kidnapping? That's not exactly in my line."

"You don't have any problem shooting somebody, but you won't grab a child to get his father off our back?"

"The feds will come out in droves," Junior said. "And little kids are the worst."

"Nobody is going to know he was kidnapped," Ames said. "We aren't calling for ransom. The only person who counts is Alex Michaels."

"What about the kid's mama? She's just going to hand him over to me, right?"

Ames laughed, putting an edge of scorn in it. "You don't think you can handle somebody's *mother*?"

Junior shook his head. "If she sees me, she can testify against me."

Ames looked at him, his eyes hard and unyielding. "Not if she isn't around to testify, she can't."

Junior sighed and sat back in his chair. "You don't want much, do you?"

"Junior, I can't impress on you enough how serious this situation is. Net Force knows who you are and what you did. They are all over your trail." He shook his head. "I can't believe you actually shot a *cop*."

When Ames had called him and told him they were in deep trouble, Junior assumed he had figured that out somehow. He'd admitted to it when Ames waved it in his face, and almost blurted out that the Atlanta cop was only one of many he'd capped. Fortunately, he had kept that to himself.

He shrugged. "It was him or me," he said.

"That's the same thing you said about the congressman."

"That's because it *was* the same thing. I had some trouble with Joan, yeah. It involved some . . . gunplay in a biker bar. Somebody else got shot. When the cop stopped me I was still carrying the gun that did that shooting. I didn't have time to get rid of it. A felon in possession of a firearm, aggravated assault, attempted murder, murder? I'd be up the creek with no paddle, and you know it. There wasn't any choice."

Ames leaned forward in his chair. "All right," he said. "What's done is done. But we're up against it, now. We need to give Alex Michaels something else to think about. So you get down to Washington, now, today, you drop by his house, and you take his son for a ride."

"I don't much like the idea of killing a kid."

"So don't kill him. Drop him off a hundred miles away at a mall, after we're done with him. Killing the woman shouldn't bother you—once you get past the first, they're all the same, right?"

Junior nodded. Probably. But since he hadn't actually gotten Joan, he wasn't past the first one yet. Still, he wasn't a virgin when it came to dropping the hammer anymore, was he? Man or woman, the bullet didn't know the difference.

"Trust me on this, Junior," Ames said. "I know this guy, this Alex Michaels. I've met him, talked to him. He'll fold, and once we get what we need, I settle with you for a nice sum and you go off to live on the Mexican coast happily ever after."

"How much settlement are we talking about here?"

"Five million seems fair. If you leave the country."

Junior blinked at that. Five million. A nice house in Mexico, servants, a mistress, tequila, and lying in the sun, not having to work? You could live like a king for the rest of your life with five million U.S. down there. You didn't even have to speak the language if you didn't want to bother—money was the universal language. You could get whatever you wanted if you had enough of it. Five million? That was lot better than being shipped back to Angola or some federal pen.

"Okay," he said.

"Call me when you get ready to move," Ames said. "The timing on this is critical. Today. As soon as you can get there."

"Yeah, yeah, okay."

Ames watched Junior leave. This was bad, all of it, and maybe it was time to take a little vacation, spend a few days or a week at his hideaway in Texas, until it blew over. Low profile was definitely the ticket.

He looked around. This was the last time he would see this place. He wasn't going to give anybody the chance to come and sneak up on him here.

Yes, it was definitely time to crank up the corporate jet and leave town for a while. He could make the call from anywhere, just as easy to do it from Texas as here. Like he'd told Junior, the timing was critical.

For Junior, it would be exactly that.

Washington, D.C.

Toni was running late. She was anxious to get back into the office and follow up on Ames. Thumper had picked his photo out of the group of twelve or so still shots she'd shown him. She'd turned Jay loose on Ames right away, and wanted to get in to see what he'd found.

But she couldn't find her car keys. She knew she had put them on the mail table by the front door, she was sure of it, but somehow, they had vanished.

"Here they are, Mrs. Michaels," Tyrone said.

She was in the kitchen, and she looked up to see Tyrone dangling the keys as he came toward her.

"Where were they?"

"In the bathroom. On the back of the toilet."

Toni shook her head. "How'd they get there?"

He shrugged. "Got me. I just find them, I don't explain them."

Toni grinned. "The boy was up half the night," she said. "He'll probably sleep late."

That was an understatement. Little Alex had a nightmare that woke him up at midnight, and he'd spent the next two hours squirming on the bed between Toni and Alex, putting his cold little feet on her and pushing, which hadn't done her sleep any good, either. When he had finally gotten back to sleep, Alex had carried him to his own bed. By then, it must have been two thirty or three A.M.

Yeah, he'd sleep until nine or ten. Toni wished she could stay in bed a couple more hours herself. They never told you that when you had a baby, you'd be in sleep-deficit for the next two or three years. . . .

"Okay, I'm gone. Are you going to need a ride home?"

"No, ma'am. My mom is picking me up. I've got shooting club practice tonight. My pop got me a new pistol, and I get to try it out this evening."

"Great. Okay. I'll be back around one. Anything you need . . ."

"Yes, ma'am. I expect I can still operate the phone." He grinned.

She returned the smile as she headed for the door. He was really a sweet kid. John and Nadine Howard had done a good job. She'd be sure to tell them that the next time she saw either of them.

She was in the car and rolling two minutes later, her mind already on the day's work. The FBI had been pleased enough with the information she and Jay had developed on Marcus Boudreaux, and while they hadn't apprehended him yet, they were working on it.

They hadn't mentioned anything about Ames yet. All they had so far was the coincidence of his name showing up at a shooting club where Marcus Boudreaux was a member, and the word of a computer hacker. For just about anyone else, that would have been enough. But not for Mitchell Ames. Not for a high-level, almost celebrity-status attorney. And certainly not for a high-level, celebrity attorney who was currently suing Net Force.

No, they had to have everything nailed down perfectly before they even breathed a word about Ames.

In the meantime, Jay was digging into Ames's personal life like a rabid steam shovel, looking for any hint of a connection with Boudreaux.

On a more personal front, Guru would be home tomorrow, she'd said. Her great-grandson was out of the woods, well enough so they had sent him home from the hospital. It was a hot, but not-too-smoggy sunny day.

Things were going along pretty well at the moment, she had to admit. But she couldn't wait to get in to work.

Net Force HQ
Quantico, Virginia

Michaels leaned back in his chair and nodded at John Howard. "So that's the situation, General."

Howard nodded. "You really think Ames is involved in this?"

"I'm sure of it."

Howard chuckled. "Wouldn't that be something, Commander? Busting the guy suing you?"

Alex grinned. "I would think it would go a long way to making his case look bad to a jury. A lawyer with his own hit man?"

"I thought they all had hit men," Howard said.

Michaels laughed.

"Well, I suppose there won't be anything for me to do, once we're ready to go with this," Howard said. "I'd guess the New York police would frown on a Net Force team storming a Park penthouse."

"Probably," Michaels agreed.

Howard left, and Michaels took another moment to relish the idea of sending a crooked lawyer to jail. Even if it turned out he wasn't guilty, it was a nice fantasy for a summer morning. . . .

36

Just after noon, Junior cruised past the house to get a good look at it.

He took deep breath. This was too hurried-up to suit him, but sometimes you had to make do. Might as well get to it.

He called Ames on the throwaway.

"Yes?"

"I'm starting that job now," he said.

"Right now?" Ames's voice was a bit crackly on the throwaway.

"Yeah."

"Okay. Call me when you get things squared away."

Junior hung up. He circled the block, then parked the rental car a couple houses down, got out, taking his time.

A cowboy suit would stand out too much in this neighborhood, so he wore a baseball cap, sunglasses, his fishing vest over a T-shirt, and shorts. Just another average Joe.

Well, okay, another average Joe with two guns hidden under his vest.

He walked to the place, looked around, still in no hurry.

He didn't see any neighbors watching him. He tried the front door, but it was locked. He circled around, found a gate in a fence to the backyard, also locked, and climbed it. No dog started barking, which was good.

He went to the back and saw a sliding glass door into a kitchen. It was closed, and the sound of a big AC rumbling on a concrete pad around the corner meant the windows would be closed, too, but unless they had a broomstick in the track or a backup lock, opening a sliding door like this was easy enough.

Junior carried a titanium "business card" in his wallet for just such occasions. The card was thin, flexible, tough, and it would take maybe fifteen seconds to jimmy the latch.

It took half that.

Net Force HQ
Quantico, Virginia

Michaels was on his way back from lunch when his virgil chirped. He pulled the unit from his belt. No caller ID, but only a handful of people had this number. He thumbed the connect button.

There was no visual.

"Yes?"

"Alex Michaels?" said a breathy female voice.

"Yes, who is calling, please?"

"That doesn't matter. What matters is, there's a man breaking into your house right now who means to kill your son."

The caller discommed.

Michaels felt a blast of cold fear slap him. Alex was home with Tyrone, Toni was still at lunch!

He pushed the call button and said, "D.C. Police, emergency!"

Washington, D.C.

Junior smiled as he slid the back door open. He thought he caught a hint of movement, just a glimpse, but it was gone before he could get a real look. Did he really see somebody?

He shook his head. He would have sworn he'd seen a black kid, skinny, a teenager. He shook his head. Could he have the wrong house? The address checked out, but far as he knew, Alex and his family were all white.

He waited, holding his breath. Nothing.

Must be his imagination.

Careful, Junior, he thought. *Don't go lettin' your nerves get to you now.*

He slid the door closed carefully behind him and stood there for a few seconds, listening. He heard the hum of the refrigerator, the more distant drone of the air conditioner. Nothing else.

Junior pulled his right-hand revolver. It wouldn't do to get bashed by the wife or a baby-sitter swinging a frying pan. And since the guy whose kid he was after was a fed, he might have a gun at home. If Junior saw somebody pointing a gun in his direction, he'd cook 'em, no question.

He eased his way through the kitchen to the hallway, peeped around the corner, and pulled his head back real fast.

Nothing.

He stepped into the hallway, his gun leading.

Ames's Corporate Jet
Somewhere over Tennessee

Ames smiled at the throwaway phone. Well, it was done.

Junior wouldn't give up when the cops came calling. There'd probably be some kind of hostage situation, and Junior would know they had him for kidnapping at the very least, plus the gun felonies, and maybe a connection to the shooting in Atlanta. He knew that Junior didn't want to spend the rest of his life in prison, or waiting to be executed. There was no way he'd give up. And eventually, if they didn't blast him right off, a SWAT sniper would line up and put a .308 round through Junior's head, and that would be that.

Adios, Junior. Give my regards to the Devil. . . .

Net Force Helipad
Quantico, Virginia

The Net Force helicopter lifted, Toni and Alex the only passengers, and veered to the left in a dizzying maneuver.

Alex had told the pilot to do whatever he had to do to get them home, fast.

"Alex?" She had to yell over the sound of the engine and rotors.

"It'll be okay!" he yelled back. "D.C. police are on the way, they'll be there before we are."

Toni was terrified.

Dear God, don't let anything happen to my baby!

Washington, D.C.

Junior thought he could hear somebody talking, low and quiet, and he crept along the wall toward the sound, his left hand coming up to grip his right, holding the revolver in a double-grip. He kept the gun pointed at about a forty-five-degree angle in front of him, toward the floor. It was easier to bring it up and target than it was to bring it down from a barrel-up position, like a lot of cops and military guys did it.

He passed a couple of rooms with doors open, peeked in quickly, and didn't see anybody.

He got to the end of the hall, where there was a closed door. He tried the knob quietly. . . .

Locked.

He put his ear against the door, but the voice—if that's what it had been—had gone quiet. He couldn't hear a thing. He was sure somebody was in the room, though. Sure of it.

Junior sweated, despite the air-conditioning. He stood there for a long time, thinking about it.

Should he back off, go around and look in the window? Assuming there wasn't a blind or curtain over it that wouldn't let him see anything. Should he demand that whoever was inside come out? That might not be a good idea. They could be standing there holding a phone with the police emergency number already dialed. That could even be what he'd heard—somebody calling the police, who could even now be on their way here.

Or maybe it was the mama in there, holding her grand-daddy's old pump shotgun, ready to shred anything that came through the door.

He shook his head. Too many questions with no way to answer them unless he moved. No, if somebody was in the room, no point in giving them any warning, any time to do anything. Best thing was to kick the door open, jump in, and catch them off guard. People got spooked by loud noises and movement, distracted by yelling things like, "How's your sister?" They got overwhelmed by too much coming at them at once, every time.

He took a deep breath, let a little of it out, and gathered himself. It was an interior door, hollow-core, with a snap-button lock. No problem.

Ames's Corporate Jet
Somewhere over Arkansas

Ames had opened a bottle of very good red wine when the jet had lifted, and it had breathed enough by now. Some wines didn't travel very well, and the lower pressure in the cabin wasn't good for wine in general, but he didn't care. He would have a glass or two, and if the rest of it didn't keep, what was a couple hundred bucks, given his income? Plenty more where that came from. He had dozens of cases of good stuff at the hideout in Texas.

He poured the wine and swirled it around in his glass, and thought about the lobbyist, Cory Skye. He hadn't heard from her in a couple of days and wondered where she was, and how she was doing in her pursuit of Net Force's commander.

He inhaled the sharp scent, then took a slow sip from the glass. Ah.

Washington, D.C.

Junior leaned into the kick, hit the door hard, and was happy to see it pop open, showing a bedroom. He leaped in—

He caught movement to his left, twisted, and saw several things at once:

There was a bathroom, and in it, crouched down under a sink, was the boy he'd come to collect.

There was also a skinny black kid—he'd been right about that!—standing in front of the door, partially blocking it.

There was a long-barreled target pistol in the skinny kid's hand, pointing at the rug—

Gun!

Junior swung his revolver around. Driven by years of practice, made smooth by countless repetitions, he moved like oil on polished steel, no hesitation, no jerkiness, no roughness.

Turn. Index. Target—

He lined up on the black kid's head, ready to squeeze off the first round. . . .

The long-barreled gun in the kid's hand blurred.

Jesus! How fast was that?

He didn't have time to wonder very long. Before his finger was halfway through the trigger squeeze, there was fire and noise, but it cut off—

—Junior's mind stopped dead. His last thought was: *How could—?*

The D.C. cops were there, but they had established a perimeter, nobody had gone inside. Toni and Alex were out of the copter and almost to the front door, despite the cops yelling at them to stay back. It was going to take more than police to stop Toni getting to her child—

There came the horrible crack of a small-caliber gunshot.

Toni screamed something wordless and primal, a cry for her mate's help, but it wasn't necessary—Alex was moving. He hit the door with his shoulder, slammed it open against the wall, hard enough to break the doorstop, never slowing—

She ran down the hall, Alex a step ahead of her, both of them yelling—

The baby!

Heedless of guns, they ran into the bedroom—

—and almost tripped over the body of a man lying face-up on the floor, a stubby gun clutched in his hand. He had been hit in the forehead. Right between the eyes.

Boudreaux!

To her left, Tyrone stood, Alex clutched in one arm on his hip, the other hand holding a sleek pistol which was now pointed at the floor.

"H-H-He k-ki-kicked in the d-d-door, Mrs. Michaels! He had a g-g-gun!"

"Mama!" Alex said. He smiled and held out his arms to her, happy to see her. He wasn't crying. Didn't even seem particularly upset.

She took the boy, a sense of relief flooding her like a tsunami.

"I-I-I—" Tyrone was sobbing too hard to get anything else out.

Tyrone and his target pistol. He had saved them from the killer.

Amazing.

Alex squatted on the floor next to the downed man. "Dead," he said.

"It's okay, Tyrone," Toni said. "You did the right thing. It's okay." She reached out and encircled him with her free arm, pulling him close. "Thank you."

Those two little words were so inadequate, but she saw Tyrone nod. Then she turned and looked back at the man by her bed and her husband. This was the second time Death had come to her house to visit. She shook her head. It was going to be the last. She wasn't going to stay here and put her child at risk anymore. She would have to make

Alex understand that. It was time to leave this town.

Alex was nodding, and she knew it was because he had read her mind. Their son was safe. And they were going to keep him that way, whatever it took.

37

Toni was at home with their son. Nadine Howard had
come and collected Tyrone. The boy was shaken, but he
seemed okay otherwise. John Howard had gone home,
seen to his boy, and now was back.

The police had gotten their forensics people in and out,
and the coroner had hauled the body away. It was late,
almost seven P.M., but Michaels was at the office, and neither Jay nor John Howard had any plans to go home.

Michaels had been profuse in his gratitude to Tyrone,
and in telling Howard how much he owed them. Howard
had been rattled and worried for his son, but under it, a
glimmer of pride showed through. In the face of deadly
danger, his son had stepped up. Against a man who was
a killer, Tyrone had prevailed. It was not every man who
could have done it, and for a teenager untrained in violence, it was even more impressive.

But now, everybody in this room was frustrated and
angry.

"No ID on the call?" Michaels said.

"No, boss," Jay said. "But we did get a location. We backwalked it to a cell tower in Tennessee."

Michaels shook his head. "Who is in Tennessee?"

"Nobody we're concerned with. But our boy Ames hopped on his private jet this morning, flight plans filed for Texas. At the time of the call to your virgil, given the jet's cruising speed and path, it would have been somewhere over Tennessee."

"We've got him, then," Howard said.

Michaels nodded. "What's in Texas?"

"Ames owns a big fallout shelter, built during the early years of the cold war."

"A fallout shelter?"

"The size of a village, just about, buried under the plains in the middle of nowhere."

"Why would he be going there?"

"Maybe he can read minds," Howard said. "Because if he sent that thug to threaten our children, he's going to have to hide somewhere. Though I am here to tell you, a fallout shelter will not be deep enough."

The rage in Howard's voice was quiet but no less deadly for that. And Michaels was a hundred percent in agreement.

"The thing is, we can't be positive he made the call," Jay said.

Both Howard and Michaels looked at him.

Jay blinked, and looked away.

"Who else?" Michaels said. "The only people likely to know that Boudreaux was going after Alex would Boudreaux and whoever sent him."

"But— Why give him up like that?"

"Because the man had become a liability," Howard said. "You and Toni made the connection. The Atlanta police are after him for two shootings—one of them a cop-killing—and the FBI is working up evidence to connect him to other murders, including the congressman. If Ames was his employer, Boudreaux would be in a position to do him a lot of damage by implicating him. But if he died in a shoot-out with the police . . ."

"Dead men tell no tales," Jay said.

"Exactly."

"It's still not enough evidence to get an indictment, Boss," Jay said, shaking his head. "Even with the hacker, it's still real thin. We can pin those murders on Junior, I'm pretty sure, but unless Ames slipped up—and as careful as he's been so far, that doesn't seem likely—we'll have a hard time proving he is the guy behind it all."

"Maybe. But at the very least, we can have a little chat with him about it."

Jay shook his head again. "You already got one lawsuit from this guy. We've got enough to keep digging, maybe even enough to start some serious prying into his affairs, but we don't have near enough to go after him physically. Not yet." He sighed. "I'm sorry, Boss."

Michaels nodded and exchanged looks with Howard. "You're right, Jay," he said, "but you know what? I'm seriously thinking about retiring. If Ames turns out to be innocent, let him sue me."

"Me, too," Howard said. "I've done about all I wanted to do after I was called back into Net Force's service. You can't get much mileage with a threat to fire a man who's ready to quit."

Jay sighed again, then gave a tight little smile and nodded. "Okay," he said. "What do you want me to do?"

"Get me some hard information on this bomb shelter," Michaels said. "Find out everything there is to know. And, Jay," he added, "this guy ran for a reason. Could be a coincidence, but it could be that he caught wind of us sniffing after his hired killer, so go carefully. Leave no tracks."

"You got it, Boss."

• • •

The thing about bureaucracy that Jay found so comforting was that there was always a record of any official governmental action. Sometimes it was buried deeply. Sometimes it was covered with so many top-secret layers it was almost impossible to get to. But it was always there, somewhere.

Much of what the U.S. government had been up to during those worrisome days when schoolchildren were taught to duck and cover when the nukes started going off had been kept secret for so long that nobody alive knew where to find it. A great deal of what went on during the cold war had not made the transition from hard copy documents to microfilm and then computer media. It was locked away in a storeroom or vault or somebody's old desk—extant, but, for all practical purposes, invisible. Finding it would be a Herculean labor. But when it came to real estate that generated income, Uncle Sam didn't drop that particular ball very often.

The plans, record of sale, and other documentation regarding the underground bunker near Odessa, Texas, had indeed made the shift from paper to pixels. It was all there. Right in the safe-deposit box of the bank vault scenario Jay was currently using.

Of course, Jay wasn't supposed to be in the vault looking at those plans. He didn't have the particular clearance necessary.

Jay grinned. That had never stopped him before. Besides, it was just plain silly. What possible threat to national security could it be for him to see it? Here was a site that had been sold to a civilian fifty years after it had been built, having never been used. Keeping this under a top-secret seal was, in a word, and not to put too fine a point on it, stupid.

If he had to guess, Ames had probably paid an additional little premium to someone to keep that top-secret flag on the files. Ames liked his privacy, no doubt about it.

Jay copied the files and exited the scenario.

Howard looked at the printout of the plans and shook his head. "Hard to imagine how worried people were about being bombed by the Russians back then."

Michaels nodded. "So, what do you think, General?"

Howard frowned. "Well, even assuming the feds pulled all the defensives they had in there when they bailed out, this one's going to be hard. This guy has money, it's for sure he's reinstalled some sort of protective system. He could have rockets, mines, Lord knows what all out there. In addition to that, this place is huge. He could hide from a small crew for a long time—and maybe even get past them if he had a good bolt hole."

"So, what exactly are you saying?" Michaels asked.

"Our only chance is to sneak up on him. If he knows we're coming, we're in trouble."

Michaels grinned. "So we wait until it gets dark, right?"

Howard laughed. "Not quite that easy, Commander. It's hard to tell by looking, but this place is in the middle of nowhere. If he has any kind of sensor gear, radar, doppler—stuff you can buy in any boat shop—he'll see us coming a long way off."

"So, how do you get around that?"

Howard smiled. "I have a couple of ideas," he said.

Odessa, Texas

Ames was able to call the hideaway on a secure phone and start the power generators by remote control, so that by the time he got there, the main building would be cooler and not so stale-smelling.

The entrance to the hydraulic automobile elevator was an upgrade he'd had installed with a triple-redundant system. There was a mechanical lock that used a magnetic key, an electronic code via a keypad, and a voxax computer chip that not only used a password, but was coded to his voice only. You had to use all three devices or the door wouldn't open, nor would the lift work. Once inside, the locks could be overridden so they no longer operated from without. The steel door itself was in a reinforced concrete and steel frame that made the average bank vault look puny. Nobody was going to get in that way without enough heavy equipment to knock down a nuclear power plant.

Not that he expected company. Still, it was nice to know no one would be dropping by unexpectedly. He had caught the newscast just before he had landed—an armed man who had broken into the home of Alex Michaels, the commander of Net Force, had been shot and killed by the family's baby-sitter, a young man whose name wasn't being revealed because of his age.

Ames had to laugh at that—ace pistoleer Junior Boudreaux shot dead by a juvenile. How galling that must have felt to Junior.

He pulled his car to a stop and got out. Walking over to the override panel, he shut off access to the lift. No point in concerning himself about Junior anymore, he was history, and good riddance.

When he thought about it, there wasn't any real reason he'd had to leave town. Net Force didn't have a link to him—and Junior certainly wasn't going to be providing one now. His exit had been driven by nerves. Not panic, exactly, but, he had to admit, he had been worried.

Well, as long as he was here, he might as well relax and enjoy himself. He deserved it.

He walked down the corridor from the garage, his footsteps echoing from the tile on floor, walls, and ceiling.

Some good wine, a steak and salad, maybe a nice baked potato, then watch a movie, really kick back.

Yeah, he was ready for a little vacation. Then he'd go back to Washington and really turn up the heat on Net Force.

38

Julio didn't hesitate even a heartbeat. "I'm in," he said.

"We might not be on firm legal ground here," Howard said.

Julio laughed. "Since when did that matter?"

"I don't want you blindsided."

"John," Julio said, "you're my boss, but you're also my best friend. When that assassin pointed a gun in Tyrone's direction, everything changed. If this guy Mitchell Ames sent that man to the commander's house, I want to be part of nailing him." He shrugged. "Besides, I can always get another job."

Howard was silent for a moment. Not that he had expected anything else. Still, it was gratifying to hear his old friend say it. "Thanks, Julio."

Julio nodded. "Okay, so what's the plan?"

They were in Howard's office. Nobody else was around. Howard fiddled with the computer controls on his workstation. A satellite view of the Texas desert appeared.

"Okay, here's what we've got. . . ."

When Michaels called Toni, she was doing a little better—not so much that she was happy, but at least she wasn't about to boil over.

He explained where they were regarding Ames.

"That's fine," she said. "I'm going to sit this one out."

"Toni—"

"Don't get me wrong, Alex. When you catch him, I'd like five minutes alone with him, assuming he lives that long. But once this is over, I'm finished with this business, Alex. Done. It's time to get away from a place where killers come to our house after our son."

He nodded, then realized that the nonvisual connection wouldn't show that and said, "I understand."

"Do you?"

"Yes. And I agree."

And he did. If something happened to his child because of the work he did, he would never forgive himself. "How is Little Alex?"

"*He* is fine, he thought it was all a game Tyrone was playing. But I am serious about this."

"I heard you the first time. I'll turn in my resignation as soon as we have Ames in custody."

"Really?"

"Really."

After he disconnected, Michaels reflected on how much he had changed over the years. There was a time when the job was everything. It had cost him his first marriage, and had distanced him from his own daughter. There was a time when an ultimatum like the one Toni had just given him would have put his back up and led to a screaming fight. But somewhere along the way, he had grown up and realized what was really important in his life. His wife and son were irreplaceable. Net Force could find another commander. His family could never replace him.

"Commander?"

General Howard stood in his doorway. "Yes?"

"Lieutenant Fernandez and I have come up with some ideas we'd like to run past you."

"I'm all ears."

Howard laid it all out, watching as Michaels took it in. When he was done, Michaels said, "Good. How soon can we get started?"

" 'We'?"

"You don't think I'm going to sit home like I'm supposed to, do you? I never have before, why start now?" He grinned. "Besides, if they fire me, maybe I can draw unemployment."

Howard grinned back and shook his head. "We're talking a small unit. A couple of little jets are already fueled up and ready to fly. No reason we can't get it set up for tomorrow night."

"Don't tell me I was right about going after dark."

Howard smiled again. "Every little bit helps. Besides, it'll give us more time to plan, and maybe run through this thing a time or two in VR." He paused. "Speaking of VR. Will Jay be coming along, too?"

Alex shook his head. "I don't think so. He'll be staying here, continuing to dig for information on Ames. When we bring him in, we'll need everything we can get to hold him and make this stick." He paused, then added, "Besides, when this is all over, Jay might be the senior man left around here."

Howard grinned. "Now there's a sobering thought."

Michaels just nodded.

"Well, sir, I had better get to it."

Michaels offered his hand, and Howard took it.

"I really appreciate this," Michaels said.

"Don't forget, my son was there, too."

Michaels nodded. "No, I won't ever forget that."

Howard met Julio at the air base. The lieutenant was supervising the loading of one of the stripped business jets Net Force's military used for relatively short-range hops.

"How are we doing, Lieutenant?"

"Just fine, sir. We got the easy stuff on board. The rest is being hauled from the warehouse by truck. We'll be packed and ready to rock by 0200."

"Good. Go home, get some sleep, and be back here by 0600."

"Yes, sir."

Howard looked at his watch. He should go home and get some sleep, too.

Washington, D.C.

When Howard got home, Tyrone was in the kitchen, fixing himself a sandwich. Dagwood would have been proud of the concoction Tyrone was cobbling together—three different kinds of meat, two cheeses, lettuce, tomato, pickles, sliced onion, three slices of bread, mayo, mustard, catsup. It was a monster.

Howard decided to keep it light. He said, "Lost your appetite, huh?"

Tyrone said, "Yeah, I can't seem to make myself eat much."

Howard waited a second, then said, "So how are you, son? You okay?"

Tyrone blew out a soft sigh. "I don't know." He paused in his sandwich construction.

Howard nodded. He'd been through this with seasoned veterans, longtime soldiers who'd trained for years but never had to actually shoot another person. When they did, it hit them, sometimes hard.

And Tyrone was no seasoned soldier. He was just a fifteen-year-old boy.

"Tell me about it, son."

Tyrone gave a little shrug. "I shot a man, Dad. This guy was alive yesterday. Now he's dead."

Howard nodded. "You're right, Tyrone," he said. "That's a serious thing, and never, ever something done lightly. But you didn't cause that situation, son."

"I know," Ty said. "That man was coming to kill Little Alex. Probably, anyway. But it's for sure that he was going to kill me. I *saw* him point that gun at me. I *saw* his finger tighten." He looked at his father. "He tried to kill me, Dad. No one's ever done that before. The thing is, I still keep feeling that I should have tried something else. Shooting him in the shoulder, maybe."

Howard shook his head. "You did the right thing, son," he said. "We've talked about weapons before, about things like stopping power and the different calibers. That .22 of yours makes a great target piece, but it's not very good at stopping a man." He looked directly into Tyrone's eyes, ignoring the sandwich, ignoring the way his son's hand had started to shake slightly, ignoring everything but the communication, the *contact*, that was happening between them at this moment. "You did the right thing, Ty. Had you tried anything else, had you shot him in the shoulder, you would probably not have stopped him. He'd have fired back at you, and he'd have killed you, and then he would have done whatever he'd come to do to Little Alex." He paused again, letting that sink in for a moment, and then he repeated. "You did the right thing. You did the only thing. He gave you no other choice."

Tyrone nodded, but Howard wasn't sure how much his words had helped. Ty was in a spot where words could only do so much. He had to work through this on his own.

His dad could be there for him, to answer some of the tough questions, and to point him in the right direction, but it was up to Ty to get through this.

John knew he would, though. He was a good kid, with a good heart, and a good head on his shoulders. And besides, everything Howard had just told him was the truth. He had done the right thing, the only thing.

"Thanks, Dad," Ty said. He picked up his sandwich and took a huge bite. "I love you."

At least, that's what it sounded like he said. It was hard to tell around that mouthful of sandwich.

Howard smiled. "I love you, too," he said. "And I am very, very proud of you, Ty."

Michaels and Toni were in bed, the baby sleeping between them. Alex had his right hand resting on Little Alex's chest, rising and falling slightly with his son's breathing. His left hand rested on the pillow, holding Toni's hand tenderly.

"Guru will be back tomorrow," she said.

"That's good."

"What time are you leaving?"

"John wants to take off around six thirty."

"You be careful," she said, giving his hand a small squeeze.

Alex smiled. "Ames is a lawyer, not a Navy SEAL."

Toni shook her head. "He has guns. He belongs to a gun club."

"I'll be careful," Alex said.

They lay quietly for a moment. "So, what do you think about Colorado?" Alex asked.

"Colorado?"

He nodded. "I got offered a job as head of corporate computer security for Aspen International, remember? Twice the money, half the work, complete with a car, expense account, and country-club membership."

She hesitated. "Maybe I was a little upset before," she said.

Alex shook his head. "No, hon, you were a lot upset. And you had a right to be. You weren't wrong. It's time to move on."

Another long pause. "We'll have to get a house big enough for Guru, and for when Susie comes to visit."

Alex smiled. "They have big houses out there. I bet we could find one."

Toni looked at him, her eyes holding his steadily for a long moment. "Are you sure about this, Alex?"

"I have never been more sure about anything, Toni. Well, except that marrying you was a good idea."

That got a big smile from her.

He loved to make her smile.

39

Odessa, Texas

Ames arose at dawn, showered, dressed, made himself a cup of coffee, and then hiked to the emergency escape hatch past the garbage dump. Once there, he climbed the three flights of stairs up to the surface. The door, a hydraulically operated vaultlike monster, was designed to keep out the riffraff fleeing atomic attack. Disc-shaped, it was slightly larger in diameter than a manhole cover, two feet thick, and hinged like a jeweler's loupe. It pivoted on a massive, tempered pin as big around as a large man's arm. It was camouflaged on the surface by a flat stretch of sand on a motorized frame that raised up on command. When the sand frame was in place, the entrance was virtually invisible. And even if you knew it was there, opening it would be a major chore without the proper keys, codes, and commands.

Ames used the periscope hidden in a creosote bush to check and make sure nobody was around. When he was certain that everything was clear, he pushed the door control button. It took thirty seconds for the sand frame to rise high enough for the door to pivot open.

He climbed up and out, standing under the sand frame, which now stood some seven feet above the ground.

This was the best time of day if you wanted to go outside here in the summer. It was as cool as it was going to get this time of year, and only the jackrabbits and birds were stirring. There were no other humans for as far as he could see, though a distant jet contrail arrowed across the pale, cloudless sky, too far away for him to hear the craft that created it.

Quiet, peaceful, and all his . . .

He spent ten minutes or so breathing the fresh air, glad to be out of the confines of the bomb shelter, laying his plans for the coming days and weeks. Satisfied, he went back inside, shut the door and lowered the frame, and headed back along the echoing tile corridor toward the kitchen. He had in mind salmon hash and eggs for breakfast this morning, and maybe a mimosa to wash in down.

He grinned. *Wonder what the poor folks are doing this morning.*

Bush Air Force Base
Odessa, Texas

The Net Force jet was nearly there by the time dawn broke locally, pacing the sun from the east. They would have all day to get set, plenty of time.

Michaels, surprisingly, had fallen asleep on the trip, and awoke as the craft began its descent toward the new Air Force base a couple of hours away from their target. Howard had arranged to borrow some trucks from the Texas National Guard, Net Force technically being a part of the

Guard, at least for accounting purposes. In theory, the vehicles should be there when the jet landed.

After they were down and the unloading process under way, John Howard joined Michaels in the back of the mobile operations center, which was essentially a canvas-covered flatbed truck. Despite this, it was air-conditioned, after a fashion.

"For the computers," Howard said. "The personal tactical units don't need it, but the bigger ones get goofy once the air temp rises above body heat."

"Is it going to get that hot here?"

"West Texas in the summer? Oh, yes. It'll be cooler after dark, but we will have to load and move out in the daylight."

Alex looked at him. "Do you really think this will work, John?" he asked. "It seems like an awfully big place to assault with only ten men."

A forklift wheeled past bearing a pair of wooden crates bigger than coffins. There were three more like them still on the jet.

General Howard said, "I think so. The truth is, though, that either we nail it with ten men or we wouldn't be able to do it with a hundred. Like you said, it's a big place, and surprise will work better for us than sheer numbers."

Alex nodded. He'd known that already, of course, but this entire operation was going forward on his say-so alone. He had the final word on go/no go, and he still could cancel it at any time up until they actually entered Ames's bomb shelter. After that things got a lot dicier.

Ames had plenty to distract him. He had full net capabilities as well as satellite-reception radio and video. He could get five hundred television channels from around the world, and local programming from the radio stations in Addis Ababa, if he wanted. He had a library to rival those in many small towns in hard copy alone, legal tomes, med-

ical books, not to mention thousands of novels, entertainment vids, and musical compositions on DVD and minis,
should his net connection somehow go out. He had a gym,
a lap pool, a shooting range, a basketball court, and even
a six-lane bowling alley. He had food, wine, and a phar-
macy deep enough to take care of a hundred people all
sick with different diseases.

He had art on his walls, paintings by masters. He had
sculptures. He had three of his favorite chairs, and a
computer-operated bed of biogel that was the most comfortable in the world.

He had everything he needed, except a challenge.

Ames shrugged. There was nothing he could do about
that right now. His plans were in place. Net Force was tied
up by the lawsuit, afraid to do anything, and every day
they delayed brought the passage of the CyberNation bill
closer to reality.

Everything was moving along nicely. All he had to do
was wait.

And that, he'd found before, was the one thing he did
not do well.

He shrugged. That's why he had this place stocked as
well as he did. He needed the distractions.

Thinking about them, he decided that he felt like doing
a few laps in the pool, then maybe a little shooting at the
range. It would be good to keep a sound body and sharp
eye to go with the sound mind. . . .

Upton County, Texas

The staging area was twelve miles away from the target,
and at five o'clock in the afternoon, it was a hundred and
three degrees Fahrenheit. The only shade came from the

trucks and a few scraggly willow trees along an almost dry creek bed.

Howard saw Julio coming toward him, wiping his face with a rag.

"I hope these things don't go belly up in this heat," Lieutenant Fernandez said.

Behind Howard, Michaels said, "Is that likely?"

"I hope not. It'll be a long walk home if they do."

The things to which Julio was referring were the five specially fitted Segway scooters that Howard, Michaels, Julio, and two troopers would be riding toward the target from the south while the other five soldiers rolled in on the position from the north.

The little electric scooters wore stealth gear, the latest generation of polycarb fiber sheathing, all sharp angles and smooth surfaces. They had used similar camo on trucks. It worked, especially on civilian-grade radar and Doppler, but it wasn't perfect. That was why the troops in the truck would be feinting from the north as Howard and the others sneaked in from the opposite direction.

If Ames was awake when they rolled in, and if he had his radar on, he would see a nice, fat blip thrown by the truck, and, with any luck, not the scooters. They wouldn't be totally invisible, but they would be fuzzy and dim enough so he probably wouldn't notice them.

The plan was to pull the truck to within a mile or so and stop it. The men would get out and move around, offering enough activity to occupy a watcher's attention. Even if he had FLIR or some kind of spookeye starlight scope, the hope was that he'd be focused on the obvious threat. Which wouldn't seem imminent, since they wouldn't be close to any of the known entrances.

Meanwhile, Howard and the strike team from the south would get there, get inside, and grab the guy before he knew what hit him.

In theory, anyway.

The commander had asked the big question: Just how did they get into a secure facility designed to keep everything up to and including nuclear radiation out? Digging through thirty or forty feet of dirt wasn't a chore for ordinary men with shovels, not if they were in hurry, and the doors were more than likely going to be locked.

Howard thought he had an answer, but that remained to be seen. If the plans they had of the place were accurate, if they could get there undetected, and if the other new gear worked, they had a shot at it.

If, if, if.

"We're pretty much ready to roll," Julio said. "I think I'm going to take a nap."

Julio ambled off and climbed into the back of the truck with the computer gear in it. Howard nodded. It was at least twenty degrees cooler in there. He'd find room—and sleeping curled in relative cool was better than stretched out on the dirt in the middle of a Texas summer day.

"It's not a bad idea, getting some rest," Howard said. "We won't start our run until midnight."

Michaels looked dubious.

"One of the first things you learn as a soldier is to eat and sleep whenever you can," Howard said. "Never know when you'll get the chance again, once things start cooking."

Ames put on an old Marx brothers' movie around six, fixed himself a sandwich and a microbrew beer when that was done, and headed for bed. Though there was no real reason for it, he was tired. A couple of hours in the magic bed would fix him right up.

Michaels looked at his watch. It was five of twelve. The day's heat had died down considerably, but it was hardly what you would call "cool"—it was still about eighty or so, he guessed.

Howard, dressed in chocolate-chip camo that matched the clothes Michaels himself wore, even to the spider-silk body armor, walked over to where Michaels stood.

"I thought it got cold at night in the desert."

"Depends on the desert," Howard said. "It probably gets colder here in the winter. You ready?"

"Yes."

"Let's go over this one more time," Howard said. "The scooters have fat tires that will work fine on dirt, though it will take most of an hour to get there. The spookeyes will make it look like daylight, and all you have to do is stay behind me. I'm tracking Julio, and he has mapped out the safest route, using GPS grids. Troopers Holder and Reaves will bring up the rear. If you can keep from falling off your scooter, you'll be fine. You had a chance to check on it, right?"

"On the nice, flat, concrete parking lot at Net Force HQ."

Howard grinned. "You'll do fine, Commander. Just remember to hang on to the little handle grip and lean. We won't be doing any fancy maneuvers out there."

Michaels nodded.

Howard looked at his watch. "Okay, people, time to mount up!"

Michaels walked to his scooter. It looked sort of like a filing cabinet with some odd bits projecting from it, angled so that one edge was leading. The back of it was hollowed out, and the whole thing was mounted on what looked like an old nonmotorized push lawnmower. The only part of his body that would be visible from the front to radar would be his head, and the stealth helmet with its built-in spookeye heads-up display shield was supposed to take care of that.

Well, they'd find out how well it worked soon enough.

Lieutenant Fernandez climbed onto his machine, leaned forward, and started to roll. Howard followed suit. Michaels mounted his own two-wheeler, put his helmet on, and flipped the motor's power switch.

"Here we go," he said quietly.

Ames awoke past midnight, almost one A.M., not sure what had awakened him. He got up and padded to the bathroom. On his way back to bed he heard a little beeping noise.

He frowned. What was that?

The control console on his bedside table flashed a red light from the screen, pulsing in time with the noise. It took a second for him to realize what it was.

The radar alarm. He had company!

He didn't bother to dress, just grabbed his pistol and ran to the computer center down the hall in his pajamas.

The radar/Doppler screen showed activity to the north, a mile or so away. Who was that, and what were they doing out here?

There were two dozen cameras on his property, with others hidden in the ground or in bushes or trees past that, all wireless remotes. He cranked up the one closest to the intruders. It was a hundred yards away from them, but the optics were very good, light-gathering intensifiers making the night scene easily visible even at almost one in the morning, although with a slight greenish cast to it.

What he saw was a big truck, a flatbed, with two guys standing next to it. The truck had the hood up, and a third guy was poking around in the engine compartment. They didn't look like any kind of official anything, just three guys attending to a malfunctioning truck. On their way from no count to no place, and broke down in the middle of nowhere. They didn't even know this place was here.

Still, he wasn't going to take his eyes off them. No sense taking chances. Not at this point.

But maybe he should put some clothes on, just in case.

• • •

Riding the scooter across the ground was both easier and
harder than Michaels had expected. The ride was bumpy
and slow. Then again, he hadn't fallen off, which was
something.

He had no idea how far they had come. It seemed as if
they had been riding for hours, though a glance at his
watch showed they'd actually been rolling for only about
forty-five minutes.

The five of them wore LOSIR gear, line-of-sight infra-
red com sets that wouldn't be picked up by ordinary radio
receivers, and on scrambled channels so that anybody else
with such gear couldn't hear them anyway. Even so, Howard had ordered com-silence except for emergencies, and
so far, at least, there hadn't been any of those.

Knock on wood . . .

The night vision devices worked well enough. It wasn't
exactly like noon, and the helmet's computer coloration
was more pastel than reality. But it didn't look like an
unlighted desert in the middle of the night, either. The
wonders of modern technology.

On point, Julio Fernandez slowed. Howard followed
suit, and Michaels leaned back a hair to slow his own
scooter. Michaels watched carefully. Once they arrived,
there was a pattern in which they would have to park the
vehicles, so as to screen them from the sensor's view.
There would be a dead zone behind the scooter screen,
Howard had told him, an invisible gap in which they could
work undetected. Well, at least unseen. They'd be making
a fair amount of noise pretty quick. . . .

Julio raised his hand and made a "stop" gesture. He
angled to his left a hair. Howard altered his course. Michaels followed Howard, knowing that he had to park his
scooter two meters to the right and a meter back. The other
two troopers would complete the pattern behind and to the
side of Michaels.

Thirty seconds later, the five were parked. Fernandez

came back and the men gathered close. "Right there," he said, pointing.

Howard said, "You heard the lieutenant. Do it."

The two troopers said, "Yes, sir!"

They looked pretty strange, outfitted in the gear they wore. Exoskeletons, Howard had called them. Specialized equipment with motors and frames that essentially turned the wearer into Hercules, several times as strong as an ordinary man. There was a mechanical hum as the power units started. The two troopers, looking like something from a science fiction movie, moved to what looked like any other patch of dirt out here and started digging. One wielded a heavy pick, the other a shovel.

Howard had examined the plans for the once-secret bunker with great care. He had talked at length with his engineers, and determined a method of attack that should work.

"There's thirty or forty feet of earth between the surface and the roof in most places," he'd said. "It would take a backhoe days to dig all the way down. And the entrances are all hardened steel and reinforced concrete, so blasting through those would be a major chore. However, there are relatively weak spots."

Howard had shown Michaels on the diagrams. "Here, at these access ports, the stairwells are open all the way down. Now, there is a big plug of concrete and rebar surrounding the actual entrance and exit, but if you go just a couple meters out, the slab is much thinner, only about a meter thick, under half a meter of earth. They couldn't make it too heavy without having to build massive support structures. Punch through that, move a little more dirt, and you are in the stairwell."

"Three feet of reinforced concrete doesn't seem like something a couple of guys with picks and shovels are going to cut through in a hurry, even wearing Spider-Man suits," Michaels had said.

"No, sir, that is true. However, they built this place back in the 1950s, and they designed it to withstand the technology they had back then. Obviously they didn't have the resources we have today. These days we have shaped charges that will go through concrete and rebar like a hot knife through butter. All we have to do is clear away the dirt and get to the hard stuff."

"That seems awful easy. Why didn't Ames update things when he moved in?"

"I'm guessing that he was banking on the fact that no one knows about this place. You don't need thick walls to guard a place no one knows about. And besides, I don't really know what he could have done about it. These weak spots are design elements. He would have had to essentially rebuild the entire bomb shelter to get rid of them, and there was no way to do that and still keep this place a secret. Like I said, though, I'm guessing here."

"Okay," Alex said. "Assuming you're right and these weak spots are still here, isn't the idea to surprise him? Won't this charge make a pretty loud 'bang' when it goes off?"

"It will. But I think we have that covered."

Howard had told him why, and Michaels had to admit, it sounded as if it might work.

The two troopers were moving dirt at an incredible rate. In just a few minutes they reached the concrete. A few more minutes and they had cleared a rough circle five feet across.

Those exoskeletons were certainly impressive.

Fernandez climbed down into the shallow hole and set a brick-shaped block the size of a loaf of bread onto the concrete.

Fernandez said, "Ready, sir."

Howard looked at his watch. He touched a control on his LOSIR headset and said, "Thirty seconds, on my mark."

Fernandez nodded and touched a control on the shaped charge.

"Mark," Howard said into his throat mike.

"Twenty meters, people, that way!" Fernandez said.

They moved. Quickly.

40

Odessa, Texas

Ames was back at the monitors drinking a cup of coffee when the truck blew up. He was looking right at it when it turned into a fireball, washing out the filters on the cameras with a bright white glare. He could feel the room vibrate, and heard the sound echo around him.

He set his coffee cup down carefully and rubbed at his eyes, still staring at his monitors.

When the images cleared, he saw what was left of the flatbed, mostly just the frame and wheels, burning like mad. Even the tires were on fire.

Of the men who had been there, there was no sign.

Blown halfway to Mexico, no doubt.

What could have happened? A fuel leak? Maybe the truck had been hauling explosives? No. He shook his head. He had seen that the thing was empty.

He shook his head, then took a sip of his coffee. What should he do about this? Anything? The men were beyond help, that was for sure. He hadn't seen them for a few minutes, had assumed they had climbed back inside, unable to fix whatever was wrong. If they had—and they must have, because he didn't see them running around out there—they were toast.

He could call the state police, he supposed, and report it, but he didn't really want to have his presence noted. Even out here, somebody passing by would spot it soon enough and call it in. Yes, he was curious—but not enough to talk to the police. It didn't concern him, and it wasn't worth giving up the privacy and secrecy he had worked so hard to establish here.

Besides, the men in that truck were beyond help. There was nothing he or anyone else could do for them now. At least they probably never knew what hit them.

Where there had been a slab of concrete and steel rods, there was now a crater. But there was still dirt to be removed.

"Reaves, Holder, front and center!" Fernandez yelled. "Get those supersuits in gear!"

The pair of exosuited troopers moved forward, not quite a zombielike lurch, but not as smooth as a normal man's walk, either. Accompanied by the hums of motors and hydraulics, they started moving dirt again.

"He surely heard our explosion," Michaels said, pointing to the crater.

"If he is down there, I'd say he did," Howard said. "That was unavoidable, which is why we had the decoy timed to go off at the exact same moment. The question is, did it work?"

"I guess we'll find out soon enough."

Ames watched the truck burn for a while, but there weren't any more explosions, and he lost interest after a few minutes. He decided to get something to eat and go back to bed. One cup of coffee wouldn't keep him from sleeping.

He loaded a fresh set of tapes into his recording devices, though. He'd check them in the morning, see how long it took the state patrol to arrive, and what they did while they were there. He also wanted to be sure they all left when they were finished. He didn't want any stragglers anywhere on his property.

"We're through, sir," Reaves said.

Behind Reaves, Holder kept one augmented hand locked onto the trooper's suit, preventing him from falling into the hole he'd just dug.

Howard nodded. "Lieutenant, the rope ladder."

Julio came forward, unrolling the nylon and cross-slat device.

"It looks like it's a good twenty feet to the landing, sir," Fernandez said. "We're going to be dangling."

"No problem," Howard said.

Michaels said, "Good. Let's go find this guy, shall we?"

"Yes, sir, Commander. My thoughts exactly."

Ames sat in the kitchen, eating a duck-egg omelet and black rye toast with marionberry jam. He paused, a bite halfway to his mouth.

What was that?

He listened carefully.

Nothing but the hum of the refrigerators. He waited a few seconds but heard nothing else.

One of the problems with a place this big and old was that it was full of creaky, groany things. Even this far under the surface, some of the heat must seep down enough to cause expansion and contraction. Unless there were resident ghosts, nobody was here but him. He was safer here than in a bank vault—nobody had a combination to *his* doors.

He finished his snack, washed and dried the dishes, and headed back to the bedroom. You didn't want to go off and leave food caked on a plate when you might not be back for six or eight months. He hadn't seen any ants, and they weren't supposed to be able to get in here. On the other hand, they had found a roach on one of the space stations a couple years back, so why tempt fate?

He sat on the bed and started to pull his shoes off when he heard another noise.

One of his sensors had gone off.

The weird thing was, it wasn't one of his perimeter alarms. Instead, it was a flashing red light that indicated a clogged air filter in one of the ventilator shafts.

What made it weird was that he had the filters cleaned and checked regularly. Out here in the desert, he had to. The only way that filter could be clogged this soon was if he'd left the door open behind him.

He stopped, felt a chill frost him.

Or if someone else had found another way in.

Michaels looked at General Howard.

Howard was studying a map on his flatscreen. After a moment he gestured down a hallway. "If Ames is still here, he should be over in that direction. The bedroom closest to the sensor room is only a hundred meters or so that way. That's where I'd be staying, anyway."

Michaels nodded.

Howard and his men carried 9mm subguns, along with their sidearms. Michaels had a pistol, one of the issue H&K tacticals, with instructions not to shoot unless somebody was in his face shooting at him. If Howard, Julio, and the two troopers all got outshot by one lawyer, the pistol probably wasn't going to do him all that much good anyhow.

"Spread out," Howard ordered. "And be quiet. Hand signals from now on."

• • •

Ames held his pistol pointed at the floor, his finger outside the trigger guard, and moved carefully down the hall. He had to be imagining this, right?

Maybe. But something isn't right. First a truck pulls up, then explodes like a big bomb, then you get a clogged filter warning light. Maybe those two things are connected?

He didn't like coincidences.

Assume for the moment a worst-case scenario: Somebody was in here. If that was true, then it was bad news, very bad news. Because that would mean they had come specifically for him. That they were organized, well-informed, and extremely resourceful, not only to have found him, but to have mounted an assault and gotten inside undetected.

No. That shouldn't be possible. They shouldn't have been able to bypass his sensors, and couldn't have gotten in if they had. No way.

Maybe there's a secret entrance you don't know about?

No. He had seen the plans. He had explored every foot of the place. There were no secret doors he didn't know about.

He stopped and listened.

Nothing.

He tried to reassure himself. The filter was wonky, or the warning system was. It had to be. It certainly made much more sense.

Maybe. But he was not going to start taking chances now. He'd check everything out, carefully, and if there was any sign at all that he wasn't alone, he'd run. Simple as that.

He felt better.

Then he turned a corner and saw the soldier with the submachine gun coming toward him—

• • •

"Target!" Julio said.

No sooner was that word out of his mouth than the target opened up with a weapon. Howard couldn't see either the man or the gun, and the helmet's sound suppressors damped the noise, but it sounded like a handgun. Three quick shots—*bam-bam-bam!*—fired almost as one.

Instinctively, Howard moved to the wall, seeking cover.

Julio, four meters ahead on point, returned fire with his subgun, a pair of three-round bursts.

Behind Howard, Michaels hit the floor and went prone. Reaves and Holder crouched, weapons seeking targets.

"He's gone!" Julio yelled.

"You hit?"

"Negative, sir."

"You hit him?"

"I don't think so. He boogied awful fast."

They moved up, but the corridor was indeed empty. There wasn't any blood on the floor.

"Okay, he knows we're here. Move in. Crank up that heat sensor, see if we can spot him that way. Commander, you bring up the rear."

Michaels didn't argue. He was smart enough to know what he didn't know.

The five of them moved, Julio clearing the way, waving a little handheld device that should be able to pick up a man's body heat.

Ames was not immediately evident.

"Easy does it, Lieutenant."

"Always, General Howard, sir."

Ames clutched his pistol, his hands sweaty on the wood and steel. He had some kind of assault team, military guys, right here with him! What was he going to do?

Who *were* they?

He didn't even have a spare magazine for his gun. How many rounds had he fired? Two? Three?

Panic flowed in him.

The voice of reason tried to rise through the surge: *What are you doing, fool?! Put the gun down and raise your hands! Let them arrest you! You're a brilliant attorney, for God's sake! They can't have anything on you that will hold up in court! And once in court,* you'll *have* them *outnumbered and outgunned.*

Ames forced himself to take a deep breath. Yes. That was true. But— What if they hadn't come to arrest him? What if this was some kind of black op deal? What if they were assassins?

They sure weren't ordinary cops. Nobody had yelled, "Police, freeze!" or anything like that. Yes, he *had* shot at them, but they shot back in a hurry, and nobody had said a thing.

They had gone to great lengths to track him here—extraordinary measures, really, just to sneak up on him. They had blown up a truck to cover themselves breaking in. And they were armed to the teeth.

Who were they? How could he get past them to the escape hatch?

Would there be others aboveground, waiting for him?

Giving up was the smart thing, right?

But if he put down his gun and raised his hands, what if they just smiled and then cut him to bloody pieces? He'd be dead, and he'd never even know who had killed him, or why. . . .

He shook his head. No, he couldn't just surrender. Not yet. He had to find out more about them, make sure it was safe first.

And to do that, he had to stay alive.

Michaels held his pistol pointed at the floor, standing fifty feet behind the last of the others. His breathing was fast, but he found he wasn't afraid. Nervous, yes, and excited, but not frightened.

The place was a maze of corridors and doorways, and they moved carefully through it, Fernandez and Howard slipping into rooms along the way to check them out while Michaels stayed in the hall.

It was a big place, a lot of spots where a man could hide. Even with the sensors, they might miss him. And wouldn't that be a snafu. It was good that he was thinking of retiring, because they would surely fire him if this didn't end well.

Ames didn't know how many of them there were, could be ten, could be fifty. He couldn't shoot it out with them. They were obviously better armed, and however many of them there were, he was outnumbered. If he wasn't going to give himself up, then the only other option was to hide and wait for an opportunity to escape.

After that? Well, he'd worry about that if he got that far.

His advantage was that he knew the place better than they possibly could, even if they had the floor plans. They couldn't know where stuff was stacked, where he had put supplies, rearranged furniture, like that. If he could hide somewhere they wouldn't immediately look, get behind them, go down one of the other halls or levels, he could maybe slip by. It was his best chance.

The main kitchen was a good place. Lots of bins, coolers, pantries. If they did find him, he could still try to surrender. If they were law enforcement of some kind, they ought not shoot him if he surrendered.

It was a chance, anyway, and right now it looked like the only one he had.

"Got a hot spot in there," Julio said. He pointed to an open doorway. "Looks like a kitchen."

Howard moved up. "Clear the left, I'll take the right. Reaves, watch the door, Holder, cover that next hallway, just ahead. Commander, if you would stay right there and make sure he doesn't somehow get behind us?"

Michaels nodded. "Got it."

"Okay, Julio, on three. One . . . two . . . *three!*"

Julio went in first, low and to the left, and Howard was right behind him, higher, and covering the other half of the large room.

It was a kitchen, sure enough. A big one, with three stoves, refrigerators, sinks, tables, and institutional-sized food trays and bins.

Julio nodded at the stoves. The two of them edged that way, guns ready.

Julio put one hand on the stove. "There's the heat source. He must have had a late supper."

"Sensor getting anything else?"

"Negative." .

"Okay. Get Reaves and Holder in here, let them search. We'll move on."

Ames heard the voices, and even though they were muffled because of his hiding place in the walk-in fridge, he recognized one of them.

It was John Howard, the leader of Net Force's military arm.

Ah. That made sense, sort of. Somehow, they had connected him to Junior. Maybe he hadn't died right away when he'd been shot. Ames grinned. Maybe Junior wasn't even dead at all. It could be some kind of misinformation campaign. Maybe Junior was alive and well and singing like a flock of canaries. . . .

The fact that it was Net Force changed things. In his lawsuit, he claimed that all the Net Force personnel were violence-prone, trigger-happy vigilantes who went out of their way to find trouble and used deadly force whenever possible, but he knew that wasn't true. And up until now he hadn't cared.

Now, however, it mattered.

He'd read the reports himself. He had to in order to be able to spin them for a jury. And he knew that he could lay his weapon down and walk out of that refrigerator and be as safe as he would in his own offices.

Except that they would take him to jail. And if Net Force was out there, they had something concrete, even though he had no idea what it possibly could be. They'd crossed the lines before, he knew, but he also knew that his own lawsuit had turned a very bright spotlight on their actions. There was no way they'd be coming for him as part of a bluff. No way.

Which meant he couldn't turn himself in. Not yet. Not until he'd had some time to think things through, maybe find out what they had—or thought they had—on him, and had a plan for dealing with it. Then he could be caught.

But not until he already had some sort of get-out-of-jail-free card in his pocket.

He frowned, then checked the bullets left in his magazine. Getting away would be a trick, that was for sure, given that more men were coming in here to look for him, and it wouldn't be a good idea for him to shoot any of them. Move, he decided. Get to the dumbwaiter, go down a level, and sneak past them. It's the only way. Go!

Michaels had his breathing under control—well, more or less—and he was still ten yards behind John. The two troopers had gone into the huge kitchen to search it. It was beginning to look to Michaels as if they might not find Ames again, which would be a real shame after all the trouble they had gone to.

He was passing a stairwell going down when he heard something.

It wasn't much, a small click, and it probably didn't mean anything. He leaned over and looked down the stairs. Nothing to see—wait, what was that? A flash of shadow, as if somebody had passed in front of a light source—

"John."

Ahead of him, Howard turned. "Yes?"

"I think he might have gone down the stairs!"

Without thinking, Michaels started down.

"Alex, wait—!"

But Michaels was already four steps down and speeding up.

There wasn't a door at the bottom of the landing, just a wide opening to the next level. Probably didn't have to worry about fire codes when they built this place.

He was cautious enough not to run full speed through the doorway. He slowed, stuck his head through, and saw a man moving quickly away from him down the corridor, a hundred feet away. Had to be Ames.

Michaels stepped out into the hall, brought his pistol up. "Freeze!" he yelled. "Net Force!"

He was aware of Howard's boots thumping down the stairs behind him.

Ames turned, saw him, and stared. He had a gun in his right hand, but it was pointed at the floor.

"Don't shoot!" Ames yelled. "I give up!"

Michaels felt himself relax a hair. Good. He wasn't sure he could have hit the man that far away with a handgun anyhow.

"Put your weapon down!"

"Okay, take it easy!" Ames bent and started to put his pistol on the floor—

—except that he didn't. He jerked the gun back up and started shooting—!

Michaels felt the bullets hit him, at least two of them, square in the chest. Even though he was wearing armor, the impact felt like being smashed with a hammer. He lurched to the side, to get out of the way, fired his own pistol in return—

Howard yelled from behind him: "Commander, down!"

Michaels went prone, shoving his pistol out in front of him as he did so.

Howard's submachine gun roared, the sound of it joining those of Michaels's and Ames's weapons.

Ames saw Michaels go down, was sure he had hit him, but then the second man was there, firing—

Why had he shot? Why hadn't he surrendered, like he said?

But he didn't have an answer for that. It hadn't been a decision. It had been a reflex, an action born of something deep within him, something he hadn't even known had been a part of him until that moment.

Fire blossomed in his chest, in his shoulder, in his leg. He spun away from the hurt, but the pain followed him. He looked down, saw the blood—

More impacts. The gun fell from his suddenly nerveless fingers, clattered on the floor, but he was past worrying about that. He felt weak, too weak to stand. He fell, hit the wall, slid to the floor in a sitting position. He was having trouble breathing. . . .

He saw the two men come toward him. He should do something, but he was suddenly so tired. . . .

I'll just rest a second here. Get my strength back. Close my eyes for a minute, then I'll be better. . . .

Howard moved quickly, Michaels now on his feet and following. Ames was down, bleeding. It didn't look as if he was breathing.

Howard kicked the fallen man's pistol down the hall, then bent and laid two fingers on Ames's right carotid.

Nothing.

Julio came running, slid to a stop as Howard shook his head.

Michaels said, "Did I hit him?"

"Hard to say, but I think that one in the leg was yours," Howard said.

"Good."

Howard looked at Michaels, wondering.

"That man sent a killer to my house," Michaels said. "He threatened my child."

Howard nodded. "Mine, too. God will judge him for his actions, but I'm not sorry He will get the chance sooner rather than later."

"Amen," Julio said.

EPILOGUE

Washington, D.C.

Michaels and Toni went for a walk to the park with Alex and Guru. The day was unseasonably cool, in the seventies. As Guru followed the boy toward the merry-go-round, Toni turned to Alex and asked, "So John is really retiring this time?"

Michaels nodded. "Yes. He's been offered a job in the private sector. An old friend is running the place, and I think he is going to go for it. More money, and he'll be dealing with a different class of people. Not necessarily better, but probably less dangerous. At least physically. I think he might find some kind of security job there for Julio Fernandez, too."

"Good for them."

He smiled at her. "And good for us, too."

"You're really going to pull the plug?"

"It's already done. I talked to the director today. You can help me draft my letter of resignation."

"You're sure?"

"Absolutely. I'll stay on long enough to bring a new commander up to speed, a few weeks at most. We can sell the condo, cash in some bonds, buy a nice house in the Colorado suburbs, and take some time off before I have to worry about a job."

She looked at him. "And what about CyberNation?"

He paused, then shrugged. "Yeah, that's a point. We've cut off some of its heads, but CyberNation is still out there, and I don't think it's going away anytime soon. The thing is, I'm not sure what I think about it anymore."

Toni frowned. "That's a switch."

He nodded. "That lobbyist I told you about, Corinna Skye, made some good points in my office one day. I can't say I agree with her, not completely, but maybe I don't disagree quite so strongly as I once did."

He reached out and took her hand. "I guess the way I see it is that CyberNation will either happen or it won't—and if it does happen, it'll either be a good thing or a bad . . . or somewhere in between. Like most things in life, it's not as simple as I'd like it to be." He shrugged. "Either way, though, it's not up to me any longer. And that's okay."

She slid her arm around his waist. "You aren't worried that we might turn into a dull, old married couple?"

He laughed. "That's not high on my list of things to worry about, no. We have already had enough excitement for ten lifetimes."

"Look, Guru is getting on the merry-go-round with the boy," she said.

"Great, that's all we need, Guru with a broken hip."

But the old lady stood in the middle of the twirling playground equipment as solidly as if she were bolted down. Little Alex was delighted, laughing as the merry-go-round twirled.

This was what life was supposed to be about, Toni

thought. Your family with you, healthy, and safe. Not necessarily living happily ever after, no one could promise that—but it was a start.

And right now, that was enough.

refresh yourself at penguin.co.uk

Visit penguin.co.uk for exclusive information and interviews with
bestselling authors, fantastic give-aways and the
inside track on all our books, from the Penguin Classics
to the latest bestsellers.

BE FIRST ▼

first chapters, first editions, first novels

EXCLUSIVES ▼

author chats, video interviews, biographies, special features

EVERYONE'S A WINNER ▼

give-aways, competitions, quizzes, ecards

READERS GROUPS ▼

exciting features to support existing groups and create new ones

NEWS ▼

author events, bestsellers, awards, what's new

EBOOKS ▼

books that click – download an ePenguin today

BROWSE AND BUY ▼

thousands of books to investigate – search, try and buy the perfect gift online – or treat yourself!

ABOUT US ▼

job vacancies, advice for writers and company history

Get Closer To Penguin . . . www.penguin.co.uk